Wyandotté

Or, The Hutted Knoll
A Tale

by

James Fenimore Cooper

Wyandotté
Or, The Hutted Knoll A Tale
by James Fenimore Cooper

ISBN: 978-93-68098-91-1

Published by

DOUBLE 9 BOOKS

2/13-B, Ansari Road
Daryaganj, New Delhi – 110002
info@double9books.com
www.double9books.com
Tel. 011-40042856

ABOUT THE AUTHOR

James Fenimore Cooper was born on September 15, 1789, was an American author. He wrote authentic romantic stories portraying colonist and Native characters from the seventeenth to the nineteenth centuries. His most popular work is The Last of the Mohicans, often regarded as a masterpiece. James Fenimore Cooper was the 11th offspring of William Cooper and Elizabeth (Fenimore) Cooper. He wedded Susan Augusta de Lancey at Mamaroneck, Westchester Area, New York on January 1, 1811. The Coopers had seven children, but only five of them live to adulthood. The Last of the Mohicans (1826) was written in New York City where Cooper and his family resided. It became one of the most-read American books of the nineteenth century. The series includes the racial friendship of Natty Bumppo with the Delaware Indians. In 1826, Cooper moved his family to Europe to acquire more income from his books. He became friends with painters Samuel Morse and Gilbert du Motier and Marquis de Lafayette. In 1832, he entered the list as a political writer in a series of letters to Le National.

CONTENTS

"I venerate the Pilgrim's cause,
Yet for the red man dare to plead:
We bow to Heaven's recorded laws,
He turns to Nature for his creed."

Sprague.

Preface

The history of the borders is filled with legends of the sufferings of isolated families, during the troubled scenes of colonial warfare. Those which we now offer to the reader, are distinctive in many of their leading facts, if not rigidly true in the details. The first alone is necessary to the legitimate objects of fiction.

One of the misfortunes of a nation, is to hear little besides its own praises. Although the American revolution was probably as just an effort as was ever made by a people to resist the first inroads of oppression, the cause had its evil aspects, as well as all other human struggles. We have been so much accustomed to hear everything extolled, of late years, that could be dragged into the remotest connection with that great event, and the principles which led to it, that there is danger of overlooking truth, in a pseudo patriotism. Nothing is really patriotic, however, that is not strictly true and just; any more than it is paternal love to undermine the constitution of a child by an indiscriminate indulgence in pernicious diet. That there were demagogues in 1776, is as certain as that there are demagogues in 1843, and will probably continue to be demagogues as long as means for misleading the common mind shall exist.

A great deal of undigested morality is uttered to the world, under the disguise of a pretended public virtue. In the eye of reason, the man who deliberately and voluntarily contracts civil engagements is more strictly bound to their fulfilment, than he whose whole obligations consist of an accident over which he had not the smallest control, that of birth; though the very reverse of this is usually maintained under the influence of popular prejudice. The reader will probably discover how we view this master, in the course of our narrative.

Perhaps this story is obnoxious to the charge of a slight anachronism, in representing the activity of the Indians a year earlier than any were actually employed in the struggle of 1775. During the century of warfare that existed between the English and French colonies, the savage tribes were important agents in furthering the views of the respective belligerents. The war was on the frontiers, and these fierce savages were, in a measure, necessary to the management of hostilities that invaded their own villages and hunting-grounds. In 1775, the enemy came from the side of the Atlantic, and it was only after the struggle had acquired force, that the operations of the interior rendered the services of such allies desirable. In other respects, without pretending to refer to any real events, the incidents of this tale are believed to be sufficiently historical for all the legitimate purposes of fiction.

In this book the writer has aimed at sketching several distinct varieties of the human race, as true to the governing impulses of their educations, habits, modes of thinking and natures. The red man had his morality, as much as his white brother, and it is well known that even Christian ethics are coloured and governed, by standards of opinion set up on purely human authority. The honesty of one Christian is not always that of another, any more than his humanity, truth, fidelity or faith. The spirit must quit its earthly tabernacle altogether, ere it cease to be influenced by its tints and imperfections.

Chapter I

"An acorn fell from an old oak tree,
And lay on the frosty ground--
'O, what shall the fate of the acorn be?'
Was whispered all around
By low-toned voices chiming sweet,
Like a floweret's bell when swung--
And grasshopper steeds were gathering fleet,
And the beetle's hoofs up-rung."

Mrs. Seba Smith.

There is a wide-spread error on the subject of American scenery. From the size of the lakes, the length and breadth of the rivers, the vast solitudes of the forests, and the seemingly boundless expanse of the prairies, the world has come to attach to it an idea of grandeur; a word that is in nearly every case, misapplied. The scenery of that portion of the American continent which has fallen to the share of the Anglo-Saxon race, very seldom rises to a scale that merits this term; when it does, it is more owing to the accessories, as in the case of the interminable woods, than to the natural face of the country. To him who is accustomed to the terrific sublimity of the Alps, the softened and yet wild grandeur of the Italian lakes, or to the noble witchery of the shores of the Mediterranean, this country is apt to seem tame, and uninteresting as a whole; though it certainly has exceptions that carry charms of this nature to the verge of loveliness.

Of the latter character is the face of most of that region which lies in the angle formed by the junction of the Mohawk with the Hudson, extending as far south, or even farther, than the line of Pennsylvania, and west to the verge of that vast rolling plain which composes Western New York. This is a region of more than ten thousand square miles of surface, embracing to-day, ten counties at least, and supporting a rural population of near half a million of souls, excluding the river towns.

All who have seen this district of country, and who are familiar with the elements of charming, rather than grand scenery it possesses, are agreed in extolling its capabilities, and, in some instances, its realities. The want of high finish is common to everything of this sort in America; and, perhaps we may add, that the absence of picturesqueness as connected with the works of man, is a general defect; still, this particular region, and all others resembling it--for they abound on the wide surface of the twenty-six states--has beauties of its own, that it would be difficult to meet with in any of the older portions of the earth.

They who have done us the honour to read our previous works, will at once understand that the district to which we allude, is that of which we have taken more than one occasion to write; and we return to it now, less with a desire to celebrate its charms, than to exhibit them in a somewhat novel, and yet perfectly historical aspect. Our own earlier labours will have told the reader, that all of this extended district of country, with the exception of belts of settlements along the two great rivers named, was a wilderness, anterior to the American revolution. There was a minor class of exceptions to this general rule, however, to which it will be proper to advert, lest, by conceiving us too literally, the reader may think he can convict us of a contradiction. In order to be fully understood, the explanations shall be given at a little length.

While it is true, then, that the mountainous region, which now contains the counties of Schoharie, Otsego, Chenango, Broome, Delaware, &c., was a wilderness in 1775, the colonial governors had begun to make grants of its lands, some twenty years earlier. The patent of the estate on which we are writing lies before us; and it bears the date of 1769, with an Indian grant annexed, that is a year or two older. This may be taken as a mean date for the portion of country alluded to; some of the deeds being older, and others still more recent. These grants of land were originally made, subject to quit-rents to the crown; and usually on the payment of heavy fees to the colonial officers, after going through the somewhat supererogatory duty of "extinguishing the Indian title," as it was called. The latter were pretty effectually "extinguished" in that day, as well as in our own; and it would be a matter of curious research to ascertain the precise nature of the purchase-money given to the aborigines. In the case of the patent before us, the Indian right was "extinguished" by means of a few rifles, blankets, kettles, and beads; though the grant covers a nominal hundred thousand, and a real hundred and ten or twenty thousand acres of land.

The abuse of the grants, as land became more valuable, induced a law, restricting the number of acres patented to any one person, at any one time, to a thousand. Our monarchical predecessors had the same facilities, and it may be added, the same propensities, to rendering a law a dead letter, as belongs to our republican selves. The patent on our table, being for a nominal hundred thousand acres, contains the names of one hundred different grantees, while three several parchment documents at its side, each signed by thirty-three of these very persons, vest the legal estate in the first named, for whose sole benefit the whole concession was made; the dates of the last instruments succeeding, by one or two days, that of the royal patent itself.

Such is the history of most of the original titles to the many estates that dotted the region we have described, prior to the revolution. Money and favouritism, however were not always the motives of these large concessions. Occasionally, services presented their claims; and many instances occur in which old officers of the army, in particular, received a species of reward, by a patent for land, the fees being duly paid, and the Indian title righteously "extinguished." These grants to ancient soldiers were seldom large, except in the cases of officers of rank; three or four thousand well-selected acres, being a sufficient boon to the younger sons of Scottish lairds, or English squires, who had been accustomed to look upon a single farm as an estate.

As most of the soldiers mentioned were used to forest life, from having been long stationed at frontier posts, and had thus become familiarized with its privations, and hardened against its dangers, it was no unusual thing for them to sell out, or go on half-pay, when the wants of a family began to urge their claims, and to retire to their "patents," as the land itself, as well as the instrument by which it was granted, was invariably termed, with a view of establishing themselves permanently as landlords.

These grants from the crown, in the portions of the colony of New York that lie west of the river counties, were generally, if not invariably, simple concessions of the fee, subject to quit-rents to the king, and reservations of mines of the precious metals, without any of the privileges of feudal seignory, as existed in the older manors on the Hudson, on the islands, and on the Sound. Why this distinction was made, it exceeds our power to say; but, that the fact was so, as a rule, we have it in proof, by means of a great number of the original patents, themselves, that have been transmitted to us from various sources. Still, the habits of "home" entailed the name, even where the thing was not to be found. Titular manors exist, in a few instances, to this day, where no manorial rights were ever granted; and manor-houses were common appellations for the residences of the landlords of large estates, that were held in fee, without any exclusive privileges, and subject to the reservation named. Some of these manorial residences were of so primitive an appearance, as to induce the belief that the names were bestowed in pleasantry; the dwellings themselves being of logs, with the bark still on them, and the other fixtures to correspond. Notwithstanding all these drawbacks, early impressions and rooted habits could easily transfer terms to such an abode; and there was always a saddened enjoyment among these exiles, when they could liken their forest names and usages to those they had left in the distant scenes of their childhood.

The effect of the different causes we have here given was to dot the region described, though at long intervals, with spots of a semi-civilized appearance, in the midst of the vast--nay, almost boundless--expanse of forest. Some of these early settlements had made considerable advances towards finish and comfort, ere the war of '76 drove their occupants to seek protection against the inroads of the savages; and long after the influx of immigration which succeeded the peace, the fruits, the meadows, and the tilled fields of these oases in the desert, rendered them conspicuous amidst the blackened stumps, piled logs, and smooty fallows of an active and bustling settlement. At even a much later day, they were to be distinguished by the smoother surfaces of their fields, the greater growth and more bountiful yield of their orchards, and by the general appearance of a more finished civilization, and of greater age. Here and there, a hamlet had sprung up; and isolated places, like Cherry Valley and Wyoming, were found, that have since become known to the general history of the country.

Our present tale now leads us to the description of one of those early, personal, or family settlements, that had grown up, in what was then a very remote part of the territory in question, under the care and supervision of an ancient officer of the name of Willoughby. Captain Willoughby, after serving many years, had married an American wife, and continuing his services until a son and daughter were born, he sold his commission, procured a grant of land, and determined to retire to his new possessions, in order to pass the close of his life in the tranquil pursuits of agriculture, and in the bosom of his family. An adopted child was also added to his cares. Being an educated as well as a provident man, Captain Willoughby had set about the execution of this scheme with deliberation, prudence, and intelligence. On the frontiers, or lines, as it is the custom to term the American boundaries, he had become acquainted with a Tuscarora, known by the English *sobriquet* of "Saucy Nick." This fellow, a sort of half-outcast from his own people, had early attached himself to the whites, had acquired their language, and owing to a singular mixture of good and bad qualities, blended with great native shrewdness, he had wormed himself into the confidence of several commanders of small garrisons, among whom was our captain. No sooner was the mind of the latter made up, concerning his future course, than he sent for Nick, who was then in the fort; when the following conversation took place:

"Nick," commenced the captain, passing his hand over his brow, as was his wont when in a reflecting mood; "Nick, I have an important movement in view, in which you can be of some service to me."

The Tuscarora, fastening his dark basilisk-like eyes on the soldier, gazed a moment, as if to read his soul; then he jerked a thumb backward, over his own shoulder, and said, with a grave smile--

"Nick understand. Want six, two, scalp off Frenchman's head; wife and child; out yonder, over dere, up in Canada. Nick do him--what you give?"

"No, you red rascal, I want nothing of the sort--it is peace now, (this conversation took place in 1764), and you know I never bought a scalp, in time of war. Let me hear no more of this."

"What you want, *den?*" asked Nick, like one who was a good deal puzzled.

"I want land--*good* land--little, but *good*. I am about to get a grant--a patent--"

"Yes," interrupted Nick, nodding; "I know *him*--paper to take away Indian's hunting-ground."

"Why, I have no wish to do that--I am willing to pay the red men reasonably for their right, first."

"Buy Nick's land, den--better dan any oder."

"Your land, knave!--You own no land--belong to no tribe--have no rights to sell."

"What for ask Nick help, den?"

"What for?--Why because you *know* a good deal, though you own literally nothing. That's what for."

"Buy Nick *know*, den. Better dan he great fader *know*, down at York."

"That is just what I do wish to purchase. I will pay you well, Nick, if you will start to-morrow, with your rifle and a pocket-compass, off here towards the head-waters of the Susquehannah and Delaware, where the streams run rapidly, and where there are no fevers, and bring me an account of three or four thousand acres of rich bottom-land, in such a way as a surveyor can find it, and I can get a patent for it. What say you, Nick; will you go?"

"He not wanted. Nick sell 'e captain, his own land: here in 'e fort."

"Knave, do you not know me well enough not to trifle, when I am serious?"

"Nick ser'ous too--Moravian priest no ser'ouser more dan Nick at dis moment. Got land to sell."

Captain Willoughby had found occasion to punish the Tuscarora, in the course of his services; and as the parties understood each other perfectly well, the former saw the improbability of the latter's daring to trifle with him.

"Where is this land of yours, Nick," he inquired, after studying the Indian's countenance for a moment. "Where does it lie, what is it like, how much is there of it, and how came you to own it?"

"Ask him just so, ag'in," said Nick, taking up four twigs, to note down the questions, *seriatim*.

The captain repeated his inquiries, the Tuscarora laying down a stick at each separate interrogatory.

"Where he be?" answered Nick, taking up a twig, as a memorandum. "He out dere--where he want him--where he say.--One day's march from Susquehanna."

"Well; proceed."

"What he like?--Like land, to be sure. T'ink he like water! Got *some* water--no too much--got some land--got no tree--got some tree. Got good sugar-bush--got place for wheat and corn."

"Proceed."

"How much of him?" continued Nick, taking up another twig; "much as he want--want little, got him--want more, got him. Want none at all, got none at all--got what he want."

"Go on."

"To be sure. How came to own him?--How a pale face come to own America? *Discover* him--ha!--Well, Nick discover land down yonder, up dere, over here."

"Nick, what the devil do you mean by all this?"

"No mean devil, at all--mean land--*good* land. *Discover* him--know where he is--catch beaver dere, three, two year. All Nick say, true as word of honour; much more too."

"Do you mean it is an old beaver-dam destroyed?" asked the captain, pricking up his ears; for he was too familiar with the woods, not to understand the value of such a thing.

"No destroy--stand up yet--good as ever.--Nick dere, last season."

"Why, then, do you tell of it? Are not the beaver of more value to you, than any price you may receive for the land?"

"Cotch him all, four, two year ago--rest run away. No find beaver to stay long, when Indian once know, two time, where to set he trap. Beaver cunninger 'an pale face--cunning as bear."

Wyandotté : Or, The Hutted Knoll A Tale | 15

"I begin to comprehend you, Nick. How large do you suppose this pond to be?"

"He 'm not as big as Lake Ontario. S'pose him smaller, what den? Big enough for farm."

"Does it cover one or two hundred acres, think you?--Is it as large as the clearing around the fort?"

"Big as two, six, four of him. Take forty skin, dere one season. Little lake; all 'e tree gone."

"And the land around it--is it mountainous and rough, or will it be good for corn?"

"All sugar-bush--what you want better? S'pose you want corn; *plant* him. S'pose you want sugar; *make* him."

Captain Willoughby was struck with this description, and he returned to the subject, again and again. At length, after extracting all the information he could get from Nick, he struck a bargain with the fellow. A surveyor was engaged, and he started for the place, under the guidance of the Tuscarora. The result showed that Nick had not exaggerated. The pond was found, as he had described it to be, covering at least four hundred acres of low bottom-land; while near three thousand acres of higher river-flat, covered with beach and maple, spread around it for a considerable distance. The adjacent mountains too, were arable, though bold, and promised, in time, to become a fertile and manageable district. Calculating his distances with judgment, the surveyor laid out his metes and bounds in such a manner as to include the pond, all the low-land, and about three thousand acres of hill, or mountain, making the materials for a very pretty little "patent" of somewhat more than six thousand acres of capital land. He then collected a few chiefs of the nearest tribe, dealt out his rum, tobacco, blankets, wampum, and gunpowder, got twelve Indians to make their marks on a bit of deer-skin, and returned to his employer with a map, a field-book, and a deed, by which the Indian title was "extinguished." The surveyor received his compensation, and set off on a similar excursion, for a different employer, and in another direction. Nick got his reward, too, and was well satisfied with the transaction. This he afterwards called "sellin' beaver when he all run away."

Furnished with the necessary means, Captain Willoughby now "sued out his patent," as it was termed, in due form. Having some influence, the affair was soon arranged; the grant was made by the governor in council, a massive seal was annexed to a famous sheet of parchment, the signatures were obtained, and "Willoughby's Patent" took its place on the records of the colony, as well as on its maps. We are wrong as respects the latter particular; it did not take *its* place, on the maps of the colony, though it took *a* place; the location given for many years afterwards, being some forty or fifty miles too far west. In this peculiarity there was nothing novel, the surveys of all new regions being liable to similar trifling mistakes. Thus it was, that an estate, lying within five-and-twenty miles of the city of New York, and in which we happen to have a small interest at this hour, was clipped of its fair proportions, in consequence of losing some miles that run over obtrusively into another colony; and, within a short distance of the spot where we are writing, a "patent" has been squeezed entirely out of existence, between the claims of two older grants.

No such calamity befell "Willoughby's Patent," however. The land was found, with all its "marked or *blazed* trees," its "heaps of stones," "large butternut corners," and "dead oaks." In a word, everything was as it should be; even to the quality of the soil, the beaver-pond, and the quantity. As respects the last, the colony never gave "struck measure;" a thousand acres on paper, seldom falling short of eleven or twelve hundred in soil. In the present instance, the six thousand two hundred and forty-six acres of "Willoughby's Patent," were subsequently ascertained to contain just seven thousand and ninety-two acres of solid ground.

Our limits and plan will not permit us to give more than a sketch of the proceedings of the captain, in taking possession; though we feel certain that a minute account of the progress of such a settlement would possess a sort of Robinson Crusoe-like interest, that might repay the reader. As usual, the adventurers commenced their operations in the spring. Mrs. Willoughby, and the children, were left with their friends, in Albany; while the captain and his party pioneered their way to the patent, in the best manner they could. This party consisted of Nick, who went in the capacity of hunter, an office of a good deal of dignity, and of the last importance, to a set of adventurers on an expedition of this nature. Then there were eight axe-men, a house-carpenter, a mason, and a mill-wright. These, with Captain Willoughby, and an invalid sergeant, of the name of Joyce, composed the party.

Our adventurers made most of their journey by water. After finding their way to the head of the Canaideraga, mistaking it for the Otsego, they felled trees, hollowed them into canoes, embarked, and, aided by a yoke of oxen that were driven along the shore, they wormed their way, through the Oaks, into the Susquehanna, descending that river until they reached the Unadilla, which stream they ascended until they came to the small river, known in the parlance of the country, by the erroneous name of a creek, that ran through the captain's new estate. The labour of this ascent was exceedingly severe; but the whole journey was completed by the end of April, and while the streams were high. Snow still lay in the woods; but the sap had started, and the season was beginning to show its promise.

The first measure adopted by our adventurers was to "hut." In the very centre of the pond, which, it will be remembered, covered four hundred acres, was an island of some five or six acres in extent. It was a rocky knoll, that rose forty feet above the surface of the water, and was still crowned with noble pines, a species of tree that had escaped the ravages of the beaver. In the pond, itself, a few "stubs" alone remained, the water having killed the trees, which had fallen and decayed. This circumstance showed that the stream had long before been dammed; successions of families of beavers having probably occupied the place, and renewed the works, for centuries, at intervals of generations. The dam in existence, however, was not very old; the animals having fled from their great enemy, man, rather than from any other foe.

To the island Captain Willoughby transferred all his stores, and here he built his hut. This was opposed to the notions of his axe-men, who, rightly enough, fancied the mainland would be more convenient; but the captain and the sergeant, after a council of war, decided that the position on the knoll would be the most military, and might be defended the longest, against man or beast. Another station was taken up, however, on the nearest shore, where such of the men were permitted to "hut," as preferred the location.

These preliminaries observed, the captain meditated a bold stroke against the wilderness, by draining the pond, and coming at once into the possession of a noble farm, cleared of trees and stumps, as it might be by a *coup de main*. This would be compressing the results of ordinary years of toil, into those of a single season, and everybody was agreed as to the expediency of the course, provided it were feasible.

The feasibility was soon ascertained. The stream which ran through the valley, was far from swift, until it reached a pass where the hills approached each other in low promontories; there the land fell rapidly away to what might be termed a lower terrace. Across this gorge, or defile, a distance of about five hundred feet, the dam had been thrown, a good deal aided by the position of some rocks that here rose to the surface, and through which the little river found its passage. The part which might be termed the key-stone of the dam, was only twenty yards wide, and immediately below it, the rocks fell away rapidly, quite sixty feet, carrying down the waste water in a sort of fall. Here the mill-wright announced his determination to commence operations at once, putting in a protest against destroying the works of the beavers. A pond of four hundred acres being too great a luxury for the region, the man was overruled, and the labour commenced.

The first blow was struck against the dam about nine o'clock, on the 2d day of May, 1765, and, by evening, the little sylvan-looking lake, which had lain embedded in the forest, glittering in the morning sun, unruffled by a breath of air, had entirely disappeared! In its place, there remained an open expanse of wet mud, thickly covered with pools and the remains of beaver-houses, with a small river winding its way slowly through the slime. The change to the eye was melancholy indeed; though the prospect was cheering to the agriculturist. No sooner did the water obtain a little passage, than it began to clear the way for itself, gushing out in a torrent, through the pass already mentioned.

The following morning, Captain Willoughby almost mourned over the works of his hands. The scene was so very different from that it had presented when the flats were covered with water, that it was impossible not to feel the change. For quite a month, it had an influence on the whole party. Nick, in particular, denounced it, as unwise and uncalled for, though he had made his price out of the very circumstance in prospective; and even Sergeant Joyce was compelled to admit that the knoll, an island no longer, had lost quite half its security as a military position. The next month, however, brought other changes. Half the pools had vanished by drainings and evaporation; the mud had begun to crack, and, in some places to pulverize; while the upper margin of the old pond had become sufficiently firm to permit the oxen to walk over it, without miring. Fences of trees, brush, and even rails, enclosed, on this portion of the flats, quite fifty acres of land; and Indian corn, oats, pumpkins, peas, potatoes, flax, and several other sorts of seed, were already in the ground. The spring proved dry, and the sun of the forty-third degree of latitude was doing its work, with great power and beneficence. What was of nearly equal importance, the age of the pond had prevented any recent accumulation of vegetable matter, and consequently spared those who laboured around the spot, the impurities of atmosphere usually consequent on its decay. Grass-seed, too, had been liberally scattered on favourable places, and things began to assume the appearance of what is termed "living."

August presented a still different picture. A saw-mill was up, and had been at work for some time. Piles of green boards began to make their appearance, and the plane of the carpenter was already in motion. Captain Willoughby was rich, in a small way; in other words, he possessed a few thousand pounds besides his land, and had yet to receive the price of his commission. A portion of these means were employed judiciously to advance his establishment; and, satisfied that there would be no scarcity of fodder for the ensuing winter, a man had been sent into the settlements for another yoke of cattle, and a couple of cows. Farming utensils were manufactured on the spot, and sleds began to take the place of carts; the latter exceeding the skill of any of the workmen present.

October offered its products as a reward for all this toil. The yield was enormous, and of excellent quality. Of Indian corn, the captain gathered several hundred bushels, besides stacks of stalks and tops. His turnips, too, were superabundant in quantity, and of a delicacy and flavour entirely unknown to the precincts of old lands. The potatoes had not done so well; to own the truth, they were a little watery, though there were enough of them to winter every hoof he had, of themselves. Then the peas and garden truck were both good and plenty; and a few pigs having been procured, there was the certainty of enjoying a plenty of that important article, pork, during the coming winter.

Late in the autumn, the captain rejoined his family in Albany, quitting the field for winter quarters. He left sergeant Joyce, in garrison, supported by Nick, a miller, the mason, carpenter, and three of the axe-men. Their duty was to prepare materials for the approaching season, to take care of the stock, to put in winter crops, to make a few bridges, clear out a road or two, haul wood to keep themselves from freezing, to build a log barn and some sheds, and otherwise to advance the interests of the settlement. They were also to commence a house for the patentee.

As his children were at school, captain Willoughby determined not to take his family immediately to the Hutted Knoll, as the place soon came to be called, from the circumstance of the original bivouack. This name was conferred by sergeant Joyce, who had a taste in that way, and as it got to be confirmed by the condescension of the proprietor and his family, we have chosen it to designate our present labours. From time to time, a messenger arrived with news from the place; and twice, in the course of the winter, the same individual went back with supplies, and encouraging messages to the different persons left in the clearing. As spring approached, however, the captain began to make his preparations for the coming campaign, in which he was to be accompanied by his wife; Mrs. Willoughby, a mild, affectionate, true-hearted New York woman, having decided not to let her husband pass another summer in that solitude without feeling the cheering influence of her presence.

In March, before the snow began to melt, several sleigh-loads of different necessaries were sent up the valley of the Mohawk, to a point opposite the head of the Otsego, where a thriving village called Fortplain now stands. Thence men were employed in transporting the articles, partly by means of "jumpers" *improvised* for the occasion, and partly on pack-horses, to the lake, which was found this time, instead of its neighbour the Canaderaiga. This necessary and laborious service occupied six weeks, the captain having been up as far as the lake once himself; returning to Albany, however, ere the snow was gone.

Chapter II

All things are new--the buds, the leaves,
That gild the elm-tree's nodding crest,
And even the nest beneath the eaves--
There are no birds in last year's nest.

Longfellow.

"I have good news for you, Wilhelmina," cried the captain, coming into the parlour where his wife used to sit and knit or sew quite half the day, and speaking with a bright face, and in a cheerful voice--"Here is a letter from my excellent old colonel; and Bob's affair is all settled and agreed on. He is to leave school next week, and to put on His Majesty's livery the week after."

Mrs. Willoughby smiled, and yet two or three tears followed each other down her cheeks, even while she smiled. The first was produced by pleasure at hearing that her son had got an ensigncy in the 60th, or Royal Americans; and the last was a tribute paid to nature; a mother's fears at consigning an only boy to the profession of arms.

"I am rejoiced, Willoughby," she said, "because *you* rejoice, and I know that Robert will be delighted at possessing the king's commission; but, he is *very* young to be sent into the dangers of battle and the camp!"

"I was younger, when I actually went into battle, for *then* it was war; now, we have a peace that promises to be endless, and Bob will have abundance of time to cultivate a beard before he smells gunpowder. As for myself"--he added in a half-regretful manner, for old habits and opinions would occasionally cross his mind--"as for myself, the cultivation of *turnips* must be my future occupation. Well, the bit of parchment is sold, Bob has got *his* in its place, while the difference in price is in my pocket, and no more need be said--and here come our dear girls, Wilhelmina, to prevent any regrets. The father of two such daughters *ought*, at least, to be happy."

At this instant, Beulah and Maud Willoughby, (for so the adopted child was called as well as the real), entered the room, having taken the lodgings of their parents, in a morning walk, on which they were regularly sent by the mistress of the boarding-school, in which they were receiving what was *then* thought to be a first-rate American female education. And much reason had their fond parents to be proud of them! Beulah, the eldest, was just eleven, while her sister was eighteen months younger. The first had a staid, and yet a cheerful look; but her cheeks were blooming, her eyes bright, and her smile sweet. Maud, the adopted one, however, had already the sunny countenance of an angel, with quite as much of the appearance of health as her sister; her face had more finesse, her looks more intelligence, her playfulness more feeling, her smile more tenderness, at times; at others, more meaning. It is scarcely necessary to say that both had that delicacy of outline which seems almost inseparable from the female form in this country. What was, perhaps, more usual in that day among persons of their class than it is in our own, each spoke her own language with an even graceful utterance, and a faultless accuracy of pronunciation, equally removed from effort and provincialisms. As the Dutch was in very common use then, at Albany, and most females of Dutch origin had a slight touch of their mother tongue in their enunciation of English, this purity of dialect in the two girls was to be ascribed to the fact that their father was an Englishman by birth; their mother an American of purely English origin, though named after a Dutch god-mother; and the head of the school in which they had now been three years, was a native of London, and a lady by habits and education.

"Now, Maud," cried the captain, after he had kissed the forehead, eyes and cheeks of his smiling little favourite--"Now, Maud, I will set you to guess what good news I have for you and Beulah."

"You and mother don't mean to go to that bad Beave Manor this summer, as some call the ugly pond?" answered the child, quick as lightning.

"That is kind of you, my darling; more kind than prudent; but you are not right."

"Try Beulah, now," interrupted the mother, who, while she too doted on her youngest child, had an increasing respect for the greater solidity and better judgment of her sister: "let us hear Beulah's guess."

"It is something about my brother, I know by mother's eyes," answered the eldest girl, looking inquiringly into Mrs. Willoughby's face.

"Oh! yes," cried Maud, beginning to jump about the room, until she ended her saltations in her father's arms--"Bob has got his commission!--I know it all well enough, now--I would not thank you to tell me--I know it all now--*dear* Bob, how he *will* laugh! and how happy I am!"

"Is it so, mother?" asked Beulah, anxiously, and without even a smile.

"Maud is right; Bob is an ensign--or, will be one, in a day or two. You do not seem pleased, my child?"

"I wish Robert were not a soldier, mother. Now he will be always away, and we shall never see him; then he may be obliged to fight, and who knows how unhappy it may make *him*?"

Beulah thought more of her brother than she did of herself; and, sooth to say, her mother had many of the child's misgivings. With Maud it was altogether different: she saw only the bright side of the picture; Bob gay and brilliant, his face covered with smiles, his appearance admired himself, and of course his sisters, happy. Captain Willoughby sympathized altogether with his pet. Accustomed to arms, he rejoiced that a career in which he had partially failed--this he did not conceal from himself or his wife--that this same career had opened, as he trusted, with better auspices on his only son. He covered Maud with kisses, and then rushed from the house, finding his heart too full to run the risk of being unmanned in the presence of females.

A week later, availing themselves of one of the last falls of snow of the season, captain Willoughby and his wife left Albany for the Knoll. The leave-taking was tender, and to the parents bitter; though after all, it was known that little more than a hundred miles would separate them from their beloved daughters. Fifty of these miles, however, were absolutely wilderness; and to achieve them, quite a hundred of tangled forest, or of difficult navigation, were to be passed. The communications would be at considerable intervals, and difficult. Still they might be held, and the anxious mother left many injunctions with Mrs. Waring, the head of the school, in relation to the health of her daughters, and the manner in which she was to be sent for, in the event of any serious illness.

Mrs. Willoughby had often overcome, as she fancied, the difficulties of a wilderness, in the company of her husband. It is the fashion highly to extol Napoleon's passage of the Alps, simply in reference to its physical obstacles. There never was a brigade moved twenty-four hours into the American wilds, that had not greater embarrassments of this nature to overcome, unless in those cases in which favourable river navigation has offered its facilities. Still, time and necessity had made a sort of military ways to all the more important frontier points occupied by the British garrisons, and the experience of Mrs. Willoughby had not hitherto been of the severe character of that she was now compelled to undergo.

The first fifty miles were passed over in a sleigh, in a few hours, and with little or no personal fatigue. This brought the travellers to a Dutch inn on the Mohawk, where the captain had often made his halts, and whither he had from time to time, sent his advanced parties in the course of the winter and spring. Here a jumper was found prepared to receive Mrs. Willoughby; and the horse being led by the captain himself, a passage through the forest was effected as far as the head of the Otsego. The distance being about twelve miles, it required two days for its performance. As the settlements extended south from the Mohawk a few miles, the first night was passed in a log cabin, on the extreme verge of civilization, if civilization it could be called, and the remaining eight miles were got over in the course of the succeeding day. This was more than would probably have been achieved in the virgin forest, and under the circumstances, had not so many of the captain's people passed over the same ground, going and returning, thereby learning how to avoid the greatest difficulties of the route, and here and there constructing a rude bridge. They had also blazed the trees, shortening the road by pointing out its true direction.

At the head of the Otsego, our adventurers were fairly in the wilderness. Huts had been built to receive the travellers, and here the whole party assembled, in readiness to make a fresh start in company. It consisted of more than a dozen persons, in all; the black domestics of the family being present, as well as several mechanics whom Captain Willoughby had employed to carry on his improvements. The men sent in advance had not been idle, any more than those left at the Hutted Knoll. They had built three or four skiffs, one small batteau, and a couple of canoes. These were all in the water, in waiting for the disappearance of the ice; which was now reduced to a mass of stalactites in form, greenish and sombre in hue, as they floated in a body, but clear and bright when separated and exposed to the sun. The south winds began to prevail, and the shore was glittering with the fast-melting piles of the frozen fluid, though it would have been vain yet to attempt a passage through it.

The Otsego is a sheet that we have taken more than one occasion to describe, and the picture it then presented, amidst its frame of mountains, will readily be imagined by most of our readers. In 1765, no sign of a settlement was visible on its shores; few of the grants of land in that vicinity extending back so far. Still the spot began to be known, and hunters had been in the habit of frequenting its bosom and its shores, for the last twenty years or more Not a vestige of their presence, however, was to be seen from the huts of the captain; but Mrs. Willoughby assured her husband, as she stood leaning on his arm, the morning after her arrival, that never before had she gazed on so eloquent, and yet so pleasing a picture of solitude as that which lay spread before her eyes.

"There is something encouraging and soothing in this bland south wind, too," she added, "which seems to promise that we shall meet with a beneficent nature, in the spot to which we are going. The south airs of spring, to me are always filled with promise."

"And justly, love; for they are the harbingers of a renewed vegetation. If the wind increase, as I think it may, we shall see this chilling sheet of ice succeeded by the more cheerful view of water. It is in this way, that all these lakes open their bosoms in April."

Captain Willoughby did not know it, while speaking, but, at that moment, quite two miles of the lower, or southern end of the lake, was clear, and the opening giving a sweep to the breeze, the latter was already driving the sheets of ice before it, towards the head, at a rate of quite a mile in the hour. Just then, an Irishman, named Michael O'Hearn, who had recently arrived in America, and whom the captain had hired as a servant of all work, came rushing up to his master, and opened his teeming thoughts, with an earnestness of manner, and a confusion of rhetoric, that were equally characteristic of the man and of a portion of his nation.

"Is it journeying south, or to the other end of this bit of wather, or ice, that yer honour is thinking of?" he cried "Well, and there'll be room for us all, and to spare; for divil a bir-r-d will be left in that quarter by night, or forenent twelve o'clock either, calculating by the clock, if one had such a thing; as a body might say."

As this was said not only vehemently, but with an accent that defies imitation with the pen, Mrs. Willoughby was quite at a loss to get a clue to the idea; but, her husband, more accustomed to men of Mike's class, was sufficiently lucky to comprehend what he was at.

"You mean the pigeons, Mike, I suppose," the captain answered, good-humouredly. "There are certainly a goodly number of them; and I dare say our hunters will bring us in some, for dinner. It is a certain sign that the winter is gone, when birds and beasts follow their instincts, in this manner. Where are you from, Mike?"

"County Leitrim, yer honour," answered the other, touching his cap.

"Ay, that one may guess," said the captain, smiling, 'but where last?"

"From looking at the bir-r-ds, sir!--Och! It's a sight that will do madam good, and contains a sartainty there'll be room enough made for us, where all these cr'atures came from. I'm thinking, yer honour, if we don't ate *them*, they'll be wanting to ate *us*. What a power of them, counting big and little; though they 're all of a size, just as much as if they had flown through a hole made on purpose to kape them down to a convanient bigness, in body and feathers."

"Such a flight of pigeons in Ireland, would make a sensation, Mike," observed the captain, willing to amuse his wife, by drawing out the County Leitrim-man, a little.

"It would make a dinner, yer honour, for every mother's son of 'em, counting the gur-r-rls, in the bargain! Such a power of bir-r-ds, would knock down 'praties, in a wonderful degree, and make even butthermilk chape and plenthiful. Will it be always such abundance with us, down at the Huts, yer honour? or is this sight only a delusion to fill us with hopes that's never to be satisfied?"

"Pigeons are seldom wanting in this country, Mike, in the spring and autumn; though we have both birds and beasts, in plenty, that are preferable for food."

"Will it be plentthier than this?--Well, it's enough to destroy human appetite, the sight of 'em! I'd give the half joe I lost among them blackguards in Albany, at their Pauss, as they calls it, jist to let my sisther's childer have their supper out of one of these flocks, such as they are, betther or no betther. Och! its pleasant to think of them childer having their will, for once, on such a power of wild, savage bir-r-ds!"

Captain Willoughby smiled at this proof of *naiveté* in his new domestic, and then led his wife back to the hut; if being time to make some fresh dispositions for the approaching movement. By noon, it became apparent to those who were waiting such an event, that the lake was opening; and, about the same time, one of the hunters came in from a neighbouring mountain, and reported that he had seen clear water, as near their position as three or four miles. By this time it was blowing fresh, and the wind, having a clear rake, drove up the honeycomb-looking sheet before it, as the scraper accumulates snow. When the sun set, the whole north shore was white with piles of glittering icicles; while the bosom of the Otsego, no longer disturbed by the wind, resembled a placid mirror. Early on the following morning, the whole party embarked. There was no wind, and men were placed at the paddles and the oars. Care was taken, on quitting the huts, to close their doors and shutters; for they were to be taverns to cover the heads of many a traveller, in the frequent journeys that were likely to be made, between the Knoll and the settlements. These stations, then, were of the last importance, and a frontier-man always had the same regard for them, that the mountaineer of the Alps has for his "refuge."

The passage down the Otsego was the easiest and most agreeable portion of the whole journey. The day was pleasant, and the oarsmen vigorous, if not very skilful, rendering the movement rapid, and sufficiently direct. But one drawback occurred to the prosperity of the voyage. Among the labourers hired by the captain, was a Connecticut man, of the name of Joel Strides, between whom and the County Leitrim-man, there had early commenced a warfare of tricks and petty annoyances; a warfare that was perfectly defensive on the part of O'Hearn, who did little more, in the way of retort, than comment on the long, lank, shapeless figure, and meagre countenance of his enemy. Joel had not been seen to smile, since he engaged with the captain; though three times had he laughed outright, and each time at the occurrence of some mishap to Michael O'Hearn the fruit of one of his own schemes of annoyance.

On the present occasion, Joel, who had the distribution of such duty, placed Mike in a skiff, by himself, flattering the poor fellow with the credit he would achieve, by rowing a boat to the foot of the lake, without assistance. He might as well have asked Mike to walk to the outlet on the surface of the water! This arrangement proceeded from an innate love of mischief in Joel, who had much of the quiet waggery, blended with many of the bad qualities of the men of his peculiar class. A narrow and conceited selfishness lay at the root of the larger portion of this man's faults. As a physical being, he was a perfect labour-saving machine, himself; bringing all the resources of a naturally quick and acute mind to bear on this one end, never doing anything that required a particle more than the exertion and strength that were absolutely necessary to effect his object. He rowed the skiff in which the captain and his wife had embarked, with his own hands; and, previously to starting, he had selected the best sculls from the other boats, had fitted his twhart with the closest attention to his own ease, and had placed a stretcher for his feet, with an intelligence and knowledge of mechanics, that would have done credit to a Whitehall waterman. This much proceeded from the predominating principle of his nature, which was, always to have an eye on the interests of Joel Strides; though the effect happened, in this instance, to be beneficial to those he served.

Michael O'Hearn, on the contrary, thought only of the end; and this so intensely, not to so say vehemently, as generally to overlook the means. Frank, generous, self-devoted, and withal accustomed to get most things wrong-end-foremost, he usually threw away twice the same labour, in effecting a given purpose, that was expended by the Yankee; doing the thing worse, too, besides losing twice the time. He never paused to think of this, however. The *masther's* boat was to be rowed to the other end of the lake, and, though he had never rowed a boat an inch in his life, he was ready and willing to undertake the job. "If a certain quantity of work will not do it," thought Mike, "I'll try as much ag'in; and the divil is in it, if *that* won't sarve the purpose of that little bit of a job."

Under such circumstances the party started. Most of the skiffs and canoes went off half an hour before Mrs. Willoughby was ready, and Joel managed to keep Mike for he last, under the pretence of wishing his aid in loading his own boat, with the bed and bedding from the hut. All was ready, at length, and taking his seat, with a sort of quiet deliberation, Joel said, in his drawling way, "You'll follow *us*, Mike, and you can't be a thousand miles out of the way." Then he pulled from the shore with a quiet, steady stroke of the sculls, that sent the skiff ahead with great rapidity, though with much ease to himself.

Michael O'Hearn stood looking at the retiring skiff, in silent admiration, for two or three minutes. He was quite alone; for all the other boats were already two or three miles on their way, and distance already prevented him from seeing the mischief that was lurking in Joel's hypocritical eyes.

"Follow *yees!*" soliloquized Mike--"The divil burn ye, for a guessing yankee as ye ar'--how am I to follow with such legs as the likes of these? If it wasn't for the masther and the missus, ra'al jontlemen and ladies they be, I'd turn my back on ye, in the desert, and let ye find that Beaver estate, in yer own disagreeable company. Ha!--well, I must thry, and if the boat won't go, it'll be no fault of the man that has a good disposition to make it."

Mike now took his seat on a board that lay across the gunwale of the skiff at a most inconvenient height, placed two sculls in the water, one of which was six inches longer than the other, made a desperate effort, and got his craft fairly afloat. Now, Michael O'Hearn was not left-handed, and, as usually happens with such men, the inequality between the two limbs was quite marked. By a sinister accident, too, it happened that the longest oar got into the strongest hand, and there it would have staid to the end of time; before Mike would think of changing it, on that account. Joel, alone, sat with his face towards the head of the lake, and he alone could see the dilemma in which the county Leitrim-man was placed. Neither the captain nor his wife thought of looking behind, and the yankee had all the fun to himself. As for Mike, he succeeded in getting a few rods from the land, when the strong arm and the longer lever asserting their superiority, the skiff began to incline to the westward. So intense, however, was the poor fellow's zeal, that he did not discover the change in his course until he had so far turned as to give him a glimpse of his retiring master; then he inferred that all was right, and pulled more leisurely. The result was, that in about ten minutes, Mike was stopped by the land, the boat touching the north shore again, two or three rods from the very point whence it had started. The honest fellow got up, looked around him, scratched his head, gazed wistfully after the fast-receding boat of his master, and broke out in another soliloquy.

"Bad luck to them that made ye, ye one-sided thing!" he said, shaking his head reproachfully at the skiff: "there's liberty for ye to do as ye ought, and ye'll not be doing it, just out of contrairiness. Why the divil can't ye do like the other skiffs, and go where ye're wanted, on the road towards thim beavers? Och, ye'll be sorry for this, when ye're left behind, out of sight!"

Then it flashed on Mike's mind that possibly some article had been left in the hut, and the skiff had come back to look after it; so, up he ran to the captain's deserted lodge, entered it, was lost to view for a minute, then came in sight again, scratching his head, and renewing his muttering--"No," he said, "divil a thing can I see, and it must be pure con*trairi*ness! Perhaps the baste will behave betther next time, so I'll thry it ag'in, and give it an occasion. Barring obstinacy, 't is as good-lookin' a skiff as the best of them."

Mike was as good as his word, and gave the skiff as fair an opportunity of behaving itself as was ever offered to a boat. Seven times did he quit the shore, and as often return to it, gradually working his way towards the western shore, and slightly down the lake. In this manner, Mike at length got himself so far on the side of the lake, as to present a barrier of land to the evil disposition of his skiff to incline to the westward. It could go no longer in that direction, at least.

"Divil burn ye," the honest fellow cried, the perspiration rolling down his face; "I think ye'll be satisfied without walking out into the forest, where I wish ye war' with all my heart, amang the threes that made ye! Now, I'll see if yer con*trairy* enough to run up a hill."

Mike next essayed to pull along the shore, in the hope that the sight of the land, and of the overhanging pines and hemlocks, would cure the boat's propensity to turn in that direction. It is not necessary to say that his expectations were disappointed, and he finally was reduced to getting out into the water, cool as was the weather, and of wading along the shore, dragging the boat after him. All this Joel saw before he passed out of sight, but no movement of his muscles let the captain into the secret of the poor Irishman's strait.

In the meanwhile, the rest of the flotilla, or *brigade* of boats, as the captain termed them, went prosperously on their way, going from one end of the lake to the other, in the course of three hours. As one of the party had been over the route several times already, there was no hesitation on the subject of the point to which the boats were to proceed. They all touched the shore near the stone that is now called the "Otsego Rock," beneath a steep wooded bank, and quite near to the place where the Susquehannah glanced out of the lake, in a swift current, beneath a high-arched tracery of branches that were not yet clothed with leaves.

Here the question was put as to what had become of Mike. His skiff was nowhere visible, and the captain felt the necessity of having him looked for, before he proceeded any further. After a short consultation, a boat manned by two negroes, father and son, named Pliny the elder, and Pliny the younger, or, in common parlance, "old Plin" and "young Plin," was sent back along the west-shore to hunt him up. Of course, a hut was immediately prepared for the reception of Mrs. Willoughby, upon the plain that stretches across the valley, at this point. This was on the site of the present village of Cooperstown, but just twenty years anterior to the commencement of the pretty little shire town that now exists on the spot.

It was night ere the two Plinies appeared towing Mike, as their great namesakes of antiquity might have brought in a Carthaginian galley, in triumph. The county Leitrim-man had made his way with excessive toil about a league ere he was met, and glad enough was he to see his succour approach. In that day, the strong antipathy which now exists between the black and the emigrant Irishman was unknown, the competition for household service commencing more than half a century later. Still, as the negro loved fun constitutionally, and Pliny the younger was somewhat of a wag, Mike did not entirely escape, scot-free.

"Why you drag 'im like ox, Irish Mike?" cried the younger negro--"why you no row 'im like other folk?"

"Ah--you're as bad as the rest of 'em," growled Mike. "They tould me Ameriky was a mighty warm country, and war-r-m I find it, sure enough, though the wather isn't as warm as good whiskey. Come, ye black divils, and see if ye can coax this *contrairy* crathure to do as a person wants."

The negroes soon had Mike in tow, and then they went down the lake merrily, laughing and cracking their jokes, at the Irishman's expense, after the fashion of their race. It was fortunate for the Leitrim-man that he was accustomed to ditching, though it may be questioned if the pores of his body closed again that day, so very effectually had they been opened. When he rejoined his master, not a syllable was said of the mishap, Joel having the prudence to keep his own secret, and even joining Mike in denouncing the bad qualities of the boat. We will only add here, that a little calculation entered into this trick, Joel perceiving that Mike was a favourite, and wishing to bring him into discredit.

Early the next morning, the captain sent the negroes and Mike down the Susquehannah a mile, to clear away some flood-wood, of which one of the hunters had brought in a report the preceding day. Two hours later, the boats left the shore, and began to float downward with the current, following the direction of a stream that has obtained its name from its sinuosities.

In a few minutes the boats reached the flood-wood, where, to Joel's great amusement, Mike and the negroes, the latter having little more calculation than the former, had commenced their operations on the upper side of the raft, piling the logs on one another, with a view to make a passage through the centre. Of course, there was a halt, the females landing. Captain Willoughby now cast an eye round him in hesitation, when a knowing look from Joel caught his attention.

"This does not seem to be right," he said--"cannot we better if a little?"

"It's right wrong, captain," answered Joel, laughing like one who enjoyed other people's ignorance. "A sensible crittur' would begin the work on such a job, at the lower side of the raft."

"Take the direction, and order things to suit yourself."

This was just what Joel liked. *Head-work* before all other work for him, and he set about the duty authoritatively and with promptitude. After rating the negroes roundly for their stupidity, and laying it on Mike without much delicacy of thought or diction, over the shoulders of the two blacks, he mustered his forces, and began to clear the channel with intelligence and readiness.

Going to the lower side of the jammed flood-wood, he soon succeeded in loosening one or two trees, which floated away, making room for others to follow. By these means a passage was effected in half an hour, Joel having the prudence to set no more timber in motion than was necessary to his purpose, lest it might choke the stream below. In this manner the party got through, and, the river being high at that season, by night the travellers were half-way to the mouth of the Unadilla. The next evening they encamped at the junction of the two streams, making their preparations to ascend the latter the following morning.

The toil of the ascent, however, did not commence, until the boats entered what was called the creek, or the small tributary of the Unadilla, on which the beavers had erected their works, and which ran through the "Manor." Here, indeed, the progress was slow and laborious, the rapidity of the current and the shallowness of the water rendering every foot gained a work of exertion and pain. Perseverance and skill, notwithstanding, prevailed; all the boats reaching the foot of the rapids, or straggling falls, on which the captain had built his mills, about an hour before the sun disappeared. Here, of course, the boats were left, a rude road having been cut, by means of which the freights were transported on a sledge the remainder of the distance. Throughout the whole of this trying day, Joel had not only worked head-work, but he had actually exerted himself with his body. As for Mike, never before had he made such desperate efforts. He felt all the disgrace of his adventure on the lake, and was disposed to wipe it out by his exploits on the rivers. Thus Mike was ever loyal to his employer. He had sold his flesh and blood for money, and a man of his conscience was inclined to give a fair penny's-worth. The tractable manner in which the boat had floated down the river, it is true, caused him some surprise, as was shown in his remark to the younger Pliny, on landing.

"This is a curious boat, afther all," said Pat. "One time it's all con*trari*ness, and then ag'in it's as obliging as one's own mother. It *followed* the day all's one like a puppy dog, while yon on the big wather there was no more *dhriving* it than a hog. Och! it's a faimale boat, by its whims!"

Chapter III

"He sleeps forgetful of his once bright flame
He has no feeling of the glory gone;
He has no eye to catch the mounting flame
That once in transport drew him on;
He lies in dull oblivious dreams, nor cares
Who the wreathed laurel bears."

Percival.

The appearance of a place in which the remainder of one's life is to be past is always noted with interest on a first visit. Thus it was that Mrs. Willoughby had been observant and silent from the moment the captain informed her that they had passed the line of his estate, and were approaching the spot where they were to dwell. The stream was so small, and the girding of the forest so close, that there was little range for the sight; but the anxious wife and mother could perceive that the hills drew together, at this point, the valley narrowing essentially, that rocks began to appear in the bed of the river, and that the growth of the timber indicated fertility and a generous soil.

When the boat stopped, the little stream came brawling down a ragged declivity, and a mill, one so arranged as to grind and saw, both in a very small way, however, gave the first signs of civilization she had beheld since quitting the last hut near the Mohawk. After issuing a few orders, the captain drew his wife's arm through his own, and hurried up the ascent, with an eagerness that was almost boyish, to show her what had been done towards the improvement of the "Knoll." There is a pleasure in diving into a virgin forest and commencing the labours of civilization, that has no exact parallel in any other human occupation. That of building, or of laying out grounds, has certainly some resemblance to it, but it is a resemblance so faint and distant as scarcely to liken the enjoyment each produces. The former approaches nearer to the feeling of creating, and is far more pregnant with anticipations and hopes, though its first effects are seldom agreeable, and are sometimes nearly hideous. Our captain, however, had escaped most of these last consequences, by possessing the advantage of having a clearing, without going through the usual processes of chopping and burning; the first of which leaves the earth dotted, for many years, with unsightly stumps, while the rains and snows do not wash out the hues of the last for several seasons.

An exclamation betrayed the pleasure with which Mrs. Willoughby got her first glimpse of the drained pond. It was when she had clambered to the point of the rocks, where the stream began to tumble downward into the valley below. A year had done a vast deal for the place. The few stumps and stubs which had disfigured the basin when it was first laid bare, had all been drawn by oxen, and burned. This left the entire surface of the four hundred acres smooth and fit for the plough. The soil was the deposit of centuries, and the inclination, from the woods to the stream, was scarcely perceptible to the eye. In fact, it was barely sufficient to drain the drippings of the winter's snows. The form of the area was a little irregular; just enough so to be picturesque; while the inequalities were surprisingly few and trifling. In a word, nature had formed just such a spot as delights the husbandman's heart, and placed it beneath a sun which, while its fierceness is relieved by winters of frost and snow, had a power to bring out all its latent resources.

Trees had been felled around the whole area, with the open spaces filled by branches, in a way to form what is termed a brush fence. This is not a sightly object, and the captain had ordered the line to be drawn *within* the woods, so that the visible boundaries of the open land were the virgin forest itself. His men had protested against this, a fence, however unseemly, being in their view an indispensable accessory to civilization. But the captain's authority, if not his better taste, prevailed; and the boundary of felled trees and brush was completely concealed in the back-ground of woods. As yet, there was no necessity for cross-fences, the whole open space lying in a single field. One hundred acres were in winter wheat. As this grain had been got in the previous autumn, it was now standing on the finest and driest of the soil, giving an air of rich fertility to the whole basin. Grass-seed had been sown along both banks of the stream, and its waters were quietly flowing between two wide belts of fresh verdure, the young plants having already started in that sheltered receptacle of the sun's rays. Other portions of the flat showed signs of improvement, the plough having actually been at work for quite a fortnight.

All this was far more than even the captain had expected, and much more than his wife had dared to hope. Mrs. Willoughby had been accustomed to witness the slow progress of a new settlement; but never before had she seen what might be done on a beaver-dam. To her all appeared like magic, and her first question would have been to ask her husband to explain what had been done with the trees and stumps, had not her future residence caught her eye. Captain Willoughby had left his orders concerning the house, previously to quitting the Knoll; and he was now well pleased to perceive that they had been attended to. As this spot will prove the scene of many of the incidents we are bound to relate, it may be proper, here, to describe it, at some length.

The hillock that rose out of the pond, in the form of a rocky little island, was one of those capricious formations that are often met with on the surface of the earth. It stood about thirty rods from the northern side of the area, very nearly central as to its eastern and western boundaries, and presented a slope inclining towards the south. Its greatest height was at its northern end, where it rose out of the rich alluvion of the soil, literally a rock of some forty feet in perpendicular height, having a summit of about an acre of level land, and falling off on its three sides; to the east and west precipitously; to the south quite gently and with regularity. It was this accidental formation which had induced the captain to select the spot as the site of his residence; for dwelling so far from any post, and in a place so difficult of access, something like military defences were merely precautions of ordinary prudence. While the pond remained, the islet was susceptible of being made very strong against any of the usual assaults of Indian warfare; and, now that the basin was drained, it had great advantages for the same purpose. The perpendicular rock to the north, even overhung the plain. It was almost inaccessible; while the formation on the other sides, offered singular facilities, both for a dwelling and for security. All this the captain, who was so familiar with the finesse of Indian stratagem, had resolved to improve in the following manner:

In the first place, he directed the men to build a massive wall of stone, for a hundred and fifty feet in length, and six feet in height. This stretched in front of the perpendicular rock, with receding walls to its verge. The latter were about two hundred feet in length, each. This was enclosing an area of two hundred, by one hundred and fifty feet, within a blind wall of masonry. Through this wall there was only a single passage; a gateway, in the centre of its southern face. The materials had all been found on the hill itself, which was well covered with heavy stones. Within this wall, which was substantially laid, by a Scotch mason, one accustomed to the craft, the men had erected a building of massive, squared, pine timber, well secured by cross partitions. This building followed the wall in its whole extent, was just fifteen feet in elevation, without the roof, and was composed, in part, by the wall itself; the latter forming nearly one-half its height, on the exterior. The breadth of this edifice was only twenty feet, clear of the stones and wood-work; leaving a court within of about one hundred by one hundred and seventy-five feet in extent. The roof extended over the gateway even; so that the space within was completely covered, the gates being closed.

This much had been done during the preceding fall and winter; the edifice presenting an appearance of rude completeness on the exterior. Still it had a sombre and goal-like air, there being nothing resembling a window visible; no aperture, indeed, on either of its outer faces, but the open gateway, of which the massive leaves were finished, and placed against the adjacent walls, but which were not yet hung. It is scarcely necessary to say, this house resembled barracks, more than an ordinary dwelling. Mrs. Willoughby stood gazing at it, half in doubt whether to admire or to condemn, when a voice, within a few yards, suddenly drew her attention in another direction.

"How you like him?" asked Nick, who was seated on a stone, at the margin of the stream, washing his feet, after a long day's hunt. "No t'ink him better dan beaver skin? Cap'in know all 'bout him; now he give Nick some more last quit-rent?"

"*Last*, indeed, it will be, then, Nick; for I have already paid you *twice* for your rights."

"Discovery wort' great deal, cap'in--see what great man he make pale-face."

"Ay, but *your* discovery, Nick, is not of that sort."

"What sort, den?" demanded Nick, with the rapidity of lightning. "Give him back 'e beaver, if you no like he discovery. Grad to see 'em back, ag'in; skin higher price dan ever."

"Nick, you're a cormorant, if there ever was one in this world! Here--there is a dollar for you; the quit-rent is paid for this year, at least. It ought to be for the last time."

"Let him go for all summer, cap'in. Yes, Nick wonderful commerant! no such eye he got, among Oneida!"

Here the Tuscarora left the side of the stream, and came up on the rock, shaking hands, good-humouredly, with Mrs. Willoughby, who rather liked the knave; though she knew him to possess most of the vices of his class.

"He very han'som beaver-dam," said Nick, sweeping his hand gracefully over the view; "bye 'nd bye, he'll bring potatoe, and corn, and cider--all 'e squaw want. Cap'in got good fort, too. Old soldier love fort; like to live in him."

"The day may come, Nick, when that fort may serve us all a good turn, out here in the wilderness," Mrs. Willoughby observed, in a somewhat melancholy tone; for her tender thoughts naturally turned towards her youthful and innocent daughters.

The Indian gazed at the house, with that fierce intentness which sometimes glared, in a manner that had got to be, in its ordinary aspects, dull and besotted. There was a startling intelligence in his eye, at such moments; the feelings of youth and earlier habit, once more asserting their power. Twenty years before, Nick had been foremost on the war-path; and what was scarcely less honourable, among the wisest around the council-fire. He was born a chief, and had made himself an outcast from his tribe, more by the excess of ungovernable passions, than from any act of base meanness.

"Cap'm tell Nick, now, what he mean by building such house, out here, among ole beaver bones?" he said, sideling up nearer to his employer, and gazing with some curiosity into his face.

"What do I mean, Nick?--Why I mean to have a place of safety to put the heads of my wife and children in, at need. The road to Canada is not so long, but a red-skin can make one pair of moccasins go over it. Then, the Oneidas and Mohawks are not all children of heaven."

"No pale-face rogue, go about, I s'pose?" said Nick, sarcastically.

"Yes, there are men of that class, who are none the worse for being locked out of one's house, at times. But, what do *you* think of the hut?--You know I call the place the 'Hut,' the Hutted Knoll."

"He hole plenty of beaver, if you cotch him!--But no water left, and he all go away. Why you make him stone, first; den you make him wood, a'ter; eh? Plenty rock; plenty tree."

"Why, the stone wall can neither be cut away, nor set fire to, Nick; that's the reason. I took as much stone as was necessary, and then used wood, which is more easily worked, and which is also drier."

"Good--Nick t'ought just dat. How you get him water if Injen come?"

"There's the stream, that winds round the foot of the hill, Nick, as you see; and then there is a delicious spring, within one hundred yards of the very gate."

"Which side of him?" asked Nick, with his startling rapidity.

"Why, here, to the left of the gate, and a little to the right of the large stone--"

"No--no," interrupted the Indian, "no left--no right--which side--*inside* gate; *outside* gate?"

"Oh!--the spring is outside the gate, certainly; but means might be found to make a covered way to it; and then the stream winds round directly underneath the rocks, behind the house, and wafer could be raised from *that*, by means of a rope. Our rifles would count for something, too, in drawing water, as well as in drawing blood."

"Good.--Rifle got long arm. He talk so, Ingin mind him. When you t'ink red-skin come ag'in your fort, cap'in, now you got him done?"

"A long time first, I hope, Nick. We are at peace with France, again; and I see no prospect of any new quarrel, very soon. So long as the French and English are at peace, the red men will not dare to touch either."

"Dat true as missionary! What a soldier do, cap'in, if so much peace? Warrior love a war-path."

"I wish it were not so, Nick. But *my* hatchet is buried, I hope, for ever."

"Nick hope cap'in know where to find him, if he want to? Very bad to put anyt'ing where he forget; partic'larly tomahawk. Sometime quarrel come, like rain, when you don't tink."

"Yes, that also cannot be denied. Yet, I fear the next quarrel will be among ourselves, Nick.--The government at home, and the people of the colonies, are getting to have bad blood between them."

"Dat very queer! Why pale-face mo'der and pale-face darter no love one anoder, like red-skin?"

"Really, Nick, you are somewhat interrogating this evening; but, my squaw must be a little desirous of seeing the inside of her house, as well as its outside, and I must refer you to that honest fellow, yonder, for an answer. His name is Mike; I hope he and you will always be good friends."

So saying, the captain nodded in a friendly manner, and led Mrs. Willoughby towards the hut, taking a foot-path that was already trodden firm, and which followed the sinuosities of the stream, to which it served as a sort of a dyke. Nick took the captain at his word, and turning about he met the county Leitrim-man, with an air of great blandness, thrusting out a hand, in the pale-face fashion, as a sign of amity, saying, at the same time--

"How do, Mike?--Sago--Sago--grad you come--good fellow to drink Santa Cruz, wid Nick."

"How do, Mike!" exclaimed the other, looking at the Tuscarora with astonishment, for this was positively the first red man the Irishman had ever seen. "How do Mike! Ould Nick be ye?--well--ye look pretty much as I expected to see you--pray, how did ye come to know *my* name?"

"Nick know him--know every t'ing. Grad to see you, Mike--hope we live together like good friend, down yonder, up here, over dere."

"Ye do, do ye! Divil burn me, now, if I want any sich company. Ould Nick's yer name, is it?"

"Old Nick--young Nick--saucy Nick; all one, all to'ther. Make no odd what you call; I come."

"Och, yer a handy one! Divil trust ye, but ye'll come when you arn't wanted, or yer not of yer father's own family. D'ye live hereabouts, masther Ould Nick?"

"Live here--out yonder--in he hut, in he wood--where he want. Make no difference to Nick."

Michael now drew back a pace or two, keeping his eyes fastened on the other intently, for he actually expected to see some prodigious and sudden change in his appearance. When he thought he had got a good position for manly defence or rapid retreat, as either might become necessary the county Leitrim-man put on a bolder front and resumed the discourse.

"If it's so indifferent to ye where ye dwell," asked Mike, "why can't you keep at home, and let a body carry these cloaks and bundles of the missuses, out yonder to the house wither she's gone?"

"Nick help carry 'em. Carry t'ing for dat squaw hundred time."

"That what! D'ye mane Madam Willoughby by yer blackguard name?"

"Yes; cap'in wife--cap'in squaw, mean him. Carry bundle, basket, hundred time for him."

"The Lord preserve me, now, from sich atrocity and impudence!" laying down the cloaks and bundles, and facing the Indian, with an appearance of great indignation--"Did a body ever hear sich a liar! Why, Misther Ould Nick, Madam Willoughby wouldn't let the likes of ye touch the ind of her garments. You wouldn't get the liberty to walk in the same path with her, much less to carry her bundles. I'll answer for it, ye're a great liar, now, ould Nick, in the bottom of your heart."

"Nick great liar," answered the Indian, good-naturedly; for he so well knew this was his common reputation, that he saw no use in denying it. "What of dat? Lie good sometime."

"That's another! Oh, ye animal; I've a great mind to set upon ye at once, and see what an honest man can do wid ye, in fair fight! If I only knew what ye'd got about yer toes, now, under them fine-looking things ye wear for shoes, once, I'd taich ye to talk of the missus, in this style."

"Speak as well as he know how. Nick never been to school. Call 'e squaw, *good* squaw. What want more?"

"Get out! If ye come a foot nearer, I'll be at ye, like a dog upon a bull, though ye gore me. What brought ye into this paiceful sittlement, where nothing but virtue and honesty have taken up their abode?"

What more Mike might have said is not known, as Nick caught a sign from the captain, and went loping across the flat, at his customary gait, leaving the Irishman standing on the defensive, and, to own the truth, not sorry to be rid of him. Unfortunately for the immediate enlightenment of Mike's mind, Joel overheard the dialogue, and comprehending its meaning, with his native readiness, he joined his companion in a mood but little disposed to clear up the error.

"Did ye see that *crathure*?" asked Mike, with emphasis.

"Sartain--he is often seen here, at the Hut. He may be said to live here, half his time."

"A pritty hut, then, ye must have of it! Why do ye tolerate the vagabond? He's not fit for Christian society."

"Oh! he's good company, sometimes, Mike. When you know him better, you'll like him better. Come; up with the bundles, and let us follow. The captain is looking after us, as you see."

"Well may he look, to see us in sich company!--Will he har-r-m the missus?"

"Not he. I tell you, you'll like him yourself when you come to know him."

"If I do, burn me! Why, he says *himself*, that he's Ould Nick, and I'm sure I never fancied the crathure but it was in just some such for-r-m. Och! he's ill-looking enough, for twenty Ould Nicks."

Lest the reader get an exaggerated notion of Michael's credulity, it may be well to say that Nick had painted a few days before, in a fit of caprice, and that one-half of his face was black, and the other a deep red, while each of his eyes was surrounded with a circle of white, all of which had got to be a little confused in consequence of a night or two of orgies, succeeded by mornings in which the toilet had been altogether neglected. His dress, too, a blanket with tawdry red and yellow trimmings, with ornamented leggings and moccasins to correspond, had all aided in maintaining the accidental mystification. Mike followed his companion, growling out his discontent, and watching the form of the Indian, as the latter still went loping over the flat, having passed the captain, with a message to the barns.

"I'll warrant ye, now, the captain wouldn't tolerate such a crathure, but he's sent him off to the woods, as ye may see, like a divil, as he is! To think of such a thing's spakeing to the missus! Will I fight him?--That will I, rather than he'll say an uncivil word to the likes of her! He's claws they tell me, though he kapes them so well covered in his fine brogues; divil burn me, but I'd grapple him by the toes."

Joel now saw how deep was Michael's delusion, and knowing it *must* soon be over, he determined to make a merit of necessity, by letting his friend into the truth, thereby creating a confidence that would open the way to a hundre'd future mischievous scenes.

"Claws!" he repeated, with an air of surprise--"And why do you think an Injin has claws, Mike?"

"An Injin! D'ye call that miscoloured crathure an Injin Joel. Isn't it one of yer yankee divils?"

"Out upon you, for an Irish ninny. Do you think the captain would *board* a devil! The fellow's a Tuscarora, and is as well known here as the owner of the Hut himself. It's Saucy Nick."

"Yes, saucy Ould Nick--had it from his very mout' and even the divil would hardly be such a blackguard as to lie about his own name. Och! he's a roarer, sure enough; and then for the tusks you mintion, I didn't see 'em, with my eyes; but the crathure has a mouth that might hould a basket-full."

Joel now perceived that he must go more seriously to work to undeceive his companion. Mike honestly believed he had met an American devil, and it required no little argumentation to persuade him of the contrary. We shall leave Joel employed in this difficult task, in which he finally succeeded, and follow the captain and his wife to the hut.

The lord and lady of the manor examined everything around their future residence, with curious eyes. Jamie Allen, the Scotch mason mentioned, was standing in front of the house, to hear what might be said of his wall, while two or three other mechanics betrayed some such agitation as the tyro in literature manifests, ere he learns what the critics have said of his first work. The exterior gave great satisfaction to the captain. The wall was not only solid and secure, but it was really handsome. This was in some measure owing to the quality of the stones, but quite as much to Jamie's dexterity in using them. The wall and chimneys, of the latter of which there were no less than six, were all laid in lime, too; it having been found necessary to burn some of the material to plaster the interior. Then the gates were massive, being framed in oak, filled in with four-inch plank, and might have resisted a very formidable assault. Their strong iron hinges were all in their places, but the heavy job of hanging had been deferred to a leisure moment, when all the strength of the manor might be collected for that purpose. There they stood, inclining against the wall, one on each side of the gateway, like indolent sentinels on post, who felt too secure from attack to raise their eyes.

The different mechanics crowded round the captain, each eager to show his own portion of what had been done. The winter had not been wasted, but, proper materials being in abundance, and on the spot, captain Willoughby had every reason to be satisfied with what he got for his money. Completely shut out from the rest of the world, the men had worked cheerfully and with little interruption; for their labours composed their recreation. Mrs. Willoughby found the cart of the building her family was to occupy, with the usual offices, done and furnished. This comprised all the front on the-eastern side of the gateway, and most of the wing, in the same half, extending back to the cliff. It is true, the finish was plain; but everything was comfortable. The ceilings were only ten feet high certainly, but it was thought prodigious in the colony in that day; and then the plastering of Jamie was by no means as unexceptionable as his stone-work; still every room had its two coats, and white-wash gave them a clean and healthful aspect. The end of the wing that came next the cliff was a laundry, and a pump was fitted, by means of which water was raised from the rivulet. Next came the kitchen, a spacious and comfortable room of thirty by twenty feet; an upper-servant's apartment succeeded; after which were the bed-rooms of the family a large parlour, and a library, or office, for the captain. As the entire range, on this particular side of the house, extended near or quite two hundred and fifty feet, there was no want of space or accommodation.

The opposite, or western half of the edifice, was devoted to more homely uses. It contained an eating-room and divers sleeping-rooms far the domestics and labourers, besides store-rooms, garners, and *omnium gatherums* of all sorts. The vast ranges of garrets, too, answered for various purposes of household and farming economy. All the windows, and sundry doors, opened into the court, while the whole of the exterior wall, both wooden and stone, presented a perfect blank, in the way of outlets. It was the captain's intention, however, to cut divers loops through the logs, at some convenient moment, so that men stationed in the garrets might command the different faces of the structure with their musketry. But, like the gates, these means of defence were laid aside for a more favourable opportunity.

Our excellent matron was delighted with her domestic arrangements. They much surpassed any of the various barracks in which she had dwelt, and a smile of happiness beamed on her handsome face, as she followed her husband from room to room, listening to his explanations. When they entered their private apartments, and these were furnished and ready to receive them, respect caused the rest to leave them by themselves, and once more they found that they were alone.

"Well, Wilhelmina," asked the gratified husband--gratified, because he saw pleasure beaming in the mild countenance and serene blue eyes of one of the best wives living--"Well, Wilhelmina," he asked, "can you give up Albany, and all the comforts of your friends' dwellings, to be satisfied in a home like this? It is not probable I shall ever build again, whatever Bob may do, when he comes after me. This structure, then, part house, part barrack, part fort, as it is, must be our residence for the remainder of our days. We are *hutted* for life."

"It is all-sufficient, Willoughby. It has space, comfort, warmth, coolness and security. What more can a wife and a mother ask, when she is surrounded by those she most loves? Only attend to the security, Hugh. Remember how far we are removed from any succour, and how sudden and fierce the Indians are in their attacks. Twice have we, ourselves, been near being destroyed by surprises, from which accident, or God's providence, protected us, rather than our own vigilance. If this could happen in garrisons, and with king's troops around us, how much more easily might it happen here, with only common labourers to watch what is going on!"

"You exaggerate the danger, wife. There are no Indians, in this part of the country, who would dare to molest a settlement like ours. We count thirteen able-bodied men in all, besides seven women, and could use seventeen or eighteen muskets and rifles on an emergency. No *tribe* would dare commence hostilities, in a time of general peace, and so near the settlements too; and, as to stragglers, who might indeed murder to rob, we are so strong, ourselves, that we may sleep in peace, so far as they are concerned."

"One never knows that, dearest Hugh. A marauding party of half-a-dozen might prove too much for many times their own number, when unprepared. I *do* hope you will have the gates hung, at least; should the girls come here, in the autumn, I could not sleep without hanging the gates."

"Fear nothing, love," said the captain, kissing his wife with manly tenderness. "As for Beulah and Maud, let them come when they please; we shall always have a welcome for them, and no place can be safer than under their father's eyes."

"I care not so much for myself, Hugh, but *do* not let the gates be forgotten until the girls come."

"Everything shall be done as you desire, wife of mine, though it will be a hard job to get two such confounded heavy loads of wood on their hinges. We must take some day when everybody is at home, and everybody willing to work. Saturday next, I intend to have a review; and, once a month, the year round, there will be a muster, when all the arms are to be cleaned and loaded, and orders given how to act in case of an alarm. An old soldier would be disgraced to allow himself to be run down by mere vagabonds. My pride is concerned, and you may sleep in peace."

"Yes, do, dearest Hugh."--Then the matron proceeded through the rooms, expressing her satisfaction at the care which had been had for her comfort, in her own rooms in particular.

Sooth to say, the interior of the hut presented that odd contrast between civilization and rude expedients, which so frequently occurs on an American frontier, where persons educated in refinement often find themselves brought in close collision with savage life. Carpets, in America, and in the year of our Lord 1765, were not quite as much a matter of course in domestic economy, as they are to-day. Still they were to be found, though it was rare, indeed, that they covered more than the centre of the room. One of these great essentials, without which no place can appear comfortable in a cold climate, was spread on the floor of Mrs. Willoughby's parlour--a room that served for both eating and as a sala, the Knight's Hall of the Hut, measuring twenty by twenty-four feet--though in fact this carpet concealed exactly two-thirds of the white clean plank. Then the chairs were massive and even rich, while one might see his face in the dark mahogany of the tables. There were cellarets--the captain being a connoisseur in wines--bureaus, secretaries, beaufets, and other similar articles, that had been collected in the course of twenty years' housekeeping, and scattered at different posts, were collected, and brought hither by means of sledges, and the facilities of the water-courses. Fashion had little to do with furniture, in that simple age, when the son did not hesitate to wear even the clothes of the father, years and years after the tailor had taken leave of them. Massive old furniture, in particular, lasted for generations, and our matron now saw many articles that had belonged to her grandfather assembled beneath the first roof that she could ever strictly call her own.

Mrs. Willoughby took a survey of the offices last. Here she found, already established, the two Plinies, with Mari', the sister of the elder Pliny, Bess, the wife of the younger, and Mony--alias Desdemona--a collateral of the race, by ties and affinities that garter-king-at-arms could not have traced genealogically; since he would have been puzzled to say whether the woman was the cousin, or aunt, or step-daughter of Mari', or all three. All the women were hard at work, Bess singing in a voice that reached the adjoining forest. Mari'--this name was pronounced with a strong emphasis on the last syllable, or like Maria, without the final vowel--Mari' was the head of the kitchen, even Pliny the elder standing in salutary dread of her authority; and her orders to her brother and nephew were pouring forth, in an English that was divided into three categories; the Anglo-Saxon, the Low

Dutch, and the Guinea dialect; a medley that rendered her discourse a droll assemblage of the vulgar and the classical.

"Here, niggers," she cried, "why you don't jump about like Paus dance? Ebbery t'ing want a hand, and some want a foot. Plate to wash, crockery to open, water to b'ile, dem knife to clean, and not'ing missed. Lord, here's a madam, and 'e whole kitchen in a diffusion."

"Well, Mari'," exclaimed the captain, good-naturedly, "here you are, scolding away as if you had been in the place these six months, and knew all its faults and weaknesses."

"Can't help a scold, master, in sich a time as dis--come away from dem plates, *you* Great Smash, and let a proper hand take hold on 'em."

Here we ought to say, that captain Willoughby had christened Bess by the sobriquet of Great Smash, on account of her size, which fell little short of two hundred, estimated in pounds, and a certain facility she possessed in destroying crockery, while 'Mony went by the milder appellation of "Little Smash;" not that bowls or plates fared any better in her hands, but because *she* weighed only one hundred and eighty.

"Dis is what I tell 'em, master," continued Mari', in a remonstrating, argumentative sort of a tone, with dogmatism and respect singularly mingled in her manner--"Dis, massa, just what I tell 'em *all*. I tell 'em, says I, this is Hunter Knoll, and not All*bon*ny--here no store--no place to buy t'ing if you break 'em; no good woman who know ebbery t'ing, to tell you where to find t'ing, if you *lose* him. If dere was only good woman, *dat* somet'ing; but no fortun'-teller out here in de bushes--no, no--when a silber spoon go, *here*, he go for good and all--Goody, massy"--staring at something in the court--"what he call *dat*, sa?"

"That--oh! that is only an Indian hunter I keep about me, to bring us game--you'll never have an empty spit, Mari', as long as *he* is with us. Fear nothing; he will not harm you. His name is Nick."

"De *Ole* Nick, massa?"

"No, only *Saucy* Nick. The fellow is a little slovenly to-day in his appearance, and you see he has brought already several partridges, besides a rabbit. We shall have venison, in the season."

Here all the negroes, after staring at Nick, quite a minute, set up a loud shout, laughing as if the Tuscarora had been created for their special amusement. Although the captain was somewhat of a martinet in his domestic discipline, it had ever altogether exceeded his authority, or his art, to prevent these bursts of merriment; and he led his wife away from the din, leaving Mari', Great Smash, and Little Smash, with the two Plinies, in ecstasies at their own uproar. Burst succeeded burst, until the Indian walked away, in offended dignity.

Such was the commencement of the domestication of the Willoughbys at the Hutted Knoll. The plan of our tale does not require us to follow them minutely for, the few succeeding years, though some further explanation may be necessary to show why this settlement varied a little from the ordinary course.

That very season, or, in the summer of 1765, Mrs. Willoughby inherited some real estate in Albany, by the death of an uncle, as well as a few thousand pounds currency, in ready money. This addition to his fortune made the captain exceedingly comfortable; or, for that day, rich; and it left him to act his pleasure as related to his lands. Situated as these last were, so remote from other settlements as to render highways, for some time, hopeless, he saw no use in endeavouring to anticipate the natural order of things. It would only create embarrassment to raise produce that could not be sent to market; and he well knew that a population of any amount could not exist, in quiet, without the usual attendants of buying and selling. Then it suited his own taste to be the commander-in-chief of an isolated establishment like this; and he was content to live in abundance, on his flats, feeding his people, his cattle, and even his hogs to satiety, and having wherewithal to send away the occasional adventurer, who entered his clearing, contented and happy.

Thus it was that he neither sold nor leased. No person dwelt on his land who was not a direct dependant, or hireling, and all that the earth yielded he could call his own. Nothing was sent abroad for sale but cattle. Every year, a small drove of fat beeves and milch cows found their way through the forest to Albany, and the proceeds returned in the shape of foreign supplies. The rents, and the interests on bonds, were left to accumulate, or were applied to aid Robert in obtaining a new step in the army. Lands began to be granted nearer and nearer to his own, and here and there some old officer like himself, or a solitary farmer, began to cut away the wilderness; but none in his immediate vicinity.

Still the captain did not live altogether as a hermit. He visited Edmeston of Mount Edmeston, a neighbour less than fifty miles distant; was occasionally seen at Johnson Hall, with Sir William; or at the bachelor establishment of Sir John, on the Mohawk; and once or twice he so far overcame his indolence, as to consent to serve as a member for a new county, that was called Tryon, after a ruling governor.

Chapter IV

Hail! sober evening! Thee the harass'd brain
And aching heart with fond orisons greet;
The respite thou of toil; the balm of pain;
To thoughtful mind the hour for musing meet,
'Tis then the sage from forth his lone retreat,
The rolling universe around espies;
'Tis then the bard may hold communion sweet
With lovely shapes unkenned by grosser eyes,
And quick perception comes of finer mysteries.
  Sands.

In the preceding chapter we closed the minuter narrative with a scene at the Hut, in the spring of 1765. We must now advance the time just ten years, opening, anew, in the month of May, 1775. This, it is scarcely necessary to tell the reader, is bringing him at once up to the earliest days of the revolution. The contest which preceded that great event had in fact occurred in the intervening time, and we are now about to plunge into the current of some of the minor incidents of the struggle itself.

Ten years are a century in the history of a perfectly new settlement. The changes they produce are even surprising, though in ordinary cases they do not suffice to erase the signs of a recent origin. The forest is opened, and the light of day admitted, it is true; but its remains are still to be seen in multitudes of unsightly stumps, dead standing trees, and ill-looking stubs. These vestiges of the savage state usually remain a quarter of a century; in certain region they are to be found for even more than twice that period. All this, however, had captain Willoughby escaped, in consequence of limiting his clearing, in a great measure, to that which had been made by the beavers, and from which time and natural decay had, long before his arrival, removed every ungainly object. It is true, here and there a few acres had been cleared on the firmer ground, at the margin of the flats, where barns and farm buildings had been built, and orchards planted; but, in order to preserve the harmony of his view, the captain had caused all the stumps to be pulled and burnt, giving to these places the same air of agricultural finish as characterized the fields on the lower land.

To this sylvan scene, at a moment which preceded the setting of the sun by a little more than an hour, and in the first week of the genial month of May, we must now bring the reader in fancy. The season had been early, and the Beaver Manor, or the part of it which was cultivated, lying low and sheltered, vegetation had advanced considerably beyond the point that is usual, at that date, in the elevated region of which we have been writing. The meadows were green with matted grasses, the wheat and rye resembled rich velvets, and the ploughed fields had the fresh and mellowed appearance of good husbandry and a rich soil. The shrubbery, of which the captain's English taste had introduced quantities, was already in leaf, and even portions of the forest began to veil their sombre mysteries with the delicate foliage of an American spring.

The site of the ancient pond was a miracle of rustic beauty. Everything like inequality or imperfection had disappeared, the whole presenting a broad and picturesquely shaped basin, with outlines fashioned principally by nature, an artist that rarely fails in effect. The flat was divided into fields by low post-and-rail fences, the captain making it a law to banish all unruly animals from his estate. The barns and out-buildings were neatly made and judiciously placed, and the three or four roads, or lanes, that led to them, crossed the low-land in such graceful curves, as greatly to increase the beauty of the landscape. Here and there a log cabin was visible, nearly buried in the forest, with a few necessary and neat appliances around it; the homes of labourers who had long dwelt in them, and who seemed content to pass their lives in the same place. As most of these men had married and become fathers, the whole colony, including children, notwithstanding the captain's policy not to settle, had grown to considerably more than a hundred souls, of whom three-and-twenty were able-bodied men. Among the latter were the millers; but, their mills were buried in the ravine where they had been first placed, quite out of sight from the picture above, concealing all the unavoidable and ungainly-looking objects of a saw-mill yard.

As a matter of course, the object of the greatest interest, as it was the most conspicuous, was the Hutted Knoll, as the house was now altogether called, and the objects it contained. Thither, then, we will now direct our attention, and describe things as they appeared ten years after they were first presented to the reader.

The same agricultural finish as prevailed on the flats pervaded every object on the Knoll, though some labour had been expended to produce it. Everything like a visible rock, the face of the cliff on the northern end excepted, had disappeared, the stones having been blasted, and either worked into walls for foundations, or walls for fence. The entire base of the Knoll, always excepting the little precipice at the rivulet, was encircled by one of the latter, erected under the superintendence of Jamie Allen, who still remained at the Hut, a bachelor, and as he said himself, a happy man. The southern-face of the Knoll was converted into lawn, there being quite two acres intersected with walks, and well garnished with shrubbery. What was unusual in America, at that day, the captain, owing to his English education, had avoided straight lines, and formal paths; giving to the little spot the improvement on nature which is a consequence of embellishing her works without destroying them. On each side of this lawn was an orchard, thrifty and young, and which were already beginning to show signs of putting forth their blossoms.

About the Hut itself, the appearance of change was not so manifest. Captain Willoughby had caused it to be constructed originally, as he intended to preserve it, and if formed no part of his plan to cover it with tawdry colours. There it stood, brown above, and grey beneath, as wood or stone was the material, with a widely projecting roof. It had no piazzas, or stoups, and was still without external windows, one range excepted. The loops had been cut, but it was more for the benefit of lighting the garrets, than for any other reason, all of them being glazed, and serving the end for which they had been pierced. The gates remained precisely in the situation in which they were, when last presented to the eye of the reader! There they stood, each leaning against the wall on its own side of the gateway, the hinges beginning to rust, by time and exposure. Ten years had not produced a day of sufficient leisure in which to hang them: though Mrs. Willoughby frequently spoke of the necessity of doing so, in the course of the first summer. Even she had got to be so familiarized to her situation, and so accustomed to seeing the leaves where they stood, that she now regarded them as a couple of sleeping lions in stone, or as characteristic ornaments, rather than as substantial defences to the entrance of the dwelling.

The interior of the Hut, however, had undergone many alterations. The western half had been completed, and handsome rooms had been fitted up for guests and inmates of the family, in the portion of the edifice occupied by the latter. Additional comforts had been introduced, and, the garners, cribs and lodgings of the labourers having been transferred to the skirts of the forest, the house was more strictly and exclusively the abode of a respectable and well-regulated family. In the rear, too, a wing had been thrown along the verge of the cliff, completely enclosing the court. This wing, which overhung the rivulet, and had, not only a most picturesque site, but a most picturesque and lovely view, now contained the library, parlour and music-room, together with other apartments devoted to the uses of the ladies, during the day; the old portions of the house that had once been similarly occupied being now converted into sleeping apartments. The new wing was constructed entirely of massive squared logs, so as to render it bullet-proof, here being no necessity for a stone foundation, standing, as it did, on the verge of a cliff some forty feet in height. This was the part of the edifice which had external windows, the elevation removing it from the danger of inroads, or hostile shot, while the air and view were both grateful and desirable. Some extra attention had been paid to the appearance of the meadows on this side of the Knoll, and the captain had studiously kept their skirts, as far as the eye could see from the windows, in virgin forest; placing the barns, cabins, and other detached buildings, so far south as to be removed from view. Beulah Willoughby, a gentle, tranquil creature, had a profound admiration of the beauties of nature; and to her, her parents had yielded the control of everything that was considered accessary to the mere charms of the eye; her taste had directed most of that which had not been effected by the noble luxuriance of nature. Wild roses were already putting forth their leaves in various fissures of the rocks, where earth had been placed for their support, and the margin of the little stream, that actually washed the base of the cliff, winding off in a charming sweep through the meadows, a rivulet of less than twenty feet in width, was garnished with willows and alder. Quitting this sylvan spot, we will return to the little shrub-adorned area in front of the Hut. This spot the captain called his *glacis*, while his daughters termed it the lawn. The hour, it will be remembered, was shortly before sunset, and thither nearly all the family had repaired to breathe the freshness of the pure air, and bathe in the genial warmth of a season, which is ever so grateful to those who have recently escaped from the rigour of a stern winter. Rude, and sufficiently picturesque garden-seats, were scattered about, and on one of these were seated the captain and his wife; he, with his hair sprinkled with grey, a hale, athletic, healthy man of sixty, and she a fresh-looking, mild-featured, and still handsome matron of forty-eight. In front, stood a venerable-looking personage, of small stature, dressed in rusty black, of the cut that denoted the attire of a clergyman, before it was considered aristocratic to wear the outward symbols of belonging to the church of God. This was the Rev. Jedidiah Woods, a native of New England, who had long served as a chaplain in the same regiment with the captain, and who, being a bachelor, on retired pay, had dwelt with his old messmate for the last eight years, in the double capacity of one who exercised the healing art as well for the soul as for the body. To his other offices, he added that of an instructor, in various branches of knowledge, to the young people. The chaplain, for so he was called by everybody in and around the Hut, was, at the moment of which we are writing, busy in expounding to his friends certain nice distinctions that existed, or which he fancied to exist, between a tom-cod and a chub, the former of which fish he very erroneously conceived he held in his hand at that moment; the Rev. Mr. Woods being a much better angler than naturalist. To his dissertation Mrs. Willoughby listened with great good-nature, endeavouring all the while to feel interested; while her husband kept uttering his "by all means," "yes," "certainly," "you're quite right, Woods," his gaze, at the same time, fastened on Joel Strides, and Pliny the elder, who were unharnessing their teams, on the flats beneath, having just finished a "land," and deeming it too late to commence another.

Beulah, her pretty face shaded by a large sun-bonnet, was superintending the labours of Jamie Allen, who, finding nothing just then to do as a mason, was acting in the capacity of gardener; his hat was thrown upon the grass, with his white locks bare, and he was delving about some shrubs with the intention of giving them the benefit of a fresh dressing of manure. Maud, however, without a hat of any sort, her long, luxuriant, silken, golden tresses covering her shoulders, and occasionally veiling her warm, rich cheek, was exercising with a battledore, keeping Little Smash, now increased in size to quite fourteen stone, rather actively employed as an assistant, whenever the exuberance of her own spirits caused her to throw the plaything beyond her reach. In one of the orchards, near by, two men were employed trimming the trees. To these the captain next turned all his attention, just as he had encouraged the chaplain to persevere, by exclaiming, "out of all question, my dear sir"--though he was absolutely ignorant that the other had just advanced a downright scientific heresy. At this critical moment a cry from Little Smash, that almost equalled a downfall of crockery in its clamour, drew every eye in her direction.

"What is the matter, Desdemona?" asked the chaplain, a little tartly, by no means pleased at having his natural history startled by sounds so inapplicable to the subject. "How often have I told you that the Lord views with displeasure anything so violent and improper as your outcries?"

"Can't help him, dominie--nebber can help him, when he take me sudden. See, masser, dere come Ole Nick!"

There was Nick, sure enough. For the first time, in more than two years, the Tuscarora was seen approaching the house, on the long, loping trot that he affected when he wished to seem busy, or honestly earning his money. He was advancing by the only road that was ever travelled by the stranger as he approached the Hut; or, he came up the valley. As the woman spoke, he had just made his appearance over the rocks, in the direction of the mills. At that distance, quite half a mile, he would not have been recognised, but for this gait, which was too familiar to all at the Knoll, however, to be mistaken.

"That is Nick, sure enough!" exclaimed the captain. "The fellow comes at the pace of a runner; or, as if he were the bearer of some important news!"

"The tricks of Saucy Nick are too well known to deceive any here," observed Mrs. Willoughby, who, surrounded by her husband and children, always felt so happy as to deprecate every appearance of danger.

"These savages will keep that pace for hours at a time," observed the chaplain; "a circumstance that has induced some naturalists to fancy a difference in the species, if not in the genus."

"Is he chub or tom-cod, Woods?" asked the captain, throwing back on the other all he recollected of the previous discourse.

"Nay," observed Mrs. Willoughby, anxiously, "I *do* think he may have some intelligence! It is now more than a twelvemonth since we have seen Nick."

"It is more than twice twelvemonth, my dear; I have not seen the fellow's face since I denied him the keg of rum for his 'discovery' of another beaver pond. He has tried to sell me a new pond every season since the purchase of this."

"Do you think he took serious offence, Hugh, at that refusal? If so, would it not be better to give him what he asks?"

"I have thought little about it, and care less, my dear. Nick and I know each other pretty well. It is an acquaintance of thirty years' standing, and one that has endured trials by flood and field, and even by the horse-whip. No less than three times have I been obliged to make these salutary applications to Nick's back, with my own hands; though it is, now, more than ten years since a blow has passed between us."

"Does a savage ever forgive a blow?" asked the chaplain, with a grave air, and a look of surprise.

"I fancy a *savage* is quite as apt to forgive it, as a *civilized* man, Woods. To you, who have served so long in His Majesty's army, a blow, in the way of punishment, can be no great novelty."

"Certainly not, as respects the soldiers; but I did not know Indians were ever flogged."

"That is because you never happened to be present at the ceremony-- but, this is Nick, sure enough; and by his trot I begin to think the fellow has some message, or news."

"How old is the man, captain? Does an Indian never break down?"

"Nick must be fairly fifty, now. I have known him more than half that period, and he was an experienced, and, to own the truth, a brave and skilful warrior, when we first met. I rate him fifty, every day of it."

By this time the new-comer was so near, that the conversation ceased, all standing gazing at him, as he drew near, and Maud gathering up her hair, with maiden bashfulness, though certainly Nick was no stranger. As for Little Smash, she waddled off to proclaim the news to the younger Pliny, Mari, and Great Smash, all of whom were still in the kitchen of the Hut, flourishing, sleek and glistening.

Soon after, Nick arrived. He came up the Knoll on his loping trot, never stopping until he was within five or six yards of the Captain, when he suddenly halted, folded his arms, and stood in a composed attitude, lest he should betray a womanish desire to tell his story. He did not even pant but appeared as composed and unmoved, as if he had walked the half-mile he had been seen to pass over on a trot.

"Sago--Sago," cried the captain, heartily--"you are welcome back, Nick; I am glad to see you still so active."

"Sago"--answered the guttural voice of the Indian, who quietly nodded his head.

"What will you have to refresh you, after such a journey, Nick--our trees give us good cider, now."

"Santa Cruz better,"--rejoined the sententious Tuscarora.

"Santa Cruz is certainly *stronger*" answered the captain laughing, "and, in that sense, you may find it better. You shall have a glass, as soon as we go to the house. What news do you bring, that you come in so fast?"

"Glass won't do. Nick bring news worth *jug*. Squaw give *two* jug for Nick's news. Is it barg'in?"

"I!" cried Mrs. Willoughby--"what concern can I have with your news. My daughters are both with me, and Heaven be praised! both are well. What *can* I care for your news, Nick?"

"Got no pap-poose but gal? T'ink you got boy--officer--great chief--up here, down yonder--over dere."

"Robert!--Major Willoughby! What can *you* have to tell me of my son?"

"Tell all about him, for *one* jug. Jug out yonder; Nick's story out here. One good as t'other."

"You shall have all you ask, Nick."--These were not temperance days, when conscience took so firm a stand between the bottle and the lips.--"You shall have all you ask, Nick, provided you can really give me good accounts of my noble boy. Speak, then; what have you to say?"

"Say you see him in ten, five minute. Sent Nick before to keep moder from too much cry."

An exclamation from Maud followed; then the ardent girl was seen rushing down the lawn, her hat thrown aside; and her bright fair hair again flowing in ringlets on her shoulders. She flew rather than ran, in the direction of the mill, where the figure of Robert Willoughby was seen rushing forward to meet her. Suddenly the girl stopped, threw herself on a log, and hid her face. In a few minutes she was locked in her brother's arms. Neither Mrs. Willoughby nor Beulah imitated this impetuous movement on the part of Maud; but the captain, chaplain, and even Jamie Allen, hastened down the road to meet and welcome the young major. Ten minutes later, Bob Willoughby was folded to his mother's heart; then came Beulah's turn; after which, the news having flown through the household, the young man had to receive the greetings of *Mari'*, both the Smashes, the younger Pliny, and all the dogs. A tumultuous quarter of an hour brought all round, again, to its proper place, and restored something like order to the Knoll. Still an excitement prevailed the rest of the day, for the sudden arrival of a guest always produced a sensation in that retired settlement; much more likely, then, was the unexpected appearance of the only son and heir to create one. As everybody bustled and was in motion, the whole family was in the parlour, and major Willoughby was receiving the grateful refreshment of a delicious cup of tea, before the sun set. The chaplain would have retired out of delicacy, but to this the captain would not listen; he would have everything proceed as if the son were a customary guest, though it might have been seen by the manner in which his mother's affectionate eye was fastened on his handsome face, as well as that in which his sister Beulah, in particular, hung about him, under the pretence of supplying his wants, that the young man was anything but an every-day inmate.

"How the lad has grown!" said the captain, tears of pride starting into his eyes, in spite of a very manful resolution to appear composed and soldier-like.

"I was about to remark that myself, captain," observed the chaplain. "I do think Mr. Robert has got to his full six feet--every inch as tall as you are yourself, my good sir."

"That is he, Woods--and taller in one sense. He is a major, already, at twenty-seven; it is a step I was not able to reach at near twice the age."

"That is owing, my dear sir," answered the son quickly, and with a slight tremor in his voice, "to your not having as kind a father as has fallen to my share--or at least one not as well provided with the means of purchasing."

"Say none at all, Bob, and you can wound no feeling, while you will tell the truth. *My* father died a lieutenant-colonel when I was a school-boy; I owed my ensigncy to my uncle Sir Hugh, the father of the present Sir Harry Willoughby; after that I owed each step to hard and long service. Your mother's legacies have helped you along, at a faster rate, though I do trust there has been some merit to aid in the preferment."

"Speaking of Sir Harry Willoughby, sir, reminds me of one part of my errand to the Hut," said the major, glancing his eye towards his father, as if to prepare him for some unexpected intelligence.

"What of my cousin?" demanded the captain, calmly. "We have not met in thirty years, and are the next thing to strangers to each other. Has he made that silly match of which I heard something when last in York? Has he disinherited his daughter as he threatened? Use no reserve here; our friend Woods is one of the family."

"Sir Harry Willoughby is not married, sir, but dead."

"Dead!" repeated the captain, setting down his cup, like one who received a sudden shock. "I hope not without having been reconciled to his daughter, and providing for her large family?"

"He died in her arms, and escaped the consequences of his silly intention to marry his own housekeeper. With one material exception, he has left Mrs. Bowater his whole fortune."

The captain sat thoughtful, for some time; every one else being silent and attentive. But the mother's feelings prompted her to inquire as to the nature of the exception.

"Why, mother, contrary to all my expectations, and I may say wishes, he has left *me* twenty-five thousand pounds in the fives. I only hold the money as my father's trustee."

"You do no such thing, Master Bob, I can tell you!" said the captain, with emphasis.

The son looked at the father, a moment, as if to see whether he was understood, and then he proceeded--

"I presume you remember, sir," said the major, "that *you* are the heir to the title?"

"I have not forgot that, major Willoughby; but what is an empty baronetcy to a happy husband and father like me, here in the wilds of America? Were I still in the army, and a colonel, the thing might be of use; as I am, I would rather have a tolerable road from this place to the Mohawk than the duchy of Norfolk, without the estate."

"Estate there is none, certainly," returned the major, in a tone of a little disappointment, "except the twenty-five thousand pounds; unless you include that which you possess where you are; not insignificant, by the way, sir."

"It will do well enough for old Hugh Willoughby, late a captain in His Majesty's 23d Regiment of Foot, but not so well for *Sir* Hugh. No, no, Bob. Let the baronetcy sleep awhile; it has been used quite enough for the last hundred years or more. Out of this circle, there are probably not ten persons in America, who know that I have any claims to it."

The major coloured, and he played with the spoon of his empty cup, stealing a glance or two around, before he answered.

"I beg your pardon, Sir Hugh--my dear father, I mean--but--to own the truth, never anticipating such a decision on your part, I have spoken of the thing to a good many friends--I dare say, if the truth were known, I've called you the baronet, or Sir Hugh, to others, at least a dozen times."

"Well, should it be so, the thing will be forgotten. A parson can be unfrocked, Woods, and a baronet can be unbaroneted, I suppose."

"But, Sir William"--so everybody called the well-known Sir William Johnson, in the colony of New York--"But, Sir William found it useful, Willoughby, and so, I dare say, will his son and successor, Sir John," observed the attentive wife and anxious mother; "and if *you* are not now in the army, Bob is. It will be a good thing for our son one day, and ought not to be lost."

"Ah, I see how it is, Beulah; your mother has no notion to lose the right of being called Lady Willoughby."

"I am sure my mother, sir, wishes to be called nothing that does not become *your* wife; if you remain Mr. Hugh Willoughby, she will remain Mrs. Hugh Willoughby. But papa, it *might* be useful to Bob."

Beulah was a great favourite with the captain, Maud being only his darling; he listened always to whatever the former said, therefore, with indulgence and respect. He often told the chaplain that his daughter Beulah had the true feelings of her sex, possessing a sort of instinct for whatever was right and becoming, in woman.

"Well, Bob may have the baronetcy, then," he said, smiling. "Major Sir Robert Willoughby will not sound amiss in a despatch."

"But, Bob *cannot* have it, father," exclaimed Maud--"No one *can* have it but *you*; and it's a pity it should be lost."

"Let him wait, then, until I am out of the way; when he may claim his own."

"*Can* that be done?" inquired the mother, to whom nothing was without interest that affected her children. "How is it, Mr. Woods?--may a title be dropped, and then picked up again?--how is this, Robert?"

"I believe it may, my dear mother--it will always exist, so long as there is an heir, and my father's disrelish for it will not be binding on me."

"Oh! in that case, then, all will come right in the end--though, as your father does not want it, I wish you could have it, now."

This was said with the most satisfied air in the world, as if the speaker had no possible interest in the matter herself, and it closed the conversation, for that time. It was not easy to keep up an interest in anything that related to the family, where Mrs. Willoughby was concerned, in which heart did not predominate. A baronetcy was a considerable dignity in the colony of New York in the year of our Lord, 1775, and it gave its possessor far more importance than it would have done in England. In the whole colony there was but one, though a good many were to be found further south; and he was known as "Sir John," as, in England, Lord Rockingham, or, in America, at a later day, La Fayette, was known as "*The* Marquis." Under such circumstances, then, it would have been no trifling sacrifice to an ordinary woman to forego the pleasure of being called "my lady." But the sacrifice cost our matron no pain, no regrets, no thought even: The same attachments which made her happy, away from the world, in the wilderness where she dwelt, supplanted all other feelings, and left her no room, or leisure, to think of such vanities. When the discourse changed, it was understood that "Sir Hugh" was not to be "Sir Hugh," and that "Sir Robert" must bide his time.

"Where did you fall in with the Tuscarora, Bob?" suddenly asked the captain, as much to bring up another subject, as through curiosity. "The fellow had been so long away, I began to think we should never see him again.

"He tells me, sir, he has been on a war path, somewhere out among the western savages. It seems these Indians fight among themselves, from time to time, and Nick has been trying to keep his hand in. I found him down at Canajoharie, and took him for a guide, though he had the honesty to own he was on the point of coming over here, had I not engaged him."

"He tells me, sir, he has been on a war path, somewhere out among the western savages. It seems these Indians fight among themselves, from time to time, and Nick has been trying to keep his hand in. I found him down at Canajoharie, and took him for a guide, though he had the honesty to own he was on the point of coming over here, had I not engaged him."

"I'll answer for it he didn't tell you *that*, until you had paid him for the job."

"Why, to own the truth, he did not, sir. He pretended something about owing money in the village, and got his pay in advance. I learned his intentions only when we were within a few miles of the Hut."

"I'm glad to find, Bob, that you give the place its proper name. How gloriously Sir Hugh Willoughby, Bart., of The *Hut*, Tryon county, New York, would sound, Woods!--Did Nick boast of the scalps he has taken from the Carthaginians?"

"He lays claim to three, I believe, though I have seen none of his trophies."

"The Roman hero!--Yet, I have known Nick rather a dangerous warrior. He was out against us, in some of my earliest service, and our acquaintance was made by my saving his life from the bayonet of one of my own grenadiers. I thought the fellow remembered the act for some years; but, in the end, I believe I flogged all the gratitude out of him. His motives, now, are concentrated in the little island of Santa Cruz."

"Here he is, father," said Maud, stretching her light, flexible form out of a window. "Mike and the Indian are seated at the lower spring, with a jug between them, and appear to be in a deep conversation."

"Ay, I remember on their first acquaintance, that Mike mistook *Saucy* Nick, for *Old* Nick. The Indian was indignant for a while, at being mistaken for the Evil Spirit, but the worthies soon found a bond of union between them, and, before six months, he and the Irishman became sworn friends. It is said whenever two human beings love a common principle, that it never fails to make them firm allies."

"And what was the principle, in this case, captain Willoughby?" inquired the chaplain, with curiosity.

"Santa Cruz. Mike renounced whiskey altogether, after he came to America, and took to rum. As for Nick, he was never so vulgar as to find pleasure in the former liquor."

The whole party had gathered to the windows, while the discourse was proceeding, and looking out, each individual saw Mike and his friend, in the situation described by Maud. The two *amateurs--connoisseurs* would not be misapplied, either--had seated themselves at the brink of a spring of delicious water, and removing the corn-cob that Pliny the younger had felt it to be classical to affix to the nozzle of a quart jug, had, some time before, commenced the delightful recreation of sounding the depth, not of the spring, but of the vessel. As respects the former, Mike, who was a wag in his way, had taken a hint from a practice said to be common in Ireland, called "potatoe and point," which means to eat the potatoe and point at the butter; declaring that "rum and p'int" was every bit as entertaining as a "p'int of rum." On this principle, then, with a broad grin on a face that opened from ear to ear whenever he laughed, the county Leitrim-man would gravely point his finger at the water, in a sort of mock-homage, and follow up the movement with such a suck at the nozzle, as, aided by the efforts of Nick, soon analyzed the upper half of the liquor that had entered by that very passage. All this time, conversation did not flag, and, as the parties grew warm, confidence increased, though reason sensibly diminished. As a part of this discourse will have some bearing on what is to follow, it may be in place to relate it, here.

"Ye're a jewel, ye be, *ould* Nick, or *young* Nick!" cried Mike, in an ecstasy of friendship, just after he had completed his first half-pint. "Ye're as wilcome at the Huts, as if ye owned thim, and I love ye as I did my own brother, before I left the county Leitrim--paice to his sowl!"

"He dead?" asked Nick, sententiously; for he had lived enough among the pale-faces to have some notions of then theory about the soul.

"That's more than I know--but, living or dead, the man must have a sowl, ye understand, Nicholas. A human crathure widout a sowl, is what I call a heretick; and none of the O'Hearns ever came to *that*."

Nick was tolerably drunk, but by no means so far gone, that he had not manners enough to make a grave, and somewhat dignified gesture; which was as much as to say he was familiar with the subject.

"All go ole fashion here?" he asked, avoiding every appearance of curiosity, however.

"That does it--that it does, Nicholas. All goes ould enough. The captain begins to get ould; and the missus is oulder than she used to be; and Joel's wife looks a hundred, though she isn't t'irty; and Joel, himself, the spalpeen- -he looks--" a gulp at the jug stopped the communication.

"Dirty, too?" added the sententious Tuscarora, who did not comprehend more than half his friend said.

"Ay, dir-r-ty--he's always *that*. He's a dirthy fellow, that thinks his yankee charactur is above all other things."

Nick's countenance became illuminated with an expression nowise akin to that produced by rum, and he fastened on his companion one of his fiery gazes, which occasionally seemed to penetrate to the centre of the object looked at.

"Why pale-face hate one anoder? Why Irishman don't love yankee?"

"Och! love the crathure, is it? You'd betther ask me to love a to'd"--for so Michael would pronounce the word 'toad.' "What is there to love about him, but skin and bone! I'd as soon love a skiliten. Yes--an immortal skiliten."

Nick made another gesture, and then he endeavoured to reflect, like one who had a grave business in contemplation. The Santa Cruz confused his brain, but the Indian never entirely lost his presence of mind; or never, at least, so long as he could either see or walk.

"Don't like him"--rejoined Nick. "Like anybody?"

"To be sure I does--I like the capt'in--och, *he's* a jontleman--and I likes the missus; she's a laddy--and I likes Miss Beuly, who's a swate young woman--and then there's Miss Maud, who's the delight of my eyes. Fegs, but isn't *she* a crathure to relish!"

Mike spoke like a good honest fellow, as he was at the bottom, with all his heart and soul. The Indian did not seem pleased, but he made no answer.

"You've been in the wars then, Nick!" asked the Irishman, after a short pause.

"Yes--Nick been chief ag'in--take scalps."

"Ach! That's a mighty ugly thrade! If you'd tell 'em that in Ireland, they'd not think it a possibility."

"No like fight in Ireland, hah?"

"I'll not say that--no, I'll not say that; for many's the jollification at which the fighting is the chafe amusement. But we likes *thumping* on the head--not *skinning* it."

"That your fashion--my fashion take scalp. You thump; I skin--which best?"

"Augh! skinnin' is a dreadthful operation; but shillaleh-work comes nately and nat'rally. How many of these said scalps, now, may ye have picked up, Nick, in yer last journey?"

"T'ree--all man and woman--no pappoose. One big enough make *two*; so call him *four*."

"Oh! Divil burn ye, Nick; but there's a spice of your namesake in ye, afther all. T'ree human crathures skinned, and you not satisfied, and so ye'll chait a bit to make 'em four! D'ye never think, now, of yer latther ind? D'ye never confess?"

"T'ink every day of *dat*. Hope to find more, before last day come. Plenty scalp *here*; ha, Mike?"

This was said a little incautiously, perhaps, but it was said under a strong native impulse. The Irishman, however, was never very logical or clear-headed; and three gills of rum had, by no means, helped to purify his brain. He heard the word "plenty," knew he was well fed and warmly clad, and just now, that Santa Cruz so much abounded, the term seemed peculiarly applicable.

"It's a plinthiful place it is, is this very manor. There's all sorts of things in it that's wanted. There's food and raiment, and cattle, and grain, and porkers, and praiching--yes, divil burn it, Nick, but there's what *goes* for praiching, though it's no more like what *we* calls praiching than yer'e like Miss Maud in comeliness, and ye'll own, yourself, Nick, yer'e no beauty."

"Got handsome hair," said Nick, surlily--"How she look widout scalp?"

"The likes of her, is it! Who ever saw one of her beauthy without the finest hair that ever was! What do you get for your scalps?--are they of any use when you find 'em?"

"Bring plenty bye'm-by. Whole country glad to see him before long--den beavers get pond ag'in."

"How's that--how's that, Indian? Baiver get pounded? There's no pound, hereabouts, and baivers is not an animal to be shut up like a hog!"

Nick perceived that his friend was past argumentation, and as he himself was approaching the state when the drunkard receives delight from he knows not what, it is unnecessary to relate any more of the dialogue. The jug was finished, each man very honestly drinking his pint, and as naturally submitting to its consequences; and this so much the more because the two were so engrossed with the rum that both forgot to pay that attention to the spring that might have been expected from its proximity.

Chapter V

The soul, my lord, is fashioned--like the lyre.
Strike one chord suddenly, and others vibrate.
Your name abruptly mentioned, casual words
Of comment on your deeds, praise from your uncle,
News from the armies, talk of your return,
A word let fall touching your youthful passion,
Suffused her cheek, call'd to her drooping eye
A momentary lustre, made her pulse
Leap headlong, and her bosom palpitate.
Hillhouse.

The approach of night, at sea and in a wilderness, has always something more solemn in it, than on land in the centre of civilization. As the curtain is drawn before his eyes, the solitude of the mariner is increased, while even his sleepless vigilance seems, in a measure, baffled, by the manner in which he is cut off from the signs of the hour. Thus, too, in the forest, or in an isolated clearing, the mysteries of the woods are deepened, and danger is robbed of its forethought and customary guards. That evening, Major Willoughby stood at a window with an arm round the slender waist of Beulah, Maud standing a little aloof; and, as the twilight retired, leaving the shadows of evening to thicken on the forest that lay within a few hundred feet of that side of the Hut, and casting a gloom over the whole of the quiet solitude, he felt the force of the feeling just mentioned, in a degree he had never before experienced.

"This is a *very* retired abode, my sisters," he said, thoughtfully. "Do my father and mother never speak of bringing you out more into the world?"

"They take us to New York every winter, now father is in the Assembly," quietly answered Beulah. "We expected to meet you there, last season, and were greatly disappointed that you did not come."

"My regiment was sent to the eastward, as you know, and having just received my new rank of major, it would not do to be absent at the moment. Do you ever see any one here, besides those who belong to the manor?"

"Oh! yes"--exclaimed Maud eagerly--then she paused, as if sorry she had said anything; continuing, after a little pause, in a much more moderated vein--"I mean occasionally. No doubt the place is very retired."

"Of what characters are your visiters?--hunters, trappers, settlers-- savages or travellers?"

Maud did not answer; but, Beulah, after waiting a moment for her sister to reply, took that office on herself.

"Some of all," she said, "though few certainly of the latter class. The hunters are often here; one or two a month, in the mild season; settlers rarely, as you may suppose, since my father will not sell, and there are not many about, I believe; the Indians come more frequently, though I think we have seen less of them, during Nick's absence than while he was more with us. Still we have as many as a hundred in a year, perhaps, counting the women. They come in parties, you know, and five or six of these will make that number. As for travellers, they are rare; being generally surveyors, land-hunters, or perhaps a proprietor who is looking up his estate. We had two of the last in the fall, before we went below."

"That is singular; and yet one might well look for an estate in a wilderness like this. Who were your proprietors?"

"An elderly man, and a young one. The first was a sort of partner of the late Sir William's, I believe, who has a grant somewhere near us, for which he was searching. His name was Fonda. The other was one of the Beekmans, who has lately succeeded his father in a property of considerable extent, somewhere at no great distance from us, and came to take a look at it. They say he has quite a hundred thousand acres, in one body."

"And did he find his land? Tracts of thousands and tens of thousands, are sometimes not to be discovered."

"We saw him twice, going and returning, and he was successful. The last time, he was detained by a snow-storm, and staid with us some days-- so long, indeed, that he remained, and accompanied us out, when we went below. We saw much of him, too, last winter, in town."

"Maud, you wrote me nothing of all this! Are visiters of this sort so very common that you do not speak of them in your letters?"

"Did I not?--Beulah will scarce pardon me for *that*. She thinks Mr. Evert Beekman more worthy of a place in a letter, than I do, perhaps."

"I think him a very respectable and sensible young man," answered Beulah quietly though there was a deeper tint on her cheek than common, which it was too dark to see. "I am not certain, however, he need fill much space in the letters of either of your sisters.'

"Well, this is *something* gleaned!" said the major, laughing--"and now, Beulah, if you will only let out a secret of the same sort about Maud, I shall be *au fait* of all the family mysteries."

"All!" repeated Maud, quickly--"would there be nothing to tell of a certain major Willoughby, brother of mine?"

"Not a syllable. I am as heart-whole as a sound oak, and hope to remain so. At all events, all I love is in this house. To tell you the truth, girls, these are not times for a soldier to think of anything but his duty. The quarrel is getting to be serious between the mother country and her colonies."

"Not so serious, brother," observed Beulah, earnestly, "as to amount to *that*. Evert Beekman thinks there will be trouble, but he does not appear to fancy it will go as far as very serious violence."

"Evert *Beekman*!--most of that family are loyal, I believe; how is it with this Evert?"

"I dare say, *you* would call him a *rebel*," answered Maud, laughing, for now Beulah chose to be silent, leaving her sister to explain, "He is not *fiery*; but he calls himself an *American*, with emphasis; and that is saying a good deal, when it means he is not an *Englishman*. Pray what do you call yourself, Bob?"

"I!--Certainly an American in one sense, but an Englishman in another. An American, as my father was a Cumberland-man, and an Englishman as a subject, and as connected with the empire."

"As St. Paul was a Roman. Heigho!--Well, I fear I have but one character--or, if I have two, they are an American, and a New York girl. Did I dress in scarlet, as you do, I might feel English too, possibly."

"This is making a trifling misunderstanding too serious," observed Beulah. "Nothing can come of all the big words that have been used, than more big words. I know that is Evert Beekman's opinion."

"I hope you may prove a true prophet," answered the major, once more buried in thought. "This place *does* seem to be fearfully retired for a family like ours. I hope my father may be persuaded to pass more of his time in New York. Does he ever speak on the subject, girls, or appear to have any uneasiness?"

"Uneasiness about what? The place is health itself: all sorts of fevers, and agues, and those things being quite unknown. Mamma says the toothache, even, cannot be found in this healthful spot."

"That is lucky--and, yet, I wish captain Willoughby--*Sir Hugh* Willoughby could be induced to live more in New York. Girls of your time of life, ought to be in the way of seeing the world, too."

"In other words, of seeing admirers, major Bob," said Maud, laughing, and bending forward to steal a glance in her brother's face. "Good night. *Sir Hugh* wishes us to send you into his library when we can spare you, and *my lady* has sent us a hint that it is ten o'clock, at which hour it is usual for sober people to retire."

The major kissed both sisters with warm affection--Beulah fancied with a sobered tenderness, and Maud thought kindly--and then they retired to join their mother, while he went to seek his father.

The captain was smoking in the library, as a room of all-*head*-work was called, in company with the chaplain. The practice of using tobacco in this form, had grown to be so strong in both of these old inmates of garrisons, that they usually passed an hour, in the recreation, before they went to bed. Nor shall we mislead the reader with any notions of fine-flavoured Havana segars; pipes, with Virginia cut, being the materials employed in the indulgence. A little excellent Cogniac and water, in which however the spring was not as much neglected, as in the orgies related in the previous chapter, moistened their lips, from time to time, giving a certain zest and comfort to their enjoyments. Just as the door opened to admit the major, he was the subject of discourse, the proud parent and the partial friend finding almost an equal gratification in discussing his fine, manly appearance, good qualities, and future hopes. His presence was untimely, then, in one sense; though he was welcome, and, indeed, expected. The captain pushed a chair to his son, and invited him to take a seat near the table, which held a spare pipe or two, a box of tobacco, a decanter of excellent brandy, a pitcher of pure water, all pleasant companions to the elderly gentlemen, then in possession.

"I suppose you are too much of a maccaroni, Bob, to smoke," observed the smiling father. "I detested a pipe at your time of life; or may say, I was afraid of it; the only smoke that was in fashion among our scarlet coats being the smoke of gunpowder. Well, how comes on Gage, and your neighbours the Yankees?"

"Why, sir," answered the major, looking behind him, to make sure that the door was shut--"Why, sir, to own the truth, my visit, here, just at this moment, is connected with the present state of that quarrel."

Both the captain and the chaplain drew the pipes from their mouths, holding them suspended in surprise and attention.

"The deuce it is!" exclaimed the former. "I thought I owed this unexpected pleasure to your affectionate desire to let me know I had inherited the empty honours of a baronetcy!"

"That was *one* motive, sir, but the least. I beg you to remember the awkwardness of my position, as a king's officer, in the midst of enemies."

"The devil! I say, parson, this exceeds heresy and schism! Do you call lodging in your father's house, major Willoughby, being in the midst of enemies? This is rebellion against nature, and is worse than rebellion against the king."

"My dear father, no one feels more secure with *you*, than I do; or, even, with Mr. Woods, here. But, there are others besides you two, in this part of the world, and your very settlement may not be safe a week longer; probably would not be, if my presence in it were known."

Both the listeners, now, fairly laid down their pipes, and the smoke began gradually to dissipate, as it might have been rising from a field of battle. One looked at the other, in wonder, and, then, both looked at the major, in curiosity.

"What is the meaning of all this, my son?" asked the captain, gravely. "Has anything new occurred to complicate the old causes of quarrel?"

"Blood has, at length, been drawn, sir; open rebellion has commenced!"

"This is a serious matter, indeed, if it be really so. But do you not exaggerate the consequences of some fresh indiscretion of the soldiery, in firing on the people? Remember, in the other affair, even the colonial authorities justified the officers."

"This is a very different matter, sir. Blood has not been drawn in a *riot*, but in a *battle*."

"Battle! You amaze me, sir! That is indeed a serious matter, and may lead to most serious consequences!"

"The Lord preserve us from evil times," ejaculated the chaplain, "and lead us, poor, dependent creatures that we are, into the paths of peace and quietness! Without his grace, we are the blind leading the blind."

"Do you mean, major Willoughby, that armed and disciplined bodies have met in actual conflict?"

"Perhaps not literally so, my dear father; but the minute-men of Massachusetts, and His Majesty's forces, have met and fought. This I know, full well; for my own regiment was in the field, and, I hope it is unnecessary to add, that its second officer was not absent."

"Of course these minute-men--rabble would be the better word--could not stand before you?" said the captain, compressing his lips, under a strong impulse of military pride.

Major Willoughby coloured, and, to own the truth, at that moment he wished the Rev. Mr. Woods, if not literally at the devil, at least safe and sound in another room; anywhere, so it were out of ear-shot of the answer.

"Why, sir," he said, hesitating, not to say stammering, notwithstanding a prodigious effort to seem philosophical and calm--"To own the truth, these minute-fellows are not quite as contemptible as we soldiers would be apt to think. It was a stone-wall affair, and dodging work; and, so, you know, sir, drilled troops wouldn't have the usual chance. They pressed us pretty warmly on the retreat."

"*Retreat*! Major Willoughby!"

"I called it retreat, sure enough; but it was only a march *in*, again, after having done the business on which we went out. I shall admit, I say, sir, that we were hard pressed, until *reinforced*."

"*Reinforced*, my dear Bob! *Your* regiment, *our* regiment could not need a reinforcement against all the Yankees in New England."

The major could not abstain from laughing, a little, at this exhibition of his father's *esprit de corps*; but native frankness, and love of truth, compelled him to admit the contrary.

"It *did*, sir, notwithstanding," he answered; "and, not to mince the matter, it needed it confoundedly. Some of our officers who have seen the hardest service of the last war, declare, that taking the march, and the popping work, and the distance, altogether, it was the warmest day *they* remember. Our loss, too, was by no means insignificant, as I hope you will believe, when you know the troops engaged. We report something like three hundred casualties."

The captain did not answer for quite a minute. All this time he sat thoughtful, and even pale; for his mind was teeming with the pregnant consequences of such an outbreak. Then he desired his son to give a succinct, but connected history of the whole affair. The major complied, beginning his narrative with an account of the general state of the country, and concluding it, by giving, as far as it was possible for one whose professional pride and political feelings were too deeply involved to be entirely impartial, a reasonably just account of the particular occurrence already mentioned.

The events that led to, and the hot skirmish which it is the practice of the country to call the Battle of Lexington, and the incidents of the day itself, are too familiar to the ordinary reader, to require repetition here. The major explained all the military points very clearly, did full justice to the perseverance and daring of the provincials, as he called his enemies--for, an American himself, he would not term them Americans--and threw in as many explanatory remarks as he could think of, by way of vindicating the "march *in*, again." This he did, too, quite as much out of filial piety, as out of self-love; for, to own the truth, the captain's mortification, as a soldier, was so very evident as to give his son sensible pain.

"The effect of all this," continued the major, when his narrative of the military movements was ended, "has been to raise a tremendous feeling, throughout the country, and God knows what is to follow."

"And this you have come hither to tell me, Robert," said the father, kindly. "It is well done, and as I would have expected from you. We might have passed the summer, here, and not have heard a whisper of so important an event."

"Soon after the affair--or, as soon as we got some notion of its effect on the provinces, general Gage sent me, privately, with despatches to governor Tryon. *He*, governor Tryon, was aware of your position; and, as I had also to communicate the death of Sir Harry Willoughby, he directed me to come up the river, privately, have an interview with Sir John, if possible, and then push on, under a feigned name, and communicate with you. He thinks, now Sir William is dead, that with your estate, and new rank, and local influence, you might be very serviceable in sustaining the royal cause; for, it is not to be concealed that this affair is likely to take the character of an open and wide-spread revolt against the authority of the crown."

"General Tryon does me too much honour," answered the captain, coldly. "My estate is a small body of wild land; my influence extends little beyond this beaver meadow, and is confined to my own household, and some fifteen or twenty labourers; and as for the *new rank* of which you speak, it is not likely the colonists will care much for *that*, if they disregard the rights of the king. Still, you have acted like a son in running the risk you do, Bob; and I pray God you may get back to your regiment, in safety."

"This is a cordial to my hopes, sir; for nothing would pain me more than to believe you think it my duty, because I was born in the colonies, to throw up my commission, and take side with the rebels."

"I do not conceive that to be your duty, any more than I conceive it to be mine to take sides against them, because I happened to be born in England. It is a weak view of moral obligations, that confines them merely to the accidents of birth, and birth-place. Such a subsequent state of things may have grown up, as to change all our duties, and it is necessary that we discharge them as they *are*; not as they may have been, hitherto, or may be, hereafter. Those who clamour so much about mere birth-place, usually have no very clear sense of their higher obligations. Over our birth we can have no control; while we are rigidly responsible for the fulfilment of obligations voluntarily contracted."

"Do you reason thus, captain?" asked the chaplain, with strong interest--"Now, I confess, I *feel*, in this matter, not only very much like a native American, but very much like a native Yankee, in the bargain. You know I was born in the Bay, and--the major must excuse me--but, it ill-becomes my cloth to deceive--I hope the major will pardon me--I--I do hope--"

"Speak out, Mr. Woods," said Robert Willoughby, smiling--"*You* have nothing to fear from your old friend the major."

"So I thought--so I thought--well, then, I was glad--yes, really rejoiced at heart, to hear that my countrymen, down-east, there, had made the king's troops scamper,"

"I am not aware that I used any such terms, sir, in connection with the manner in which we marched in, after the duty we went out on was performed," returned the young soldier, a little stiffly. "I suppose it is natural for one Yankee to sympathize with another; but, my father, Mr. Woods, is an *Old* England, and not a *New*-England-man; and he may be excused if he feel more for the servants of the crown."

"Certainly, my dear major--certainly, my dear Mr. Robert--my old pupil, and, I hope, my friend--all this is true enough, and very natural. I allow captain Willoughby to wish the best for the king's troops, while I wish the best for my own countrymen."

"This is natural, on both sides, out of all question, though it by no means follows that it is right. 'Our country, right or wrong,' is a high-sounding maxim, but it is scarcely the honest man's maxim. Our country, after all, cannot have nearer claims upon us, than our parents for instance; and who can claim a moral right to sustain even his own father, in error, injustice, or crime? No, no--I hate your pithy sayings; they commonly mean nothing that is substantially good, at bottom."

"But one's country, in a time of actual war, sir!" said the major, in a tone of as much remonstrance as habit would allow him to use to his own father.

"Quite true, Bob; but the difficulty here, is to know which *is* one's country. It is a family quarrel, at the best, and it will hardly do to talk about foreigners, at all. It is the same as if I should treat Maud unkindly, or harshly, because she is the child of only a friend, and not my own natural daughter. As God is my judge, Woods, I am unconscious of not loving Maud

Meredith, at this moment, as tenderly as I love Beulah Willoughby. There was a period, in her childhood, when the playful little witch had most of my heart, I am afraid, if the truth were known. It is use, and duty, then, and not mere birth, that ought to tie our hearts."

The major thought it might very well be that one child should be loved more than another, though he did not understand how there could be a divided allegiance. The chaplain looked at the subject with views still more narrowed, and he took up the cudgels of argument in sober earnest, conceiving this to be as good an opportunity as another, for disposing of the matter.

"I am all for birth, and blood, and natural ties," he said, "always excepting the peculiar claims of Miss Maud, whose case is *sui generis*, and not to be confounded with any other case. A man can have but one country, any more than he can have but one nature; and, as he is forced to be true to that nature, so ought he morally to be true to that country. The captain says, that it is difficult to determine which is one's country, in a civil war; but I cannot admit the argument. If Massachusetts and England get to blows, Massachusetts is my country; if Suffolk and Worcester counties get into a quarrel, my duty calls me to Worcester, where I was born; and so I should carry out the principle from country to country, county to county, town to town, parish to parish; or, even household to household."

"This is an extraordinary view of one's duty, indeed, my dear Mr. Woods," cried the major, with a good deal of animation; "and if one-half the household quarrelled with the other, you would take sides with that in which you happened to find yourself, at the moment."

"It is an extraordinary view of one's duty, for a *parson;*" observed the captain. "Let us reason backward a little, and ascertain where we shall come out. You put the head of the household out of the question. Has he no claims? Is a father to be altogether overlooked in the struggle between the children? Are his laws to be broken--his rights invaded--or his person to be maltreated, perhaps, and his curse disregarded, because a set of unruly children get by the ears, on points connected with their own selfishness?"

"I give up the household," cried the chaplain, "for the bible settles that; and what the bible disposes of, is beyond dispute--'Honour thy father and thy mother, that thy days may be long in the land which the Lord thy God giveth thee'--are terrible words, and must not be disobeyed. But the decalogue has not another syllable which touches the question. 'Thou shalt not kill,' means murder only; common, vulgar murder--and 'thou shalt not steal,' 'thou shalt not commit adultery,' &c., don't bear on civil war, as I see. 'Remember the Sabbath to keep it holy'--'Thou shalt not covet the ox nor the ass'--'Thou shalt not take the name of the Lord thy God in vain'--none of these, not one of them, bears, at all, on this question."

"What do you think of the words of the Saviour, where he tells us to 'render unto Cæsar the things which are Cæsar's? Has Cæsar no rights here? Can Massachusetts and my Lord North settle their quarrels in such a manner as to put Cæsar altogether out of view?"

The chaplain looked down a moment, pondered a little, and then he came up to the attack, again, with renewed ardour.

"Cæsar is out of the question here. If His Majesty will come and take sides with us, we shall be ready to honour and obey him; but if he choose to remain alienated from us, it is his act, not ours."

"This is a new mode of settling allegiance! If Cæsar will do as we wish, he shall still be Cæsar; but, if he refuse to do as we wish, then down with Cæsar. I am an old soldier, Woods, and while I feel that this question has two sides to it, my disposition to reverence and honour the king is still strong."

The major appeared delighted, and, finding matters going on so favourably, he pleaded fatigue and withdrew, feeling satisfied that, if his father fairly got into a warm discussion, taking the loyal side of the question, he would do more to confirm himself in the desired views, than could be effected by any other means. By this time, the disputants were so warm as scarcely to notice the disappearance of the young man, the argument proceeding.

The subject is too hackneyed, and, indeed, possesses too little interest, to induce us to give more than an outline of what passed. The captain and the chaplain belonged to that class of friends, which may be termed argumentative. Their constant discussions were a strong link in the chain of esteem; for they had a tendency to enliven their solitude, and to give a zest to lives that, without them, would have been exceedingly monotonous. Their ordinary subjects were theology and war; the chaplain having some practical knowledge of the last, and the captain a lively disposition to the first. In these discussions, the clergyman was good-natured and the soldier polite; circumstances that tended to render them far more agreeable to the listeners than they might otherwise have proved.

On the present occasion, the chaplain rang the changes diligently, on the natural feelings, while his friend spoke most of the higher duties. The *ad captandum* part of the argument, oddly enough, fell to the share of the minister of the church; while the intellectual, discriminating, and really logical portion of the subject, was handled by one trained in garrisons and camps, with a truth, both of ethics and reason, that would have done credit to a drilled casuist. The war of words continued till past midnight, both disputants soon getting back to their pipes, carrying on the conflict amid a smoke that did no dishonour to such a well-contested field. Leaving the captain and his friend thus intently engaged, we will take one or two glimpses into different parts of the house, before we cause all our characters to retire for the night.

About the time the battle in the library was at its height, Mrs. Willoughby was alone in her room, having disposed of all the cares, and most of the duties of the day. The mother's heart was filled with a calm delight that it would have been difficult for herself to describe. All she held most dear on earth, her husband, her kind-hearted, faithful, long-loved husband; her noble son, the pride and joy of her heart; Beulah, her own natural-born daughter, the mild, tractable, sincere, true-hearted child that so much resembled herself; and Maud, the adopted, one rendered dear by solicitude and tenderness, and now so fondly beloved on her own account, were all with her, beneath her own roof, almost within the circle of her arms. The Hutted Knoll was no longer a solitude; the manor was not a wilderness to *her*; for where her heart was, there truly was her treasure, also. After passing a few minutes in silent, but delightful thought, this excellent, guileless woman knelt and poured out her soul in thanksgivings to the Being, who had surrounded her lot with so many blessings. Alas! little did she suspect the extent, duration, and direful nature of the evils which, at that very moment, were pending over her native country, or the pains that her own affectionate hear? was to endure! The major had not suffered a whisper of the real nature of his errand to escape him, except to his father and the chaplain; and we will now follow him to his apartment, and pass a minute, *tête-à-tête*, with the young soldier, ere he too lays his head on his pillow.

A couple of neat rooms were prepared and furnished, that were held sacred to the uses of the heir. They were known to the whole household, black and white, as the "young captain's quarters;" and even Maud called them, in her laughing off-handedness, "Bob's Sanctum." Here, then, the major found everything as he left it on his last visit, a twelvemonth before; and some few things that were strangers to him, in the bargain. In that day, toilets covered with muslin, more or less worked and ornamented, were a regular appliance of every bed-room, of a better-class house, throughout America. The more modern "Duchesses," "Psyches," "dressing-tables," &c. &c., of our own extravagant and benefit-of-the-act-taking generation, were then unknown; a moderately-sized glass, surrounded by curved, gilded ornaments, hanging against the wall, above the said muslin-covered table, quite as a matter of law, if not of domestic faith.

As soon as the major had set down his candle, he looked about him, as one recognises old friends, pleased at renewing his acquaintance with so many dear and cherished objects. The very playthings of his childhood were there; and, even a beautiful and long-used hoop, was embellished with ribbons, by some hand unknown to himself. "Can this be my mother?" thought the young man, approaching to examine the well-remembered hoop, which he had never found so honoured before; "can my kind, tender-hearted mother, who never will forget that I am no longer a child, can she have really done this? I must laugh at her, to-morrow, about it, even while I kiss and bless her." Then he turned to the toilet, where stood a basket, filled with different articles, which, at once, he understood were offerings to himself. Never had he visited the Hut without finding such a basket in his room at night. It was a tender proof how truly and well he was remembered, in his absence.

"Ah!" thought the major, as he opened a bundle of knit lamb's-wool stockings, "here is my dear mother again, with her thoughts about damp feet, and the exposure of service. And a dozen shirts, too, with 'Beulah' pinned on one of them--how the deuce does the dear girl suppose I am to carry away such a stock of linen, without even a horse to ease me of a bundle? My kit would be like that of the commander-in-chief, were I to take away all that these dear relatives design for me. What's this?--a purse! a handsome silken purse, too, with Beulah's name on it. Has Maud nothing, here? Why has Maud forgotten me! Ruffles, handkerchiefs, garters--yes, here is a pair of my good mother's own knitting, but nothing of Maud's-- Ha! what have we here? As I live, a beautiful silken scarf--netted in a way to make a whole regiment envious. Can this have been bought, or has it been the work of a twelvemonth? No name on it, either. Would my father have done this? Perhaps it is one of his old scarfs--if so, it is an old *new* one, for I do not think it has ever been worn. I must inquire into this, in the morning--I wonder there is nothing of Maud's!"

As the major laid aside his presents, he kissed the scarf, and then--I regret to say without saying *his* prayers--the young man went to bed.

The scene must now be transferred to the room where the sisters--in affection, if not in blood--were about to seek their pillows also. Maud, ever the quickest and most prompt in her movements, was already in her night-clothes; and, wrapping a shawl about herself, was seated waiting for Beulah to finish her nightly orisons. It was not long before the latter rose from her knees, and then our heroine spoke.

"The major must have examined the basket by this time," she cried, her cheek rivalling the tint of a riband it leaned against, on the back of the chair. "I heard his heavy tramp--tramp--tramp--as he went to his room--how differently these men walk from us girls, Beulah!"

"They do, indeed; and Bob has got to be so large and heavy, now, that he quite frightens me, sometimes. Do you not think he grows wonderfully like papa?"

"I do not see it. He wears his own hair, and it's a pity he should ever cut it off, it's so handsome and curling. Then he is taller, but lighter--has more colour--is so much younger--and everyway so different, I wonder you think so. I do not think him in the least like father."

"Well, that is odd, Maud. Both mother and myself were struck with the resemblance, this evening, and we were both delighted to see it. Papa is quite handsome, and so I think is Bob. Mother says he is not *quite* as handsome as father was, at his age, but *so* like him, it is surprising!"

"Men may be handsome and not alike. Father is certainly one of the handsomest elderly men of my acquaintance--and the major is so-so-ish--but, I wonder you can think a man of seven-and-twenty so *very* like one of sixty odd. Bob tells me he can play the flute quite readily now, Beulah."

"I dare say; he does everything he undertakes uncommonly well. Mr. Woods said, a few days since, he had never met with a boy who was quicker at his mathematics."

"Oh! All Mr. Wood's geese are swans. I dare say there have been other boys who were quite as clever. I do not believe in *non-pareils*, Beulah."

"You surprise me, Maud--you, whom I always supposed such a friend of Bob's! He thinks everything *you* do, too, so perfect! Now, this very evening, he was looking at the sketch you have made of the Knoll, and he protested he did not know a regular artist in England, even, that would have done it better."

Maud stole a glance at her sister, while the latter was speaking, from under her cap, and her cheeks now fairly put the riband to shame; but her smile was still saucy and wilful.

"Oh nonsense," she said--"Bob's no judge of drawings--*He* scarce knows a tree from a horse!"

"I'm surprised to hear you say so, Maud," said the generous-minded and affectionate Beulah, who could see no imperfection in Bob; "and that of your brother. When he taught *you* to draw, you thought him well skilled as an artist."

"Did I?--I dare say I'm a capricious creature--but, somehow, I don't regard Bob, just as I used to. He has been away from us so much, of late, you know--and the army makes men so formidable--and, they are not like us, you know--and, altogether, I think Bob excessively changed."

"Well, I'm glad mamma don't hear this, Maud. She looks upon her son, now he is a major, and twenty-seven, just as she used to look upon him, when he was in petticoats--nay, I think she considers us all exactly as so many little children."

"She is a dear, good mother, I know," said Maud, with emphasis, tears starting to her eyes, involuntarily, almost *impetuously*--"whatever she says, does, wishes, hopes, or thinks, is right."

"Oh! I knew you would come to, as soon as there was a question about mother! Well, for my part, I have no such horror of men, as not to feel just as much tenderness for father or brother, as I feel for mamma, herself."

"Not for Bob, Beulah. Tenderness for Bob! Why, my dear sister, that is feeling tenderness for a *Major of Foot*, a very different thing from feeling it for one's mother. As for papa--dear me, he is glorious, and I do so love him!"

"You ought to, Maud; for you were, and I am not certain that you are not, at this moment, *his* darling."

It was odd that this was said without the least thought, on the part of the speaker, that Maud was not her natural sister--that, in fact, she was not in the least degree related to her by blood. But so closely and judiciously had captain and Mrs. Willoughby managed the affair of their adopted child, that neither they themselves, Beulah, nor the inmates of the family or household, ever thought of her, but as of a real daughter of her nominal parents. As for Beulah, her feelings were so simple and sincere, that they were even beyond the ordinary considerations of delicacy, and she took precisely the same liberties with her titular, as she would have done with a natural sister. Maud alone, of all in the Hut, remembered her birth, and submitted to some of its most obvious consequences. As respects the captain, the idea never crossed her mind, that she was adopted by him; as respects her mother, she filled to her, in every sense, that sacred character; Beulah, too, was a sister, in thought and deed; but, Bob, he had so changed, had been so many years separated from her; had once actually called her Miss Meredith--somehow, she knew not how herself--it was fully six years since she had begun to remember that *he* was not her brother.

"As for my father," said Maud, rising with emotion, and speaking with startling emphasis--"I will not say I *love* him--I *worship* him!"

"Ah! I know that well enough, Maud; and to say the truth, you are a couple of idolaters, between you. Mamma says this, sometimes; though she owns she is not jealous. But it would pain her excessively to hear that you do not feel towards Bob, just as we all feel."

"But, ought I?--Beulah, I cannot!"

"Ought you!--Why not, Maud? Are you in your senses, child?"

"But--you know--I'm sure--you ought to remember--"

"*What?*" demanded Beulah, really frightened at the other's excessive agitation.

"That I am *not* his real--true--*born* sister!"

This was the first time in their lives, either had ever alluded to the fact, in the other's presence. Beulah turned pale; she trembled all over, as if in an ague; then she luckily burst into tears, else she might have fainted.

"Beulah--my sister--my *own* sister!" cried Maud, throwing herself into the arms of the distressed girl.

"Ah! Maud, you *are*, you *shall* for ever be, my only, only sister."

Chapter VI

O! It is great for our country to die, where ranks are contending;
Bright is the wreath of our fame; Glory awaits us for aye--
Glory, that never is dim, shining on with light never ending--
Glory, that never shall fade, never, O! never away.

Percival.

Notwithstanding the startling intelligence that had so unexpectedly reached it, and the warm polemical conflict that had been carried on within its walls, the night passed peacefully over the roof of the Hutted Knoll. At the return of dawn, the two Plinys, both the Smashes, and all the menials were again afoot; and, ere long, Mike, Saucy Nick Joel, and the rest were seen astir, in the open fields, or in the margin of the woods. Cattle were fed, cows milked fires lighted, and everything pursued its course, in the order of May. The three wenches, as female negroes were then termed, *ex officio*, in America, opened their throats, as was usual at that hour, and were heard singing at their labours, in a way nearly to deaden the morning carols of the tenants of the forest. *Mari'* in particular, would have drowned the roar of Niagara. The captain used to call her his clarion.

In due time, the superiors of the household made their appearance. Mrs. Willoughby was the first out of her room, as was ever the case when there was anything to be done. On the present occasion, the "fatted calf" was to be killed, not in honour of the return of a prodigal son, however, but in behalf of one who was the pride of her eyes, and the joy of her heart. The breakfast that she ordered was just the sort of breakfast, that one must visit America to witness. France can set forth a very scientific *déjeuner à la fourchette*, and England has laboured-and ponderous imitations; but, for the spontaneous, superabundant, unsophisticated, natural, all-sufficing and all-subduing morning's meal, take America, in a better-class house, in the country, and you reach the *ne plus ultra*, in that sort of thing. Tea, coffee, and chocolate, of which the first and last were excellent, and the second respectable; ham, fish, eggs, toast, cakes, rolls, marmalades, &c. &c. &c., were thrown together in noble confusion; frequently occasioning the guest, as Mr. Woods naively confessed, an utter confusion of mind, as to which he was to attack, when all were inviting and each would be welcome.

Leaving Mrs. Willoughby in deep consultation with Mari' on the subject of this feast, we will next look after the two sweet girls whom we so abruptly deserted in the last chapter. When Maud's glowing cheeks were first visible that morning, signs of tears might have been discovered on them, as the traces of the dew are found on the leaf of the rose; but they completely vanished under the duties of the toilet, and she came forth from her chamber, bright and cloudless as the glorious May-morning, which had returned to cheer the solitude of the manor. Beulah followed, tranquil, bland and mild as the day itself, the living image of the purity of soul, and deep affections, of her honest nature.

The sisters went into the breakfast-room, where they had little lady-like offices of their own to discharge, too, in honour of the guest; each employing herself in decorating the table, and in seeing that it wanted nothing in the proprieties As their pleasing tasks were fulfilled, the discourse did not flag between them. Nothing, however, had been said, that made the smallest allusion to the conversation of the past night. Neither felt any wish to revive that subject; and, as for Maud, bitterly did she regret ever having broached it. At times, her cheeks burned with blushes, as she recalled her words; and yet she scarce knew the reason why. The feeling of Beulah was different. She wondered her sister could ever think she was a Meredith, and not a Willoughby. At times she feared some unfortunate oversight of her own, some careless allusion, or indiscreet act, might have served to remind Maud of the circumstances of her real birth. Yet there was nothing in the last likely to awaken unpleasant reflections, apart from the circumstance that she was not truly a child of the family into which she had been transplanted. The Merediths were, at least, as nonourable a family as the Willoughbys, in the ordinary worldly view of the matter; nor was Maud, by any means, a dependant, in the way of money. Five thousand pounds, in the English funds, had been settled on her, by the marriage articles of her parents; and twenty years of careful husbandry, during which every shilling had been scrupulously devoted to accumulation, had quite doubled the original amount. So far from being penniless, therefore, Maud's fortune was often alluded to by the captain, in a jocular way, as if purposely to remind her that she had the means of independence, and duties connected with it. It is true, Maud, herself, had no suspicion that she had been educated altogether by her "father," and that her own money had not been used for this purpose. To own the truth, she thought little about it; knew little about it, beyond the fact, that she had a fortune of her own, into the possession of which she must step, when she attained her majority. How she came by it, even, was a question she never asked though there were moments when tender regrets and affectionate melancholy would come over her heart, as she thought of her natural parents, and of their early deaths. Still, Maud implicitly reposed on the captain and Mrs. Willoughby, as on a father and mother; and it was not owing to *them*, or anything connected with their love, treatment, words, or thoughts, that she was reminded that they were not so in very fact, as well as in tenderness.

"Bob will think *you* made these plum sweetmeats, Beulah," said Maud, with a saucy smile, as she placed a glass plate on the table--"He never thinks I *can* make anything of this sort; and, as he is so fond of plums, he will be certain to taste them; then *you* will come in for the praise!"

"You appear to think, that *praise* he must. Perhaps he may not fancy them good."

"If I thought so, I would take them away this instant," cried Maud, standing in the attitude of one in doubt. "Bob does *not* think much of such things in girls, for he says ladies need not be cooks; and yet when one *does* make a thing of this sort, one would certainly like to have it *well* made."

"Set your heart at ease, Maud; the plums are delicious--much the best we ever had, and we are rather famous for them, you know. I'll answer for it, Bob will pronounce them the best he has ever tasted."

"And if he shouldn't, why should I care--that is, not *very much*--about it. You know they are the first I ever made, and one may be permitted to fail on a first effort. Besides, a man *may* go to England, and see fine sights, and live in great houses, and all that, and not understand when he has good plum sweetmeats before him, and when bad. I dare say there are many *colonels* in the army, who are ignorant on this point."

Beulah laughed, and admitted the truth of the remark; though, in her secret mind, she had almost persuaded herself that Bob knew everything.

"Do you not think our brother improved in appearance, Maud," she asked, after a short pause. "The visit to England has done him that service, at least."

"I don't see it, Beulah--I see no change. To me, Bob is just the same to-day, that he has ever been; that is, ever since he grew to be a man--with boys, of course, it is different. Ever since he was made a captain, I mean."

As major Willoughby had reached that rank the day he was one-and-twenty, the reader can understand the precise date when Maud began to take her present views of his appearance and character.

"I am surprised to hear you say so, Maud! Papa says he is better 'set up,' as he calls it, by his English drill, and that he looks altogether more like a soldier than he did."

"Bob has always had a martial look!" cried Maud, quickly--"He got that in garrison, when a boy."

"If so, I hope he may never lose it!" said the subject of the remark, himself, who had entered the room unperceived, and overheard this speech. "Being a soldier, one would wish to look like what he is, my little critic."

The kiss that followed, and that given to Beulah, were no more than the usual morning salutations of a brother to his sisters, slight touches of rosy cheeks; and yet Maud blushed; for, as she said to herself, she had been taken by surprise.

"They say listeners never hear good of themselves," answered Maud, with a vivacity that betokened confusion. "Had you come a minute sooner, master Bob, it might have been an advantage."

"Oh! Beulah's remarks I do not fear; so long as I get off unscathed from yours, Miss Maud, I shall think myself a lucky fellow. But what has brought me and my training into discussion, this morning?"

"It is natural for sisters to speak about their brother after so long----"

"Tell him nothing about it, Beulah," interrupted Maud. "Let him listen, and eaves-drop, and find out as he may, if he would learn our secrets. There, major Willoughby, I hope that is a promise of a breakfast, which will satisfy even your military appetite!"

"It looks well, indeed, Maud--and there, I perceive, are some of Beulah's excellent plums, of which I am so fond--know they were made especially for me, and I must kiss you, sister, for this proof of remembrance."

Beulah, to whose simple mind it seemed injustice to appropriate credit that belonged to another, was about to tell the truth; but an imploring gesture from her sister induced her to smile, and receive the salute in silence.

"Has any one seen captain Willoughby and parson Woods this morning?" inquired the major. "I left them desperately engaged in discussion, and I really feel some apprehension as to the remains left on the field of battle."

"Here they both come," cried Maud, glad to find the discourse taking so complete a change; "and there is mamma, followed by Pliny, to tell Beulah to take her station at the coffee, while I go to the chocolate, leaving the tea to the only hand that can make it so that my father will drink it."

The parties mentioned entered the room, in the order named; the usual salutations followed, and all took their seats at table. Captain Willoughby was silent and thoughtful at first, leaving his son to rattle on, in a way that betokened care, in his view of the matter, quite as much as it betokened light-heartedness in those of his mother and sisters. The chaplain was rather more communicative than his friend; but he, too, seemed restless, and desirous of arriving at some point that was not likely to come uppermost, in such a family party. At length, the impulses of Mr. Woods got the better of his discretion, even, and he could conceal his thoughts no longer.

"Captain Willoughby," he said, in a sort of apologetic, and yet simple and natural manner, "I have done little since we parted, seven hours since, but think of the matter under discussion."

"If you have, my dear Woods, there has been a strong sympathy between us; I have scarcely slept. I may say I have thought of nothing else, myself, and am glad you have broached the subject, again."

"I was about to say, my worthy sir, that reflection, and my pillow, and your sound and admirable arguments, have produced an entire change in my sentiments. I think, now, altogether with you."

"The devil you do, Woods!" cried the captain, looking up from his bit of dry toast, in astonishment. "Why, my dear fellow--this is odd--excessively odd, if the truth must be said.--To own the real state of the case, chaplain, you have won *me* over, and I was just about to make proper acknowledgments of your victory!"

It need scarcely be added that the rest of the company were not a little amazed at these cross-concessions, while Maud was exceedingly amused. As for Mrs. Willoughby, nothing laughable ever occurred in connection with her husband; and then she would as soon think of assailing the church itself, as to ridicule one of its ministers. Beulah could see nothing but what was right in her father, at least; and, as for the major, he felt too much concerned at this unexpected admission of his father's, to perceive anything but the error.

"Have you not overlooked the injunction of scripture, my excellent friend?" rejoined the chaplain. "Have you left to the rights of Cæsar, all their weight and authority? 'The king's name is a tower of strength.'"

"Have not you, Woods, forgotten the superior claims of reason and right, over those of accident and birth--that man is to be considered as a reasoning being, to be governed by principles and ever-varying facts, and not a mere animal left to the control of an instinct that perishes with its usefulness?"

"What *can* they mean, mother?" whispered Maud, scarce able to repress the laughter that came so easily to one with a keen sense of the ludicrous.

"They have been arguing about the right of parliament to tax the colonies, I believe, my dear, and *over-persuaded* each other, that's all. It *is* odd, Robert, that Mr. Woods should convert your father."

"No, my dearest mother, it is something even more serious than that." By this time, the disputants, who sat opposite each other, were fairly launched into the discussion, again, and heeded nothing that passed--"No, dearest mother, it is far worse than even *that*. Pliny, tell my man to brush the hunting-jacket--and, see he has his breakfast, in good style--he is a grumbling rascal, and will give the house a bad character, else--you need not come back, until we ring for you--yes, mother, yes dearest girls, this is a far more serious matter than you suppose, though it ought not to be mentioned idly, among the people. God knows now they may take it--and bad news flies swift enough, of itself."

"Merciful Providence!" exclaimed Mrs. Willoughby-"What *can* you mean, my son?"

"I mean, mother, that civil war has actually commenced in the colonies, and that the people of your blood and race are, in open arms, against the people of my father's native country--in a word, against me."

"How can that be, Robert? Who would *dare* to strike a blow against the king?"

"When men get excited, and their passions are once inflamed, they will do much, my mother, that they might not dream of, else."

"This must be a mistake! Some evil-disposed person has told you this, Robert, knowing your attachment to the crown."

"I wish it were so, dear madam; but my own eyes have seen--I may say my own flesh has felt, the contrary."

The major then related what had happened, letting his auditors into the secret of the true state of the country. It is scarcely necessary to allude to the degree of consternation and pain, with which he was heard, or to the grief which succeeded.

"You spoke of yourself, dear Bob," said Maud, naturally, and with strong feeling--"*You* were not hurt, in this cruel, cruel battle."

"I ought not to have mentioned it, although I did certainly receive a smart contusion--nothing more, I assure you--here in the shoulder, and it now scarcely inconveniences me."

By this time all were listening, curiosity and interest having silenced even the disputants, especially as this was the first they had heard of the major's casualty. Then neither felt the zeal which had warmed him in the previous contest, but was better disposed to turn aside from its pursuit.

"I hope it did not send you to the rear, Bob?" anxiously inquired the father.

"I *was* in the rear, sir, when I got the hurt," answered the major, laughing. "The rear is the post of honour, on a retreat, you know, my dear father; and I believe our march scarce deserves another name."

"That is hard, too, on king's troops! What sort of fellows had you to oppose, my son?"

"A rather intrusive set, sir. Their object was to persuade us to go into Boston, as fast as possible; and, it was a little difficult, at times, not to listen to their arguments. If my Lord Percy had not come out, with a strong party, and two pieces of artillery, we might not have stood it much longer. Our men were fagged like hunted deer, and the day proved oppressively hot."

"Artillery, too!" exclaimed the captain, his military pride reviving a little, to unsettle his last convictions of duty. "Did you open your columns, and charge your enemies, in line?"

"It would have been charging air. No sooner did we halt, than our foes dispersed; or, no sooner did we renew the march, than every line of wall, along our route, became a line of hostile muskets. I trust you will do us justice, sir--you know the regiments, and can scarce think they misbehaved."

"British troops seldom do that; although I have known it happen. No men, however, are usually more steady, and then these provincials are formidable as skirmishers. In that character, I know *them*, too. What has been the effect of all this on the country, Bob?--You told us something of it last night; complete the history."

"The provinces are in a tumult. As for New England, a flame of fire could scarce be more devastating; though I think this colony is less excited. Still, here, men are arming in thousands."

"Dear me--dear me"--ejaculated the peacefully-inclined chaplain--"that human beings can thus be inclined to self destruction!"

"Is Tryon active?--What do the royal authorities, all this time?"

"Of course they neglect nothing feasible; but, they must principally rely on the loyalty and influence of the gentry, until succour can arrive from Europe. If *that* fail them, their difficulties will be much increased."

Captain Willoughby understood his son; he glanced towards his unconscious wife, as if to see how far she felt with him.

"Our own families are divided, of course, much as they have been in the previous discussions," he added. "The De Lanceys, Van Cortlandts, Philipses, Bayards, and most of that town connection, with a large portion of the Long Island families, I should think, are with the crown; while the

Livingstons, Morrises, Schuylers, Rensselaers, and their friends, go with the colony. Is not this the manner in which they are divided?"

"With some limitations, sir. All the De Lanceys, with most of their strong connections and influence, are with *us*--with the *king*, I mean--while all the Livingstons and Morrises are against us. The other families are divided-- as with the Cortlandts, Schuylers, and Rensselaers. It is fortunate for the Patroon, that he is a boy."

"Why so, Bob?" asked the captain, looking inquiringly up, at his son.

"Simply, sir, that his great estate may not be confiscated. So many of his near connections are against us, that he could hardly escape the contamination; and the consequences would be inevitable."

"Do you consider that so certain, sir? As there are two sides to the question, may there not be two results to the war?"

"I think not, sir. England is no power to be defied by colonies insignificant as these."

"This is well enough for a king's officer, major Willoughby; but all large bodies of men are formidable when they are right, and nations--these colonies are a nation, in extent and number--are not so easily put down, when the spirit of liberty is up and doing among them."

The major listened to his father with pain and wonder. The captain spoke earnestly, and there was a flush about his fine countenance, that gave it sternness and authority. Unused to debate with his father, especially when the latter was in such a mood, the son remained silent, though his mother, who was thoroughly loyal in her heart--meaning loyal as applied to a sovereign--and who had the utmost confidence in her husband's tenderness and consideration for herself, was not so scrupulous.

"Why, Willoughby," she cried, "you really incline to rebellion! I, even I, who was born in the colonies, think them very wrong to resist their anointed king, and sovereign prince."

"Ah, Wilhelmina," answered the captain, more mildly, "you have a true colonist's admiration of *home*. But I was old enough, when I left England, to appreciate what I saw and knew, and cannot feel all this provincial admiration."

"But surely, my dear captain, England is a very great country," interrupted the chaplain--"a prodigious country; one that can claim all our respect and love. Look at the church, now, the purified continuation of the ancient visible authority of Christ on earth! It is the consideration of this church that has subdued my natural love of birth-place, and altered my sentiments."

"All very true, and all very well, in *your* mouth, chaplain; yet even the visible church may err. This doctrine of divine right would have kept the Stuarts on the throne, and it is not even English doctrine; much less, then, need it be American. I am no Cromwellian, no republican, that wishes to oppose the throne, in order to destroy it. A good king is a good thing, and a prodigious blessing to a country; still, a people needs look to its political privileges if it wish to preserve them. You and I will discuss this matter another time, parson. There will be plenty of opportunities," he added, rising, and smiling good-humouredly; "I must, now, call my people together, and let them know this news. It is not fair to conceal a civil war."

"My dear sir!" exclaimed the major, in concern--"are you not wrong?--precipitate, I mean--Is it not better to preserve the secret, to give yourself time for reflection--to await events?--I can discover no necessity for this haste. Should you see things differently, hereafter, an incautious word uttered at this moment might bring much motive for regret."

"I have thought of all this, Bob, during the night--for hardly did I close my eyes--and you cannot change my purpose. It is honest to let my people know how matters stand; and, so far from being hazardous, as you seem to think, I consider it wise. God knows what time will bring forth; but, in every, or any event, fair-dealing can scarcely injure him who practises it. I have already sent directions to have the whole settlement collected on the lawn, at the ringing of the bell, and I expect every moment we shall hear the summons."

Against this decision there was no appeal. Mild and indulgent as the captain habitually was, his authority was not to be disputed, when he chose to exercise it. Some doubts arose, and the father participated in them, for a moment, as to what might be the effect on the major's fortunes; for, should a very patriotic spirit arise among the men, two-thirds of whom were native Americans, and what was more, from the eastern colonies, he might be detained; or, at least, betrayed on his return, and delivered into the hands of the revolted authorities. This was a very serious consideration, and it detained the captain in the house, some time after the people were assembled, debating the chances, in the bosom of his own family.

"We exaggerate the danger," the captain, at length, exclaimed. "Most of these men have been with me for years, and I know not one among them who I think would wish to injure me, or even you, my son, in this way. There is far more danger in attempting to deceive them, than in making them confidants. I will go out and tell the truth; then we shall, at least, have the security of self-approbation. If you escape the danger of being sold by Nick, my son, I think you have little to fear from any other."

"By Nick!" repeated half-a-dozen voices, in surprise--Surely, father--surely, Willoughby--surely, my dear captain, you cannot suspect as old and tried a follower, as the Tuscarora!"

"Ay, he is an *old* follower, certainly, and he has been *punished* often enough, if he has not been *tried*. I have never suffered my distrust of that fellow to go to sleep--it is unsafe, with an Indian, unless you have a strong hold on his gratitude."

"But, Willoughby, he it was who found this manor for us," rejoined the wife. "Without him, we should never have been the owners of this lovely place, this beaver-dam, and all else that we so much enjoy."

"True, my dear; and without good golden guineas, we should not have had Nick."

"But, sir, I pay as liberally as he can wish," observed the major. "If bribes will buy him, mine are as good as another's."

"We shall see--under actual circumstances, I think we shall be, in every respect, safer, by keeping nothing back, than by telling all to the people."

The captain now put on his hat, and issued through the undefended gateway, followed by every individual of his family. As the summons had been general, when the Willoughbys and the chaplain appeared on the lawn, every living soul of that isolated settlement, even to infants in the arms, was collected there. The captain commanded the profound respect of all his dependants, though a few among them did not love him. The fault was not his, however, but was inherent rather in the untoward characters of the disaffected themselves. His habits of authority were unsuited to their habits of a presuming equality, perhaps; and it is impossible for the comparatively powerful and affluent to escape the envy and repinings of men, who, unable to draw the real distinctions that separate the gentleman from the low-minded and grovelling, impute their advantages to accidents and money. But, even the few who permitted this malign and corrupting tendency to influence their feelings, could not deny that their master was just and benevolent, though he did not always exhibit this justice and benevolence precisely in the way best calculated to soothe their own craving self-love, and exaggerated notions of assumed natural claims. In a word, captain Willoughby, in the eyes of a few unquiet and bloated imaginations among his people, was obnoxious to the imputation of pride; and this because he saw and felt the consequences of education, habits, manners, opinions and sentiments that were hidden from those who not only had no perception of their existence, but who had no knowledge whatever of the qualities that brought them into being. Pope's familiar line of "what can we reason but from what we know?" is peculiarly applicable to persons of this class; who are ever for dragging all things down to standards created by their own ignorance; and who, slaves of the basest and meanest passions, reason as if they were possessors of all the knowledge, sensibilities and refinements of their own country and times. Of this class of men, comes the ordinary demagogue, a wretch equally incapable of setting an example of any of the higher qualities, in his own person or practice, and of appreciating it when exhibited by others. Such men abound under all systems where human liberty is highly privileged, being the moral *fungi* of freedom, as the rankest weeds are known to be the troublesome and baneful productions of the richest soils.

It was no unusual thing for the people of the Hutted Knoll to be collected, in the manner we have described. We are writing of a period, that the present enlightened generation is apt to confound with the darker ages of American knowledge, in much that relates to social usages at least, though it escaped the long-buried wisdom of the Mormon bible, and Miller's interpretations of the prophecies. In that day, men were not so silly as to attempt to appear always wise; but some of the fêtes and festivals of our Anglo-Saxon ancestors were still tolerated among us; the all-absorbing and all-*swallowing* jubilee of "Independence-day" not having yet overshadowed everything else in the shape of a holiday. Now, captain Willoughby had brought with him to the colonies the love of festivals that is so much more prevalent in the old world than in the new; and it was by no means an uncommon thing for him to call his people together, to make merry on a birth-day, or the anniversary of some battle in which he had been one of the victors. When he appeared on the lawn, on the present occasion, therefore, it was expected he was about to meet them with some such announcement.

The inhabitants of the manor, or the estate of the Hutted Knoll, might be divided into three great physical, and we might add moral categories, or races, viz: the Anglo-Saxon, the Dutch, both high and low, and the African. The first was the most numerous, including the families of the millers, most of the mechanics, and that of Joel Strides, the land-overseer; the second was composed chiefly of labourers; and the last were exclusively household servants, with the exception of one of the Plinys, who was a ploughman, though permitted to live with his kinsfolk in the Hut. These divisions, Maud, in one of her merry humours, had nick-named the three tribes; while her father, to make the enumeration complete, had classed the serjeant, Mike, and Jamie Allen, as supernumeraries.

The three tribes, and the three supernumeraries, then, were all collected on the lawn, as the captain and his family approached. By a sort of secret instinct, too, they had divided themselves into knots, the Dutch keeping a little aloof from the Yankees; and the blacks, almost as a matter of religion, standing a short distance in the rear, as became people of their colour, and slaves. Mike and Jamie, however, had got a sort of neutral position, between the two great divisions of the whites, as if equally indifferent to their dissensions or antipathies. In this manner all parties stood, impatiently awaiting an announcement that had been so long delayed. The captain advanced to the front, and removing his hat, a ceremony he always observed on similar occasions, and which had the effect to make his listeners imitate his own courtesy, he addressed the crowd.

"When people live together, in a wilderness like this," commenced the captain, "there ought to be no secrets between them, my friends, in matters that touch the common interests. We are like men on a remote island; a sort of colony of our own; and we must act fairly and frankly by each other. In this spirit, then, I am now about to lay before you, all that I know myself, concerning an affair of the last importance to the colonies, and to the empire." Here Joel pricked up his ears, and cast a knowing glance at 'the miller,' a countryman and early neighbour of his own, who had charge of the grinding for the settlement, and who went by that appellation '*par excellence!*' "You all know," continued the captain, "that there have been serious difficulties between the colonies and parliament, now, for more than ten years; difficulties that have been, once or twice, partially settled, but which have as often broken out, in some new shape, as soon as an old quarrel was adjusted."

Here the captain paused a moment; and Joel, who was the usual spokesman of 'the people,' took an occasion to put a question.

"The captain means, I s'pose," he said, in a sly, half-honest, half-jesuitical manner, "the right of parliament to tax us Americans, without our own consent, or our having any members in their legyslatoore?"

"I mean what you say. The tax on tea, the shutting the port of Boston, and other steps, have brought larger bodies of the king's troops among us, than have been usual. Boston, as you probably know, has had a strong garrison, now, for some months. About six weeks since, the commander-in-chief sent a detachment out as far as Concord, in New Hampshire, to destroy certain stores. This detachment had a meeting with the minute-men, and blood was drawn. A running fight ensued, in which several hundreds have been killed and wounded; and I think I know both sides sufficiently well, to predict that a long and bloody civil war is begun. These are facts you should know, and accordingly I tell them to you."

This simple, but explicit, account was received very differently, by the different listeners. Joel Strides leaned forward, with intense interest, so as not to lose a syllable. Most of the New Englanders, or Yankees, paid great attention, and exchanged meaning glances with each other, when the captain had got through. As for Mike, he grasped a shillelah that he habitually carried, when not at work, looking round, as if waiting for orders from the captain, on whom to begin. Jamie was thoughtful and grave, and, once or twice, as the captain proceeded, he scratched his head in doubt. The Dutch seemed curious, but bewildered, gaping at each other like men who might make up their minds, if you would give them time, but who certainly had not yet. As for the blacks, their eyes began to open like saucers, when they heard of the quarrel; when it got to the blows, their mouths were all grinning with the delight of a thing so exciting. At the mention of the number of the dead, however, something like awe passed over them, and changed their countenances to dismay. Nick alone was indifferent. By the cold apathy of his manner, the captain saw at once that the battle of Lexington had not been a secret to the Tuscarora, when he commenced his own account. As the captain always encouraged a proper familiarity in his dependants, he now told them he was ready to answer any questions they might think expedient to put to him, in gratification of their natural curiosity.

"I s'pose this news comes by the major?" asked Joel.

"You may well suppose that, Strides. My son is here, and we have no other means of getting it."

"Will yer honour be wishful that we shoulther our fire-arms, and go out and fight one of them sides, or t'other?" demanded Mike.

"I wish nothing of the sort, O'Hearn. It will be time enough for us to take a decided part, when we get better ideas of what is really going on."

"Doesn't the captain, then, think matters have got far enough towards a head, for the Americans to make up their minds conclusively, as it might be?" put in Joel, in his very worst manner.

"I think it will be wiser for us all to remain where we are, and *as* we are. Civil war is a serious matter, Strides, And no man should rush blindly into its dangers and difficulties."

Joel looked at the miller, and the miller looked at Joel. Neither said anything, however, at the time. Jamie Allen had been *out* in the 'forty-five,' when thirty years younger than he was that day; and though he had his predilections and antipathies, circumstances had taught him prudence.

"Will the parliament, think ye, no be bidding the soldiery to wark their will on the puir unairmed folk, up and down the country, and they not provided with the means to resist them?"

"Och, Jamie!" interrupted Mike, who did not appear to deem it necessary to treat this matter with even decent respect--"where will be yer valour and stomach, to ask sich a question as *that*! A man is always reathy, when he has his ar-r-ms and legs free to act accorthing to natur'. What would a rigiment of throops do ag'in the likes of sich a place as this? I'm sure it's tin years I've been *in* it, and I've niver been able to find my way *out* of it. Set a souldier to rowing on the lake forenent the rising sun, with orders to get to the other ind, and a pretty job he 'd make of marching on that same! I knows it, for I've thried it, and it is not a new beginner that will make much of *sich* oare; barring he knows nothin' about them."

This was not very intelligible to anybody but Joel, and *he* had ceased to laugh at Mike's voyage, now, some six or seven years; divers other disasters, all having their origin in a similar confusion of ideas, having, in the interval, supplanted that calamity, as it might be, *seriatim.* Still it was an indication that Mike might be set down as a belligerent, who was disposed to follow his leader into the battle, without troubling him with many questions concerning the merits of the quarrel. Nevertheless, the county Leitrim-man acknowledged particular principles, all of which had a certain influence on his conduct, whenever he could get at them, to render them available. First and foremost, he cordially disliked a Yankee; and he hated an Englishman, both as an oppressor and a heretic; yet he loved his master and all that belonged to him. These were contradictory feelings, certainly; but Mike was all contradiction, both in theory and in practice.

The Anglo-Saxon tribe now professed a willingness to retire, promising to *think of the matter*, a course against which Mike loudly protested, declaring he never knew any good come of thinking, when matters had got as far as blows. Jamie, too, went off scratching his head, and he was seen to make many pauses, that day, between the shovels-full of earth he, from time to time, threw around his plants, as if pondering on what he had heard. As for the Dutch, their hour had not come. No one expected them to decide the day they first heard of argument.

The negroes got together, and began to dwell on the marvels of a battle in which so many Christians had been put to death. Little Smash placed the slain at a few thousands; but Great Smash, as better became her loftier appellation and higher spirit, affirmed that the captain had stated *hundreds* of thousands; a loss, with less than which, as she contended, no great battle could possibly be fought.

When the captain was housed, Serjeant Joyce demanded an audience; the object of which was simply to ask for *orders*, without the least reference to *principles*.

Chapter VII

We are all here!
    Father, mother,
    Sister, brother,
All who hold each other dear.
Each chair is fill'd--we're all *at home*;
To-night let no cold stranger come:
It is not often thus around
Our old familiar hearth we're found:
Bless, then, the meeting and the spot;
For once be every care forgot;
Let gentle Peace assert her power,
And kind Affection rule the hour;
    We're all--all here.

    Sprague.

Although most of the people retired to their dwellings, or their labours, as soon as the captain dismissed them, a few remained to receive his farther orders. Among these last were Joel, the carpenter, and the blacksmith. These men now joined the chief of the settlement and his son, who had lingered near the gateway, in conversation concerning the alterations that the present state of things might render necessary, in and about the Hut.

"Joel," observed the captain, when the three men were near enough to hear his orders, "this great change in the times will render some changes in our means of defence prudent, if not necessary."

"Does the captain s'pose the people of the colony will attack *us*?" asked the wily overseer, with emphasis.

"Perhaps not the people of the colony, Mr. Strides, for we have not *yet* declared ourselves their enemies; but there are other foes, who are more to be apprehended than the people of the colony."

"I should think the king's troops not likely to trouble themselves to ventur' here--the road might prove easier to come than to return. Besides, our plunder would scarce pay for such a march."

"Perhaps not--but there never has yet been a war in these colonies that some of the savage tribes were not engaged in it, before the whites had fairly got themselves into line."

"Do you really think, sir, there can be much serious danger of *that*!" exclaimed the major, in surprise.

"Beyond a question, my son. The scalping-knife will be at work in six months, if it be not busy already, should one-half of your reports and rumours turn out to be true. Such is American history."

"I rather think, sir, your apprehensions for my mother and sisters may mislead you. I do not believe the American authorities will ever allow themselves to be driven into a measure so perfectly horrible and unjustifiable; and were the English ministry sufficiently cruel, or unprincipled, to adopt the policy, the honest indignation of so humane a people would be certain to drive them from power."

As the major ceased speaking, he turned and caught the expression of Joel's countenance, and was struck with the look of intense interest with which the overseer watched his own warm and sincere manner.

"Humanity is a very pretty stalking-horse for political orations, Bob," quietly returned the father; "but it will scarcely count for much with an old campaigner. God send you may come out of this war with the same ingenuous and natural feelings as you go into it."

"The major will scarce dread the savages, should he be on the side of his nat'ral friends!" remarked Joel; "and if what he says about the humanity of the king's advisers be true, he will be safe from *them*."

"The major will be on the side to which duty calls him, Mr. Strides, if it may be agreeable to your views of the matter," answered the young man, with a little more *hauteur* than the occasion required.

The father felt uneasy, and he regretted that his son had been so indiscreet; though he saw no remedy but by drawing the attention of the men to the matter before them.

"Neither the real wishes of the people of America, nor of the people of England, will avail much, in carrying on this war," he said. "Its conduct will fall into the hands of those who will look more to the ends than to the means; and success will be found a sufficient apology for any wrong. This has been the history of all the wars of my time, and it is likely to prove the history of this. I fear it will make little difference to us on which side we may be in feeling; there will be savages to guard against in either case. This gate must be hung, one of the first things, Joel; and I have serious thoughts of placing palisades around the Knoll. The Hut, well palisaded, would make a work that could not be easily carried, without artillery."

Joel seemed struck with the idea, though it did not appear that it was favourably. He stood studying the house and the massive gates for a minute or two, ere he delivered his sentiments on the subject. When he did speak, it was a good deal more in doubt, than in approbation.

"It's all very true, captain," he said; the house would *seem* to be a good deal more safe like, if the gates were up; but, a body don't know; sometimes gates be a security, and sometimes they isn't. It all depends on which side the danger comes. Still, as these are *made*, and finished all to hanging, it's 'most a pity, too, they shouldn't be used, if a body could find *time*."

"The time *must* be found, and the gates be hung," interrupted the captain, too much accustomed to Joel's doubting, 'sort-o'-concluding manner, to be always patient under the infliction. "Not only the gates, but the palisades must be got out, holes dug, and the circumvallation completed."

"It must be as the captain says, of course, he being master here. But time's precious in May. There's half our plantin' to be done yet, and some of the ground hasn't got the last ploughin'. Harvest won't come without seed-time; for no man, let him be great, or let him be small--and it does seem to me a sort o' wastin' of the Lord's blessin's, to be hangin' gates, and diggin' holes for that--the thing the captain mentioned--when there's no visible danger in sight to recommend the measure to prudence, as it might be."

"That may be your opinion, Mr. Strides, but it is not mine. I intend to guard against a visible danger that is *out* of sight, and I will thank you to have these gates hung, this very day."

"This very day!--The captain's a mind to be musical about the matter! Every hand in the settlement couldn't get them gates in their places in less than a week."

"It appears to me, Strides, you are 'playing on the music,' as you call it, yourself, now?"

"No, indeed, captain; them gates will have to be hung on the mechanic principle; and it will take at least two or three days for the carpenter and blacksmith to get up the works that's to do it. Then the hanging, itself, I should think would stand us in hand a day for each side. As for the circumvalley, what between the cuttin', and haulin', and diggin', and settin', that would occupy all hands until after first hoein'. That is, hoein' would come afore the plantin'."

"It does not appear to me, Bob, such a heavy job as Joel represents! The gates are heavy, certainly, and may take us a day or two; but, as for stockading--I've seen barracks stockaded in, in a week, if I remember right. You know something of this--what is your opinion?"

"That this house can be stockaded in, in the time you mention; and, as I have a strong reluctance to leave the family before it is in security, with your permission I will remain and superintend the work."

The offer was gladly accepted, on more accounts than one; and the captain, accustomed to be obeyed when he was in earnest, issued his orders forthwith, to let the work proceed. Joel, however, was excused, in order that he might finish the planting he had commenced, and which a very few hands could complete within the required time. As no ditch was necessary, the work was of a very simple nature, and the major set about his portion of it without even re-entering the house.

The first thing was to draw a line for a trench some six or seven feet deep, that was to encircle the whole building, at a distance of about thirty yards from the house. This line ran, on each side of the Hut, on the very verge of the declivities, rendering the flanks far more secure than the front, where it crossed the lawn on a gently inclining surface. In one hour the major had traced this lines with accuracy; and he had six or eight men at work with spades, digging the trench. A gang of hands was sent into the woods, with orders to cut the requisite quantify of young chestnuts; and, by noon, a load of the material actually appeared on the ground. Still, nothing was done to the gates.

To own the truth, the captain was now delighted. The scene reminded him of some in his military life, and he bustled about, giving his orders, with a good deal of the fire of youth renewed, taking care, however, in no manner to interfere with the plans of his son. Mike buried himself like a mole, and had actually advanced several feet, before either of the Yankees had got even a fair footing on the bottom of his part of the trench. As for Jamie Allen, he went to work with deliberation; but it was not long before his naked gray hairs were seen on a level with the surface of the ground. The digging was not hard, though a little stony, and the work proceeded with spirit and success. All that day, and the next, and the next, and the next, the Knoll appeared alive, earth being cast upward, teams moving, carpenters sawing, and labourers toiling. Many of the men protested that their work was useless, unnecessary, *unlawful* even; but no one dared hesitate under the eyes of the major, when his father had once issued a serious command. In the mean time, Joel's planting was finished, though he made many long pauses while at work on the flats, to look up and gaze at the scene of activity and bustle that was presented at the Knoll. On the fourth day, towards evening, he was obliged to join the general "bee," with the few hands he had retained with himself.

By this time, the trench was dug, most of the timber was prepared, and the business of setting up the stockade was commenced. Each young tree was cut to the length of twenty feet, and pointed at one end. Mortices, to receive cross-pieces, were cut at proper distances, and holes were bored to admit the pins. This was all the preparation, and the timbers were set in the trench, pointed ends uppermost. When a sufficient number were thus arranged, a few inches from each other, the cross-pieces were pinned on, bringing the whole into a single connected frame, or bent. The bent was then raised to a perpendicular, and secured, by pounding the earth around the lower ends of the timbers. The latter process required care and judgment, and it was entrusted to the especial supervision of the deliberate Jamie, the major having discovered that the Yankees, in general, were too impatient to get on, and to make a show. Serjeant Joyce was particularly useful in dressing the rows of timber, and in giving the whole arrangement a military air.

"*Guid* wark is far better than *quick* wark," observed the cool-headed Scotchman, as he moved about among the men, "and it's no the fuss and bustle of acteevity that is to give the captain pleasure. The thing that is well done, is done with the least noise and confusion. Set the stockades mair pairpendic'lar, my men."

"Ay--dress them, too, my lads"--added the venerable ex-serjeant.

"This is queer plantin', Jamie," put in Joel, "and queerer grain will come of it. Do you think these young chestnuts will ever grow, ag'in, that you put them out in rows, like so much corn?"

"Now it's no for the growth we does it, Joel, but to presairve the human growth we have. To keep the savage bairbers o' the wilderness fra' clippin' our polls before the shearin' time o' natur' has gathered us a' in for the hairvest of etairnity. They that no like the safety we're makin' for them, can gang their way to 'ither places, where they '11 find no forts, or stockades to trouble their een."

"I'm not critical at all, Jamie, though to my notion a much better use for your timber plantation would be to turn it into sheds for cattle, in the winter months. I can see some good in *that*, but none in *this*."

"Bad luck to ye, then, Misther Sthroddle," cried Mike, from the bottom of the trench, where he was using a pounding instrument with the zeal of a paviour--"Bad luck to the likes of ye, say I, Misther Strides. If ye've no relish for a fortification, in a time of war, ye've only to shoulther yer knapsack, and go out into the open counthry, where ye'll have all to yer own satisfaction. Is it forthify the house, will we? That we will, and not a hair of the missuss's head, nor of the young ladies' heads, nor of the masther's head, though he's mighty bald as it is, but not a hair of *all* their heads shall be harmed, while Jamie, and Mike, and the bould ould serjeant, here, can have their way. I wish I had the trench full of yer savages, and a gineral funeral we'd make of the vagabonds! Och! They're the divil's imps, I hear from all sides, and no love do I owe them."

"And yet you're the bosom friend of Nick, who's anything but what I call a specimen of his people."

"Is it Nick ye 're afther? Well, Nick's half-civilized accorthin' to yer Yankee manners, and he's no spicimen, at all. Let him hear you call him by sich a name, if ye want throuble."

Joel walked away, muttering, leaving the labourers in doubt whether he relished least the work he was now obliged to unite in furthering, or Mike's hit at his own peculiar people. Still the work proceeded, and in one week from the day it was commenced, the stockade was complete, its gate excepted. The entrance through the palisades was directly in front of that to the house, and both passages still remained open, one set of gates not being completed, and the other not yet being hung.

It was on a Saturday evening when the last palisade was placed firmly in the ground, and all the signs of the recent labour were removed, in order to restore as much of the former beauty of the Knoll as possible. It had been a busy week; so much so, indeed, as to prevent the major from holding any of that confidential intercourse with his mother and sisters, in which it had been his habit to indulge in former visits. The fatigues of the days sent everybody to their pillows early; and the snatches of discourse which passed, had been affectionate and pleasant, rather than communicative. Now that the principal job was so near being finished, however, and the rubbish was cleared away, the captain summoned the family to the lawn again, to enjoy a delicious evening near the close of the winning month of May. The season was early, and the weather more bland, than was usual, even in that sheltered and genial valley. For the first time that year, Mrs. Willoughby consented to order the tea-equipage to be carried to a permanent table that had been placed under the shade of a fine elm, in readiness for any *fête champêtre* of this simple character.

"Come, Wilhelmina, give us a cup of your fragrant hyson, of which we have luckily abundance, tax or no tax. I should lose *caste*, were it known how much American treason we have gulped down, in this way; but, a little tea, up here in the forest, can do no man's conscience any great violence, in the long run. I suppose, major Willoughby, His Majesty's forces do not disdain tea, in these stirring times."

"Far from it, sir; we deem it so loyal to drink it, that it is said the port and sherry of the different messes, at Boston, are getting to be much neglected. I am an admirer of tea, for itself, however, caring little about its collateral qualities. Farrel"--turning to his man, who was aiding Pliny the elder, in arranging the table--"when you are through here, bring out the basket you will find on the toilet, in my room."

"True, Bob," observed the mother, smiling--"that basket has scarce been treated with civility. Not a syllable of thanks have I heard, for all the fine things it contains."

"My mind has been occupied with care for your safety, dear mother, and that must be my excuse. Now, however, there is an appearance of security which gives one a breathing-time, and my gratitude receives a sudden impulse. As for you, Maud, I regret to be compelled to say that you stand convicted of laziness; not a single thing do I owe to your labours, or recollection of me."

"Is that possible!" exclaimed the captain, who was pouring water into the tea-pot. "Maud is the last person I should suspect of neglect of this nature; I do assure you, Bob, no one listens to news of your promotions and movements with more interest than Maud."

Maud, herself, made no answer. She bent her head aside, in a secret consciousness that her sister might alone detect, and form her own conclusions concerning the colour that she felt warming her cheeks. But, Maud's own sensitive feelings attributed more to Beulah than the sincere and simple-minded girl deserved. So completely was she accustomed to regard Robert and Maud as brother and sister, that even all which had passed produced no effect in unsettling her opinions, or in giving her thoughts a new direction. Just at this moment Farrel came back, and placed the basket on the bench, at the side of his master.

"Now, my dearest mother, and you, girls"--the major had begun to drop the use of the word 'sisters' when addressing *both* the young ladies-- "Now, my dearest mother, and you, girls, I am about to give each her due. In the first place, I confess my own unworthiness, and acknowledge, that I do not deserve one-half the kind attention I have received in these various presents, after which we will descend to particulars."

The major, then, exposed every article contained in the basket, finding the words "mother" and "Beulah" pinned on each, but nowhere any indication that his younger sister had even borne him in mind. His father looked surprised at this, not to say a little grave; and he waited, with evident curiosity, for the gifts of Maud, as one thing after another came up, without any signs of her having recollected the absentee.

"This is odd, truly," observed the father, seriously; "I hope, Bob, you have done nothing to deserve this? I should be sorry to have my little girl affronted!"

"I assure you, sir, that I am altogether ignorant of any act, and I can solemnly protest against any intention, to give offence. If guilty, I now pray Maud to pardon me."

"You have done nothing, Bob--*said* nothing, Bob--*thought* nothing to offend me," cried Maud, eagerly.

"Why, then, have you forgotten him, darling, when your mother and sister have done so much in the way of recollection?" asked the captain.

"Forced gifts, my dear father, are no gifts. I do not like to be compelled to make presents."

This was uttered in a way to induce the major to throw all the articles back into the basket, as if he wished to get rid of the subject, without further comment. Owing to this precipitation, the scarf was not seen. Fortunately for Maud, who was ready to burst into tears, the service of the tea prevented any farther allusion to the matter.

"You have told me, major," observed captain Willoughby, "that your old regiment has a new colonel; but you have forgotten to mention his name. I hope it is my old messmate, Tom Wallingford, who wrote me he had some such hopes last year."

"General Wallingford has got a light-dragoon regiment--general Meredith has my old corps; he is now in this country, at the head of one of Gage's brigades."

It is a strong proof of the manner in which Maud--Maud Willoughby, as she was ever termed--had become identified with the family of the Hutted Knoll, that, with two exceptions, not a person present thought of her, when the name of this general Meredith was mentioned; though, in truth, he was the uncle of her late father. The exceptions were the major and herself. The former now never heard the name without thinking of his beautiful little playfellow, and nominal sister; while Maud, of late, had become curious and even anxious on the subject of her natural relatives. Still, a feeling akin to awe, a sentiment that appeared as if it would be doing violence to a most solemn duty, prevented her from making any allusion to her change of thought, in the presence of those whom, during childhood, she had viewed only as her nearest relatives, and who still continued so to regard her. She would have given the world to ask Bob a few questions concerning the kinsman he had mentioned, but could not think of doing so before her mother, whatever she might be induced to attempt with the young man, when by himself.

Nick next came strolling along, gazing at the stockade, and drawing near the table with an indifference to persons and things that characterized his habits. When close to the party he stopped, keeping his eye on the recent works.

"You see, Nick, I am about to turn soldier again, in my old days," observed the captain. "It is now many years since you and I have met within a line of palisades. How do you like our work?"

"What you make him for, cap'in?"

"So as to be secure against any red-skins who may happen to long for our scalps."

"Why want *your* scalp? Hatchet hasn't been dug up, atween us--bury him so deep can't find him in ten, two, six year."

"Ay, it has long been buried, it is true; but you red gentlemen have a trick of digging it up, with great readiness, when there is any occasion for it. I suppose you know, Nick, that there are troubles in the colonies?"

"Tell Nick all about him,"--answered the Indian, evasively--"No read--no hear--don't talk much--talk most wid Irisher--can't understand what he want--say t'ing one way, den say him, anoder."

"Mike is not very lucid of a certainty," rejoined the captain, laughing, all the party joining in the merriment--"but he is a sterling good fellow, and is always to be found, in a time of need."

"Poor rifle--nebber hit--shoot one way, look t'other?"

"He is no great shot, I will admit; but he is a famous fellow with a shillaleh. Has he given you any of the news?"

"All he say, news--much news ten time, as one time. Cap'in lend Nick a quarter dollar, yesterday."

"I did lend you a quarter, certainly, Nick; and I supposed it had gone to the miller for rum, before this. What am I to understand by your holding it out in this manner?--that you mean to repay me!"

"Sartain--good quarter--just like him cap'in lent Nick. Like as one pea. Nick man of honour; keep his word."

"This does look more like it than common, Nick. The money was to be returned to-day, but I did not expect to see it, so many previous contracts of that nature having been vacated, as the lawyers call it."

"Tuscarora chief alway gentleman. What he say, he do. Good quarter dollar, dat, cap'in?"

"It is unexceptionable, old acquaintance; I'll not disdain receiving it, as it may serve for a future loan."

"No need bye'm-by--take him, now--cap'in, lend Nick dollar; pay him to-morrow."

The captain protested against the *sequitur* that the Indian evidently wished to establish; declining, though in a good-natured manner, to lend the larger sum. Nick was disappointed, and walked sullenly away, moving nearer to the stockade, with the air of an offended man.

"That is an extraordinary fellow, sir!" observed the major--"I really wonder you tolerate him so much about the Hut. It might be a good idea to banish him, now that the war has broken out."

"Which would be a thing more easily said than done. A drop of water might as readily be banished from that stream, as an Indian, from any part of the forest he may choose to visit. You brought him here yourself, Bob, and should not blame us for tolerating his presence."

"I brought him, sir, because I found he recognised me even in this dress, and it was wise to make a friend of him. Then I wanted a guide, and I was well assured he knew the way, if any man did. He is a surly scoundrel, however, and appears to have changed his character, since I was a boy."

"If there be any change, Bob, it is in yourself. Nick has been Nick these thirty years, or as long as I have known him. Rascal he is, or his tribe would not have cast him out. Indian justice is stern, but it is natural justice. No man is ever put to the ban among the red men, until they are satisfied he is not fit to enjoy savage rights. In garrison, we always looked upon Nick as a clever knave, and treated him accordingly. When one is on his guard against such a fellow, he can do little harm, and this Tuscarora has a salutary dread of me, which keeps him in tolerable order, during his visits to the Hut. The principal mischief he does here, is to get Mike and Jamie deeper in the Santa Cruz than I could wish; but the miller has his orders to sell no more rum."

"I hardly think you do Nick justice, Willoughby," observed the right-judging and gentle wife. "He has *some* good qualities; but you soldiers always apply martial-law to the weaknesses of your fellow-creatures."

"And you tender-hearted women, my dear Wilhelmina, think everybody as good as yourselves."

"Remember, Hugh, when your son, there, had the canker-rash, how actively and readily the Tuscarora went into the forest to look for the gold-thread that even the doctors admitted cured him. It was difficult to find, Robert; but Nick remembered a spot where he had seen it, fifty miles off; and, without a request even, from us, he travelled that distance to procure it."

"Yes, this is true"--returned the captain, thoughtfully--"though I question if the cure was owing to the gold-thread, as you call it, Wilhelmina. Every man has some good quality or other; and, I much fear, some bad ones also.--But, here is the fellow coming back, and I do not like to let him think himself of sufficient consequence to be the subject of our remarks."

"Very true, sir--it adds excessively to the trouble of such fellows, to let them fancy themselves of importance."

Nick, now, came slowly back, after having examined the recent changes to his satisfaction. He stood a moment in silence, near the table, and then, assuming an air of more dignity than common, he addressed the captain.

"Nick ole *chief*" he said. "Been at Council Fire, often as cap'in. Can't tell, all he know; want to hear about new war."

"Why, Nick, it is a family quarrel, this time. The French have nothing to do with it."

"Yengeese fight Yengeese--um?"

"I am afraid it will so turn out. Do not the Tuscaroras sometimes dig up the hatchet against the Tuscaroras?"

"Tuscarora man kill Tuscarora man--good--he quarrel, and kill he enemy. But Tuscarora warrior nebber take scalp of Tuscarora squaw and pappoose! What you t'ink he do dat for? Red man no hog, to eat pork."

"It must be admitted, Nick, you are a very literal logician--'dog won't eat dog,' is our English saying. Still the *Yankee* will fight the Yengeese, it would seem. In a word, the Great Father, in England, has raised the hatchet against his American children."

"How you like him, cap'in--um? Which go on straight path, which go on crooked? How you like him?"

"I like it little, Nick, and wish with all my heart the quarrel had not taken place."

"Mean to put on regimentals--hah! Mean to be cap'in, ag'in? Follow drum and fife, like ole time?"

"I rather think not, old comrade. After sixty, one likes peace better than war; and I intend to stay at home."

"What for, den, build fort? Why you put fence round a house, like pound for sheep?"

"Because I intend to *stay* there. The stockade will be good to keep off any, or every enemy who may take it into their heads to come against us. You have known me defend a worse position than this."

"He got no gate," muttered Nick--"What he good for, widout gate? Yengeese, Yankees, red man, French man, walk in just as he please. No good to leave such squaw wid a door wide open."

"Thank you, Nick," cried Mrs. Willoughby. "I knew you were *my* friend, and have not forgotten the gold-thread."

"He *very* good," answered the Indian, with an important look. "Pappoose get well like not'ing. He a'most die, to-day; to-morrow he run about and play. Nick do him, too; cure him wid gold-thread."

"Oh! you are, or were quite a physician at one time, Nick. I remember when you had the smallpox, yourself."

The Indian turned, with the quickness of lightning, to Mrs. Willoughby, whom he startled with his energy, as he demanded--

"You remember dat, Mrs. cap'in! Who gib him--who cure him--um?"

"Upon my word, Nick, you almost frighten me. I fear I gave you the disease, but it was for your own good it was done. You were inoculated by myself, when the soldiers were dying around us, because they had never had that care taken of them. All I inoculated lived; yourself among the number."

The startling expression passed away from the fierce countenance of the savage, leaving in its place another so kind and amicable as to prove he not only was aware of the benefit he had received, but that he was deeply grateful for it. He drew near to Mrs. Willoughby, took her still white and soft hand in his own sinewy and dark fingers, then dropped the blanket that he had thrown carelessly across his body, from a shoulder, and laid it on a mark left by the disease, by way of pointing to her good work. He smiled, as this was done.

"Ole mark," he said, nodding his head--"sign we good friend--he nebber go away while Nick live."

This touched the captain's heart, and he tossed a dollar towards the Indian, who suffered it, however, to lie at his feet unnoticed. Turning to the stockade, he pointed significantly at the open gateways.

"Great danger go t'rough little 'ole," he said, sententiously, walking away as he concluded. "Why you leave big 'ole open?"

"We *must* get those gates hung next week," said the captain, positively; "and yet it is almost absurd to apprehend anything serious in this remote settlement, and that at so early a period in the war."

Nothing further passed on the lawn worthy to be recorded. The sun set, and the family withdrew into the house, as usual, to trust to the overseeing care of Divine Providence, throughout a night passed in a wilderness. By common consent, the discourse turned upon things noway connected with the civil war, or its expected results, until the party was about to separate for the night, when the major found himself alone with his sisters, in his own little parlour, dressing-room, or study, whatever the room adjoining his chamber could properly be called.

"You will not leave us soon, Robert," said Beulah, taking her brother's hand, with confiding affection, "I hardly think my father young and active enough, or rather *alarmed* enough, to live in times like these!"

"He is a soldier, Beulah, and a good one; so good that his son can teach him nothing. I wish I could say that he is as good a *subject*: I fear he leans to the side of the colonies."

"Heaven be praised!" exclaimed Beulah--"Oh! that his son would incline in the same direction."

"Nay, Beulah," rejoined Maud, reproachfully; "you speak without reflection. Mamma bitterly regrets that papa sees things in the light he does. *She* thinks the parliament right, and the colonies wrong."

"What a thing is a civil war!" ejaculated the major--"Here is husband divided against wife--son against father--brother against sister. I could almost wish I were dead, ere I had lived to see this!"

"Nay, Robert, it is not so bad as that, either," added Maud. "My mother will never oppose my father's will or judgment. Good wives, you know, never do *that*. She will only pray that he may decide right, and in a way that his children will never have cause to regret. As for me, I count for nothing, of course."

"And Beulah, Maud; is she nothing, too? Here will Beulah be praying for her brother's defeat, throughout this war. It has been some presentiment of this difference of opinion that has probably induced you to forget me, while Beulah and my mother were passing so many hours to fill that basket."

"Perhaps you do Maud injustice, Robert," said Beulah, smiling. "I think I can say none loves you better than our dear sister--or no one has thought of you more, in your absence."

"Why, then, does the basket contain no proof of this remembrance--not even a chain of hair--a purse, or a ring--nothing, in short, to show that I have not been forgotten, when away."

"Even if this be so," said Maud, with spirit, "in what am I worse than yourself. What proof is there that you have remembered *us?*"

"This," answered the major, laying before his sisters two small packages, each marked with the name of its proper owner. "My mother has her's, too, and my father has not been forgotten."

Beulah's exclamations proved how much she was gratified with her presents; principally trinkets and jewelry, suited to her years and station. First kissing the major, she declared her mother must see what she had received, before she retired for the night, and hurried from the room. That Maud was not less pleased, was apparent by her glowing cheeks and tearful eyes; though, for a wonder, she was far more restrained in the expression of her feelings. After examining the different articles, with pleasure, for a minute or two, she went, with a quick impetuous movement, to the basket, tumbled all its contents on the table, until she reached the scarf, which she tossed towards the major, saying, with a faint laugh--

"There, unbeliever--heathen--is *that* nothing? Was that made in a minute, think you?"

"*This!*" cried the major, opening the beautiful, glossy fabric in surprise. "Is not this one of my father's old sashes, to which I have fallen heir, in the order of nature?"

Maud dropped her trinkets, and seizing two corners of the sash, she opened it, in a way to exhibit its freshness and beauty.

"Is this *old*, or *worn?*" she asked, reproachfully. "Your father never even saw it, Bob. It has not yet been around the waist of man."

"It is not possible!--This would be the work of months--is *so* beautiful--you cannot have purchased it."

Maud appeared distressed at his doubts. Opening the folds still wider, she raised the centre of the silk to the light, pointed to certain letters that had been wrought into the fabric, so ingeniously as to escape ordinary observation, and yet so plainly as to be distinctly legible when the attention was once drawn to them. The major took the sash into his own hands altogether, held it opened before the candles, and read the words "Maud Meredith" aloud. Dropping the sash, he turned to seek the face of the donor, but she had fled the room. He followed her footsteps and entered the library, just as she was about to escape from it, by a different door.

"I am offended at your incredulity," said Maud, making an effort to laugh away the scene, "and will not remain to hear lame excuses. Your new regiment can have no nature in it, or brothers would not treat sisters thus."

"Maud *Meredith* is not my sister," he said, earnestly, "though Maud *Willoughby* may be. Why is the name Meredith?"

"As a retort to one of your own allusions--did you not call me Miss Meredith, one day, when I last saw you in Albany?"

"Ay, but that was in jest, my dearest Maud. It was not a deliberate thing, like the name on that sash."

"Oh! jokes may be premeditated as well as murder; and many a one *is* murdered, you know. Mine is a prolonged jest."

"Tell me, does my mother--does Beulah know who made this sash?"

"How else could it have been made, Bob? Do you think I went into the woods, and worked by myself, like some romantic damsel who had an unmeaning secret to keep against the curious eyes of persecuting friends!"

"I know not what I thought--scarce know what I think now. But, my mother; does she know of this *name?*"

Maud blushed to the eyes; but the habit and the love of truth were so strong in her, that she shook her head in the negative.

"Nor Beulah?--*She*, I am certain, would not have permitted 'Meredith' to appear where 'Willoughby' should have been."

"Nor Beulah, either, major Willoughby," pronouncing the name with an affectation of reverence. "The honour of the Willoughbys is thus preserved from every taint, and all the blame must fall on poor Maud Meredith."

"You dislike the name of Willoughby, then, and intend to drop it, in future--I have remarked that you sign yourself only 'Maud,' in your last letters--never before, however, did I suspect the reason."

"Who wishes to live for ever an impostor? It is not my legal name, and I shall soon be called on to perform legal acts. Remember, Mr. Robert Willoughby, I am twenty; when it comes to pounds, shillings, and pence, I must not forge. A little habit is necessary to teach me the use of my own *bonâ fide* signature."

"But ours--the name is not hateful to you--you do not throw it aside, seriously, for ever!"

"*Yours*! What, the honoured name of my dear, dearest father--of my mother--of Beulah--of yourself, Bob!"

Maud did not remain to terminate her speech. Bursting into tears, she vanished.

Chapter VIII

The village tower--'tis joy to me!--I cry, the Lord is here!
The village bells! They fill the soul with ecstasy sincere.
And thus, I sing, the light hath shined to lands in darkness hurled,
Their sound is now in all the earth, their words
throughout the world.
  Coxe.

Another night past in peace within the settlement of the Hutted Knoll. The following morning was the Sabbath, and it came forth, balmy, genial, and mild; worthy of the great festival of the Christian world. On the subject of religion, captain Willoughby was a little of a martinet; understanding by liberty of conscience, the right of improving by the instruction of those ministers who belonged to the church of England. Several of his labourers had left him because he refused to allow of any other ministrations on his estate; his doctrine being that every man had a right to do as he pleased in such matters; and as he did not choose to allow of schism, within the sphere of his own influence, if others desired to be schismatics they were at liberty to go elsewhere, in order to indulge their tastes. Joel Strides and Jamie Allen were both disaffected to this sort of orthodoxy, and they had frequent private discussions on its propriety; the former in his usual wily and jesuitical mode of sneering and insinuating, and the latter respectfully as related to his master, but earnestly as it concerned his conscience. Others, too, were dissentients, but with less repining; though occasionally they would stay away from Mr. Wood's services. Mike, alone, took an open and manly stand in the matter, and he a little out-Heroded Herod; or, in other words, he exceeded the captain himself in strictness of construction. On the very morning we have just described, he was present at a discussion between the Yankee overseer and the Scotch mason, in which these two dissenters, the first a congregationalist, and the last a seceder, were complaining of the hardships of a ten years' abstinence, during which no spiritual provender had been fed out to them from a proper source. The Irishman broke out upon the complainants in a way that will at once let the reader into the secret of the county Leitrim-man's principles, if he has any desire to know them.

"Bad luck to all sorts of religion but the right one!" cried Mike, in a most tolerant spirit. "Who d'ye think will be wishful of hearing mass and pr'aching that comes from *any* of your heretick parsons? Ye're as dape in the mire yerselves, as Mr. Woods is in the woods, and no one to lade ye out of either, but an evil spirit that would rather see all mankind br'iling in agony, than dancing at a fair."

"Go to your confessional, Mike," returned Joel, with a sneer--"It's a month, or more, sin' you seen it, and the priest will think you have forgotten him, and go away offended."

"Och! It's such a praist, as the likes of yees has no nade of throubling! Yer conscience is aisy, Misther Straddle, so that yer belly is filled, and yer wages is paid. Bad luck o sich religion!"

The allusion of Joel related to a practice of Michael's that is deserving of notice. It seems that the poor fellow, excluded by his insulated position from any communication with a priest of his own church, was in the habit of resorting to a particular rock in the forest, where he would kneel and acknowledge his sins, very much as he would have done had the rock been a confessional containing one authorized to grant him absolution. Accident revealed the secret, and from that time Michael's devotion was a standing jest among the dissenters of the valley. The county Leitrim-man was certainly a little too much addicted to Santa Cruz, and he was accused of always visiting his romantic chapel after a debauch. Of course, he was but little pleased with Joel's remark on the present occasion; and being, like a modern newspaper, somewhat more vituperative than logical, he broke out as related.

"Jamie," continued Joel, too much accustomed to Mike's violence to heed it, "it does seem to me a hardship to be obliged to frequent a church of which a man's conscience can't approve. Mr. Woods, though a native colonist, is an Old England parson, and he has so many popish ways about him, that I am under considerable concern of *mind*"--concern, of *itself*, was not sufficiently emphatic for one of Joel's sensitive feelings--"I am under considerable *concern of mind* about the children. They *sit under* no other preaching; and, though Lyddy and I do all we can to gainsay the sermons, as soon as meetin' is out, some of it *will* stick. You may worry the best Christian into idolatry and unbelief, by parseverance and falsehood. Now that things look so serious, too, in the colonies, we ought to be most careful."

Jamie did not clearly understand the application of the present state of the colonies, nor had he quite made up his mind, touching the merits of the quarrel between parliament and the Americans. As between the Stuarts and the House of Hanover, he was for the former, and that mainly because he thought them Scotch, and it was surely a good thing for a Scotchman to govern England; but, as between the *Old* countries and the *New*, he was rather inclined to think the rights of the first ought to predominate; there being something opposed to natural order, agreeably to his notions, in permitting the reverse of this doctrine to prevail. As for presbyterianism, however, even in the mitigated form of New England church government, he deemed it to be so much better than episcopacy, that he would have taken up arms, old as he was, for the party that it could be made to appear was fighting to uphold the last. We have no wish to mislead the reader. Neither of the persons mentioned, Mike included, actually *knew* anything of the points in dispute between the different sects, or churches, mentioned; but only *fancied* themselves in possession of the doctrines, traditions, and authorities connected with the subject. These fancies, however, served to keep alive a discussion that soon had many listeners; and never before, since his first ministration in the valley, did Mr. Woods meet as disaffected a congregation, as on this day.

The church of the Hutted Knoll, or, as the clergyman more modestly termed it, the chapel, stood in the centre of the meadows, on a very low swell of their surface, where a bit of solid dry ground had been discovered, fit for such a purpose. The principal object had been to make it central; though some attention had been paid also to the picturesque. It was well shaded with young elms, just then opening into leaf; and about a dozen graves, principally of very young children, were memorials of the mortality of the settlement. The building was of stone, the work of Jamie Allen's own hands, but small, square, with a pointed roof, and totally without tower, or belfry. The interior was of unpainted cherry, and through a want of skill in the mechanics, had a cold and raw look, little suited to the objects of the structure. Still, the small altar, the desk and the pulpit, and the large, square, curtained pew of the captain, the only one the house contained, were all well ornamented with hangings, or cloth, and gave the place somewhat of an air of clerical comfort and propriety. The rest of the congregation sat on benches, with kneeling-boards before them. The walls were plastered, and, a proof that parsimony had no connection with the simple character of the building, and a thing almost as unusual in America at that period as it is to-day in parts of Italy, the chapel was entirely finished.

It has been said that the morning of the particular Sabbath at which we have now arrived, was mild and balmy. The sun of the forty-third degree of latitude poured out its genial rays upon the valley, gilding the tender leaves of the surrounding forest with such touches of light as are best known to the painters of Italy. The fineness of the weather brought nearly all the working people of the settlement to the chapel quite an hour before the ringing of its little bell, enabling the men to compare opinions afresh, on the subject of the political troubles of the times, and the women to gossip about their children.

On all such occasions, Joel was a principal spokesman, nature having created him for a demagogue, in a small way; an office for which education had in no degree unfitted him. As had been usual with him, of late, he turned the discourse on the importance of having correct information of what was going on, in the inhabited parts of the country, and of the expediency of sending some trustworthy person on such an errand. He had frequently intimated his own readiness to go, if his neighbours wished it.

"We're all in the dark here," he remarked, "and might stay so to the end of time, without some one to be relied on, to tell us the news. Major Willoughby is a fine man"--Joel meant *morally*, not *physically*--"but he's a king's officer, and nat'rally feels inclined to make the best of things for the rig'lars. The captain, too, was once a soldier, himself, and his feelin's turn, as it might be, unav'idably, to the side he has been most used to. We are like people on a desart island, out here in the wilderness--and if ships won't arrive to tell us how matters come on, we must send one out to l'arn it for us. I'm the last man at the Dam"--so the *oi polloi* called the valley--"to say anything hard of either the captain or his son; but one is English born, and the other is English bred; and each will make a difference in a man's feelin's."

To this proposition the miller, in particular, assented; and, for the twentieth time, he made some suggestion about the propriety of Joel's going himself, in order to ascertain how the land lay.

"You can be back by hoeing," he added, "and have plenty of time to go as far as Boston, should you wish to."

Now, while the great events were in progress, which led to the subversion of British power in America, an under-current of feeling, if not of incidents, was running in this valley, which threatened to wash away the foundations of the captain's authority. Joel and the miller, if not downright conspirators, had hopes, calculations, and even projects of their own, that never would have originated with men of the same class, in another state of society; or, it might almost be said, in another part of the world. The sagacity of the overseer had long enabled him to foresee that the issue of the present troubles would be insurrection; and a sort of instinct which some men possess for the strongest side, had pointed out to him the importance of being a patriot. The captain, he little doubted, would take part with the crown, and then no one knew what might be the consequences. It is not probable that Joel's instinct for the strongest side predicted the precise confiscations that subsequently ensued, some of which had all the grasping lawlessness of a gross abuse of power; but he could easily foresee that if the owner of the estate should be driven off, the property and its proceeds, probably for a series of years, would be very apt to fall under his own control and management. Many a patriot has been made by anticipations less brilliant than these; and as Joel and the miller talked the matter over between them, they had calculated all the possible emolument of fattening beeves, and packing pork for hostile armies, or isolated frontier posts, with a strong gusto for the occupation. Should open war but fairly commence, and could the captain only be induced to abandon the Knoll, and take refuge within a British camp, everything might be made to go smoothly, until settling day should follow a peace. At that moment, *non est inventus* would be a sufficient answer to a demand for any balance.

"They tell me," said Joel, in an aside to the miller, "that law is as good as done with in the Bay colony, already; and you know if the law has run out *there*, it will quickly come to an end, here. York never had much character for law."

"That's true, Joel; then you know the captain himself is the only magistrate hereabout; and, when he is away, we shall have to be governed by a committee of safety, or something of that natur'."

"A committee of safety will be the thing!"

"What is a committee of safety, Joel?" demanded the miller, who had made far less progress in the arts of the demagogue than his friend, and who, in fact, had much less native fitness for the vocation; "I have heer'n tell of them regulations, but do not rightly understand 'em, a'ter all."

"You know what a committee is?" asked Joel, glancing inquiringly at his friend.

"I s'pose I do--it means men's takin' on themselves the trouble and care of public business."

"That's it--now a committee of safety means a few of us, for instance, having the charge of the affairs of this settlement, in order to see that no harm shall come to anything, especially to the people."

"It would be a good thing to have one, here. The carpenter, and you, and I might be members, Joel."

"We'll talk about it, another time. The corn is just planted, you know; and it has got to be hoed *twice*, and topped, before it can be gathered. Let us wait and see how things come on at Boston."

While this incipient plot was thus slowly coming to a head, and the congregation was gradually collecting at the chapel, a very different scene was enacting in the Hut. Breakfast was no sooner through, than Mrs. Willoughby retired to her own sitting-room, whither her son was shortly summoned to join her. Expecting some of the inquiries which maternal affection might prompt, the major proceeded to the place named with alacrity; but, on entering the room, to his great surprise he found Maud with his mother. The latter seemed grave and concerned, while the former was not entirely free from alarm. The young man glanced inquiringly at the young lady, and he fancied he saw tears struggling to break out of her eyes.

"Come hither, Robert"--said Mrs. Willoughby, pointing to a chair at her side--with a gravity that struck her son as unusual--"I have brought you here to listen to one of the old-fashioned lectures, of which you got so many when a boy."

"Your advice, my dear mother--or even your reproofs--would be listened to with far more reverence and respect, now, than I fear they were then," returned the major, seating himself by the side of Mrs. Willoughby, and taking one of her hands, affectionately, in both his own. "It is only in after-life that we learn to appreciate the tenderness and care of such a parent as you have been; though what I have done lately, to bring me in danger of the guard-house, I cannot imagine. Surely *you* cannot blame me for adhering to the crown, at a moment like this!"

"I shall not interfere with your conscience in this matter, Robert; and my own feelings, American as I am by birth and family, rather incline me to think as you think. I have wished to see you, my son, on a different business."

"Do not keep me in suspense, mother; I feel like a prisoner who is waiting to hear his charges read. What have I done?"

"Nay, it is rather for *you* to tell *me* what you have done. You cannot have forgotten, Robert, how very anxious I have been to awaken and keep alive family affection, among my children; how very important both your father and I have always deemed it; and how strongly we have endeavoured to impress this importance on all your minds. The tie of family, and the love it ought to produce, is one of the sweetest of all our earthly duties. Perhaps we old people see its value more than you young; but, to us, the weakening of it seems like a disaster only a little less to be deplored than death."

"Dearest--dearest mother! What *can* you--what *do* you mean?--What can *I*--what can *Maud* have to do with this?"

"Do not your consciences tell you, both? Has there not been some misunderstanding--perhaps a quarrel--certainly a coldness between you? A mother has a quick and a jealous eye; and I have seen, for some time, that there is not the old confidence, the free natural manner, in either of you, that there used to be, and which always gave your father and me so much genuine happiness. Speak, then, and let me make peace between you."

Robert Willoughby would not have looked at Maud, at that moment, to have been given a regiment; as for Maud, herself, she was utterly incapable of raising her eyes from the floor. The former coloured to the temples, a proof of consciousness, his mother fancied; while the latter's face resembled ivory, as much as flesh and blood.

"If you think, Robert," continued Mrs. Willoughby, "that Maud has forgotten you, or shown pique for any little former misunderstanding, during your last absence, you do her injustice. No one has done as much for you, in the way of memorial; that beautiful sash being all her own work, and made of materials purchased with her own pocket-money. Maud loves you truly, too; for, whatever may be the airs she gives herself, while you are together, when absent, no one seems to care more for your wishes and happiness, than that very wilful and capricious girl."

"Mother!--mother!" murmured Maud, burying her face in both her hands.

Mrs. Willoughby was woman in all her feelings, habits and nature. No one would have been more keenly alive to the peculiar sensibilities of her sex, under ordinary circumstances, than herself; but she was now acting and thinking altogether in her character of a mother; and so long and intimately had she regarded the two beings before her, in that common and sacred light, that it would have been like the dawn of a new existence for her, just then, to look upon them as not really akin to each other.

"I shall not, nor can I treat either of you as a child," she continued, "and must therefore appeal only to your own good sense, to make a peace. I know it can be nothing serious; but, it is painful to me to see even an affected coldness among my children. Think, Maud, that we are on the point of a war, and how bitterly you would regret it, should any accident befall your brother, and your memory not be able to recall the time passed among us, in his last visit, with entire satisfaction."

The mother's voice trembled; but tears no longer struggled about the eyelids of Maud. Her face was pale as death, and it seemed as if every ordinary fountain of sorrow were dried up.

"Dear Bob, this is too much!" she said eagerly, though in husky tones. "Here is my hand--nay, here are *both*. Mother must not think this cruel charge is--*can* be true."

The major arose, approached his sister, and impressed a kiss on her cold cheek. Mrs. Willoughby smiled at these tokens of amity, and the conversation continued in a less earnest manner.

"This is right, my children," said the single-hearted Mrs. Willoughby, whose sensitive maternal love saw nothing but the dreaded consequences of weakened domestic affections; "and I shall be all the happier for having witnessed it. Young soldiers, Maud, who are sent early from their homes, have too many inducements to forget them and those they contain; and we women are so dependent on the love of our male friends, that it is wisdom in *us* to keep alive all the earlier ties as long and as much as possible."

"I am sure, dearest mother," murmured Maud, though in a voice that was scarcely audible, "*I* shall be the last to wish to weaken this family tie. No one can feel a warmer--more proper--a more *sisterly* affection for Robert, than I do--he was always so kind to me when a child--and so ready to assist me--and so manly--and so everything that he ought to be--it is surprising you should have fancied there was any coldness between us!"

Major Willoughby even bent forward to listen, so intense was his curiosity to hear what Maud said; a circumstance which, had she seen it, would probably have closed her lips. But her eyes were riveted on the floor, her cheeks were bloodless, and her voice so low, that nothing but the breathless stillness he observed, would have allowed the young man to hear it, where he sat.

"You forget, mother"--rejoined the major, satisfied that the last murmur had died on his ears--"that Maud will probably be transplanted into another family, one of these days, where we, who know her so well, and have reason to love her so much, can only foresee that she will form new, and even stronger ties than any that accident may have formed for her here."

"Never--never"--exclaimed Maud, fervently--"I can never love any as well as I love those who are in this house."

The relief she wanted stopped her voice, and, bursting into tears, she threw-herself into Mrs. Willoughby's arms, and sobbed like a child. The mother now motioned to her son to quit the room, while she remained herself to soothe the weeping girl, as she so often had done before, when overcome by her infantile, or youthful griefs. Throughout this interview, habit and single-heartedness so exercised their influence, that the excellent matron did not, in the most remote manner, recollect that her son and Maud were not natural relatives. Accustomed herself to see the latter every day, and to think of her, as she had from the moment when she was placed in her arms, an infant of a few weeks old the effect that separation might produce on others, never presented itself to her mind. Major Willoughby, a boy of eight when Maud was received in the family, had known from the first her precise position; and it was perhaps morally impossible that *he* should not recall the circumstance in their subsequent intercourse; more especially as school, college, and the army, had given him so much leisure to reflect on such things, apart from the influence of family habits; while it was to be expected that a consequence of his own peculiar mode of thinking on this subject, would be to produce something like a sympathetic sentiment in the bosom of Maud. Until within the last few years, however, she had been so much of a child herself, and had been treated so much like a child by the young soldier, that it was only through a change in him, that was perceptible only to herself, and which occurred when he first met her grown into womanhood, that she alone admitted any feelings that were not strictly to be referred to sisterly regard. All this, nevertheless, was a profound mystery to every member of the family, but the two who were its subjects; no other thoughts than the simplest and most obvious, ever suggesting themselves to the minds of the others.

In half an hour, Mrs. Willoughby had quieted all Maud's present troubles, and the whole family left the house to repair to the chapel. Michael, though he had no great reverence for Mr. Wood's ministrations, had constituted himself sexton, an office which had devolved on him in consequence of his skill with the spade. Once initiated into one branch of this duty, he had insisted on performing all the others; and it was sometimes a curious spectacle to see the honest fellow, busy about the interior of the building, during service, literally stopping one of his ears with a thumb, with a view, while he acquitted himself of what he conceived to be temporal obligations, to exclude as much heresy as possible. One of his rules was to refuse to commence tolling the bell, until he saw Mrs. Willoughby and her daughter, within a reasonable distance of the place of worship; a rule that had brought about more than one lively discussion between himself and the levelling-minded, if not heavenly-minded Joel Strides. On the present occasion, this simple process did not pass altogether without a dispute.

"Come, Mike; it's half-past ten; the people have been waiting about the meetin' 'us, some time; you should open the doors and toll the bell. People can't wait, for ever for anybody; not even for your church."

"Then let 'em just go home, ag'in, and come when they're called. Because, the ould women, and the young women, and the childer, and the likes o' them, wishes to scandalize their fellow cr'atures, Christians I will not call 'em, let 'em mate in the mill, or the school-house, and not come forenent a church on sich a business as that. Is it toll the bell, will I, afore the Missus is in sight?--No--not for a whole gineration of ye, Joel; and every one o' them, too, a much likelier man than ye bees yerself."

"Religion is no respecter of persons"--returned the philosophical Joel. "Them that likes masters and mistresses may have them, for all me; but it riles me to meet with meanness."

"It does!" cried Mike, looking up at his companion, with a very startling expression of wonder. "If that be true, ye must be in a mighty throubled state, most of the live-long day, ye must!"

"I tell you, Michael O'Hearn, religion is no respecter of persons. The Lord cares jist as much for *me*, as he does for captain Willoughby, or his wife, or his son, or his darters, or anything that is his."

"Divil burn me, now, Joel, if I believe *that*!" again cried Mike, in his dogmatic manner. "Them that understands knows the difference between mankind, and I'm sure it can be no great sacret to the Lord, when it is so well known to a poor fellow like myself. There's a plenty of fellow-cr'atures that has a mighty good notion of their own excellence, but when it comes to r'ason and thruth, it's no very great figure ye all make, in proving what ye say. This chapel is the master's, if chapel the heretical box can be called, and yonder bell was bought wid his money; and the rope is his; and the hands that mane to pull it, is his; and so there's little use in talking ag'in rocks, and ag'in minds that's made up even harder than rocks, and to spare."

This settled the matter. The bell was not tolled until Mrs. Willoughby, and her daughters, had got fairly through the still unprotected gateway of the stockade, although the recent discussion of political questions had so far substituted discontent for subordination in the settlement, that more than half of those who were of New England descent, had openly expressed their dissatisfaction at the delay. Mike, however, was as unmoved as the little chapel itself, refusing to open the door until the proper moment had arrived, according to his own notion of the fitness of things. He then proceeded to the elm, against which the little bell was hung, and commenced tolling it with as much seriousness as if the conveyer of sounds had been duly consecrated.

When the family from the Hut entered the chapel, all the rest of the congregation were in their customary seats. This arrival, however, added materially to the audience, Great Smash and Little Smash, the two Plinys, and some five or six coloured children, between the ages of six and twelve, following in the train of their master. For the blacks, a small gallery had been built, where they could sit apart, a proscribed, if not a persecuted race. Little did the Plinys or the Smashes, notwithstanding, think of this. Habit had rendered their situation more than tolerable, for it had created notions and usages that would have rendered them uncomfortable, in closer contact with the whites. In that day, the two colours never ate together, by any accident; the eastern castes being scarcely more rigid in the observance of their rules, than the people of America were on this great point. The men who would toil together, joke together, and pass their days in familiar intercourse, would not sit down at the same board. There seemed to be a sort of contamination, according to the opinions of one of these castes, in breaking bread with the other. This prejudice often gave rise to singular scenes, more especially in the households of those who habitually laboured in company with their slaves. In such families, it not unfrequently happened that a black led the councils of the farm. He might be seen seated by the fire, uttering his opinions dogmatically, reasoning warmly against his own master, and dealing out his wisdom *ex cathedra*, even while he waited, with patient humility, when he might approach, and satisfy his hunger, after all of the other colour had quitted the table.

Mr. Woods was not fortunate in the selection of his subject, on the occasion of which we are writing. There had been so much personal activity, and so much political discussion during the past week, as to prevent him from writing a new sermon, and of course he was compelled to fail back on the other end of the barrel. The recent arguments inclined him to maintain his own opinions, and he chose a discourse that he had delivered to the garrison of which he had last been chaplain. To this choice he had been enticed by the text, which was, "Render unto Cæsar the things that are Cæsar's," a mandate that would be far more palatable to an audience composed of royal troops, than to one which had become a good deal disaffected by the arts and arguments of Joel Strides and the miller. Still, as the sermon contained a proper amount of theological truisms, and had a sufficiency of general orthodoxy to cover a portion of its political bearing, it gave far more dissatisfaction to a few of the knowing, than to the multitude. To own the truth, the worthy priest was so much addicted to continuing his regimental and garrison course of religious instruction, that his ordinary listeners would scarcely observe this tendency to loyalty; though it was far different with those who were eagerly looking for causes of suspicion and denunciation, in the higher quarters.

"Well," said Joel, as he and the miller, followed by their respective families, proceeded towards the mill, where the household of the Strides' were to pass the remainder of the day, "well, this is a bold sermon for a minister to preach in times like these! I kind o' guess, if Mr. Woods was down in the Bay, 'render unto Cæsar the things that are Cæsars,' wouldn't be doctrine to be so quietly received by every congregation. What's your notion about that, Miss Strides?"

Miss Strides thought exactly as her husband thought, and the miller and his wife were not long in chiming in with her, accordingly. The sermon furnished material for conversation throughout the remainder of the day, at the mill, and divers conclusions were drawn from it, that were ominous to the preacher's future comfort and security.

Nor did the well-meaning parson entirely escape comment in the higher quarters.

"I wish, Woods, you had made choice of some other subject," observed the captain, as he and his friend walked the lawn together, in waiting for a summons to dinner.

"In times like these, one cannot be too careful of the political notions he throws out; and to own the truth to you, I am more than half inclined to think that Cæsar is exercising quite as much authority, in these colonies, as justly falls to his share."

"Why, my dear captain, you have heard this very sermon three or four times already, and you have more than once mentioned it with commendation!"

"Ay, but that was in garrison, where one is obliged to teach subordination. I remember the sermon quite well, and a very good one it was, twenty years since, when you first preached it; but--"

"I apprehend, captain Willoughby, that '*tempora mutantur, et, nos mutamus in illis.*' That the mandates and maxims of the Saviour are far beyond the mutations and erring passions of mortality. His sayings are intended for all times."

"Certainly, as respects their general principles and governing truths. But no text is to be interpreted without some reference to circumstances. All I mean is, that the preaching which might be very suitable to a battalion of His Majesty's Fortieth might be very unsuitable for the labourers of the Hutted Knoll; more especially so soon after what I find is called the Battle of Lexington."

The summons to dinner cut short the discourse; and probably prevented a long, warm, but friendly argument.

That afternoon and evening, captain Willoughby and his son had a private and confidential discourse. The former advised the major to rejoin his regiment without delay, unless he were prepared to throw up his commission and take sides with the colonists, altogether. To this the young soldier would not listen, returning to the charge, in the hope of rekindling the dormant flame of his father's loyalty.

The reader is not to suppose that captain Willoughby's own mind was absolutely made up to fly into open rebellion. Far from it. He had his doubts and misgivings on the subjects of both principles and prudence, but he inclined strongly to the equity of the demands of the Americans. Independence, or separation, if thought of at all in 1775 entered into the projects of but very few; the warmest wish of the most ardent of the whigs of the colonies being directed toward compromise, and a distinct recognition of their political franchises. The events that followed so thickly were merely the consequences of causes which, once set in motion, soon attained an impetus that defied ordinary human control. It was doubtless one of the leading incidents of the great and mysterious scheme of Divine Providence for the government of the future destinies of man, that political separation should commence, in this hemisphere, at that particular juncture, to be carried out, ere the end of a century, to its final and natural conclusion.

But the present interview was less to debate the merits of any disputed question, than to consult on the means of future intercourse, and to determine on what was best to be done at the present moment. After discussing the matter, pro and con, it was decided that the major should quit the Knoll the next day, and return to Boston, avoiding Albany and those points of the country in which he would be most exposed to detection. So many persons were joining the American forces that were collecting about the besieged town, that his journeying on the proper road would excite no suspicion; and once in the American camp, nothing would be easier than to find his way into the peninsula. All this young Willoughby felt no difficulty in being able to accomplish, provided he could get into the settlements without being followed by information of his real character. The period of spies, and of the severe exercise of martial-law, was not yet reached; and all that was apprehended was detention. Of the last, however, there was great danger; positive certainty, indeed, in the event of discovery; and major Willoughby had gleaned enough during his visit, to feel some apprehensions of being betrayed. He regretted having brought his servant with him; for the man was a European, and by his dulness and speech might easily get them both into difficulties. So serious, indeed, was this last danger deemed by the father, that he insisted on Robert's starting without the man, leaving the last to follow, on the first suitable occasion.

As soon as this point was settled, there arose the question of the proper guide. Although he distrusted the Tuscarora, captain Willoughby, after much reflection, came to the opinion that it would be safer to make an ally of him, than to give him an opportunity of being employed by the other side. Nick was sent for, and questioned. He promised to take the major to the Hudson, at a point between Lunenburg and Kinderhook, where he would be likely to cross the river without awakening suspicion; his own reward to depend on his coming back to the Hutted Knoll with a letter from the major, authorizing the father to pay him for his services. This plan, it was conceived, would keep Nick true to his faith, for the time being, at least.

Many other points were discussed between the father and son, the latter promising if anything of importance occurred, to find the means of communicating it to his friends at the Knoll, while Parrel was to follow his master, at the end of six weeks or two months, with letters from the family. Many of the captain's old army-friends were now in situations of authority and command, and he sent to them messages of prudence, and admonitions to be moderate in their views, which subsequent events proved were little regarded. To general Gage he even wrote, using the precaution not to sign the letter, though its sentiments were so much in favour of the colonies, that had it been intercepted, it is most probable the Americans would have forwarded the missive to its direction.

These matters arranged, the father and son parted for the night, some time after the house-clock had struck the hour of twelve.

Chapter IX

Though old in cunning, as in years,
He is so small, that like a child
In face and form, the god appears,
And sportive like a boy, and wild;
Lightly he moves from place to place,
In none at rest, in none content;
Delighted some new toy to chase--
On childish purpose ever bent.
Beware! to childhood's spirits gay
Is added more than childhood's power;
And you perchance may rue the hour
That saw you join his seeming play.

Griffen

The intention of the major to quit the Knoll that day, was announced to the family at breakfast, on the following morning. His mother and Beulah heard this intelligence, with a natural and affectionate concern, that they had no scruples in avowing; but Maud seemed to have so schooled her feelings, that the grief she really felt was under a prudent control. To her, it appeared as if her secret were constantly on the point of exposure, and she believed *that* would cause her instant death. To survive its shame was impossible in her eyes, and all the energies of her nature were aroused, with the determination of burying her weakness in her own bosom. She had been so near revealing it to Beulah, that even now she trembled as she thought of the precipice over which she had been impending, strengthening her resolution by the recollection of the danger she had run.

As a matter of necessary caution, the intended movements of the young man were kept a profound secret from all in the settlement. Nick had disappeared in the course of the night, carrying with him the major's pack, having repaired to a designated point on the stream, where he was to be joined by his fellow-traveller at an hour named. There were several forest-paths which led to the larger settlements. That usually travelled was in the direction of old Fort Stanwix, first proceeding north, and then taking a south-eastern direction, along the shores of the Mohawk. This was the route by which the major had come. Another struck the Otsego, and joined the Mohawk at the point more than once mentioned in our opening chapters. As these were the two ordinary paths--if paths they could be called, where few or no traces of footsteps were visible--it was more than probable any plan to arrest the traveller would be laid in reference to their courses. The major had consequently resolved to avoid them both, and to strike boldly into the mountains, until he should reach the Susquehanna, cross that stream on its flood wood, and finding one of its tributaries that flowed in from the eastward, by following its banks to the high land, which divides the waters of the Mohawk from this latter river, place himself on a route that would obliquely traverse the water-courses, which, in this quarter of the country, have all a general north or south direction. Avoiding Schenectady and Albany, he might incline towards the old establishments of the descendants of the emigrants from the Palatinate, on the Schoharie, and reach the Hudson at a point deemed safe for his purposes, through some of the passes of the mountains in their vicinity. He was to travel in the character of a land-owner who had been visiting his patent, and his father supplied him with a map and an old field-book, which would serve to corroborate his assumed character, in the event of suspicion, or arrest. Not much danger was apprehended, however, the quarrel being yet too recent to admit of the organization and distrust that subsequently produced so much vigilance and activity.

"You will contrive to let us hear of your safe arrival in Boston, Bob," observed the father, as he sat stirring his tea, in a thoughtful way--"I hope to God the matter will go no farther, and that our apprehensions, after all, have given this dark appearance to what has already happened."

"Ah, my dear father; you little know the state of the country, through which I have so lately travelled!" answered the major, shaking his head. "An alarm of fire, in an American town, would scarce create more movement, and not so much excitement. The colonies are alive, particularly those of New England, and a civil war is inevitable; though I trust the power of England will render it short."

"Then, Robert, do not trust yourself among the people of New England"--cried the anxious mother. "Go rather to New York, where we have so many friends, and so much influence. It will be far easier to reach New York than to reach Boston."

"That may be true, mother, but it will scarcely be as creditable. My regiment is in Boston, and its enemies are *before* Boston; an old soldier like captain Willoughby will tell you that the major is a very necessary officer to a corps. No--no--my best course is to fall into the current of adventurers who are pushing towards Boston, and appear like one of their number, until I can get an opportunity of stealing away from them, and join my own people."

"Have a care, Bob, that you do not commit a military crime. Perhaps these provincial officers may take it into their heads to treat you as a spy, should you fall into their hands!"

"Little fear of that, sir; at present it is a sort of colonial scramble for what they fancy liberty. That they will fight, in their zeal, I know; for I have seen it; but matters have not at all gone as far as you appear to apprehend. I question if they would even stop Gage, himself, from going through their camp, were he outside, and did he express a desire to return."

"And yet you tell me, arms and ammunition are seized all over the land; that several old half-pay officers of the king have been arrested, and put under a sort of parole!"

"Such things were talked of, certainly, though I question if they have yet been done. Luckily for yourself, under your present opinions at least, *you* are not on half-pay, even."

"It is fortunate, Bob, though you mention it with a smile. With my present feelings, I should indeed be sorry to be on half-pay, or quarter-pay, were there such a thing. I now feel myself my-own master, at liberty to follow the dictates of my conscience, and the suggestions of my judgment."

"Well, sir, you are a little fortunate, it must be acknowledged. I cannot see how any man *can* be at liberty to throw off the allegiance he owes his natural sovereign. What think you, Maud?"

This was said half in bitterness, half in jest, though the appeal at its close was uttered in a serious manner, and a little anxiously. Maud hesitated, as if to muster her thoughts, ere she replied.

"My feelings are against rebellion," she said, at length; "though I fear my reason tells me there is no such thing as a natural sovereign. If the parliament had not given us the present family, a century since, by what rule of nature would it be our princes, Bob?"

"Ah! these are some of the flights of your rich imagination, my dear-- Maud; it is parliament that has made them our princes, and parliament, at least, is our legal, constitutional master."

"That is just the point in dispute. Parliament may be the rightful governors of England, but are they the rightful governors of America?"

"Enough," said the captain, rising from table--"We will not discuss such a question, just as we are about to separate. Go, my son; a duty that is to be performed, cannot be done too soon. Your fowling-piece and ammunition are ready for you, and I shall take care to circulate the report that you have gone to pass an hour in the woods, in search of pigeons. God bless you, Bob; however we may differ in this matter--you are my son--my *only* son--my dear and well-beloved boy--God for ever bless you!"

A profound stillness succeeded this burst of nature, and then the young man took his leave of his mother and the girls. Mrs. Willoughby kissed her child. She did not even weep, until she was in her room; then, indeed, she went to her knees, her tears, and her prayers. Beulah, all heart and truth as she was, wept freely on her brother's neck; but Maud, though pale and trembling, received his kiss without returning it; though she could not help saying with a meaning that the young man had in his mind all that day, ay, and for many succeeding days--"be careful of yourself, and run into no unnecessary dangers; God bless you, dear, *dear* Bob."

Maud alone followed the movements of the gentlemen with her eyes. The peculiar construction of the Hut prevented external view from the south windows; but there was a loop in a small painting-room of the garret that was especially under her charge. Thither, then, she flew, to ease her nearly bursting heart with tears, and to watch the retiring footsteps of Robert. She saw him, accompanied by his father and the chaplain, stroll leisurely down the lawn, conversing and affecting an indifferent manner, with a wish to conceal his intent to depart. The glass of the loop was open, to admit the air, and Maud strained her sense of hearing, in the desire to catch, if possible, another tone of his voice. In this she was unsuccessful; though he stopped and gazed back at the Hut, as if to take a parting look. Her father and Mr. Woods did not turn, and Maud thrust her hand through the opening and waved her handkerchief. "He will think it Beulah or I," she thought, "and it may prove a consolation to him to know how much *we* love him." The major saw the signal, and returned it. His father unexpectedly turned, and caught a glimpse of the retiring hand, as it was disappearing within the loop. "That is our precious Maud," he said, without other thought than of her sisterly affection. "It is *her* painting-room; Beulah's is on the other side of the gateway; but the window does not seem to be open."

The major started, kissed his hand fervently, five or six times, and then he walked on. As if to change the conversation, he said hastily, and with a little want of connection with what had just passed--

"Yes, sir, that gate, sure enough--have it hung, at once, I do entreat of you. I shall not be easy until I hear that both the gates are hung--that in the stockade, and that in the house, itself."

"It was my intention to commence to-day," returned the father, "but your departure has prevented it. I will wait a day or two, to let your mother and sisters tranquillize their minds a little, before we besiege them with the noise and clamour of the workmen."

"Better besiege them with *that*, my dear sir, than leave them exposed to an Indian, or even a rebel attack."

The major then went on to give some of his more modern military notions, touching the art of defence. As one of the old school, he believed his father a miracle of skill; but what young man, who had enjoyed the advantages of ten or fifteen years of the most recent training in any branch of knowledge, ever believed the educations of those who went before him beyond the attacks of criticism. The captain listened patiently, and with an old man's tolerance for inexperience, glad to have any diversion to unhappy thoughts.

All this time Maud watched their movements from the loop, with eyes streaming with tears. She saw Robert pause, and look back, again and again; and, once more, she thrust out the handkerchief. It was plain, however, he did not see it; for he turned and proceeded, without any answering signal.

"He never *can* know whether it was Beulah or I," thought Maud; "yet, he may fancy we are *both* here."

On the rocks, that overhung the mills, the gentlemen paused, and conversed for quite a quarter of an hour. The distance prevented Maud from discerning their countenances; but she could perceive the thoughtful, and as she fancied melancholy, attitude of the major, as, leaning on his fowling-piece, his lace was turned towards the Knoll, and his eyes were really riveted on the loop. At the end of the time mentioned, the young soldier shook hands hastily and covertly with his companions, hurried towards the path, and descended out of sight, following the course of the stream. Maud saw him no more, though her father and Mr. Woods stood on the rocks quite half an hour longer, catching occasional glimpses of his form, as it came out of the shadows of the forest, into the open space of the little river; and, indeed, until the major was within a short distance of the spot where he was to meet the Indian. Then they heard the reports of both barrels of his fowling-piece, fired in quick succession, the signals that he had joined his guide. This welcome news received, the two gentlemen returned slowly towards the house.

Such was the commencement of a day, which, while it brought forth nothing alarming to the family of the Hutted Knoll, was still pregnant with important consequences. Major Willoughby disappeared from the sight of his father about ten in the morning; and before twelve, the settlement was alive with the rumours of a fresh arrival. Joel knew not whether to rejoice or to despair, as he saw a party of eight or ten armed men rising above the rock, and holding their course across the flats towards the house. He entertained no doubt of its being a party sent by the provincial authorities to arrest the captain, and he foresaw the probability of another's being put into the lucrative station of receiver of the estate, during the struggle which was in perspective. It is surprising how many, and sometimes how pure patriots are produced by just such hopes as those of Joel's. At this day, there is scarce an instance of a confiscated estate, during the American revolution, connected with which racy traditions are not to be found, that tell of treachery very similar to this contemplated by the overseer in some instances of treachery effected by means of kinsmen and false friends.

Joel had actually got on his Sunday coat, and was making his way towards the Knoll, in order to be present, at least, at the anticipated scene, when, to his amazement, and somewhat to his disappointment, he saw the captain and chaplain moving down the lawn, in a manner to show that these unexpected arrivals brought not unwelcome guests. This caused him to pause; and when he perceived that the only two among the strangers who had the air of gentlemen, were met with cordial shakes of the hand, he turned back towards his own tenement, a half-dissatisfied, and yet half contented man.

The visit which the captain had come out to receive, instead of producing any uneasiness in his family, was, in truth, highly agreeable, and very opportune. It was Evert Beekman, with an old friend, attended by a party of chain-bearers, hunters, &c., on his way from the "Patent" he owned in the neighbourhood--that is to say, within fifty miles--and halting at the Hutted Knoll, under the courteous pretence of paying his respects to the family, but, in reality, to bring the suit he had now been making to Beulah for quite a twelvemonth, to a successful termination.

The attachment between Evert Beekman and Beulah Willoughby was of a character so simple, so sincere, and so natural, as scarce to furnish materials for a brief episode. The young man had not made his addresses without leave obtained from the parents; he had been acceptable to the daughter from the commencement of their acquaintance; and she had only asked time to reflect, ere she gave her answer, when he proposed, a day or two before the family left New York.

To own the truth, Beulah was a little surprised that her suitor had delayed his appearance till near the close of May, when she had expected to see him at the beginning of the month. A letter, however, was out of the question, since there was no mode of transmitting it, unless the messenger were sent expressly; and the young man had now come in person, to make his own apologies.

Beulah received Evert Beekman naturally, and without the least exaggeration of manner, though a quiet happiness beamed in her handsome face, that said as much as lover could reasonably desire. Her parents welcomed him cordially, and the suitor must have been dull indeed, not to anticipate all he hoped. Nor was it long before every doubt was removed. The truthful, conscientious Beulah, had well consulted her heart; and, while she blushed at her own temerity, she owned her attachment to her admirer. The very day of his arrival they became formally betrothed. As our tale, however, has but a secondary connection with this little episode, we shall not dwell on it more than is necessary to the principal object. It was a busy morning, altogether; and, though there were many tears, there were also many smiles. By the time it was usual, at that bland season, for the family to assemble on the lawn, everything, even to the day, was settled between Beulah and her lover, and there was a little leisure to think of other things. It was while the younger Pliny and one of the Smashes were preparing the tea, that the following conversation was held, being introduced by Mr. Woods, in the way of digressing from feelings in which he was not quite as much interested as some of the rest of the party.

"Do you bring us anything new from Boston?" demanded the chaplain. "I have been dying to ask the question these two hours--ever since dinner, in fact; but, somehow, Mr. Beekman, I have not been able to edge in an inquiry."

This was said good-naturedly, but quite innocently; eliciting smiles, blushes, and meaning glances in return. Evert Beekman, however, looked grave before he made his reply.

"To own the truth, Mr. Woods," he said, "things are getting to be very serious. Boston is surrounded by thousands of our people; and we hope, not only to keep the king's forces in the Peninsula, but, in the end, to drive them out of the colony."

"This is a bold measure, Mr. Beekman!--a very bold step to take against Cæsar!"

"Woods preached about the rights of Cæsar, no later than yesterday, you ought to know, Beekman," put in the laughing captain; "and I am afraid he will be publicly praying for the success of the British arms, before long."

"I *did* pray for the Royal Family," said the chaplain, with spirit, "and hope I shall ever continue to do so."

"My dear fellow, I do not object to *that*. Pray for all conditions of men, enemies and friends alike; and, particularly, pray for our princes; but pray also to turn the hearts of their advisers."

Beekman seemed uneasy. He belonged to a decidedly whig family, and was himself, at the very moment, spoken of as the colonel of one of the regiments about to be raised in the colony of New York. He held that rank in the militia, as it was; and no one doubted his disposition to resist the British forces, at the proper moment. He had even stolen away from what he conceived to be very imperative duties, to secure the woman of his heart before he went into the field. His answer, in accordance, partook essentially of the bias of his mind.

"I do not know, sir, that it is quite wise to pray so very willingly for the Royal Family," he said. "We may wish them worldly happiness, and spiritual consolation, as part of the human race; but political and specific prayers, in times like these, are to be used with caution. Men attach more than the common religious notion, just now, to prayers for the king, which some interpret into direct petitions against the United Colonies."

"Well," rejoined the captain, "I cannot agree to this, myself. If there were a prayer to confound parliament and its counsels, I should be very apt to join in it cordially; but I am not yet ready to throw aside king, queen, princes and princesses, all in a lump, on account of a few taxes, and a tittle tea."

"I am sorry to hear this from you, sir," answered Evert. "When your opinions were canvassed lately at Albany, I gave a sort of pledge that you were certainly more with us than against us."

"Well then, I think, Beekman, you drew me in my true outlines. In the main, I think the colonies right, though I am still willing to pray for the king."

"I am one of those, captain Willoughby, who look forward to the most serious times. The feeling throughout the colonies is tremendous, and the disposition on the part of the royal officers is to meet the crisis with force."

"You have a brother a captain of foot in one of the regiments of the crown, colonel Beekman--what are his views in this serious state of affairs?"

"He has already thrown up his commission--refusing even to sell out, a privilege that was afforded him. His name is now before congress for a majority in one of the new regiments that are to be raised."

The captain looked grave; Mrs. Willoughby anxious; Beulah interested; and Maud thoughtful.

"This has a serious aspect, truly," observed the first. "When men abandon all their early hopes, to assume new duties, there must be a deep and engrossing cause. I had not thought it like to come to this!"

"We have had hopes major Willoughby might do the same; I know that a regiment is at his disposal, if he be disposed to join us. No one would be more gladly received. We are to have Gates, Montgomery, Lee, and many other old officers, from regular corps, on our side."

"Will colonel Lee be put at the head of the American forces?"

"I think not, sir. He has a high reputation, and a good deal of experience, but he is a humourist; and what is something, though you will pardon it, he is not an American born."

"It is quite right to consult such considerations, Beekman; were I in congress, they would influence *me*, Englishman as I am, and in many things must always remain."

"I am glad to hear you say that, Willoughby," exclaimed the chaplain--" right down rejoiced to hear you say so! A man is bound to stand by his birth-place, through thick and thin."

"How do you, then, reconcile your opinions, in this matter, to *your* birth-place, Woods?" asked the laughing captain.

To own the truth, the chaplain was a little confused. He had entered into the controversy with so much zeal, of late, as to have imbibed the feelings of a thorough partisan; and, as is usual, with such philosophers, was beginning to overlook everything that made against his opinions, and to exaggerate everything that sustained them.

"How?"--he cried, with zeal, if not with consistency--"Why, well enough. I am an Englishman too, in the general view of the case, though born in Massachusetts. Of English descent, and an English subject."

"Umph!--Then Beekman, here, who is of Dutch descent, is not bound by the same principles as we are ourselves?"

"Not by the same *feelings* possibly; but, surely, by the same principles. Colonel Beekman is an Englishman by construction, and you are by birth. Yes, I'm what may be called a *constructive* Englishman."

Even Mrs. Willoughby and Beulah laughed at this, though not a smile had crossed Maud's face, since her eye had lost Robert Willoughby from view. The captain's ideas seemed to take a new direction, and he was silent some little time before he spoke.

"Under the circumstances in which we are now placed, as respects each other, Mr. Beekman," he said, "it is proper that there should be no concealments on grave points. Had you arrived an hour or two earlier, you would have met a face well known to you, in that of my son, major Willoughby."

"Major Willoughby, my dear sir!" exclaimed Beekman, with a start of unpleasant surprise; "I had supposed him with the royal army, in Boston. You say he has left the Knoll--I sincerely hope not for Albany."

"No--I wished him to go in that direction, at first, and to see you, in particular; but his representations of the state of the country induced me to change my mind; he travels by a private way, avoiding all the towns of note, or size."

"In that he has done well, sir. Near to me as a brother of Beulah's must always seem, I should be sorry to see Bob, just at this moment. If there be no hope of getting him to join us, the farther we are separated the better."

This was said gravely, and it caused all who heard it fully to appreciate the serious character of a quarrel that threatened to arm brother against brother. As if by common consent, the discourse changed, all appearing anxious, at a moment otherwise so happy, to obliterate impressions so unpleasant from their thoughts.

The captain, his wife, Beulah and the colonel, had several long and private communications in the course of the evening. Maud was not sorry to be left to herself, and the chaplain devoted his time to the entertainment of the friend of Beekman, who was in truth a surveyor, brought along partly to preserve appearances, and partly for service. The chain-bearers, hunters, &c., had been distributed in the different cabins of the settlement, immediately on the arrival of the party.

That night, when the sisters retired, Maud perceived that Beulah had something to communicate, out of the common way. Still, she did not know whether it would be proper for her to make any inquiries, and things were permitted to take their natural course. At length Beulah, in her gentle way, remarked--"It is a fearful thing, Maud, for a woman to take upon herself the new duties, obligations and ties of a wife."

"She should *not* do it, Beulah, unless she feels a love for the man of her choice, that will sustain her in them. You, who have *real* parents living, ought to feel this fully, as I doubt not you do."

"*Real* parents! Maud, you frighten me! Are not *my* parents *yours?*--Is not all our love common?"

"I am ashamed of myself, Beulah. Dearer and better parents than mine, no girl ever had. I am ashamed of my words, and beg you will forget them."

"That I shall be very ready to do. It was a great consolation to think that should I be compelled to quit home, as compelled I must be in the end,

I should leave with my father and mother a child as dutiful, and one that loves them as sincerely as yourself, Maud."

"You have thought right, Beulah. I do love them to my heart's core! Then you are right in another sense; for I shall *never* marry. My mind is made up to *that*"

"Well, dear, many are happy that never marry--many women are happier than those that do. Evert has a kind, manly, affectionate heart, and I know will do all he can to prevent my regretting home; but we can never have more than *one* mother, Maud!"

Maud did not answer, though she looked surprised that Beulah should say this to *her*.

"Evert has reasoned and talked so much to my father and mother," continued the *fiancée*, blushing, "that they have thought we had better be married at once. Do you know, Maud, that it has been settled this evening, that the ceremony is to take place to-morrow!"

"This is sudden, indeed, Beulah! Why have they determined on so unexpected a thing?"

"It is all owing to the state of the country. I know not how he has done it--but Evert has persuaded my father, that the sooner I am his wife, the more secure we shall *all* be, here at the Knoll."

"I hope you love Evert Beekman, dearest, dearest Beulah?"

"What a question, Maud! Do you suppose I could stand up before a minister of God, and plight my faith to a man I did not love?--Why have you seemed to doubt it?"

"I do not doubt it--I am very foolish, for I know you are conscientious as the saints in heaven--and yet, Beulah, I think *I* could scarce be so tranquil about one I loved."

The gentle Beulah smiled, but she no longer felt uneasiness. She understood the impulses and sentiments of her own pure but tranquil nature too well, to distrust herself; and she could easily imagine that Maud would not be as composed under similar circumstances.

"Perhaps it is well, sister of mine," she answered laughing, though blushing, "that you are so resolved to remain single; for one hardly knows where to find a suitor sufficiently devoted and ethereal for your taste. No one pleased you last winter, though the least encouragement would have Brought a dozen to your feet; and here there is no one you can possibly have, unless it be dear, good, old Mr. Woods."

Maud compressed her lips, and really looked stern, so determined was she to command herself; then she answered somewhat in her sister's vein--

"It is very true," she said, "there is no hero for me to accept, unless it be dear Mr. Woods; and he, poor man, has had one wife that cured him of any desire to possess another, they say."

"Mr. Woods! I never knew that he was married. Who can have told you this, Maud?"

"I got it from Robert"--answered the other, hesitating a little. "He was talking one day of such things."

"What things, dear?"

"Why--of getting married--I believe it was about marrying relatives--or connections--or, some such thing; for Mr. Woods married a cousin-german, it would seem--and so he told me all about it. Bob was old enough to know his wife, when she died. Poor man, she led him a hard life--he must be far from the Knoll, by this time, Beulah!"

"Mr. Woods!--I left him with papa, a few minutes since, talking over the ceremony for to-morrow!"

"I meant Bob----"

Here the sisters caught each other's eyes, and both blushed, consciousness presenting to them, at the same instant, the images that were uppermost in their respective minds. But, no more was said. They continued their employments in silence, and soon each was kneeling in prayer.

The following day, Evert Beekman and Beulah Willoughby were married. The ceremony took place, immediately after breakfast, in the little chapel; no one being present but the relatives, and Michael O'Hearn, who quieted his conscience for not worshipping with the rest of the people, by acting as their sexton. The honest county Leitrim man was let into the secret--as a great secret, however--at early dawn; and he had the place swept and in order in good season, appearing in his Sunday attire to do honour to the occasion, as he thought became him.

A mother as tender as Mrs. Willoughby, could not resign the first claim on her child, without indulging her tears, Maud wept, too; but it was as much in sympathy for Beulah's happiness, as from any other cause. The marriage in other respects, was simple, and without any ostentatious manifestations of feeling. It was, in truth, one of those rational and wise connections, which promise to wear well, there being a perfect fitness, in station, wealth, connections, years, manners and habits, between the parties. Violence was done to nothing, in bringing this discreet and well-principled couple together. Evert was as worthy of Beulah, as she was worthy of him. There was confidence in the future, on every side; and not a doubt, or a misgiving of any sort, mingled with the regrets, if regrets they could be called, that were, in some measure, inseparable from the solemn ceremony.

The marriage was completed, the affectionate father had held the weeping but smiling bride on his bosom, the tender mother had folded her to her heart, Maud had pressed her in her arms in a fervent embrace, and the chaplain had claimed his kiss, when the well-meaning sexton approached.

"Is it the likes of yees I wish well to!" said Mike--"Ye may well say *that*; and to yer husband, and childer, and all that will go before, and all that have come after ye! I know'd ye, when ye was mighty little, and that was years agone; and niver have I seen a cross look on yer pretthy face. I've app'inted to myself, many's the time, a consait to tell ye all this, by wor-r-d of mouth; but the likes of yees, and of the Missus, and of Miss Maud there--och! isn't she a swate one! and many's the pity, there's no sich tall, handsome jontleman to take *her*, in the bargain, bad luck to him for staying away; and so God bless ye, all, praist in the bargain, though he's no praist at all; and here's my good wishes said and done."

Chapter X

Ho! Princes of Jacob! the strength and the stay
Of the daughters of Zion;--now up, and away;
Lo, the hunters have struck her, and bleeding alone
Like a pard in the desert she maketh her moan:
Up with war-horse and banner, with spear and with sword,
On the spoiler go down in the might of the Lord!

Lunt.

The succeeding fortnight, or three weeks, brought no material changes, beyond those connected with the progress of the season. Vegetation was out in its richest luxuriance, the rows of corn and potatoes, freshly hoed, were ornamenting the flats, the wheat and other grains were throwing up their heads, and the meadows were beginning to exchange their flowers for the seed. As for the forest, it had now veiled its mysteries beneath broad curtains of a green so bright and lively, that one can only meet it, beneath a generous sun, tempered by genial rains, and a mountain air. The chain-bearers, and other companions of Beekman, quitted the valley the day after the wedding, leaving no one of their party behind but its principal.

The absence of the major was not noted by Joel and his set, in the excitement of receiving so many guests, and in the movement of the wedding. But, as soon as the fact was ascertained, the overseer and miller made the pretence of a 'slack-time' in their work, and obtained permission to go to the Mohawk, on private concerns of their own. Such journeys were sufficiently common to obviate suspicion; and, the leave had, the two conspirators started off, in company, the morning of the second day, or forty-eight hours after the major and Nick had disappeared. As the latter was known to have come in by the Fort Stanwix route, it was naturally enough supposed that he had returned by the same; and Joel determined to head him on the Mohawk, at some point near Schenectady, where he might make a merit of his own patriotism, by betraying the son of his master. The reader is not to suppose Joel intended to do all this openly; so far from it, his plan was to keep himself in the back-ground, while he attracted attention to the supposed toryism of the captain, and illustrated his own attachment to the colonies.

It is scarcely necessary to say that this plan failed, in consequence of the new path taken by Nick. At the very moment when Joel and the miller were lounging about a Dutch inn, some fifteen or twenty miles above Schenectady, in waiting for the travellers to descend the valley of the Mohawk, Robert Willoughby and his guide were actually crossing the Hudson, in momentary security at least. After remaining at his post until satisfied his intended prey had escaped him, Joel, with his friend, returned to the settlement. Still, the opportunity had been improved, to make himself better acquainted with the real state of the country; to open communications with certain patriots of a moral calibre about equal to his own, but of greater influence; to throw out divers injurious hints, and secret insinuations concerning the captain; and to speculate on the propriety of leaving so important a person to work his will, at a time so critical. But the pear was not yet ripe, and all that could now be done was to clear the way a little for something important in future.

In the meantime, Evert Beekman having secured his gentle and true-hearted wife, began, though with a heavy heart, to bethink him of his great political duties. It was well understood that he was to have a regiment of the new levies, and Beulah had schooled her affectionate heart to a degree that permitted her to part with him, in such a cause, with seeming resignation. It was, sooth to say, a curious spectacle, to see how these two sisters bent all their thoughts and wishes, in matters of a public nature, to favour the engrossing sentiments of their sex and natures; Maud being strongly disposed to sustain the royal cause, and the bride to support that in which her husband had enlisted, heart and hand.

As for captain Willoughby, he said little on the subject of politics; but the marriage of Beulah had a powerful influence in confirming his mind in the direction it had taken after the memorable argument with the chaplain. Colonel Beekman was a man of strong good sense, though without the least brilliancy; and his arguments were all so clear and practical, as to carry with them far more weight than was usual in the violent partisan discussions of the period. Beulah fancied him a Solon in sagacity, and a Bacon in wisdom. Her father, without proceeding quite as far as this, was well pleased with his cool discriminating judgment, and much disposed to defer to his opinions. The chaplain was left out of the discussions as incorrigible.

The middle of June was passed, at the time colonel Beekman began to think of tearing himself from his wife, in order to return into the active scenes of preparation he had quitted, to make this visit. As usual, the family frequented the lawn, at the close of the day, the circumstance of most of the windows of the Hut looking on the court, rendering this resort to the open air more agreeable than might otherwise have been the case. Evert was undecided whether to go the following morning, or to remain a day longer, when the lawn was thus occupied, on the evening of the 25th of the month, Mrs. Willoughby making the tea, as usual, her daughters sitting near her, sewing, and the gentlemen at hand, discussing the virtues of different sorts of seed-corn.

"There is a stranger!" suddenly exclaimed the chaplain, looking towards the rocks near the mill, the point at which all arrivals in the valley were first seen from the Hut. "He comes, too, like a man in haste, whatever may be his errand."

"God be praised," returned the captain rising; "it is Nick, on his usual trot, and this is about the time he should be back, the bearer of good news. A week earlier might have augured better; but this will do. The fellow moves over the ground as if he really had something to communicate!"

Mrs. Willoughby and her daughters suspended their avocations, and the gentlemen stood, in silent expectation, watching the long, loping strides of the Tuscarora, as he came rapidly across the plain. In a few minutes the Indian came upon the lawn, perfectly in wind, moving with deliberation and gravity, as he drew nearer to the party. Captain Willoughby, knowing his man, waited quite another minute, after the red-man was leaning against an apple-tree, before he questioned him.

"Welcome back, Nick," he then said. "Where did you leave my son?"

"He tell dere," answered the Indian, presenting a note, which the captain read.

"This is all right, Nick; and it shows you have been a true man. Your wages shall be paid to-night. But, this letter has been written on the eastern bank of the Hudson, and is quite three weeks old--why have we not seen you, sooner?"

"Can't see, when he don't come."

"That is plain enough; but why have you not come back sooner? That is my question."

"Want to look at country--went to shore of Great Salt Lake."

"Oh!--Curiosity, then, has been at the bottom of your absence?"

"Nick warrior--no squaw--got no cur'osity."

"No, no--I beg your pardon, Nick; I did not mean to accuse you of so womanish a feeling. Far from it; I know you are a man. Tell us, however, how far, and whither you went?"

"Bos'on," answered Nick, sententiously.

"Boston! That has been a journey, indeed. Surely my son did not allow you to travel in his company through Massachusetts?"

"Nick go alone. Two path; one for major; one for Tuscarora. Nick got dere first."

"That I can believe, if you were in earnest. Were you not questioned by the way?"

"Yes. Tell 'em I'm Stockbridge--pale-face know no better. T'ink he fox; more like wood-chuck."

"Thank you, Nick, for the compliment. Had my son reached Boston before you came away?"

"Here he be"--answered the Indian, producing another missive, from the folds of his calico shirt.

The captain received the note which he read with extreme gravity, and some surprise.

"This is in Bob's handwriting," he said, "and is dated 'Boston, June 18th, 1775;' but it is without signature, and is not only Bob, but Bob Short."

"Read, dear Willoughby," exclaimed the anxious mother. "News from *him*, concerns us all."

"News, Wilhelmina!--They may call this news in Boston, but one is very little the better for it at the Hutted Knoll. However, such as it is, there is no reason for keeping it a secret, while there is *one* reason, at least, why it should be known. This is all. 'My dearest sir--Thank God I am unharmed; but we have had much to make us reflect; you know what duty requires--my best and endless love to my mother, and Beulah--and dear, laughing, capricious, *pretty* Maud. Nick was present, and can tell you all. I do not think he will extenuate, or aught set down in malice.'" And this without direction, or signature; with nothing, in fact, but place and date. What say *you* to all this, Nick?"

"He very good-- major dere; he know. Nick dere--hot time--a t'ousand scalp--coat red as blood."

"There has been another battle!" exclaimed the captain; "that is too plain to admit of dispute. Speak out at once, Nick--which gained the day; the British or the Americans?"

"Hard to tell--one fight, t'other fight. Red-coat take de ground; Yankee kill. If Yankee could take scalp of all he kill, he whip. But, poor warriors at takin' scalp. No know how."

"Upon my word, Woods, there does seem to be something in all this! It can hardly be possible that the Americans would dare to attack Boston, defended as it is, by a strong army of British regulars."

"That would they not," cried the chaplain, with emphasis. "This has been only another skirmish."

"What you call skirmge?" asked Nick, pointedly. "It skirmge to take t'ousand scalp, ha?"

"Tell us what *has* happened, Tuscarora?" said the captain, motioning his friend to be silent.

"Soon tell--soon done. Yankee on hill; reg'lar in canoe. Hundred, t'ousand, fifty canoe--full of red-coat. Great chief, dere!--ten--six--two--all go togeder. Come ashore--parade, pale-face manner--march--booh--booh--dem cannon; pop, pop--dem gun. Wah! how he run!"

"Run!--who ran, Nick?--Though I suppose it must have been the poor Americans, of course."

"Red-coat run," answered the Indian, quietly.

This reply produced a general sensation, even the ladies starting, and gazing at each other.

"Red-coat run"--repeated the captain, slowly. "Go on with your history, Nick--where was this battle fought?"

"T'other Bos'on--over river--go in canoe to fight, like Injin from Canada."

"That must have been in Charlestown, Woods--you may remember Boston is on one peninsula, and Charlestown on another. Still, I do not recollect that the Americans were in the latter, Beekman--you told me nothing of that?"

"They were not so near the royal forces, certainly, when I left Albany, sir," returned the colonel. "A few direct questions to the Indian, however, would bring out the whole truth."

"We must proceed more methodically. How many Yankees were in this fight, Nick?--Calculate as we used to, in the French war."

"Reach from here to mill--t'ree, two deep, cap'in. All farmer; no sodger. Carry gun, but no carry baggonet; no carry knapsack. No wear red-coat. *Look* like town-meetin'; *fight* like devils."

"A line as long as from this to the mill, three deep, would contain about two thousand men, Beekman. Is that what you wish to say, Nick?"

"That about him--pretty near--just so."

"Well, then, there were about two thousand Yankees on this hill--how many king's troops crossed in the canoes, to go against them?"

"Two time--one time, so many; t'other time, half so many. Nick close by; count *him*."

"That would make three thousand in all! By George, this does look like work. Did they all go together, Nick?"

"No; one time go first; fight, run away. Den two time go, fight good deal--run away, too. Den try harder--set fire to wigwam--go up hill; Yankee run away."

"This is plain enough, and quite graphical. Wigwam on fire? Charlestown is not burnt, Nick?"

"Dat he--Look like old Council Fire, gone out. Big canoe fire--booh--booh-- Nick nebber see such war before--wah! Dead man plenty as leaves on tree; blood run like creek!"

"Were you in this battle, Nick? How came you to learn so much about it?"

"Don't want to be in it--better out--no scalp taken. Red-man not'in' to do, dere. How know about him?--*See* him--dat all. Got eye; why no see him, behind stone wall. Good see, behind stone wall."

"Were you across the water yourself, or did you remain in Boston, and see from a distance?"

"Across in canoe--tell red-coat, general send letter by Nick--major say, he *my* friend--let Nick go."

"My son was in this bloody battle, then!" said Mrs. Willoughby. "He writes, Hugh, that he is safe?"

"He does, dearest Wilhelmina; and Bob knows us too well, to attempt deception, in such a matter."

"Did you see the major in the field, Nick--after you crossed the water, I mean?"

"See him, all. Six--two--seven t'ousand. Close by; why not see major stand up like pine--no dodge he head, *dere*. Kill all round him--no hurt *him*! Fool to stay dere--tell him so; but he no come away. Save he scalp, too."

"And how many slain do you suppose there might have been left on the ground--or, did you riot remain to see?"

"Did see--stay to get gun--knapsack--oder good t'ing--plenty about; pick him up, fast as want him." Here Nick coolly opened a small bundle, and exhibited an epaulette, several rings, a watch, five or six pairs of silver buckles, and divers other articles of plunder, of which he had managed to strip the dead. "All good t'ing--plenty as stone--have him widout askin'."

"So I see, Master Nick--and is this the plunder of Englishmen, or of Americans?"

"Red-coat nearest--got most t'ing, too. Go farder, fare worse; as pale-face say."

"Quite satisfactory. Were there more red-coats left on the ground, or more Americans?"

"Red-coat so," said Nick, holding up *four* fingers--Yankee, so; "holding up *one*. Take big grave to hold red-coat. Small grave won't hold Yankee. Hear what he count; most red-coat. More than t'ousand warrior! British groan, like squaw dat lose her hunter."

Such was Saucy Nick's description of the celebrated, and, in some particulars, unrivalled combat of Bunker Hill, of which he had actually been an eye-witness, on the ground, though using the precaution to keep his body well covered. He did not think it necessary to state the fact that he had given the *coup-de-grace*, himself, to the owner of the epaulette, nor did he deem it essential to furnish all the particulars of his mode of obtaining so many buckles. In other respects, his account was fair enough, "nothing extenuating, or setting down aught in malice." The auditors had listened with intense feeling; and Maud, when the allusion was made to Robert Willoughby, buried her pallid face in her hands, and wept. As for Beulah, time and again, she glanced anxiously at her husband, and bethought her of the danger to which he might so soon be exposed.

The receipt of this important intelligence confirmed Beekman in the intention to depart. The very next morning he tore himself away from Beulah, and proceeded to Albany. The appointment of Washington, and a long list of other officers, soon succeeded, including his own as a colonel; and the war may be said to have commenced systematically. Its distant din occasionally reached the Hutted Knoll; but the summer passed away, bringing with it no event to affect the tranquillity of that settlement. Even Joel's schemes were thwarted for a time, and he was fain to continue to wear the mask, and to gather that harvest for another, which he had hoped to reap for his own benefit.

Beulah had all a young wife's fears for her husband; but, as month succeeded month, and one affair followed another, without bringing him harm, she began to submit to the anxieties inseparable from her situation, with less of self-torment, and more of reason. Her mother and Maud were invaluable friends to her, in this novel and trying situation, though each had her own engrossing cares on account of Robert Willoughby. As no other great battle, however, occurred in the course of the year '75, Beekman remained in safety with the troops that invested Boston, and the major with the army within it. Neither was much exposed, and glad enough were these gentle affectionate hearts, when they learned that the sea separated the combatants.

This did not occur, however, until another winter was passed. In November, the family left the Hut, as had been its practice of late years, and went out into the more inhabited districts to pass the winter. This time it came only to Albany, where colonel Beekman joined it, passing a few happy weeks with his well-beloved Beulah. The ancient town mentioned was not gay at a moment like that; but it had many young officers in it, on the American side of the question, who were willing enough to make themselves acceptable to Maud. The captain was not sorry to see several of these youths manifesting assiduity about her he had so long been accustomed to consider as his youngest daughter; for, by this time, his opinions had taken so strong a bias in favour of the rights of the colonies, that Beekman himself scarce rejoiced more whenever he heard of any little success alighting on the American arms.

"It will all come right in the end," the worthy captain used to assure his friend the chaplain. "They will open their eyes at home, ere long, and the injustice of taxing the colonies will be admitted. Then all will come round again; the king will be as much beloved as ever, and England and America will be all the better friends for having a mutual respect. I know my countrymen well; they mean right, and will do right, as soon as their stomachs are a little lowered, and they come to look at the truth, coolly. I'll answer for it, the Battle of Bunker's Hill made *us*"--the captain had spoken in this way, now, for some months--"made *us* a thousand advocates, where we had one before. This is the nature of John Bull; give him reason to respect you, and he will soon do you justice; but give him reason to feel otherwise, and he becomes a careless, if not a hard master."

Such were the opinions captain Willoughby entertained of his native land; a land he had not seen in thirty years, and one in which he had so recently inherited unexpected honours, without awakening a desire to return and enjoy them. His opinions were right in part, certainly; for they depended on a law of nature, while it is not improbable they were wrong in all that was connected with the notions of any peculiarly manly quality, in any particular part of christendom. No maxim is truer than that which teaches us "like causes produce like effects;" and as human beings are governed by very similar laws all over the face of this round world of ours, nothing is more certain than the similarity of their propensities.

Maud had no smiles, beyond those extracted by her naturally sweet disposition, and a very prevalent desire to oblige, for any of the young soldiers, or young civilians, who crowded about her chair, during the Albany winter mentioned. Two or three of colonel Beekman's military friends, in particular, would very gladly have become connected with an officer so much respected, through means so exceedingly agreeable; but no encouragement emboldened either to go beyond the attention and assiduities of a marked politeness.

"I know not how it is," observed Mrs. Willoughby, one day, in a *tête-à-tête* with her husband; "Maud seems to take less pleasure than is usual with girls of her years, in the attentions of your sex. That her heart is affectionate--warm--even tender, I am very certain; and yet no sign of preference, partiality, or weakness, in favour of any of these fine young men, of whom we see so many, can I discover in the child. They all seem alike to her!"

"Her time will come, as it happened to her mother before her," answered the captain. "Whooping-cough and measles are not more certain to befall children, than love to befall a young woman. You were all made for it, my dear Willy, and no fear but the girl will catch the disease, one of these days; and that, too, without any inoculation."

"I am sure, I have no wish to separate from my child"--so Mrs. Willoughby always spoke of, and so she always felt towards Maud--"I am sure, I have no wish to separate from my child; but as we cannot always remain, it is perhaps better this one should marry, like the other. There is young Verplanck much devoted to her; he is everyway a suitable match; and then he is in Evert's own regiment."

"Ay, he would do; though to my fancy Luke Herring is the far better match."

"That is because he is richer and more powerful, Hugh--you men cannot think of a daughter's establishment, without immediately dragging in houses and lands, as part of the ceremony."

"By George, wife of mine, houses and lands in moderation, are very good sweeteners of matrimony!"

"And yet, Hugh, I have been very happy as a wife, nor have you been very miserable as a husband, without any excess of riches to sweeten the state!" answered Mrs. Willoughby, reproachfully. "Had you been a full general, I could not have loved you more than I have done as a mere captain."

"All very true, Wilhelmina, dearest," returned the husband, kissing the faithful partner of his bosom with strong affection--"very true, my dear girl; for girl you are and ever will be in my eyes; but *you* are one in a million, and I humbly trust there are not ten hundred and one, in every thousand, just like myself. For my part, I wish dear, saucy, capricious little Maud, no worse luck in a husband, than Luke Herring."

"She will never be *his* wife; I know her, and my own sex, too well to think it. You are wrong, however, Willoughby, in applying such terms to the child. Maud is not in the least capricious, especially in her affections. See with what truth and faithfulness of sisterly attachment she clings to Bob. I do declare I am often ashamed to feel that even his own mother has less solicitude about him than this dear girl."

"Pooh, Willy; don't be afflicted with the idea that you don't make yourself sufficiently miserable about the boy. Bob will do well enough, and will very likely come out of this affair a lieutenant-colonel. I may live yet to see him a general officer; certainly, if I live to be as old as my grandfather, Sir Thomas. As for Maud, she finds Beulah uneasy about Beekman; and having no husband herself, or any over that she cares a straw about, why she just falls upon Bob as a *pis aller*. I'll warrant you she cares no more for him than any of the rest of us--than myself, for instance; though as an old soldier, I don't scream every time I fancy a gun fired over yonder at Boston."

"I wish it were well over. It is *so* unnatural for Evert and Robert to be on opposite sides."

"Yes, it is out of the common way, I admit; and yet 'twill all come round, in the long run. This Mr. Washington is a clever fellow, and seems to play his cards with spirit and judgment. He was with us, in that awkward affair of Braddock's; and between you and me, Wilhelmina, he covered the regulars, or we should all have laid our bones on that accursed field. I wrote you at the time, what I thought of him, and now you see it is all coming to pass."

It was one of the captain's foibles to believe himself a political prophet; and, as he had really both written and spoken highly of Washington, at the time mentioned, it had no small influence on his opinions to find himself acting on the same side with this admired favourite. Prophecies often produce their own fulfilment, in cases of much greater gravity than this; and it is not surprising that our captain found himself strengthened in his notions by the circumstance.

The winter passed away without any of Maud's suitors making a visible impression on her heart. In March, the English evacuated Boston, Robert Willoughby sailing with his regiment for Halifax, and thence with the expedition against Charleston, under Sir Henry Clinton. The next month, the family returned to the Knoll, where it was thought wiser, and even safer to be, at a moment so critical, than even in a more frequented place. The war proceeded, and, to the captain's great regret, without any very visible approaches towards the reconciliation he had so confidently anticipated. This rather checked his warmth in favour of the colonial cause; for, an Englishman by birth, he was much opposed at bottom to anything like a dissolution of the tie that connected America with the mother country; a political event that now began seriously to be talked of among the initiated.

Desirous of thinking as little as possible of disagreeable things, the worthy owner of the valley busied himself with his crops, his mills, and his improvements. He had intended to commence leasing his wild lands about this time, and to begin a more extended settlement, with an eye to futurity; but the state of the country forbade the execution of the project, and he was fain to limit his efforts by their former boundaries. The geographical position of the valley put it beyond any of the ordinary exactions of military service; and, as there was a little doubt thrown around its owner's opinions, partly in consequence of his son's present and his own previous connection with the royal army, and partly on account of Joel's secret machinations, the authorities were well content to let the settlement alone, provided it would take care of itself. Notwithstanding the prominent patriotism of Joel Strides and the miller, they were well satisfied, themselves, with this state of things; preferring peace and quietness to the more stirring scenes of war. Their schemes, moreover, had met with somewhat of a check, in the feeling of the population of the valley, which, on an occasion calculated to put their attachment to its owner to the proof, had rather shown that they remembered his justice, liberality, and upright conduct, more than exactly comported with their longings. This manifestation of respect was shown at an election for a representative in a local convention, in which every individual at the Hutted Knoll, who had a voice at all, the two conspirators excepted, had given it in favour of the captain. So decided was this expression of feeling, indeed, that it compelled Joel and the miller to chime in with the cry of the hour, and to vote contrary to their own wishes.

One, dwelling at the Hutted Knoll, in the summer of 1776, could never have imagined that he was a resident of a country convulsed by a revolution, and disfigured by war. There, everything seemed peaceful and calm, the woods sighing with the airs of their sublime solitude, the genial sun shedding its heats on a grateful and generous soil, vegetation ripening and yielding with all the abundance of a bountiful nature, as in the more tranquil days of peace and hope.

"There is something frightful in the calm of this valley, Beulah!" exclaimed Maud one Sunday, as she and her sister looked out of the library window amid the breathing stillness of the forest, listening to the melancholy sound of the bell that summoned them to prayers. "There is a frightful calm over this place, at an hour when we know that strife and bloodshed are so active in the country. Oh! that the hateful congress had never thought of making this war!"

"Evert writes me all is well, Maud; that the times will lead to good; the people are right; and America will now be a nation--in time, he thinks, a great, and a very great nation."

"Ah! It is this ambition of greatness that hurries them all on! Why can they not be satisfied with being respectable subjects of so great a country as England, that they must destroy each other for this phantom of liberty? Will it make them wiser, or happier, or better than they are?"

Thus reasoned Maud, under the influence of one engrossing sentiment. As our tale proceeds, we shall have occasion to show, perhaps, how far was that submission to events which she inculcated, from the impulses of her true character. Beulah answered mildly, but it was more as a young American wife:

"I know Evert thinks it all right, Maud; and you will own he is neither fiery nor impetuous. If *his* cool judgment approve of what has been done, we may well suppose that it has not been done in too much haste, or needlessly."

"Think, Beulah," rejoined Maud, with an ashen cheek, and in trembling tones, "that Evert and Robert may, at this very moment, be engaged in strife against each other. The last messenger who came in, brought us the miserable tidings that Sir William Howe was landing a large army near New York, and that the Americans were preparing to meet it. We are certain that Bob is with his regiment; and his regiment we know is in the army. How can we think of this liberty, at a moment so critical?"

Beulah did not reply; for in spite of her quiet nature, and implicit confidence in her husband, she could not escape a woman's solicitude. The colonel had promised to write at every good occasion, and that which he promised was usually performed. She thought, and thought rightly, that a very few days would bring them intelligence of importance; though it came in a shape she had little anticipated, and by a messenger she had then no desire to see.

In the meantime, the season and its labours advanced. August was over, and September with its fruits had succeeded, promising to bring the year round without any new or extraordinary incidents to change the fortunes of the inmates of the Hutted Knoll. Beulah had now been married more than a twelvemonth, and was already a mother; and of course all that time had elapsed since the son quitted his father's house. Nick, too, had disappeared shortly after his return from Boston; and throughout this eventful summer, his dark, red countenance had not been seen in the valley.

Chapter XI

And now 'tis still! no sound to wake
The primal forest's awful shade;
And breathless lies the covert brake,
Where many an ambushed form is laid:
I see the red-man's gleaming eye,
Yet all so hushed the gloom profound,
That summer birds flit heedlessly,
And mocking nature smiles around.

Lunt.

The eventful summer of 1776 had been genial and generous in the valley of the Hutted Knoll. With a desire to drive away obtrusive thoughts, the captain had been much in his fields, and he was bethinking himself of making a large contribution to the good cause, in the way of fatted porkers, of which he had an unusual number, that he thought might yet be driven through the forest to Fort Stanwix, before the season closed. In the way of intelligence from the seat of war, nothing had reached the family but a letter from the major, which he had managed to get sent, and in which he wrote with necessary caution. He merely mentioned the arrival of Sir William Howe's forces, and the state of his own health. There was a short postscript, in the following words, the letter having been directed to his father:--"Tell dearest Maud," he said, "that charming women have ceased to charm me; glory occupying so much of my day-dreams, like an *ignis fatuus*, I fear; and that as for love, *all* my affections are centred in the dear objects at the Hutted Knoll. If I had met with a single woman I admired half as much as I do her pretty self, I should have been married long since." This was written in answer to some thoughtless rattle that the captain had volunteered to put in his last letter, as coming from Maud, who had sensitively shrunk from sending a message when asked; and it was read by father, mother, and Beulah, as the badinage of a brother to a sister, without awaking a second thought in either. Not so with Maud, herself, however. When her seniors had done with this letter, she carried it to her own room, reading and re-reading it a dozen times; nor could she muster resolution to return it; but, finding at length that the epistle was forgotten, she succeeded in retaining it without awakening attention to what she had done. This letter now became her constant companion, and a hundred times did the sweet gill trace its characters, in the privacy of her chamber, or in that of her now solitary walks in the woods.

As yet, the war had produced none of those scenes of ruthless frontier violence, that had distinguished all the previous conflicts of America. The enemy was on the coast, and thither the efforts of the combatants had been principally directed. It is true, an attempt on Canada had been made, but it failed for want of means; neither party being in a condition to effect much, as yet, in that quarter. The captain had commented on this peculiarity of the present struggle; all those which had preceded it having, as a matter of course, taken the direction of the frontiers between the hostile provinces.

"There is no use, Woods, in bothering ourselves about these things, after all," observed captain Willoughby, one day, when the subject of hanging the long-neglected gates came up between them. "It's a heavy job, and the crops will suffer if we take off the hands this week. We are as safe, here, as we should be in Hyde Park; and safer too; for there house-breakers and foot-pads abound; whereas, *your* preaching has left nothing but very vulgar and everyday sinners at the Knoll."

The chaplain had little to say against this reasoning; for, to own the truth, he saw no particular cause for apprehension. Impunity had produced the feeling of security, until these gates had got to be rather a subject of amusement, than of any serious discussion. The preceding year, when the stockade was erected, Joel had managed to throw so many obstacles in the way of hanging the gates, that the duty was not performed throughout the whole of the present summer, the subject having been mentioned but once or twice, and then only to be postponed to a more fitting occasion.

As yet no one in the valley knew of the great event which had taken place in July. A rumour of a design to declare the provinces independent had reached the Hut, in May; but the major's letter was silent on this important event, and positive information had arrived by no other channel; otherwise, the captain would have regarded the struggle as much more serious than he had ever done before; and he might have set about raising these all-important gates in earnest. As it was, however, there they stood; each pair leaning against its proper wall or stockade, though those of the latter were so light as to have required but eight or ten men to set them on their hinges, in a couple of hours at most.

Captain Willoughby still confined his agricultural schemes to the site of the old Beaver Pond. The area of that was perfectly beautiful, every unsightly object having been removed, while the fences and the tillage were faultlessly neat and regular. Care had been taken, too, to render the few small fields around the cabins which skirted this lovely rural scene, worthy of their vicinage. The stumps had all been dug, the surfaces levelled, and the orchards and gardens were in keeping with the charms that nature had so bountifully scattered about the place.

While, however, all in the shape of tillage was confined to this one spot, the cattle ranged the forest for miles. Not only was the valley, but the adjacent mountain-sides were covered with intersecting paths, beaten by the herds, in the course of years. These paths led to many a glen, or look-out, where Beulah and Maud had long been in the habit of pursuing their rambles, during the sultry heats of summer, Though so beautiful to the eye, the flats were not agreeable for walks; and it was but natural for the lovers of the picturesque to seek the eminences, where they could overlook the vast surfaces of leaves that were spread before them; or to bury themselves in ravines and glens, within which the rays of the sun scarce penetrated. The paths mentioned led near, or to, a hundred of these places, all within a mile or two of the Hut. As a matter of course, then, they were not neglected.

Beulah had now been a mother several months. Her little Evert was born at the Knoll, and he occupied most of those gentle and affectionate thoughts which were not engrossed by his absent father. Her marriage, of itself, had made some changes in her intercourse with Maud; but the birth of the child had brought about still more. The care of this little being formed Beulah's great delight; and Mrs. Willoughby had all that peculiar interest in her descendant, which marks a grandmother's irresponsible love. These two passed half their time in the nursery, a room fitted between their respective chambers; leaving Maud more alone than it was her wont to be, and of course to brood over her thoughts and feelings. These periods of solitude our heroine was much accustomed to pass in the forest. Use had so far emboldened her, that apprehension never shortened her walks, or lessened their pleasure. Of danger, from any ordinary source, there was literally next to none, man never having been known to approach the valley, unless by the regular path; while the beasts of prey had been so actively hunted, as rarely to be seen in that quarter of the country. The panther excepted, no wild quadruped was to be in the least feared in summer; and, of the first, none had ever been met with by Nick, or any of the numerous woodsmen who had now frequented the adjacent hills for two lustrums.

About three hours before the setting of the sun, on the evening of the 23d of September, 1776, Maud Willoughby was pursuing her way, quite alone, along one of the paths beaten by the cattle, at some little distance from a rocky eminence, where there was a look-out, on which Mike, by her father's orders, had made a rude seat. It was on the side of the clearing most remote from all the cabins; though once on the elevation, she could command a view of the whole of the little panorama around the site of the ancient pond. In that day, ladies wore the well-known gipsey hat, a style that was peculiarly suited to the face of our heroine. Exercise had given her cheeks a rich glow; and though a shade of sadness, or at least of reflection, was now habitually thrown athwart her sweet countenance, this bloom added an unusual lustre to her eyes, and a brilliancy to her beauty, that the proudest belle of any drawing-room might have been glad to possess. Although living so retired, her dress always became her rank; being simple, but of the character that denotes refinement, and the habits and tastes of a gentlewoman. In this particular, Maud had ever been observant of what was due to herself; and, more than all, had she attended to her present appearance since a chance expression of Robert Willoughby's had betrayed how much he prized the quality in her.

Looking thus, and in a melancholy frame of mind, Maud reached the rock, and took her place on its simple seat, throwing aside her hat, to catch a little of the cooling air on her burning cheeks. She turned to look at the lovely view again, with a pleasure that never tired. The rays of the sun were streaming athwart the verdant meadows and rich corn, lengthening the shadows, and mellowing everything, as if expressly to please the eye of one like her who now gazed upon the scene. Most of the people of the settlement were in the open air, the men closing their day's works in the fields, and the women and children busied beneath shades, with their wheels and needles; the whole presenting such a picture of peaceful, rural life, as a poet might delight to describe, or an artist to delineate with his pencil.

"The landscape smiles Calm in the sun; and silent are the hills And valleys, and the blue serene of air."

The Vanished Lark.

"It is very beautiful!" thought Maud. "Why cannot men be content with such scenes of loveliness and nature as this, and love each other, and be at peace, as God's laws command? Then we might all be living happily together, Mere, without trembling lest news of some sad misfortune should reach us, from hour to hour. Beulah and Evert would not be separated; but both could remain with their child--and my dear, dear father and mother would be so happy to have us all around them, in security--and, then, Bob, too--perhaps Bob might bring a wife from the town, with him, that I could love as I do Beulah"--It was one of Maud's day-dreams to love the wife of Bob, and make him happy by contributing to the happiness of those he most prized--"No; I could never love her as I do *Beulah*; but I should make her very dear to me, as I ought to, since she would be Bob's wife."

The expression of Maud's face, towards the close of this mental soliloquy, was of singular sadness; and yet it was the very picture of sincerity and truth. It was some such look as the windows of the mind assume, when the feelings struggle against nature and hope, for resignation and submission to duty.

At this instant, a cry arose from the valley! It was one of those spontaneous, involuntary outbreakings of alarm, that no art can imitate, no pen describe; but which conveys to the listener's ear, terror in the very sound. At the next instant, the men from the mill were seen rushing up to the summit of the cliff that impended over their dwellings, followed by their wives dragging children after them, making frantic gestures, indicative of alarm. The first impulse of Maud was to fly; but a moment's reflection told her it was much too late for that. To remain and witness what followed would be safer, and more wise. Her dress was dark, and she would not be likely to be observed at the distance at which she was placed; having behind her, too, a back-ground of gloomy rock. Then the scene was too exciting to admit of much hesitation or delay in coming to a decision; a fearful species of maddened curiosity mingling with her alarm. Under such circumstances, it is not surprising that Maud continued gazing on what she saw, with eyes that seemed to devour the objects before them.

The first cry from the valley was followed by the appearance of the fugitives from the mill. These took the way towards the Hut, calling on the nearest labourers by name, to seek safety in flight. The words could not be distinguished at the rock, though indistinct sounds might; but the gestures could not be mistaken. In half a minute, the plain was alive with fugitives; some rushing to their cabins for their children, and all taking the direction of the stockade, as soon as the last were found. In five minutes the roads and lanes near the Knoll were crowded with men, women and children, hastening forward to its protection, while a few of the former had already rushed through the gateways, as Maud correctly fancied, in quest of their arms.

Captain Willoughby was riding among his labourers when this fearful interruption to a tranquillity so placid first broke upon his ear. Accustomed to alarms, he galloped forward to meet the fugitives from the mill, issuing orders as he passed to several of the men nearest the house. With the miller, who thought little of anything but safety at that instant, he conversed a moment, and then pushed boldly on towards the verge of the cliffs. Maud trembled as she saw her father in a situation which she thought must be so exposed; but his cool manner of riding about proved that he saw no enemy very near. At length he waved his hat to some object, or person in the glen beneath; and she even thought she heard his shout. At the next moment, he turned his horse, and was seen scouring along the road towards the Hut. The lawn was covered with the fugitives as the captain reached it, while a few armed men were already coming out of the court-yard. Gesticulating as if giving orders, the captain dashed through them all, without drawing the rein, and disappeared in the court. A minute later, he re-issued, bearing his arms, followed by his wife and Beulah, the latter pressing little Evert to her bosom.

Something like order now began to appear among the men. Counting all ages and both colours, the valley, at this particular moment, could muster thirty-three males capable of bearing arms. To these might be added some ten or fifteen women who had occasionally brought down a deer, and who might be thought more or less dangerous, stationed at a loop, with a rifle or a musket. Captain Willoughby had taken some pains to drill the former, who could go through some of the simpler light-infantry evolutions. Among them he had appointed sundry corporals, while Joel Strides had been named a serjeant. Joyce, now an aged and war-worn veteran, did the duty of adjutant. Twenty men were soon drawn up in array, in front of the open gateway on the lawn, under the immediate orders of Joyce; and the last woman and child, that had been seen approaching the place of refuge, had passed within the stockade. At this instant captain Willoughby called a party of the stragglers around him, and set about hanging the gates of the outer passage, or that which led through the palisades.

Maud would now have left the rock, but, at that moment, a dark body of Indians poured up over the cliffs, crowning it with a menacing cloud of at least fifty armed warriors. The rivulet lay between her and the Hut, and the nearest bridge that crossed it would have brought her within reach of danger. Then it would require at least half an hour to reach that bridge by the circuitous path she would be compelled to take, and there was little hope of getting over it before the strangers should have advanced. It was better to remain where she could behold what was passing, and to be governed by events, than to rush blindly into unseen risks.

The party that crowned the cliffs near the mills, showed no impatience to advance. It was evidently busy in reconnoitring, and in receiving accessions to its numbers. The latter soon increased to some seventy or eighty warriors. After waiting several minutes in inaction, a musket, or rifle, was fired towards the Hut, as if to try the effect of a summons and the range of a bullet. At this hint the men on the lawn retired within the stockade, stacked their arms, and joined the party that was endeavouring to get the gates in their places. From the circumstance that her father directed all the women and children to retire within the court, Maud supposed that the bullet might have fallen somewhere near them. It was quite evident, however, that no one was injured.

The gates intended for the stockade, being open like the rest of that work, were materially lighter than those constructed for the house itself. The difficulty was in handling them with the accuracy required to enter the hinges, of which there were three pairs. This difficulty existed on account of their great height. Of physical force, enough could be applied to toss them over the stockade itself, if necessary; but finesse was needed, rather than force, to effect the principal object, and that under difficult circumstances. It is scarcely possible that the proximity of so fierce an enemy as a body of savages in their war-paint, for such the men at the mill had discovered was the guise of their assailants, would in any measure favour the coolness and tact of the labourers. Poor Maud lost the sense of her own danger, in the nervous desire to see the long-forgotten gates hung; and she rose once or twice, in feverish excitement, as she saw that the leaf which was raised fell in or out, missing its fastenings. Still the men persevered, one or two sentinels being placed to watch the Indians, and give timely notice of their approach, should they advance.

Maud now kneeled, with her face bowed to the seat, and uttered a short but most fervent prayer, in behalf of the dear beings that the Hut contained. This calmed her spirits a little, and she rose once more to watch the course of events. The body of men had left the gate at which they had just been toiling, and were crowding around its fellow. One leaf was hung! As an assurance of this, she soon after saw her father swing it backward and forward on its hinges, to cause it to settle into its place. This was an immense relief, though she had heard too many tales of Indian warfare, to think there was any imminent danger of an attack by open day, in the very face of the garrison. The cool manner in which her father proceeded, satisfied her that he felt the same security, for the moment; his great object being, in truth, to make suitable provision against the hours of darkness.

Although Maud had been educated as a lady, and possessed the delicacy and refinement of her class, she had unavoidably caught some of the fire and resolution of a frontier life. To her, the forest, for instance, possessed no fancied dangers; but when there was real ground for alarm, she estimated its causes intelligently, and with calmness. So it was, also, in the present crisis. She remembered all she had been taught, or had heard, and quick of apprehension, her information was justly applied to the estimate of present circumstances.

The men at the Hut soon had the second leaf of the gate ready to be raised. At this instant, an Indian advanced across the flat alone, bearing a branch of a tree in his hand, and moving swiftly. This was a flag of truce, desiring to communicate with the pale-faces. Captain Willoughby met the messenger alone, at the foot of the lawn, and there a conference took place that lasted several minutes. Maud could only conjecture its objects, though she thought her father's attitude commanding, and his gestures stern. The red-man, as usual, was quiet and dignified. This much our heroine saw, or fancied she saw; but beyond this, of course, all was vague conjecture. Just as the two were about to part, and had even made courteous signs of their intention, a shout arose from the workmen, which ascended, though faintly, as high as the rock. Captain Willoughby turned, and then Maud saw his arm extended towards the stockade. The second leaf of the gate was in its place, swinging to and fro, in a sort of exulting demonstration of its uses! The savage moved away, more slowly than he had advanced, occasionally stopping to reconnoitre the Knoll and its defences.

Captain Willoughby now returned to his people, and he was some time busied in examining the gates, and giving directions about its fastenings. Utterly forgetful of her own situation, Maud shed tears of joy, as she saw that this great object was successfully effected. The stockade was an immense security to the people of the Hut. Although it certainly might be scaled, such an enterprise would require great caution, courage, and address; and it could hardly be effected, at all, by daylight. At night, even, it would allow the sentinels time to give the alarm, and with a vigilant look-out, might be the means of repelling an enemy. There was also another consideration connected with this stockade. An enemy would not be fond of trusting himself *inside* of it, unless reasonably certain of carrying the citadel altogether; inasmuch as it might serve as a prison to place him in the hands of the garrison. To recross it under a fire from the loops, would be an exploit so hazardous that few Indians would think of undertaking it. All this Maud knew from her father's conversations, and she saw how much had been obtained in raising the gates. Then the stockade, once properly closed, afforded great security to those moving about within it; the timbers would be apt to stop a bullet, and were a perfect defence against a rush; leaving time to the women and children to get into the court, even allowing that the assailants succeeded in scaling the palisades.

Maud thought rapidly and well, in the strait in which she was placed. She understood most of the movements, on both sides, and she also saw the importance of her remaining where she could note all that passed, if she intended to make an attempt at reaching the Hut, after dark. This necessity determined her to continue at the rock, so long as light remained. She wondered she was not missed, but rightly attributed the circumstance to the suddenness of the alarm, and the crowd of other thoughts which would naturally press upon the minds of her friends, at such a fearful moment. "I will stay where I am," thought Maud, a little proudly, "and prove, if I am not really the daughter of Hugh Willoughby, that I am not altogether unworthy of his love and care! I can even pass the night in the forest, at this warm season, without suffering."

Just as these thoughts crossed her mind, in a sort of mental soliloquy, a stone rolled from a path above her, and fell over the rock on which the seat was placed. A footstep was then heard, and the girl's heart beat quick with apprehension. Still she conceived it safest to remain perfectly quiet. She scarce breathed in her anxiety to be motionless. Then it occurred to her, that some one beside herself might be out from the Hut, and that a friend was near. Mike had been in the woods that very afternoon, she knew; for she had seen him; and the true-hearted fellow would indeed be a treasure to her, at that awful moment. This idea, which rose almost to certainty as soon as it occurred, induced her to spring forward, when the appearance of a man, whom she did not recognise, dressed in a hunting-shirt, and otherwise attired for the woods, carrying a short rifle in the hollow of his arm, caused her to stop, in motionless terror. At first, her presence was not observed; but, no sooner did the stranger catch a glimpse of her person, than he stopped, raised his hands in surprise, laid his rifle against a tree, and sprang forward; the girl closing her eyes, and sinking on the seat, with bowed head, expecting the blow of the deadly tomahawk.

"Maud--dearest, *dearest* Maud--do you not know me!" exclaimed one, leaning over the pallid girl, while he passed an arm round her slender waist, with an affection so delicate and reserved, that, at another time, it might have attracted attention. "Look up, dear girl, and show that at least you fear not *me!*"

"Bob," said the half-senseless Maud. "Whence come you?--*Why* do you come at this fearful instant!--Would to God your visit had been better timed!"

"Terror makes you say this, my poor Maud! Of all the family, I had hoped for the warmest welcome from *you*. We think alike about this war-- then you are not so much terrified at the idea of my being found here, but can hear reason. Why do you say this, then, my dearest Maud?"

By this time Maud had so far recovered as to be able to look up into the major's face, with expression in which alarm was blended with unutterable tenderness. Still she did not throw her arms around him, as a sister would clasp a beloved brother; but, rather, as he pressed her gently to his bosom, repelled the embrace by a slight resistance. Extricating herself, however, she turned and pointed towards the valley.

"Why do I say this? See for yourself--the savages have at length come, and the whole dreadful picture is before you."

Young Willoughby's military eye took in the scene at a glance. The Indians were still at the cliff, and the people of the settlement were straining at the heavier gates of the Hut, having already got one of them into a position where it wanted only the proper application of a steady force to be hung. He saw his father actively employed in giving directions; and a few pertinent questions drew all the other circumstances from Maud. The enemy had now been in the valley more than an hour, and the movements of the two parties were soon related.

"Are you alone, dearest Maud? are you shut out by this sudden inroad?" demanded the major, with concern and surprise.

"So it would seem. I can see no other--though I did think Michael might be somewhere near me, in the woods, here; I at first mistook your footsteps for his."

"That is a mistake"--returned Willoughby, levelling a small pocket spy-glass at the Hut--"Mike is tugging at that gate, upholding a part of it, like a corner-stone. I see most of the faces I know there, and my dear father is as active, and yet as cool, as if at the head of a regiment."

"Then I am alone--it is perhaps better that as many as possible should be in the house to defend it."

"Not alone, my sweet Maud, so long as I am with you. Do you still think my visit so ill-timed?"

"Perhaps not, after all. Heaven knows what I should have done, by myself, when it became dark!"

"But are we safe on this seat?--May we not be seen by the Indians, since we so plainly see them?"

"I think not. I have often remarked that when Evert and Beulah have been here, their figures could not be perceived from the lawn; owing, I fancy, to the dark back-ground of rock. My dress is not light, and you are in green; which is the colour of the leaves, and not easily to be distinguished. No other spot gives so good a view of what takes place in the valley. We must risk a little exposure, or act in the dark."

"You are a soldier's daughter, Maud"--This was as true of major Meredith as of captain Willoughby, and might therefore be freely said by even Bob--"You are a soldier's daughter, and nature has clearly intended you to be a soldier's wife. This is a *coup-d'-oeil* not to be despised."

"I shall never be a wife at all"--murmured Maud, scarce knowing what she said; "I may not live to be a soldier's daughter, even, much longer. But, why are *you* here?--surely, surely *you* can have no connection with those savages!--I have heard of such horrors; but *you* would not accompany *them*, even though it were to *protect* the Hut."

"I'll not answer for that, Maud. One would do a great deal to preserve his paternal dwelling from pillage, and his father's grey hairs from violence. But I came alone; that party and its objects being utterly strangers to me."

"And *why* do you come at all, Bob?" inquired the anxious girl, looking up into his face with open affection--"The situation of the country is now such, as to make your visits very hazardous."

"Who could know the regular major in this hunting-shirt, and forest garb? I have not an article about my person to betray me, even were I before a court. No fear for me then, Maud; unless it be from these demons in human shape, the savages. Even they do not seem to be very fiercely inclined, as they appear at this moment more disposed to eat, than to attack the Hut. Look for yourself; those fellows are certainly preparing to take their food; the group that is just now coming over the cliffs, is dragging a deer after it."

Maud took the glass, though with an unsteady hand, and she looked a moment at the savages. The manner in which the instrument brought these wild beings nearer to her eye, caused her to shudder, and she was soon satisfied.

"That deer was killed this morning by the miller," she said; "they have doubtless found it in or near his cabin. We will be thankful, however, for this breathing-time--it may enable my dear father to get up the other gate. Look, Robert, and see what progress they make?"

"One side is just hung, and much joy does it produce among them! Persevere, my noble old father, and you will soon be safe against your enemies. What a calm and steady air he has, amid it all! Ah! Maud, Hugh Willoughby ought, at this moment, to be at the head of a brigade, helping to suppress this accursed and unnatural rebellion. Nay, more; he *may* be there, if he will only listen to reason and duty."

"And *this* is then your errand here, Bob?" asked his fair companion, gazing earnestly at the major.

"It is, Maud--and I hope you, whose feelings I know to be right, can encourage me to hope."

"I fear not. It is now too late. Beulah's marriage with Evert has strengthened his opinions--and then"

"What, dearest Maud? You pause as if that 'then' had a meaning you hesitated to express."

Maud coloured; after which she smiled faintly, and proceeded: "We should speak reverently of a father--and such a father, too. But does it not seem probable to you, Bob, that the many discussions he has with Mr. Woods may have a tendency to confirm each in his notions?"

Robert Willoughby would have answered in the affirmative, had not a sudden movement at the Hut prevented.

Chapter XII

From Flodden ridge
The Scots beheld the English host
Leave Barmore wood, their evening post,
And heedful watched them as they crossed
The Till by Twisal Bridge.

Scott

It was just at this instant that most of the women of the settlement rushed from the court, and spread themselves within the stockade, Mrs. Willoughby and Beulah being foremost in the movement. The captain left the gate, too, and even the men, who were just about to raise the last leaf, suspended their toil. It was quite apparent some new cause for uneasiness or alarm had suddenly awoke among them. Still the stack of arms remained untouched, nor was there any new demonstration among the Indians. The major watched everything, with intense attention, through the glass.

"What is it, dear Bob?" demanded the anxious Maud. "I see my dearest mother--she seems alarmed."

"Was it known to her that you were about to quit the house, when you came out on this walk?"

"I rather think not. She and Beulah were in the nursery with little Evert, and my father was in the fields. I came out without speaking to any person, nor did I meet any before entering the forest."

"Then you are now first missed. Yes, that is it--and no wonder, Maud, it creates alarm. Merciful God! How must they all feel, at a moment like this!"

"Fire your rifle, Bob--that will draw their eyes in this direction, and I will wave my handkerchief--perhaps *that* might be seen. Beulah has received such signals from me, before."

"It would never do. No, we must remain concealed, watching their movements, in order to be able to aid them at the proper time. It is painful to endure this suspense, beyond a doubt; but the pain must be borne in order to ensure the safety of one who is so very, very precious to us all."

Notwithstanding the fearful situation in which she was placed, Maud felt soothed by these words. The language of affection, as coming from Robert Willoughby, was very dear to her at all times, and never more than at a moment when it appeared that even her life was suspended, as it might be, by a hair.

"It is as you say," she answered gently, giving him her hand with much of her ancient frankness of manner; "we should be betrayed, and of course lost--but what means the movement at the Hut?"

There was indeed a movement within the stockade. Maud's absence was now clearly ascertained, and it is needless to describe the commotion the circumstance produced. No one thought any longer of the half of the gate that still remained to be hung, but every supposable part of the house and enclosure had been examined in quest of her who was missing. Our heroine's last remark, however, was produced by certain indications of an intention to make a descent from one of the external windows of the common parlour, a room it will be remembered that stood on the little cliff, above the rivulet that wound beneath its base. This cliff was about forty feet high, and though it offered a formidable obstacle to any attempt to scale it, there was no great difficulty in an active man's descending, aided by a rope. The spot, too, was completely concealed from the view of the party which still remained on the rock, near the mill, at a distance of quite half a mile from the gates of the stockade. This fact greatly facilitated the little sortie, since, once in the bed of the rivulet, which was fringed with bushes, it would be very practicable, by following its windings, to gain the forest unseen. The major levelled his glass at the windows, and immediately saw the truth of all that has here been mentioned.

"They are preparing to send a party out," he said, "and doubtless in quest of you, Maud. The thing is very feasible, provided the savages remain much longer in their present position. It is matter of surprise to me, that the last have not sent a force in the rear of the Hut, where the windows are at least exposed to fire, and the forest is so close as to afford a cover to the assailants. In front there is literally none, but a few low fences, which is the reason I presume that they keep so much aloof."

"It is not probable they know the valley. With the exception of Nick, but few Indians have ever visited us, and that rarely. Those we have seen have all been of the most peaceable and friendly tribes; not a true warrior, as my father says, ever having been found among them. Nick is the only one of them all that can thus be termed."

"Is it possible that fellow has led this party? I have never more than half confided in him, and yet he is too old a friend of the family, I should think, to be guilty of such an act of baseness."

"My father thinks him a knave, but I question if he has an opinion of him as bad as that. Besides, *he* knows the valley, and would have led the Indians round into the rear of the house, if it be a place so much more favourable for the attack, as you suppose. These wretches have come by the common paths, all of which first strike the river, as you know, below the mills."

"That is true. I lost my way, a few miles from this, the path being very blind on the eastern route, which I travelled as having gone it last with Nick, and thinking it the safest. Fortunately I recognised the crest of this mountain above us, by its shape, or I might never have found my way; although the streams, when struck, are certain guides to the woodsman. As soon as I hit the cow-paths, I knew they would lead me to the barns and sheds. See! a man is actually descending from a window!"

"Oh! Bob, I hope it is not my father! He is too old--it is risking too much to let him quit the house."

"I will tell you better when he reaches the ground. Unless mistaken--ay--it is the Irishman, O'Hearn."

"Honest Mike! He is always *foremost* in everything, though he so little knows how anything but digging ought to be done. Is there not another following him--or am I deceived?"

"There is--he has just reached the ground, too. This might be spared, did they know how well you are guarded, Maud. By one who would die cheerfully to prevent harm from reaching you!"

"They little dream of that, Bob," answered Maud, in a low tone. "Not a human being in that valley fancies you nearer to him than the royal armies are, at this moment. But they do not send a third--I am glad they weaken their own force no further."

"It is certainly best they should not. The men had their rifles slung when they descended, and they are now getting them ready for service. It is Joel Strides who is with Mike."

"I am sorry for it. *That* is a man I little like, Bob, and I should be sorry he knew of your being here."

This was said quickly, and with a degree of feeling that surprised the major, who questioned Maud earnestly as to her meaning and its reasons. The latter told him she scarce knew herself; that she disliked the man's manner, had long thought his principles bad, and that Mike in his extraordinary way had said certain things to her, to awaken distrust.

"Mike speaks in hieroglyphics," said the major, laughing, in spite of the serious situation in which he and his companion were placed, "and one must never be too sure of *his* meaning. Joel has now been many years with my father, and he seems to enjoy his confidence."

"He makes himself useful, and is very guarded in what he says at the Hut. Still--I wish him not to know of your being here."

"It will not be easy to prevent it, Maud. I should have come boldly into the valley, but for this accidental meeting with you, trusting that my father has no one about him so base as to betray his son."

"Trust not Joel Strides. I'll answer for Mike with my life; but sorry indeed should I be that Joel Strides knew of your being among us. It were better, perhaps, that most of the workmen should not be in the secret. See-- the two men are quitting the foot of the rocks."

This was true, and Robert Willoughby watched their movements with the glass. As had been expected, they first descended into the bed of the rivulet, wading along its shore, under the cover of the bushes, until they soon became concealed even from the view of one placed on a height as elevated as that occupied by Robert and Maud. It was sufficiently apparent, however, that their intention was to reach the forest in this manner, when they would probably commence their search for the missing young lady. Nor was it long before Robert and Maud plainly saw the two adventurers quit the bed of the stream and bury themselves in the forest. The question now seriously arose as to the best course for the major and his companion to pursue. Under ordinary circumstances, it would have been wisest, perhaps, to descend at once and meet the messengers, who might soon be found at some of the usual haunts of the girl; but against this the latter so earnestly protested, and that in a manner so soothing to the young man's feelings, that he scarce knew how to oppose her wishes. She implored him not to confide in Joel Strides too hastily, at least. It might be time enough, when there was no alternative; until the true character of the party then in the valley was known, it would be premature. Nothing was easier than to conceal himself until it was dark, when he might approach the Hut, and be admitted without his presence being known to any but those on whom the family could certainly rely. The major urged the impossibility of his quitting Maud, until she was joined by the two men sent in quest of her, and then it would be too late, as he must be seen. Although he might escape immediate recognition in his present dress, the presence of a stranger would excite suspicions, and compel an explanation. To this Maud replied in the following manner: Her customary places of resort, when in the woods, were well known; more especially to Michael, who was frequently employed in their vicinity. These were a little water-fall, that was situated a hundred rods up the rivulet, to which a path had been made expressly, and where an arbour, seat, and little table had been arranged, for the purposes of working, reading, or taking refreshments. To this spot the men would unquestionably proceed first. Then, there was a deep ravine, some distance farther, that was often visited for its savage beauty, and whither she more frequently went, perhaps, than to any other place. Thither Michael would be certain to lead his companion. These two places visited, they might infallibly expect to see the men at the rock, where the two were then seated, as the last spot in which Maud might naturally be expected to be found. It would require an hour to visit the two places first named, and to examine the surrounding woods; and by that time, not only would the sun be set, but the twilight would be disappearing. Until that moment, then, the major might remain at her side, and on the sound of the approaching footsteps of the messengers, he had only to retire behind a projection of the rocks, and afterwards follow towards the Knoll, at a safe distance.

This plan was too plausible to be rejected; and giving Robert an hour of uninterrupted discourse with his companion, it struck him as having more advantages than any other mentioned. The party near the mills, too, remaining perfectly quiet, there was less occasion for any change of their own, than might otherwise have been the case. So far, indeed, from appearing to entertain any hostile intention, not a cabin had been injured, if approached, and the smoke of the conflagration which had been expected to rise from the mills and the habitations in the glen, did not make its appearance. If any such ruthless acts as applying the brand and assaulting the people were in contemplation, they were at least delayed until night should veil them in a fitting darkness.

It is always a great relief to the mind, in moments of trial, to have decided on a course of future action. So the major and Maud now found; for, taking his seat by her side, he began to converse with his companion more connectedly, and with greater calmness than either had yet been able to achieve. Many questions were asked, and answers given, concerning the state of the family, that of his father and mother, and dear Beulah and her infant, the latter being as yet quite a stranger to the young soldier.

"Is he like his rebel of a father?" asked the royal officer, smiling, but as his companion fancied, painfully; "or has he more of the look of the Willoughbys. Beekman is a good-looking Dutchman; yet, I would rather have the boy resemble the good old English stock, after all."

"The sweet little fellow resembles both father and mother; though the first the most, to Beulah's great delight. Papa says he is true 'Holland's come of', as they call it, though neither mamma nor I will allow of any such thing. Colonel Beekman is a very worthy man, Bob, and a most affectionate and attentive husband. Beulah, but for this war, could not be happier."

"Then I forgive him one-half of his treason--for the remainder let him take his luck. Now I am an uncle, my heart begins to melt a little towards the rebel. And you, Maud, how do the honours of an aunt sit upon your feelings? But women are all heart, and would love a rat."

Maud smiled, but she answered not. Though Beulah's child were almost as dear to her as one of her own could have been, she remembered that she was *not* its aunt, in fact; and, though she knew not why, in that company, and even at that grave moment, the obtrusive thought summoned a bright flush to her cheeks. The major probably did not notice this change of countenance, since, after a short pause, he continued the conversation naturally.

"The child is called Evert, is it not, *aunt* Maud?" he asked, laying an emphasis on 'aunt.'

Maud wished this word had not been used; and yet Robert Willoughby, could the truth have been known, had adverted to it with an association in his own mind, that would have distressed her, just then, still more. *Aunt* Maud was the name that others, however, were most fond of adopting, since the birth of the child; and remembering this, our heroine smiled.

"That is what Beulah has called me, these six months," she said--"or ever since Evert was born. I became an aunt the day he became a nephew; and dear, good Beulah has not once called me *sister* since, I think."

"These little creatures introduce new ties into families," answered the major, thoughtfully. "They take the places of the generations before them, and edge us out of our hold on the affections, as in the end they supplant us in our stations in life. If Beulah love me only as an *uncle*, however, she may look to it. I'll be supplanted by no Dutchman's child that was ever born!"

"*You*, Bob!" cried Maud, starting. "You are its *real* uncle; Beulah must ever remember *you*, and *love* you, as her *own* brother!"

Maud's voice became suddenly hushed, like one who feared she had said too much. The major gazed at her intently, but he spoke not; nor did his companion see his look, her own eyes being cast meekly and tremblingly on the earth at her feet. A considerable pause succeeded, and then the conversation reverted to what was going on in the valley.

The sun was now set, and the shadows of evening began to render objects a little indistinct beneath them. Still it was apparent that much anxiety prevailed in and about the Hut, doubtless on account of our heroine's absence. So great was it, indeed, as entirely to supersede the hanging of the remaining leaf of the gate, which stood in the gap where it belonged, stayed by pieces of timber, but unhung. The major thought some disposition had been made, however, by which the inmates might pass and repass by the half that was suspended, making a tolerable defence, when all was closed.

"Hist!" whispered Maud, whose faculties were quickened by the danger of her companion; "I hear the voice of Michael, and they approach. No sense of danger can repress poor O'Hearn's eloquence; his ideas seeming to flow from his tongue very much as they rise to his thoughts, chance directing which shall appear first."

"It is true, dear girl; and as you seem so strongly to wish it, I will withdraw. Depend on my keeping near you, and on my presence, should it be required."

"You will not forget to come beneath the windows, Bob," said Maud, anxiously, but in great haste; for the footsteps of the men drew rapidly near; "at the very spot where the others descended."

The major bent forward and kissed a cheek that was chilled with apprehension, but which the act caused to burn like fire; then he disappeared behind the projection of rock he had himself pointed out. As for Maud, she sat in seeming composure, awaiting the approach of those who drew near.

"The divil bur-r-n me, and all the Injins in Ameriky along wid me," said Mike, scrambling up the ascent by a short cut, "but I think we'll find the young Missus, here, or I don't think we'll be finding her the night. It's a cursed counthry to live in, Misther Strides, where a young lady of the loveliness and pithiful beauty of Miss Maud can be lost in the woods, as it might be a sheep or a stray baste that was for tasting the neighbour's pastures."

"You speak too loud, Mike, and you speak foolishness into the bargain," returned the wary Joel.

"Is it I, you mane! Och! don't think ye 're goin' to set me a rowin' a boat once more, ag'in my inclinations and edication, as ye did in ould times. I've rung ye into yer ma'tin', and out of yer m'atin', too, twenty times too often to be catched in that same trap twice. It's Miss Maud I wants, and Miss Maud I'll find, or ---- Lord bless her swate face and morals, and her charackter, and all belonging to her!--isn't that, now, a prathy composure for the likes of her, and the savages at the mill, and the Missus in tears, and the masther mighty un'asy, and all of us bothered! See how she sits on that bit of a sate that I puts there for her wid my own hands, as a laddy should, looking jist what she is, the quane of the woods, and the delight of our eyes!"

Maud was too much accustomed to the rhapsodies of the county Leitrim-man to think much of this commencement; but resolute to act her part with discretion, she rose to meet him, speaking with great apparent self-possession.

"Is it possible you are in quest of me?" she said--"why has this happened?--I usually return about this hour."

"Hoors is it! Don't talk of hoors, beauthiful young laddy, when a single quarther may be too late," answered Mike, dogmatically. "It's your own mother that's not happy at yer being in the woods the night, and yer ould father that has moore un'asiness than he'll confess; long life to the church in which confession is held to be right, and dacent, and accorthing to the gospel of St. Luke, and the whole calender in the bargain. Ye'll not be frightened, Miss Maud, but take what I've to tell ye jist as if ye didn't bel'ave a wo-r-r-d of it; but, divil bur-r-n me, if there arn't Injins enough on the rocks, forenent the mill, to scalp a whole province, and a county along wid it, if ye'll give 'em time and knives enough."

"I understand you, Michael, but am not in the least alarmed," answered Maud, with an air of great steadiness; such, indeed, as would have delighted the captain. "Something of what has been passing below have I seen; but, by being calm and reasonable, we shall escape the danger. Tell me only, that all is safe in the Hut--that my dear mother and sister are well."

"Is it the Missus? Och, she's as valiant as a peacock, only strick down and overcome about your own self! As for Miss Beuly, where's the likes of her to be found, unless it's on this same bit of a rock? And it's agraable to see the captain, looking for all the wor-r-ld like a commander-in-chaif of six or eight rijiments, ordering one this-a-way, and another that-a-way--By St. Patrick, young laddy, I only hopes them vagabonds will come on as soon as yourself is inside the sticks, jist to give the ould jontleman a better occasion to play souldier on 'em. Should they happen to climb over the sticks, I've got the prattiest bit of a shillaleh ready that mortal eyes iver adorned! 'Twould break a head and niver a hat harmed--a thousand's the pities them chaps wears no hats. Howsever, we'll see."

"Thank you, Mike, for the courage you show, and the interest you take in all our welfares--Is it not too soon to venture down upon the flats, Joel? I must trust to *you* as a guide."

"I think Miss Maud would do full as well if she did. Mike must be told, too, not to talk so much, and above all, not to speak so loud. He may be heard, sometimes, a dozen rods."

"Tould!" exclaimed the county Leitrim-man, in heat--"And isn't tould I've been twenty times already, by your own smooth conversation? Where's the occasion to tell a thing over and over ag'in, when a man is not wanting in ears. It's the likes of you that loves to converse."

"Well, Mike, for my sake, you will be silent, I hope," said Maud. "Remember, I am not fitted for a battle, and the first thing is to get safely into the house. The sooner we are down the hill, perhaps, the better it may be. Lead the way, then, Joel, and I will follow. Michael will go next to you, in readiness for any enemy, and I will bring up the rear. It will be better for all to keep a dead silence, until it be necessary to speak."

This arrangement was made, and the party proceeded, Maud remaining a little behind, in order that the major might catch glimpses of her person, in the sombre light of the hour and the forest, and not miss the road. A few minutes brought them all upon the level land, where, Joel, instead of entering the open fields, inclined more into the woods, always keeping one of the many paths. His object was to cross the rivulet under cover, a suitable place offering a short distance from the point where the stream glided out of the forest. Towards this spot Joel quietly held his way, occasionally stopping to listen if any movement of importance had occurred on the flats. As for Maud, her eyes were frequently cast behind her, for she was fearful Robert Willoughby might miss the path, having so little acquaintance with the thousand sinuosities he encountered. She caught glimpses of his person, however, in the distance, and saw that he was on the right track. Her chief concern, therefore, soon became an anxiety that he should not be seen by her companions. As they kept a little in advance, and the underbrush was somewhat thick, she had strong hopes that this evil would be avoided.

The path being very circuitous, it took some time to reach the spot Joel sought. Here he, Mike, and Maud, crossed the rivulet on a tree that had been felled expressly to answer the purposes of a rustic foot-bridge; a common expedient of the American forest. As our heroine had often performed this exploit when alone, she required no assistance, and she felt as if half the danger of her critical situation had vanished, when she found herself on the same side of the stream as the Hut. Joel, nothing suspecting, and keeping all his faculties on the sounds and sights that might occur in front, led the way diligently, and soon reached the verge of the woods. Here he paused for his companions to join him.

Twilight had, by this time, nearly disappeared. Still, enough remained to enable Maud to perceive that many were watching for her, either at the windows above the cliff, or through different parts of the stockades. The distance was so small, that it might have been possible, by raising the voice, even to converse; but this would be an experiment too hazardous, as some hostile scouts, at that hour might very well be fearfully near.

"I see nothing, Miss Maud," observed Joel, after taking a good look around him. "By keeping the path that follows the edge of the brook, though it is so crooked, we shall be certain of good walking, and shall be half hid by the bushes. It's best to walk quick, and to be silent."

Maud bade him go on, waiting herself behind a tree, to let the two men precede her a short distance. This was done, and the major stole up to her side unseen. A few words of explanation passed, when the young lady ran after her guides, leaving Robert Willoughby seated on a log. It was a breathless moment to Maud, that in which she was passing this bit of open land. But the distance was so short, that it was soon gotten over; and the three found themselves beneath the cliff. Here they passed the spring, and following a path which led from it, turned the edge of the rocks, and ascended to the foot of the stockades. It remained to turn these also, in order to reach the so recently suspended gates. As Maud passed swiftly along, almost brushing the timbers with her dress, she saw, in the dim light, fifty faces looking at her, and thrust between the timbers; but she paused not, spoke not--scarcely breathed. A profound stillness reigned on the Knoll; but when Joel arrived at the gate, it was instantly opened, and he glided in. Not so with Mike, who stopped and waited until she he had been in quest of entered before him, and was in safety.

Maud found herself in her mother's arms, the instant the gate was passed. Mrs. Willoughby had been at the angle of the cliff, had followed her child, in her swift progress round the stockade, and was ready to receive her, the moment she entered. Beulah came next, and then the captain embraced, kissed, wept over, and scolded his little favourite.

"No reproaches now, Hugh"--said the more considerate wife, and gentle woman--"Maud has done no more than has long been her custom, and no one could have foreseen what has happened."

"Mother--father"--said Maud, almost gasping for breath--"let us bless God for my safety, and for the safety of all that are dear to us--thank you, dear Mr. Woods--there is a kiss, to thank you--now let us go into the house; I have much to tell you--come dear sir--come dearest mother, do not lose a moment; let us all go to the library."

As this was the room in which the family devotions were usually held, the auditors fancied the excited girl wished to return her thanks in that mode, one not unfrequent in that regulated family, and all followed her, who dared, with tender sympathy in her feelings, and profoundly grateful for her safety. As soon as in the room, Maud carefully shut the door, and went from one to another, in order to ascertain who were present. Finding none but her father, mother, sister, and the chaplain, she instantly related all that had passed, and pointed out the spot where the major was, at that moment, waiting for the signal to approach. It is unnecessary to dwell on the astonishment and delight, mingled with concern, that this intelligence produced.

Maud then rapidly recounted her plan, and implored her father to see it executed. The captain had none of her apprehensions on the subject of his people's fidelity, but he yielded to the girl's earnest entreaties. Mrs. Willoughby was so agitated with all the unlooked-for events of the day, that she joined her daughter in the request, and Maud was told to proceed with the affair, in her own way.

A lamp was brought, and placed by Maud in a pantry that was lighted by a single, long, narrow, external window, at the angle of the building next the offices, and the door was closed on it. This lamp was the signal for the major to approach, and with beating hearts the females bent forward from the windows, secure of not being seen in the night, which had now fairly closed on the valley, to listen to his approaching footsteps beneath. They did not wait long ere he was not only heard, but dimly seen, though totally out of the line of sight from all in the Hut, with the exception of those above his head. Captain Willoughby had prepared a rope, one end of which was dropped, and fastened by the major, himself, around his body. A jerk let those above know when he was ready.

"What shall we do next?" asked the captain, in a sort of despair. "Woods and I can never drag that tall, heavy fellow up such a distance. He is six feet, and weighs a hundred and eighty, if he weighs a pound."

"Peace," half-whispered Maud, from a window. "All will be right in a moment." Then drawing in her body, the pale but earnest girl begged her father to have patience. "I have thought of all. Mike and the blacks may be trusted with our lives--I will call them."

This was done, and the county Leitrim-man and the two Plinys were soon in the room.

"O'Hearn," said Maud, inquiringly--"I think you are my friend?"

"Am I my own!--Is it yees, is the question? Well, jist wish for a tooth, and ye may take all in my head for the asking. Och, I 'd be a baste, else! I'd ate the remain of my days wid not'ing but a spoon to obleege ye."

"As for you, Pliny, and your son here, you have known us from children. Not a word must pass the lips of either, as to what you see--now pull, but with great care, lest the rope break."

The men did as ordered, raising their load from the ground, a foot or two at a time. In this manner the burthen approached, yard after yard, until it was evidently drawing near the window.

"It's the captain hoisting up the big baste of a hog, for provisioning the hoose, ag'in a saige," whispered Mike to the negroes, who grinned as they tugged; "and when the cr'atur squails, see to it, that ye do not squail yerselves."

At that moment the head and shoulders of a man appeared at the window, Mike let go the rope, seized a chair, and was about to knock the intruder on the head; but the captain arrested the blow.

"It's one of the vagabond Injins that has undermined the hog, and coome up in its stead," roared Mike."

"It's my son"--answered the captain, mildly--"see that you are silent, and secret."

Chapter XIII

And glory long has made the sages smile,
Tis something, nothing, words, illusion, wind--
Depending more upon the historian's style
Than on the name a person leaves behind.
Troy owes to Homer what whist owes to Hoyle
The present century was growing blind
To the great Marlborough's skill in giving knocks,
Until his late Life by Archdeacon Coxe.
Byron.

Major Willoughby's feet were scarcely on the library floor, when he was clasped in his mother's arms. From these he soon passed into Beulah's; nor did his father hesitate about giving him an embrace nearly as warm. As for Maud, she stood by, weeping in sympathy and in silence.

"And you, too, old man," said Robert Willoughby, dashing the tears from his eyes, and turning to the elder black, holding out a hand--"this is not the first time, by many, old Pliny, that you have had me between heaven and earth. Your son was my old play-fellow, and we must shake hands also. As for O'Hearn, steel is not truer, and we are friends for life."

The negroes were delighted to see their young master, for, in that day, the slaves exulted in the honour, appearance, importance and dignity of their owners, far more than their liberated descendants do now in their own. The major had been their friend when a boy; and he was, at present, their pride and glory. In their view of the matter, the English army did not contain his equal in looks, courage, military skill, or experience; and it was treason *per se* to fight against a cause that he upheld. The captain had laughingly related to his wife a conversation to this effect he had not long before overheard between the two Plinys.

"Well, Miss Beuly do a pretty well"--observed the elder, "but, den he all'e better, if he no get 'Merican 'mission. What you call raal colonel, eh? Have 'e paper from 'e king like Masser Bob, and wear a rigimental like a head of a turkey cock, so! Dat bein' an up and down officer."

"P'rhaps Miss Beuly bring a colonel round, and take off a blue coat, and put on a scarlet," answered the younger.

"Nebber!--nebber see dat, Plin, in a rebbleushun. Dis got to be a rebbleushun; and when *dat* begin in 'arnest, gib up all idee of 'mendment. Rebbleushuns look all one way--nebber see two side, any more dan coloured man see two side in a red-skin."

As we have not been able to trace the thought to antiquity, this expression may have been the original of the celebrated axiom of Napoleon, which tells us that "revolutions never go backwards." At all events, such was the notion of Pliny Willoughby, Sen., as the namesake of the great Roman styled himself; and it was greatly admired by Pliny Willoughby, Jun., to say nothing of the opinions of Big Smash and Little Smash, both of whom were listeners to the discourse.

"Well, I wish a colonel Beekman"--To this name the fellow gave the true Doric sound of *Bakeman*--"I wish a colonel Beekman only corprul in king's troops, for Miss Beuly's sake. Better be sarjun dere, dan briggerdeer-ginral in 'Merikan company; dat *I* know."

"What a briggerdeer mean, Plin?" inquired Little Smash, with interest. "Who he keep company wid, and what he do? Tell a body, do--so many officer in 'e army, one nebber know all he name."

"'Mericans can't hab 'em. Too poor for *dat*. Briggerdeer great gentleum, and wear a red coat. Ole time, see 'em in hundreds, come to visit Masser, and Missus, and play wid Masser Bob. Oh! no rebbleushun in dem days; but ebbery body know he own business, and *do* it, too."

This will serve to show the political sentiments of the Plinys, and may also indicate the bias that the Smashes were likely to imbibe in such company. As a matter of course, the major was gladly welcomed by these devoted admirers; and when Maud again whispered to them the necessity of secresy, each shut his mouth, no trifling operation in itself, as if it were to be henceforth hermetically sealed.

The assistants were now dismissed, and the major was left alone with his family. Again and again Mrs. Willoughby embraced her son; nor had her new ties at all lessened Beulah's interest in her brother. Even the captain kissed his boy anew, while Mr. Woods shook hands once more with his old pupil, and blessed him. Maud alone was passive in this scene of feeling and joy.

"Now, Bob, let us to business," said the captain, as soon as tranquillity was a little restored. "You have not made this difficult and perilous journey without an object; and, as we are somewhat critically situated ourselves, the sooner we know what it is, the less will be the danger of its not producing its proper effect."

"Heaven send, dear sir, that it fail not in its effect, indeed," answered the son. "But is not this movement in the valley pressing, and have I not come opportunely to take a part in the defence of the house?"

"That will be seen a few hours later, perhaps. Everything is quiet now, and will probably so remain until near morning; or Indian tactics have undergone a change. The fellows have lighted camp-fires on their rocks, and seem disposed to rest for the present, at least. Nor do I know that they are bent on war at all. We have no Indians near us, who would be likely to dig up the hatchet; and these fellows profess peace, by a messenger they have sent me."

"Are they not in their war-paint, sir? I remember to have seen warriors, when a boy, and my glass has given these men the appearance of being on what they call 'a war-path.'"

"Some of them are certainly in that guise, though he who came to the Knoll was not. *He* pretended that they were a party travelling towards the Hudson in order to learn the true causes of the difficulties between their Great English and their Great American Fathers. He asked for meal and meat to feed his young men with. This was the whole purport of his errand."

"And your answer, sir; is it peace, or war, between you?"

"Peace in professions, but I much fear war in reality. Still one cannot know. An old frontier garrison-man, like myself, is not apt to put much reliance on Indian faith. We are now, God be praised! all within the stockade; and having plenty of arms and ammunition, are not likely to be easily stormed. A siege is out of the question; we are too well provisioned to dread that."

"But you leave the mills, the growing grain, the barns, even the cabins of your workmen, altogether at the mercy of these wretches."

"That cannot well be avoided, unless we go out and drive them off, in open battle. For the last, they are too strong, to say nothing of the odds of risking fathers of families against mere vagabonds, as I suspect these savages to be. I have told them to help themselves to meal, or grain, of which they will find plenty in the mill. Pork can be got in the houses, and they have made way with a deer already, that I had expected the pleasure of dissecting myself. The cattle roam the woods at this season, and are tolerably safe; but they can burn the barns and other buildings, should they see fit. In this respect, we are at their mercy. If they ask for rum, or cider, that may bring matters to a head; for, refusing may exasperate them, and granting either, in any quantity, will certainly cause them all to get intoxicated."

"Why would not that be good policy, Willoughby?" exclaimed the chaplain. "If fairly disguised once, our people might steal out upon them, and take away all their arms. Drunken men sleep very profoundly."

"It would be a canonical mode of warfare, perhaps, Woods," returned the chaplain, smiling, "but not exactly a military. I think it safer that they should continue sober; for, as yet, they manifest no great intentions of hostility. But of this we can speak hereafter. Why are you here, my son, and in this guise?"

"The motive may as well be told now, as at another time," answered the major, giving his mother and sisters chairs, while the others imitated their example in being seated. "Sir William Howe has permitted me to come out to see you--I might almost say *ordered* me out; for matters have now reached a pass when we think every loyal gentleman in America must feel disposed to take sides with the crown."

A general movement among his auditors told the major the extent of the interest they felt in what was expected to follow. He paused an instant to survey the dark-looking group that was clustering around him; for no lights were in the room on account of the open windows, and he spoke in a low voice from motives of prudence; then he proceeded:

"I should infer from the little that passed between Maud and myself," he said, "that you are ignorant of the two most important events that have yet occurred in this unhappy conflict?"

"We learn little here," answered the father. "I have heard that my Lord Howe and his brother Sir William have been named commissioners by His Majesty to heal all the differences. I knew them both, when young men, and their elder brother before them. Black Dick, as we used to call the admiral, is a discreet, well-meaning man; though I fear both of them owe their appointments more to their affinity to the sovereign than to the qualities that might best fit them to deal with the Americans."

"Little is known of the affinity of which you speak[*], and less said in the army," returned the major, "but I fear there is no hope of the object of the commission's being effected. The American congress has declared the colonies altogether independent of England; and so far as this country is concerned, the war is carried on as between nation and nation. All allegiance, even in name, is openly cast aside."

[* The mother of the three Lords Howe, so well known in American history, viz: *George*, killed before Ticonderoga, in the war of '56; *Richard*, the celebrated admiral, and the hero of the 1st June; and Sir *William*, for several years commander-in-chief in this country, and the 5th and last viscount; was a Mademoiselle Kilmansegge, who was supposed to be a natural daughter of George I. This would make these three officers and George II. first-cousins; and George III their great-nephew *a la mode de Bretagne*. Walpole, and various other English writers, speak openly, not only of the connection, but of the family resemblance. Indeed, most of the gossiping writers of that age seem to allow that Lord Howe was a grandson of the first English sovereign of the House of Brunswick.]

"You astonish me, Bob! I did not think it could ever come to this!"

"I thought your native attachments would hardly endure as strong a measure as this has got to be," answered the major, not a little satisfied with the strength of feeling manifested by his father. "Yet has this been done, sir, and done in a way that it will not be easy to recall. Those who now resist us, resist for the sake of throwing off all connection with England."

"Has France any agency in this, Bob?--I own it startles me, and has a French look."

"It has driven many of the most respectable of our enemies into our arms, sir. We have never considered you a direct enemy, though unhappily inclining too much against us; 'but this will determine Sir Hugh,' said the commander-in-chief in our closing interview--I suppose you know, my dear father, that all your old friends, knowing what has happened, insist on calling you Sir Hugh. I assure you, I never open my lips on the subject; and yet Lord Howe drank to the health of Sir Hugh Willoughby, openly at his own table, the last time I had the honour to dine with him."

"Then the next time he favours you with an invitation, Bob, be kind enough to thank him. I want no empty baronetcy, nor do I ever think of returning to England to live. Were all I had on earth drummed together, it would barely make out a respectable competency for a private gentleman in that extravagant state of society; and what is a mere name to one in such circumstances? I wish it were transferable, my dear boy, in the old Scotch mode, and you should be Sir Bob before you slept."

"But, Willoughby, it may be useful to Robert, and why should he not have the title, since neither you nor I care for it?" asked the considerate mother.

"So he may, my dear; though he must wait for an event that I fancy you are not very impatient to witness--my death. When I am gone, let him be Sir Robert, in welcome. But, Bob--for plain, honest Bob must you remain till then, unless indeed you earn your spurs in this unhappy war--have you any military tidings for us? We have heard nothing since the arrival of the fleet on the coast."

"We are in New York, after routing Washington on Long Island. The rebels"--the major spoke a little more confidently than had been his wont--"The rebels have retreated into the high country, near the borders of Connecticut, where they have inveterate nests of the disaffected in their rear."

"And has all this been done without bloodshed? Washington had staff in him, in the old French business."

"*His* stuff is not doubted, sir; but his men make miserable work of it. Really I am sometimes ashamed of having been born in the country. These Yankees fight like wrangling women, rather than soldiers."

"How's this!--You spoke honestly of the affair at Lexington, and wrote us a frank account of the murderous work at Bunker Hill. Have their natures changed with the change of season?"

"To own the truth, sir, they did wonders on the Hill, and not badly in the other affair; but all their spirit seems gone. I am quite ashamed of them. Perhaps this declaration of independence, as it is called, has damped their ardour."

"No, my son--the change, if change there is, depends on a general and natural law. Nothing but discipline and long training can carry men with credit through a campaign, in the open field. Fathers, and husbands, and brothers and lovers, make formidable enemies, in sight of their own chimney-tops; but the most flogging regiments, we used to say, were the best fighting regiments for a long pull. But, have a care, Bob; you are now of a rank that may well get you a separate command, and do not despise your enemy. I know these Yankees well--you are one, yourself, though only half-blooded; but I know them well, and have often seen them tried. They are very apt to be badly commanded, heaven cursing them for their sins, in this form more than any other--but get them fairly at work, and the guards will have as much as they can wish, to get along with. Woods will swear to *that*."

"Objecting to the *mode* of corroboration, my dear sir, I can support its substance. Inclined as I am to uphold Cæsar, and to do honour to the Lord's anointed, I will not deny my countrymen's courage; though I think,

Willoughby, now I recall old times, it was rather the fashion of our officers to treat it somewhat disrespectfully."

"It was, indeed," answered the captain, thoughtfully--"and a silly thing it was. They mistook the nature of a mild and pacific people, totally without the glitter and habits of military life, for a timid people; and I have often heard the new hands in the colonies speak of their inhabitants with contempt on this very head. Braddock had that failing to a great degree; and yet this very major Washington saved his army from annihilation, when it came to truly desperate work. Mark the words of a much older soldier than yourself, Bob; you may have more of the bravery of apparel, and present a more military aspect; may even gain advantages over them by means of higher discipline, better arms, and more accurate combinations; but, when you meet them fairly, depend on it you will meet dangerous foes, and men capable of being sooner drilled into good soldiers than any nation I have met with. Their great curse is, and probably will be, in selecting too many of their officers from classes not embued with proper military pride, and altogether without the collaterals of a good military education."

To all this the major had nothing very material to object, and remembering that the silent but thoughtful Beulah had a husband in what he called the rebel ranks, he changed the subject. Arrangements were now made for the comfort and privacy of the unlooked-for guest. Adjoining the library, a room with no direct communication with the court by means of either door, or window, was a small and retired apartment containing a cot-bed, to which the captain was accustomed to retire in the cases of indisposition, when Mrs. Willoughby wished to have either of her daughters with herself, on their account, or on her own. This room was now given to the major, and in it he would be perfectly free from every sort of intrusion. He might eat in the library, if necessary; though, all the windows of that wing of the house opening outward, there was little danger of being seen by any but the regular domestics of the family, all of whom were to be let into the secret of his presence, and all of whom were rightly judged to be perfectly trustworthy.

As the evening promised to be dark, it was determined among the gentlemen that the major should disguise himself still more than he was already, and venture outside of the building, in company with his father, and the chaplain, as soon as the people, who were now crowded into the vacant rooms in the empty part of the house, had taken possession of their respective quarters for the night. In the meantime a hearty supper was provided for the traveller in the library, the bullet-proof window-shutters of which room, and indeed of all the others on that side of the building, having first been closed, in order that lights might be used, without drawing a shot from the adjoining forest.

"We are very safe, here," observed the captain, as his son appeased his hunger, with the keen relish of a traveller. "Even Woods might stand a siege in a house built and stockaded like this. Every window has solid bullet-proof shutters, with fastenings not easily broken; and the logs of the buildings might almost defy round-shot. The gates are all up, one leaf excepted, and that leaf stands nearly in its place, well propped and supported. In the morning it shall be hung like the others. Then the stockade is complete, and has not a speck of decay about it yet. We shall keep a guard of twelve men up the whole night, with three sentinels outside of the buildings; and all of us will sleep in our clothes, and on our arms. My plan, should an assault be made, is to draw in the sentinels, as soon as they have discharged their pieces, to close the gate, and man the loops. The last are all open, and spare arms are distributed at them. I had a walk made within the ridge of the roofs this spring, by which men can run round the whole Hut, in the event of an attempt to, set fire to the shingles, or fire over the ridge at an enemy at the stockades. It is a great improvement, Bob; and, as it is well railed, will make a capital station in a warm conflict, before the enemy make their way within the stockade."

"We must endeavour not to let them get there, sir," answered the major--"but, as soon as your people are housed, I shall have an opportunity to reconnoitre. Open work is most to the taste of us regulars."

"Not against an Indian enemy. You will be glad of such a fortress as this, boy, before the question of independence, or no independence, shall be finally settled. Did not Washington entrench in the town?"

"Not much on that side of the water, sir; though he was reasonably well in the ground on Long Island. *There* he had many thousands of men, and works of some extent."

"And how did he get off the island?" demanded the captain, turning round to look his son in the face. "The arm of the sea is quite half-a-mile in width, at that point--how did he cross it in the face of a victorious army?--or did he only save himself, while you captured his troops?"

The major coloured a little, and then he looked at Beulah and smiled good-naturedly.

"I am so surrounded by rebels here," he said, "that it is not easy to answer all your questions, sir. Beat him we did, beyond a question, and that with a heavy loss to his army--and out of New York we have driven him, beyond a question--but--I will not increase Beulah's conceit by stating any more!"

"If you can tell me anything kind of Evert, Bob, you will act like a brother in so doing," said the gentle wife.

"Ay, Beekman did well too, they said. I heard some of our officers extolling a charge he made; and to own the truth, I was not sorry to be able to say he was my sister's husband, since a fierce rebel she would marry. All our news of *him* is to his credit; and now I shall get a kiss for my pains."

The major was not mistaken. With a swelling heart, but smiling countenance, his sister threw herself into his arms, when she kissed and was kissed until the tears streamed down her cheeks.

"It was of Washington I intended to speak, sir," resumed the major, dashing a tear or two from his own eyes, as Beulah resumed her chair. "His retreat from the island is spoken of as masterly, and has gained him great credit. He conducted it in person, and did not lose a man. I heard Sir William mention it as masterly."

"Then by heaven, America will prevail in this contest!" exclaims I the captain, striking his fist upon the table, with a suddenness and force that caused all in the room to start. "If she has a general who can effect such a movement skilfully, the reign of England is over, here. Why, Woods, Xenophon never did a better thing! The retreat of the ten thousand was boy's play to getting across that water. Besides, your victory could have been no great matter, Bob, or it would never have been done."

"Our victory was respectable, sir, while I acknowledge that the retreat was great. No one among us denies it, and Washington is always named with respect in the army."

In a minute more, Big Smash came in, under the pretence of removing the dishes, but, in reality to see Master Bob, and to be noticed by him. She was a woman of sixty, the mother of Little Smash, herself a respectable matron of forty; and both had been born in the household of Mrs. Willoughby's father, and had rather more attachment for any one of her children than for all of their own, though each had been reasonably prolific. The *sobriquets* had passed into general use, and the real names of Bess and M*ari'* were nearly obsolete. Still, the major thought it polite to use the latter on the present occasion.

"Upon my word, Mrs. Bess," he said, shaking the old woman cordially by the hand, though he instinctively shrunk back from the sight of a pair of lips that were quite ultra, in the way of pouting, which used often to salute him twenty years before--"Upon my word, Mrs. Bess, you improve in beauty, everytime I see you. Old age and you seem to be total strangers to each other. How do you manage to remain so comely and so young?"

"God send 'e fus', Masser Bob, heabben be praise, and a good conscience do 'e las'. I *do* wish you could make ole Plin hear *dat*! He nebber t'ink any good look, now-a-day, in a ole wench."

"Pliny is half blind. But that is the way with most husbands, Smash; they become blind to the charms of their spouses, after a few years of matrimony."

"Nebber get marry, Masser Bob, if dat be 'e way."

Then Great Smash gave such a laugh, and such a swing of her unwieldy body, that one might well have apprehended her downfall. But, no such thing. She maintained the equilibrium; for, renowned as she had been all her life at producing havoc among plates, and cups, and bowls, she was never known to be thrown off her own centre of gravity. Another hearty shake of the hand followed, and the major quitted the table. As was usual on all great and joyous occasions in the family, when the emotions reached the kitchen, that evening was remarkable for a "smash," in which half the crockery that had just been brought from the table, fell an unresisting sacrifice. This produced a hot discussion between "The Big" and "The Little" as to the offender, which resulted, as so often happens, in these inquiries into the accidents of domestic life, in the conclusion that "nobody" was alone to blame.

"How 'e t'ink he *can* come back, and not a plate crack!" exclaimed Little Smash, in a vindicatory tone, she being the real delinquent--"Get in 'e winder, too! Lor! *dat* enough to break all 'e dish in 'e house, and in 'e mill, too! I *do* wish ebbery plate we got was an Injin--den you see fun! Can nebber like Injin; 'em so red, and so sabbage!"

"Nebber talk of Injin, now," answered the indignant mother--"better talk of plate. Dis make forty t'ousand dish you break, Mari', sin' you war' a young woman. S'pose you t'ink Masser made of plate, dat you break 'em up so! Dat what ole Plin say--de nigger! He say all men made of clay, and plate made of clay, too--well, bot' clay, and bot' *break*. All on us wessels, and all on us break to pieces some day, and den dey'll t'row *us* away, too."

A general laugh succeeded this touch of morality, Great Smash being a little addicted to ethical remarks of this nature; after which the war was renewed on the subject of the broken crockery. Nor did it soon cease; wrangling, laughing, singing, toiling, a light-heartedness that knew no serious cares, and affection, making up the sum of the everyday existence of these semi-civilized beings. The presence of the party in the valley, however, afforded the subject of an episode; for a negro has quite as much of the *de haut en bas* in his manner of viewing the aborigines, as the whites have in their speculations on his own race. Mingled with this contempt, notwithstanding, was a very active dread, neither of the Plinys, nor of their amiable consorts, in the least relishing the idea of being shorn of the wool, with shears as penetrating as the scalping-knife. After a good deal of discussion on this subject, the kitchen arrived at the conclusion that the visit of the major was ordered by Providence, since it was out of all the rules of probability and practice to have a few half-clad savages get the better of "Masser Bob," who was born a soldier, and had so recently been fighting for the king.

On the latter subject, we ought to have stated that the captain's kitchen was ultra-loyal. The rude, but simple beings it contained, had a reverence for rank and power that even a "rebbelushun" could not disturb, and which closely associated, in their minds, royal authority with divine power. Next to their own master, they considered George III, as the greatest man of the age; and there was no disposition in them to rob him of his rights or his honours.

"You seem thoughtful, Woods," said the captain, while his son had retired to his own room, in order to assume a disguise less likely to attract attention in the garrison than a hunting-shirt. "Is it this unexpected visit of Bob's that furnishes food for reflection?"

"Not so much his visit, my dear Willoughby, as the news he brings us. God knows what will befall the church, should this rebellion make serious head. The country is in a dreadful way, already, on the subject of religion; but it will be far worse if these 'canters' get the upper hand of the government."

The captain was silent and thoughtful for a moment; then he laughingly replied--

"Fear nothing for the church, chaplain. It is of God, and will outlast a hundred political revolutions."

"I don't know that, Willoughby--I don't know that"--The chaplain did not exactly mean what he said--"'Twouldn't surprise me if we had '*taking up collections,*' '*sitting under preaching,*' '*providentially happening,*' '*exercised in mind,*' and '*our Zion*' finding their way into dictionaries."

"Quite likely, Woods"--returned the captain, smiling--"Liberty is known to produce great changes in *things*; why not in language?"

"Liberty, indeed! Yes; '*liberty* in prayer' is another of their phrases. Well, captain Willoughby, if this rebellion should succeed, we may give up all hopes for the church. What sort of government shall we have, do you imagine, sir?"

"Republican, of course," answered the captain, again becoming thoughtful, as his mind reverted to the important results that were really dependent on the present state of things. "Republican--it *can* be no other. These colonies have always had a strong bias in that direction, and they want the elements necessary to a monarchy. New York has a landed gentry, it is true; and so has Maryland, and Virginia, and the Carolinas; but they are not strong enough to set up a political aristocracy, or to prop a throne; and then this gentry will probably be much weakened by the struggle. Half the principal families are known to be with the crown, as it is; and new men will force them out of place, in a revolution. No, Woods, if this revolution prosper, the monarchy is done in America, for at least a century."

"And the prayers for the king and royal family--what will become of *them*?"

"I should think they must cease, also. I question if a people will continue long to pray for authorities that they refuse to obey."

"I shall stick to the rubrics as long as I have a tongue in my head. I trust, Willoughby, *you* will not stop these prayers, in your settlement?"

"It is the last mode in which I should choose to show hostility. Still, you must allow it is a little too much to ask a congregation to pray that the king shall overcome his enemies, when they are among those very enemies? The question presents a dilemma."

"And, yet, I have never failed to read that prayer, as well as all the rest. You have not objected, hitherto."

"I have not, for I have considered the war as being waged with parliament and the ministers, whereas it is now clearly with the king. This paper is certainly a plain and forcible document."

"And what is that paper? Not the Westminster Confession of Faith, or the Saybrook Platform, I hope; one of which will certainly supersede the Thirty-nine Articles in all our churches, if this rebellion prosper."

"It is the manifesto issued by congress, to justify their declaration of independence. Bob has brought it with him, as a proof how far matters have been carried; but, really, it seems to be a creditable document, and is eloquently reasoned."

"I see how it is, Willoughby--I see how it is. We shall find you a rebel general yet; and I expect to live to hear *you* talk about 'our Zion' and 'providential accidents.'"

"Neither, Woods. For the first, I am too old; and, for the last, I have too much taste, I trust. Whether I shall always pray for the king is another matter. But, here is the major, ready for his sortie. Upon my word, his masquerade is so complete, I hardly know him myself."

Chapter XIV

He could not rest, he could not stay
Within his tent to wait for day;
But walked him forth along the sand,
Where thousand sleepers strewed the strand.

Siege of Corinth.

It was now so late that most of the men of the Hut, and all the women and children, were housed for the night, provided no alarm occurred. There was consequently little risk in the major's venturing forth, disguised as he was, should care be taken not to approach a light. The great number of the latter, streaming through the windows of the western wing of the building, showed how many were now collected within the walls, and gave an unusual appearance of life and animation to the place. Still, the court was clear, the men seeking their pallets, in readiness for their coming watches, while the women were occupied with those great concerns of female life, the care of children.

The captain, major, and chaplain, each carrying a rifle, and the two former pistols, moved rapidly across the court, and passed the gate. The moveable leaf of the latter was left unbarred, it being the orders of the captain to the sentinels without, on the approach of an enemy, to retire within the court, and then to secure the fastenings.

The night was star-light, and it was cool, as is common to this region of country. There being neither lamp nor candle on the exterior of the house, even the loops being darkened, there was little danger in moving about within the stockades. The sentinels were directed to take their posts so near the palisades as to command views of the open lawn without, a precaution that would effectually prevent the usual stealthy approach of an enemy without discovery. As the alarm had been very decided, these irregular guardians of the house were all at their posts, and exceedingly watchful, a circumstance that enabled the captain to avoid them, and thus further remove the danger of his son's being recognised. He accordingly held himself aloof from the men, keeping within the shadows of the sides of the Hut.

As a matter of course, the first object to which our two soldiers directed their eyes, was the rock above the mill. The Indians had lighted fires, and were now apparently bivouacked at no great distance from them, having brought boards from below with that especial object. Why they chose to remain in this precise position, and why they neglected the better accommodations afforded by some fifteen or twenty log-cabins, that skirted the western side of the valley in particular, were subjects of conjecture. That they were near the fires the board shanties proved, and that they were to the last degree careless of the proximity of the people of the place, would seem also to be apparent in the fact that they had not posted, so far as could be ascertained, even a solitary sentinel.

"This is altogether surprising for Indian tactics," observed the captain, in a low voice; for everything that was uttered that night without the building was said in very guarded tones. "I have never before known the savages to cover themselves in that manner; nor is it usual with them to light fires to point out the positions they occupy, as these fellows seem to have done."

"Is it not all *seeming*, sir?" returned the major. "To me that camp, if camp it can be called, has an air of being deserted."

"There is a look about it of premeditated preparation that one ought always to distrust in war."

"Is it not unmilitary, sir, for two soldiers like ourselves to remain in doubt on such a point? My professional pride revolts at such a state of things; and, with your leave, I will go outside, and set the matter at rest by reconnoitring."

"Professional pride is a good thing, Bob, rightly understood and rightly practised. But the highest point of honour with the really good soldier is to do that for which he was precisely intended. Some men fancy armies were got together just to maintain certain exaggerated notions of military honour; whereas, military honour is nothing but a moral expedient to aid in effecting the objects for which they are really raised. I have known men so blinded as to assert that a soldier is bound to maintain his honour at the expense of the law; and this in face of the fact that, in a free country, a soldier is in truth nothing but one of the props of the law, in the last resort. So with us; we are here to defend this house, and those it contains; and our military honour is far more concerned in doing that effectually, and by right means, than in running the risk of not doing it at all, in order to satisfy an abstract and untenable notion of a false code. Let us do what is *right*, my son, and feel no concern that our honour suffer."

Captain Willoughby said this, because he fancied it a fault in his son's character, sometimes to confound the end with the means, in appreciating the ethics of his profession. This is not an uncommon error among those who bear arms, instances not being wanting in which bodies of men that are the mere creatures of authority, have not hesitated to trample the power that brought them into existence under foot, rather than submit to mortify the feelings of a purely conventional and exaggerated pride. The major was rebuked rather than convinced, it not being the natural vocation of youth to perceive the justice of all the admonitions of age.

"But, if one can be made auxiliary to the other, sir," the son remarked, "then you will allow that professional *esprit*, and professional prudence, may very well march hand in hand."

"Of that there can be no doubt, though I think it far wiser and more soldier-like, even, to use all proper precautions to guard this house, under our actual circumstances, than to risk anything material in order to satisfy our doubts concerning the state of that camp."

"But the cabins, and all the property that lies exposed to fire and other accidents, including the mills? Is it not worth your while to let me make a little excursion, in order to ascertain the state of things, as connected with them?"

"Perhaps it would, Bob"--returned the father, after a little reflection. "It would be a great point gained, to send a man to look after the buildings, and the horses. The poor beasts may be suffering for water; and, as you say, the first thing will be to ascertain where our wild visiters really are, and what they are actually bent on. Woods, go with us to the gate, and let us out. I rely on your saying nothing of our absence, except to explain to the two nearest sentinels who we are, and to be on the look-out for us, against the moment we may return."

"Will it not be very hazardous to be moving in front of the stockade, in the dark? Some of our own people may fire upon you."

"You will tell them to be cautious, and we shall use great circumspection in our turn. I had better give you a signal by which we shall be known."

This was done, and the party moved from under the shadows of the Hut, down to the gate. Here the two soldiers halted for several minutes, taking a deliberate and as thorough a survey of the scene without, as the darkness permitted. Then the chaplain opened the gate, and they issued forth, moving with great caution down the lawn, towards the fleets. As a matter of course, captain Willoughby was perfectly familiar with all the lanes, ditches, bridges and fields of his beautiful possessions. The alluvial soil that lay spread around him was principally the result of ages of deposit while the place was covered with water; but, as the overflowing of the water had been produced by a regular dam, the latter once removed, the meadows were free, from the excessive moisture which generally saturates drained lands. Still, there were two or three large open ditches, to collect the water that came down the adjacent mountains or bubbled up from springs near the margin of the woods Across these ditches the roads led, by bridges, and the whole valley was laid out, in this manner, equally with a view to convenience and rural beauty. A knowledge of all the windings was of great use, on the present occasion, even on the advance; while, on the retreat, it might clearly be the means of preserving the lives, or liberties, of the two adventurers.

The captain did not proceed by the principal road which led from the Hut to the mills, the great thoroughfare of the valley, since it might be watched, in order to prevent a hostile sortie against the camp; but he inclined to the right, or to the westward, in order to visit the cabins and barns in that quarter. It struck him his invaders might have quietly taken possession of the houses, or even have stolen his horses and decamped. In this direction, then, he and his son proceeded, using the greatest caution in their movements, and occasionally stopping to examine the waning fires at the rock, or to throw a glance behind them at the stockade. Everything remained in the quiet which renders a forest settlement so solemn and imposing, after the daily movements of man have ceased. The deepest and most breathless attention could not catch an unaccustomed sound. Even the bark of a dog was not heard, all those useful animals having followed their masters into the Hut, as if conscious that their principal care now lay in that direction. Each of the sentinels had one of these animals near him, crouched under the stockade, in the expectation of their giving the alarm, should any strange footstep approach. In this manner most of the distance between the Knoll and the forest was crossed, when the major suddenly laid a hand on his father's arm.

"Here is something stirring on our left," whispered the former--"It seems, too, to be crouching under the fence."

"You have lost your familiarity with our rural life, Bob," answered the father, with a little more confidence of tone, but still guardedly, "or this fragrant breath would tell you we are almost on a cow. It is old Whiteback; I know her by her horns. Feel; she is here in the lane with us, and within reach of your hand. A gentler animal is not in the settlement. But, stop--pass your hand on her udder--she will not stir--how is it, full or not?"

"If I can judge, sir, it is nothing remarkable in the way of size."

"I understand this better. By Jupiter, boy, that cow has been milked! It is certain none of our people have left the house to do it, since the alarm was first given. This is ominous of neighbours."

The major made no reply, but he felt to ascertain if his arms were in a state for immediate service. After a moment's further pause the captain proceeded, moving with increased caution. Not a word was now uttered, for they were getting within the shadows of the orchard, and indeed of the forest, where objects could not well be distinguished at the distance of a very few yards. A cabin was soon reached, and it was found empty; the fire reduced to a few embers, and quite safe. This was the residence of the man who had the care of the horses, the stables standing directly behind it. Captain Willoughby was a thoughtful and humane man, and it struck him the animals might now be turned into a field that joined the barn-yard, where there was not only rich pasture, but plenty of sweet running water. This he determined to do at once, the only danger being from the unbridled movements of cattle that must be impatient from unusual privation, and a prolonged restraint.

The major opened the gate of the field, and stationed himself in a way to turn the animals in the desired direction, while his father went into the stable to set them free. The first horse came out with great deliberation, being an old animal well cooled with toil at the plough, and the major had merely to swing his arm, to turn him into the field. Not so with the next, however. This was little better than a colt, a creature in training for his master's saddle; and no sooner was it released than it plunged into the yard, then bounded into the field, around which it galloped, until it found the water. The others imitated this bad example; the clatter of hoofs, though beaten on a rich turf, soon resounding in the stillness of the night, until it might be heard across the valley. The captain then rejoined his son.

"This is a good deed somewhat clumsily done, Bob," observed the father, as he picked up his rifle and prepared to proceed. "An Indian ear, however, will not fail to distinguish between the tramping of horses and a charge of foot."

"Faith, sir, the noise may serve us a good turn yet. Let us take another look at the fires, and see if this tramping has set any one in motion near them. We can get a glimpse a little further ahead."

The look was taken, but nothing was seen. While standing perfectly motionless, beneath the shadows of an apple-tree, however, a sound was heard quite near them, which resembled that of a guarded footstep. Both gentlemen drew up, like sportsmen expecting the birds to rise, in waiting for the sound to approach. It did draw nearer, and presently a human form was seen moving slowly forward in the path, approaching the tree, as if to get within its cover. It was allowed to draw nearer and nearer, until captain

Willoughby laid his hand, from behind the trunk, on the stranger's shoulder, demanding sternly, but in a low voice, "who are you?"

The start, the exclamation, and the tremor that succeeded all denoted the extent of this man's surprise. It was some little time, even, before he could recover from his alarm, and then he let himself be known by his answer.

"Massy!" exclaimed Joel Strides, who ordinarily gave this doric sound to the word 'mercy'--"Massy, captain, is it *you!* I should as soon thought of seeing a ghost! What in natur' has brought you out of the stockade, sir?"

"I think that is a question I might better ask you, Mr. Strides. My orders were to keep the gate close, and for no one to quit the court-yard even, until sent on post, or called by an alarm."

"True, sir--quite true--true as gospel. But let us moderate a little, captain, and speak lower; for the Lord only knows who's in our neighbourhood. Who's that with you, sir?--Not the Rev. Mr. Woods, is it?"

"No matter who is with me. *He* has the authority of my commands for being here, whoever he may be, while you are here in opposition to them. You know me well enough, Joel, to understand nothing but the simple truth will satisfy me."

"Lord, sir, I am one of them that never wish to tell you anything *but* truth. The captain has known me now long enough to understand my natur', I should think; so no more need be said about *that.*"

"Well, sir--give me the reason--and see that it is given to me without reserve."

"Yes, sir; the captain shall have it. He knows we scrambled out of our houses this afternoon a little onthinkingly, Injin alarms being skeary matters. It was an awful hurrying time! Well, the captain understands, too, we don't work for him without receiving our wages; and I have been laying up a little, every year, until I've scraped together a few hundred dollars, in good half-joes; and I bethought me the money might be in danger, should the savages begin to plunder; and I've just came out to look a'ter the money."

"If this be true, as I hope and can easily believe to be the case, you must have the money about you, Joel, to prove it."

The man stretched forth his arm, and let the captain feel a handkerchief, in which, sure enough, there was a goodly quantity of coin. This gave him credit for truth, and removed all suspicion of his present excursion being made with any sinister intention. The man was questioned as to his mode of passing the stockade, when he confessed he had fairly clambered over it, an exploit of no great difficulty from the inside. As the captain had known

Joel too long to be ignorant of his love of money, and the offence was very pardonable in itself, he readily forgave the breach of orders. This was the only man in the valley who did not trust his little hoard in the iron chest at the Hut; even the miller reposing that much confidence in the proprietor of the estate; but Joel was too conscious of dishonest intentions himself to put any unnecessary faith in others.

All this time, the major kept so far aloof as not to be recognised, though Joel, once or twice, betrayed symptoms of a desire to ascertain who he was. Maud had awakened suspicions that now became active, in both father and son, when circumstances so unexpectedly and inconveniently threw the man in their way. It was consequently the wish of the former to get rid of his overseer as soon as possible. Previously to doing this, however, he saw fit to interrogate him a little further.

"Have you seen anything of the Indians since you left the stockade, Strides?" demanded the captain. "We can perceive no other traces of their presence than yonder fires, though we think that some of them must have passed this way, for Whiteback's udder is empty."

"To own the truth, captain, I haven't. I some think that they've left the valley; though the Lord only can tell when they'll be back ag'in. Such critturs be beyond calcilation! They outdo arithmetic, nohow. As for the cow, I milked her myself; for being the crittur the captain has given to Phoebe for her little dairy, I thought it might hurt her not to be attended to. The pail stands yonder, under the fence, and the women and children in the Hut may be glad enough to see it in the morning."

This was very characteristic of Joel Strides. He did not hesitate about disobeying orders, or even to risk his life, in order to secure his money; but, determined to come out, he had the forethought and care to bring a pail, in order to supply the wants of those who were now crowded within the stockade, and who were too much accustomed to this particular sort of food, not to suffer from its absence. If we add, that, in the midst of all this prudent attention to the wants of his companions, Joel had an eye to his personal popularity and what are called "ulterior events", and that he selected his own cow for the precise reason given, the reader has certain distinctive traits of the man before him.

"This being the case," returned the captain, a good deal relieved at finding that the savages had not been the agents in this milking affair, since it left the probability of their remaining stationary--"This being the case, Joel, you had better find the pail, and go in. As soon as day dawns, however, I recommend that all the cows be called up to the stockade and milked generally. They are feeding in the lanes, just now, and will come readily, if properly invited. Go, then, but say nothing of having met me, and--"

"Who else did the captain say?" inquired Joel, curiously, observing that the other paused.

"Say nothing of having met us at all, I tell you. It is very important that my movements should be secret."

The two gentlemen now moved on, intending to pass in front of the cabins which lined this part of the valley, by a lane which would bring them out at the general highway which led from the Knoll to the mill. The captain marched in front, while his son brought up the rear, at a distance of two or three paces. Each walked slowly and with caution, carrying his rifle in the hollow of his arm, in perfect readiness for service. In this manner both had proceeded a few yards, when Robert Willoughby felt his elbow touched, and saw Joel's face, within eighteen inches of his own, as the fellow peered under his hat. It was an action so sudden and unexpected, that the major saw, at once, nothing but perfect coolness could avert his discovery.

"Is't you, Dan'el"--so was the miller named. "What in natur' has brought the old man on this tramp, with the valley filled with Injins?" whispered Joel, prolonging the speech in order to get a better view of a face and form that still baffled his conjectures. "Let's know all about it."

"You'll get me into trouble," answered he major, shaking off his unwelcome neighbour, moving a step further from him, and speaking also in a whisper. "The captain's bent on a scout, and you know he'll not bear contradiction. Off with you, then, and don't forget the milk."

As the major moved away, and seemed determined to baffle him, Joel had no choice between complying and exposing his disobedience of orders to the captain. He disliked doing the last, for his cue was to seem respectful and attached, and he was fain to submit. Never before, however, did Joel Strides suffer a man to slip through his fingers with so much reluctance. He saw that the captain's companion was not the miller, while the disguise was too complete to enable him to distinguish the person or face. In that day, the different classes of society were strongly distinguished from each other, by their ordinary attire; and, accustomed to see major Willoughby only in the dress that belonged to his station, he would not be likely to recognise him in his present guise, had he even known of or suspected his visit. As it was, he was completely at fault; satisfied it was not his friend Daniel, while unable to say who it was.

In this doubting state of mind, Joel actually forgot the savages, and the risks he might run from their proximity. He walked, as it might be mechanically, to the place where he had left the pail, and then proceeded slowly towards the Knoll, pondering at every step on what he had just seen. He and the miller had secret communications with certain active agents of the revolutionists, that put them in possession of facts, notwithstanding their isolated position, with which even their employer was totally unacquainted. It is true, these agents were of that low caste that never fail to attach themselves to all great political enterprises, with a sole view to their own benefit; still, as they were active, cunning and bold, and had the sagacity to make themselves useful, they passed in the throng of patriots created by the times, and were enabled to impart to men of similar spirits much available information.

It was through means like these, that Joel knew of the all-important measure of the declaration of independence, while it still remained a secret to captain Willoughby. The hope of confiscations was now active in the bosoms of all this set, and many of them had even selected the portions of property that they intended should be the reward of their own love of freedom and patriotism. It has been said that the English ministry precipitated the American revolution, with a view to share, among their favourites, the estates that it was thought it would bring within the gift of the crown, a motive so heinous as almost to defy credulity, and which may certainly admit of rational doubts. On the other hand, however, it is certain that individuals, who will go down to posterity in company with the many justly illustrious names that the events of 1776 have committed to history, were actuated by the most selfish inducements, and, in divers instances, enriched themselves with the wrecks of estates that formerly belonged to their kinsmen or friends. Joel Strides was of too low a class to get his name enrolled very high on the list of heroes, nor was he at all ambitious of any such distinction; but he was not so low that he could not and did not aspire to become the owner of the property of the Hutted Knoll. In an ordinary state of society, so high a flight would seem irrational in so low an aspirant; but Joel came of a people who seldom measure their pretensions by their merits, and who imagine that to boldly aspire, more especially in the way of money, is the first great step to success. The much talked of and little understood doctrine of political equality has this error to answer for, in thousands of cases; for nothing can be more hopeless, in the nature of things, than to convince a man of the necessity of possessing qualities of whose existence he has not even a faint perception, ere he may justly pretend to be put on a level with the high-minded, the just, the educated, and the good. Joel, therefore, saw no other reason than the law, against his becoming the great landlord, as well as captain Willoughby; and could the law be so moulded as to answer his purposes, he had discreetly resolved to care for no other considerations. The thought of the consequences to Mrs. Willoughby and her daughters gave him no concern whatever; they had already possessed the advantages of their situation so long, as to give Phoebe and the miller's wife a sort of moral claim to succeed them. In a word, Joel, in his yearnings after wealth, had only faintly shadowed forth the modern favourite doctrine of "rotation in office."

The appearance of a stranger in company with captain Willoughby could not fail, therefore, to give rise to many conjectures in the mind of a man whose daily and hourly thoughts were running on these important changes. "Who *can* it be," thought Joel, as he crawled along the lane, bearing the milk, and lifting one leg after the other, as if lead were fastened to his feet. "Dan'el it is not--nor is it any one that I can consait on, about the Hut. The captain is mightily strengthened by this marriage of his da'ter with colonel Beekman, that's sartain. The colonel stands wonderful well with our folks, and he 'll not let all this first-rate land, with such capital betterments, go out of the family without an iffort, I conclude--but then I calciate on *his* being killed--there must be a disperate lot on 'em shot, afore the war's over, and *he* is as likely to be among 'em as another. Dan'el thinks the colonel has the look of a short-lived man. Waal; to-morrow will bring about a knowledge of the name of the captain's companion, and then a body may calciate with greater sartainty!"

This is but an outline of what passed through Joel's mind as he moved onward. It will serve, however, to let the reader into the secret of his thoughts, as well as into their ordinary train, and is essentially connected with some of the succeeding events of our legend. As the overseer approached the stockade, his ideas were so abstracted that he forgot the risk he ran; but walking carelessly towards the palisades, the dogs barked, and then he was saluted by a shot. This effectually aroused Joel, who called out in his natural voice, and probably saved his life by so doing. The report of the rifle, however, produced an alarm, and by the time the astounded overseer had staggered up to the gate, the men were pouring out from the court, armed, and expecting an assault. In the midst of this scene of confusion, the chaplain admitted Joel, as much astonished as the man himself, at the whole of the unexpected occurrence.

It is unnecessary to say that many questions were asked. Joel got rid of them, by simply stating that he had gone out to milk a cow, by the captain's private orders, and that he had forgotten to arrange any signal, by which his return might be known. He ventured to name his employer, because he knew he was not there to contradict him; and Mr. Woods, being anxious to ascertain if his two friends had been seen, sent the men back to their lairs, without delay, detaining the overseer at the gate for a minute's private discourse. As the miller obeyed, with the rest, he asked for the pail with an eye to his own children's comfort; but, on receiving it, he found it empty! The bullet had passed through it, and the contents had escaped.

"Did you see any *thing, or person*, Strides?" demanded the chaplain, as soon as the two were alone.

"Lord, Mr. Woods, I met the captain!--The sight on him came over me a'most as cruelly as the shot from the rifle; for I no more expected it than I do to see you rise up to heaven, in your clothes, like Elijah of old. Sure enough, *there* was the captain, himself, and--and--"

Here Joel sneezed, repeating the word "and" several times, in hopes the chaplain would supply the name he so much wished to hear.

"But you saw no savages?--I know the captain is out, and you will be careful not to mention it, lest it get to Mrs. Willoughby's ears, and make her uneasy. You saw nothing of the savages?"

"Not a bit--the critturs lie cluss enough, if they haven't actually tramped. *Who* did you say was with the captain, Mr. Woods?"

"I said nothing about it--I merely asked after the Indians, who, as you say, do keep themselves very close. Well, Joel, go to your wife, who must be getting anxious about you, and be prudent."

Thus dismissed, the overseer did not dare to hesitate; but he entered the court, still pondering on the late meeting.

As for the two adventurers, they pursued their march in silence. As a matter of course, they heard the report of the rifle, and caught some faint sounds from the alarm that succeeded; but, readily comprehending the cause, they produced no uneasiness; the stillness which succeeded soon satisfying them that all was right. By this time they were within a hundred yards of the flickering fires. The major had kept a strict watch on the shanties at the report of the rifle; but not a living thing was seen moving in their vicinity. This induced him to think the place deserted, and he whispered as much to his father.

"With any other enemy than an Indian", answered the latter, "you might be right enough, Bob; but with these rascals one is never certain. We must advance with a good deal of their own caution."

This was done, and the gentlemen approached the fires in the most guarded manner, keeping the shantees between them and the light. By this time, however, the flames were nearly out, and there was no great difficulty in looking into the nearest shantee, without much exposure. It was deserted, as proved to be the case with all the others, on further examination. Major

Willoughby now moved about on the rock with greater confidence; for, naturally brave, and accustomed to use his faculties with self-command in moments of trial, he drew the just distinctions between real danger and unnecessary alarm; the truest of all tests of courage.

The captain, feeling a husband's and a father's responsibility, was a little more guarded; but success soon gave him more confidence, and the spot was thoroughly explored. The two then descended to the mills, which, together with the adjacent cabins, they entered also, and found uninjured and empty. After this, several other suspected points were looked at, until the captain came to the conclusion that the party had retired, for the night at least, if not entirely. Making a circuit, however, he and his son visited the chapel, and one or two dwellings on that side of the valley, when they bent their steps towards the Knoll.

As the gentlemen approached the stockade, the captain gave a loud hem, and clapped his hands. At the signal the gate flew open, and they found themselves in company with their friend the chaplain once more. A few words of explanation told all they had to say, and then the three passed into the court, and separated; each taking the direction towards his own room. The major, fatigued with the toils of a long march, was soon in a soldier's sleep; but it was hours before his more thoughtful, and still uneasy father, could obtain the rest which nature so much requires.

Chapter XV

----"I could teach you,
How to choose right, but then I am forsworn;
So will I never be; so may you miss me;
But if you do, you'll make me wish a sin
That I had been forsworn."----

Portia.

Captain Willoughby knew that the hour which preceded the return of light, was that in which the soldier had the most to apprehend, when in the field. This is the moment when it is usual to attempt surprises; and it was, in particular, the Indian's hour of blood. Orders had been left, accordingly, to call him at four o'clock, and to see that all the men of the Hut were afoot, and armed also. Notwithstanding the deserted appearance of the valley, this experienced frontier warrior distrusted the signs of the times; and he looked forward to the probability of an assault, a little before the return of day, with a degree of concern he would have been sorry to communicate to his wife and daughters.

Every emergency had been foreseen, and such a disposition made of the forces, as enabled the major to be useful, in the event of an attack, without exposing himself unnecessarily to the danger of being discovered. He was to have charge of the defence of the rear of the Hut, or that part of the buildings where the windows opened outwards; and Michael and the two Plinys were assigned him as assistants. Nor was the ward altogether a useless one. Though the cliff afforded a material safeguard to this portion of the defences, it might be scaled; and, it will be remembered, there was no stockade at all, on this, the northern end of the house.

When the men assembled in the court, therefore, about an hour before the dawn, Robert Willoughby collected his small force in the dining-room, the outer apartment of the *suite*, where he examined their arms by lamp-light, inspected their accoutrements, and directed them to remain until he issued fresh orders. His father, aided by serjeant Joyce, did the same in the court; issuing out, through the gate of the buildings, with his whole force, as soon as this duty was performed. The call being general, the women and children were all up also; many of the former repairing to the loops, while the least resolute, or the less experienced of their number, administered to the wants of the young, or busied themselves with the concerns of the household. In a word, the Hut, at that early hour, resembled a hive in activity, though the different pursuits had not much affinity to the collection of honey.

It is not to be supposed that Mrs. Willoughby and her daughters still courted their pillows on an occasion like this. They rose with the others, the grandmother and Beulah bestowing their first care on the little Evert, as if *his* life and safety were the considerations uppermost in their thoughts. This seemed so natural, that Maud wondered she too could not feel all this absorbing interest in the child, a being so totally dependent on the affection of its friends and relatives to provide for its wants and hazards, in an emergency like the present.

"*We* will see to the child, Maud," observed her mother, ten or fifteen minutes after all were up and dressed. "Do you go to your brother, who will be solitary, alone in his citadel. He may wish, too, to send some message to his father. Go, then, dear girl, and help to keep up poor Bob's spirits."

What a service for Maud! Still, she went, without hesitation or delay; for the habits of her whole infancy were not to be totally overcome by the natural and more engrossing sentiments of her later years. She could not feel precisely the reserve and self-distrust with one she had so long regarded as a brother, as might have been the case with a stranger youth in whom she had begun to feel the interest she entertained for Robert Willoughby. But, Maud did not hesitate about complying. An order from her mother to her was law; and she had no shame, no reserves on the subject of contributing to Bob's comfort or happiness.

Her presence was a great relief to the young man himself, whom she found in the library. His assistants were posted without, as sentinels to keep off intruders, a disposition that left him quite alone, anxious and uneasy. The only intercourse he could have with his father was by means of messages; and the part of the building he occupied was absolutely without any communication with the court, except by a single door near the offices, at which he had stationed O'Hearn.

"This is kind, and like yourself, dearest Maud," exclaimed the young man, taking the hand of his visiter, and pressing it in both his own, though he strangely neglected to kiss her cheek, as he certainly would have done had it been Beulah--"This is kind and like yourself; now I shall learn something of the state of the family. How is my mother?"

It might have been native coyness, or even coquetry, that unconsciously to herself influenced Maud's answer. She knew not why--and yet she felt prompted to let it be understood she had not come of her own impulses.

"Mother is well, and not at all alarmed," she said. "She and Beulah are busy with little Evert, who crows and kicks his heels about as if *he* despised danger as becomes a soldier's son, and has much amused even *me*; though I am accused of insensibility to his perfections. Believing you might be solitary, or might wish to communicate with some of us, my mother desired me to come and inquire into your wants."

"Was such a bidding required, Maud! How long has an order been necessary to bring *you* to console *me*?"

"That is a calculation I have never entered into, Bob," answered Maud, slightly blushing, and openly smiling, and that in a way, too, to take all the sting out of her words--"as young ladies can have more suitable occupations, one might think. You will admit I guided you faithfully and skilfully into the Hut last evening, and such a service should suffice for the present. But, my mother tells me we have proper causes of complaint against you, for having so thoughtlessly left the place of safety into which you were brought, and for going strolling about the valley, after we had retired, in a very heedless and boyish manner!"

"I went with my father; surely I could not have been in better company."

"At his suggestion, or at your own, Bob?" asked Maud, shaking her head.

"To own the truth, it was, in some degree, at my own. It seemed so very unmilitary for two old soldiers to allow themselves to be shut up in ignorance of what their enemies were at, that I could not resist the desire to make a little *sortie*. You must feel, dear Maud, that our motive was *your* safety--the safety, I mean, of my mother, and Beulah, and nil of you together--and you ought to be the last to blame us."

The tint on Maud's cheek deepened as Robert Willoughby laid so heavy an emphasis on "*your* safety;" but she could not smile on an act that risked so much more than was prudent.

"This is well enough as to motive," she said, after a pause; "but frightfully ill-judged, I should think, as to the risks. You do not remember the importance our dear father is to us all--to my mother--to Beulah--even to me, Bob."

"Even to *you*, Maud!--And why not as much to *you* as to any of us?"

Maud could speak to Beulah of her want of natural affinity to the family; but, it far exceeded her self-command to make a direct allusion to it to Robert Willoughby. Still, it was now rarely absent from her mind; the love she bore the captain and his wife, and Beulah, and little Evert, coming to her heart through a more insidious and possibly tenderer tie, than that of purely filial or sisterly affection. It was, indeed, this every-day regard, strangely deepened and enlivened by that collateral feeling we so freely bestow on them who are bound by natural ties to those who have the strongest holds on our hearts, and which causes us to see with their eyes, and to feel with their affections. Accordingly, no reply was made to the question; or, rather, it was answered by putting another.

"Did you see anything, after all, to compensate for so much risk?" asked Maud, but not until a pause had betrayed her embarrassment.

"We ascertained that the savages had deserted their fires, and had not entered any of the cabins. Whether this were done to mislead us, or to make a retreat as sudden and unexpected as their inroad, we are altogether in the dark. My father apprehends treachery, however; while, I confess, to me it seems probable that the arrival and the departure may be altogether matters of accident. The Indians are in motion certainly, for it is known that our agents are busy among them; but, it is by no means so clear that *our* Indians would molest captain Willoughby--Sir Hugh Willoughby, as my father is altogether called, at head-quarters."

"Have not the Americans savages on their side, to do us this ill office?"

"I think not. It is the interest of the rebels to keep the savages out of the struggle; they have so much at risk, that this species of warfare can scarcely be to *their* liking."

"And ought it to be to the liking of the king's generals, or ministers either, Bob!"

"Perhaps not, Maud. I do not defend it; but I have seen enough of politics and war, to know that results are looked to, far more than principles. Honour, and chivalry, and humanity, and virtue, and right, are freely used in terms; but seldom do they produce much influence on facts. Victory is the end aimed at, and the means are made to vary with the object."

"And where is all we have read together?--Yes, *together*, Bob? for I owe you a great deal for having directed my studies--where is all we have read about the glory and truth of the English name and cause?"

"Very much, I fear, Maud, where the glory and truth of the American name and cause will be, as soon as this new nation shall fairly burst the shell, and hatch its public morality. There are men among us who believe in this public honesty, but I do not."

"You are then engaged in a bad cause, major Willoughby, and the sooner you abandon it, the better."

"I would in a minute, if I knew where to find a better. Rely on it, dearest Maud, all causes are alike, in this particular; though one side may employ instruments, as in the case of the savages, that the other side finds it its interest to decry. Men, as individuals, *may* be, and sometimes *are*, reasonably upright--but, *bodies* of men, I much fear, never. The latter escape responsibility by dividing it."

"Still, a good cause may elevate even bodies of men," said Maud, thoughtfully.

"For a time, perhaps; but not in emergencies. You and I think it a good cause, my good and frowning Maud, to defend the rights of our sovereign lord the king. Beulah I have given up to the enemy; but on you I have implicitly replied."

"Beulah follows her heart, perhaps, as they say it is natural to women to do. As for myself, I am left free to follow my own opinion of my duties."

"And they lead you to espouse the cause of the king, Maud!"

"They will be very apt to be influenced by the notions of a certain captain Willoughby, and Wilhelmina, his wife, who have guided me aright on so many occasions, that I shall not easily distrust their opinions on this."

The major disliked this answer; and yet, when he came to reflect on it, as reflect he did a good deal in the course of the day, he was dissatisfied with himself at being so unreasonable as to expect a girl of twenty-one not to think with her parents, real or presumed, in most matters. At the moment, however, he did not wish further to press the point.

"I am glad to learn, Bob," resumed Maud, looking more cheerful and smiling, "that you met with no one in your rash sortie--for rash I shall call it, even though sanctioned by my father."

"I am wrong in saying that. We did meet with one man, and that was no less a person than your bug-bear, Joel Strides--as innocent, though as meddling an overseer as one could wish to employ."

"Robert Willoughby, what mean you! Does this man know of your presence at the Knoll?"

"I should hope not--*think* not." Here the major explained all that is known to the reader on this head, when he continued--"The fellow's curiosity brought his face within a few inches of mine; yet I do not believe he recognised me. This disguise is pretty thorough; and what between his ignorance, the darkness and the dress, I must believe he was foiled."

"Heaven be praised!" exclaimed Maud, breathing more freely. "I have long distrusted that man, though he seems to possess the confidence of every one else. Neither my father nor my mother will see him, as I see him; yet to me his design to injure you is *so* clear--*so* obvious!--I wonder, often wonder, that others cannot view it as I do. Even Beulah is blind!"

"And what do you see so clearly, Maud? I have consented to keep myself incog. in submission to your earnest request; and yet, to own the truth, I can discover no particular reason why Strides is to be distrusted more than any one else in the valley--than Mike, for instance."

"Mike! I would answer for *his* truth with my life. *He* will never betray you, Bob."

"But why is Joel so much the object of your distrust?--and why am *I* the particular subject of your apprehensions?"

Maud felt the tell-tale blood flowing again to her cheeks; since, to give a simple and clear reason for her distrust, exceeded her power. It was nothing but the keen interest which she took in Robert Willoughby's safety that had betrayed to her the truth; and, as usually happens, when anxiety leads the way in discoveries of this sort, logical and plausible inferences are not always at command. Still, Maud not only thought herself right, but, in the main, she *was* right; and this she felt so strongly as to be enabled to induce others to act on her impressions.

"*Why* I believe in Strides' sinister views is more than I may be able to explain to you, in words, Bob," she replied, after a moment's thought; "still, I *do* believe in them as firmly as I believe in my existence. His looks, his questions, his journeys, and an occasional remark, have all aided in influencing the belief; nevertheless, no one proof may be perfectly clear and satisfactory. Why *you* should be the subject of his plans, however, is simple enough, since you are the only one among us he can seriously injure. By betraying you, he might gain some great advantage to himself."

"To whom can he betray me, dear? My father is the only person here, in any authority, and of him I have no cause to be afraid."

"Yet, you were so far alarmed when last here, as to change your route back to Boston. If there were cause for apprehension then, the same reason may now exist."

"That was when many strangers were in the valley, and we knew not exactly where we stood. I have submitted to your wishes, however, Maud, and shall lie *perdu*, until there is a serious alarm; then it is understood I am to be permitted to show myself. In a moment of emergency my unexpected appearance among the men might have a dramatic effect, and, of itself, give us a victory. But tell me of my prospects--am I likely to succeed with my father? Will he be brought over to the royal cause?"

"I think not. All common inducements are lost on him. His baronetcy, for instance, he will never assume; *that*, therefore, cannot entice him. Then his feelings are with his adopted country, which he thinks right, and which he is much disposed to maintain; more particularly since Beulah's marriage, and our late intercourse with all that set. My mother's family, too, has much influence with him. They, you know, are all whigs."

"Don't prostitute the name, Maud. Whig does not mean rebel; these misguided men are neither more nor less than rebels. I had thought this declaration of independence would have brought my father at once to our side."

"I can see it has disturbed him, as did the Battle of Bunker's Hill. But he will reflect a few days, and decide now, as he did then, in favour of the Americans. He has English partialities, Bob, as is natural to one born in that country; but, on this point, his mind is very strongly American."

"The accursed Knoll has done this! Had he lived in society, as he ought to have done, among his equals and the educated, we should now see him at the head--Maud, I know I can confide in *you*."

Maud was pleased at this expression of confidence, and she looked up in the major's face, her full blue eyes expressing no small portion of the heartfelt satisfaction she experienced. Still, she said nothing.

"You may well imagine," the major continued, "that I have not made this journey entirely without an object--I mean some object more important, even, than to see you all. The commander-in-chief is empowered to raise several regiments in this country, and it is thought useful to put men of influence in the colonies at their head. Old Noll de Lancey, for instance, so well known to us all, is to have a brigade; and I have a letter in my pocket offering to Sir Hugh Willoughby one of his regiments. One of the Allens of Pennsylvania, who was actually serving against us, has thrown up his commission from congress, since this wicked declaration, and has consented to take a battalion from the king. What think you of all this? Will it not have weight with my father?"

"It may cause him to reflect, Bob; but it will not induce him to change his mind. It may suit Mr. Oliver de Lancey to be a general, for he has been a soldier his whole life; but my father has retired, and given up all thoughts of service. He tells us he never liked it, and has been happier here at the Knoll, than when he got his first commission. Mr. Allen's change of opinion may be well enough, he will say, but I have no need of change; I am here, with my wife and daughters, and have them to care for, in these troubled times. What think you he said, Bob, in one of his conversations with us, on this very subject?"

"I am sure I cannot imagine--though I rather fear it was some wretched political stuff of the day."

"So far from this, it was good natural feeling that belongs, or ought to belong to all days, and all ages," answered Maud, her voice trembling a little as she proceeded. "'There is my son,' he said; 'one soldier is enough in a family like this. *He* keeps all our hearts anxious, and may cause them all to mourn.'"

Major Willoughby was mute for quite a minute, looking rebuked and thoughtful.

"I fear I do cause my parents concern," he at length answered; "and why should I endeavour to increase that of my excellent mother, by persuading her husband to return to the profession? If this were ordinary service, I could not think of it. I do not know that I ought to think of it, as it is!"

"Do not, dear Robert. We are all--that is, mother is often miserable on your account; and why would you increase her sorrows? Remember that to tremble for one life is sufficient for a woman."

"My mother is miserable on *my* account!" answered the young man, who was thinking of anything but his father, at that instant. "Does Beulah never express concern for me? or have her new ties completely driven her brother from her recollection? I know she can scarce wish me success; but she might still feel some uneasiness for an only brother. We are but two--"

Maud started, as if some frightful object glared before her eyes; then she sat in breathless silence, resolute to hear what would come next. But Robert Willoughby meant to pursue that idea no farther. He had so accustomed himself--had endeavoured even so to accustom himself to think of Beulah as his only sister, that the words escaped him unconsciously. They were no sooner uttered, however, than the recollection of their possible effect on Maud crossed his mind. Profoundly ignorant of the true nature of her feelings towards himself, he had ever shrunk from a direct avowal of his own sentiments, lest he might shock her; as a sister's ear would naturally be wounded by a declaration of attachment from a brother; and there were bitter moments when he fancied delicacy and honour would oblige him to carry his secret with him to the grave. Two minutes of frank communication might have dissipated all these scruples for ever; but, how to obtain those minutes, or how to enter on the subject at all, were obstacles that often appeared insurmountable to the young man. As for Maud, she but imperfectly understood her own heart--true, she had conscious glimpses of its real state; but, it was through those sudden and ungovernable impulses that were so strangely mingled with her affections. It was years, indeed, since she had ceased to think of Robert Willoughby as a brother, and had begun to view him with different eyes; still, she struggled with her feelings, as against a weakness. The captain and his wife were her parents; Beulah her dearly, dearly beloved sister; little Evert her nephew; and even the collaterals, in and about Albany, came in for a due share of her regard; while Bob, though called Bob as before; though treated with a large portion of the confidence that was natural to the intimacy of her childhood; though loved with a tenderness he would have given even his high-prized commission to know, was no longer thought of as a brother. Often did Maud find herself thinking, if never saying, "Beulah may do that, for Beulah is his sister; but it would be wrong in me. I may write to him, talk freely and even confidentially with him, and be affectionate to him; all this is right, and I should be the most ungrateful creature on earth to act differently; but I cannot sit on his knee as Beulah sometimes does; I cannot throw my arms around his neck when I kiss him, as Beulah does; I cannot pat his cheek, as Beulah does, when he says anything to laugh at; nor can I pry into his secrets, as Beulah does, or affects to do, to tease him. I should be more reserved with one who has not a drop of my blood in his veins--no, not a single drop." In this way, indeed, Maud was rather fond of disclaiming any consanguinity with the family of Willoughby, even while she honoured and loved its two heads, as parents. The long pause that succeeded the major's broken sentence was only interrupted by himself.

"It is vexatious to be shut up here, in the dark, Maud," he said, "when every minute *may* bring an attack. This side of the house might be defended by you and Beulah, aided and enlightened by the arm and counsels of that young 'son of liberty,' little Evert; whereas the stockade in front may really need the presence of men who have some knowledge of the noble art. I wish there were a look-out to the front, that one might at least see the danger as it approached."

"If your presence is not indispensable here, I can lead you to my painting-room, where there is a loop directly opposite to the gate. That half of the garrets has no one in it."

The major accepted the proposal with joy, and forthwith he proceeded to issue a few necessary orders to his subordinates, before he followed Maud. When all was ready, the latter led the way, carrying a small silver lamp that she had brought with her on entering the library. The reader already understands that the Hut was built around a court, the portion of the building in the rear, or on the cliff, alone having windows that opened outward. This was as true of the roofs as of the perpendicular parts of the structure, the only exceptions being in the loops that had been cut in the half-story, beneath the eaves. Of course, the garrets were very extensive. They were occupied in part, however, by small rooms, with dormer-windows, the latter of which opened on the court, with the exception of those above the cliff. It was on the roofs of these windows that captain Willoughby had laid his platform, or walk, with a view to extinguish fires, or to defend the place. There were many rooms also that were lighted only by the loops, and which, of course, were on the outer side of the buildings. In addition to these arrangements, the garret portions of the Hut were divided into two great parts, like the lower floor, without any doors of communication. Thus, below, the apartments commenced at the gateway, and extended along one-half the front; the whole of the east wing, and the whole of the rear, occupying five-eighths of the entire structure. This part contained all the rooms occupied by the family and the offices. The corresponding three-eighths, or the remaining half of the front, and the whole of the west wing, were given to visiters, and were now in possession of the people of the valley; as were all the rooms and garrets above them. On the other hand, captain Willoughby, with a view to keep his family to itself, had excluded every one, but the usual inmates, from his own portion of the house, garret-rooms included.

Some of the garret-rooms, particularly those over the library, drawing-room, and parlour, were convenient and well-furnished little apartments, enjoying dormer-windows that opened on the meadows and forest, and possessing a very tolerable elevation, for rooms of that particular construction. Here Mr. Woods lodged and had his study. The access was by a convenient flight of steps, placed in the vestibule that communicated with the court. A private and narrower flight also ascended from the offices.

Maud now led the way up the principal stairs, Mike being on post at the outer door to keep off impertinent eyes, followed by Robert Willoughby. Unlike most American houses, the Hut had few passages on its principal floor; the rooms communicating *en suite*, as a better arrangement where the buildings were so long, and yet so narrow. Above, however, one side was left in open garret; sometimes in front and sometimes in the rear, as the light came from the court, or from without. Into this garret, then, Maud conducted the major, passing a line of humble rooms on her right, which belonged to the families of the Plinys and the Smashes, with their connections, until she reached the front range of the buildings. Here the order was changed along the half of the structure reserved to the use of the family; the rooms being on the outer side lighted merely by the loops, while opposite to them was an open garret with windows that overlooked the court.

Passing into the garret just mentioned, Maud soon reached the door of the little room she sought. It was an apartment she had selected for painting, on account of the light from the loop, which in the morning was particularly favourable, though somewhat low. As she usually sat on a little stool, however, this difficulty was in some measure obviated; and, at all events, the place was made to answer her purposes. She kept the key herself, and the room, since Beulah's marriage in particular, was her sanctum; no one entering it unless conducted by its mistress. Occasionally, Little Smash was admitted with a broom; though Maud, for reasons known to herself, often preferred sweeping the small carpet that covered the centre of the floor, with her own fair hands, in preference to suffering another to intrude.

The major was aware that Maud had used this room for the last seven years. It was here he had seen her handkerchief waving at the loop, when he last departed; and hundreds of times since had he thought of this act of watchful affection, with doubts that led equally to pain or pleasure, as images of merely sisterly care, or of a tenderer feeling, obtruded themselves. These loops were four feet long, cut in the usual bevelling manner, through the massive timbers; were glazed, and had thick, bullet-proof, inside shutters, that in this room were divided in equal parts, in order to give Maud the proper use of the light she wanted. All these shutters were now closed by command of the captain, in order to conceal the lights that would be flickering through the different garrets; and so far had caution become a habit, that Maud seldom exposed her person at night, near the loop, with the shutter open.

On the present occasion, she left the light without, and threw open the upper-half of her heavy shutter, remarking as she did so, that the day was just beginning to dawn.

"In a few minutes it will be light," she added; "then we shall be able to see who is and who is not in the valley. Look--you can perceive my father near the gate, at this moment."

"I do, to my shame, Maud. He should not be there, I am cooped up here, behind timbers that are almost shot-proof."

"It will be time for you to go to the front, as you soldiers call it, when there is an enemy to face. You cannot think there is any danger of an attack upon the Hut this morning."

"Certainty not. It is now too late. If intended at all, it would have been made before that streak of light appeared in the east."

"Then close the shutter, and I will bring in the lamp, and show you some of my sketches. We artists are thirsting always for praise; and I know you have a taste, Bob, that one might dread."

"This is kind of you, dear Maud," answered the major, closing the shutter; "for they tell me you are niggardly of bestowing such favours. I hear you have got to likenesses--little Evert's, in particular."

Chapter XVI

Anxious, she hovers o'er the web the while,
Reads, as it grows, thy figured story there;
Now she explains the texture with a smile,
And now the woof interprets with a tear.

Fawcett.

All Maud's feelings were healthful and natural. She had no exaggerated sentiments, and scarcely art enough to control or to conceal any of the ordinary impulses of her heart. We are not about to relate a scene, therefore, in which a long-cherished but hidden miniature of the young man is to play a conspicuous part, and to be the means of revealing to two lovers the state of their respective hearts; but one of a very different character. It is true, Maud had endeavoured to make, from memory, one or two sketches of "Bob's" face; but she had done it openly, and under the cognizance of the whole family. This she might very well do, indeed, in her usual character of a sister, and excite no comments. In these efforts, her father and mother, and Beulah, had uniformly pronounced her success to be far beyond their hopes; but Maud, herself, had thrown them all aside, half-finished, dissatisfied with her own labours. Like the author, whose fertile imagination fancies pictures that defy his powers of description, her pencil ever fell far short of the face that her memory kept so constantly in view. This sketch wanted animation, that gentleness, another fire, and a fourth candour; in short, had Maud begun a thousand all would have been deficient, in her eyes, in some great essential of perfection. Still, she had no secret about her efforts, and half-a-dozen of these very sketches lay uppermost in her portfolio, when she spread it, and its contents, before the eyes of the original.

Major Willoughby thought Maud had never appeared more beautiful than as she moved about making her little preparations for the exhibition. Pleasure heightened her colour; and there was such a mixture of frank, sisterly regard, in every glance of her eye, blended, however, with sensitive feeling, and conscious womanly reserve, as made her a thousand times-- measuring amounts by the young man's sensations--more interesting than he had ever seen her. The lamp gave but an indifferent light for a gallery, but it was sufficient to betray Maud's smiles, and blushes, and each varying emotion of her charming countenance.

"Now, Bob," she said, opening her portfolio, with all her youthful frankness and confidence, "you know well enough I am not one of those old masters of whom you used to talk so much, but your own pupil--the work of your own hands; and if you find more faults than you have expected, you will have the goodness to remember that the master has deserted his peaceful pursuits to go a campaigning--there--that is a caricature of your own countenance, staring you in the face, as a preface!"

"This is like, I should think--was it done from memory, dear Maud?"

"How else should it be done? All our entreaties have never been able to persuade you to send us even a miniature. You are wrong in this, Bob"--by no accident did Maud now ever call the major, Robert, though Beulah often did. There was a desperate sort of familiarity in the *Bob*, that she could easily adopt; but the 'Robert' had a family sound that she disliked; and yet a more truly feminine creature than Maud Meredith did not exist--"You are wrong, Bob; for mother actually pines to possess your picture, in some shape or other. It was this wish that induced me to attempt these things."

"And why has no one of them ever been finished?--Here are six or eight beginnings, and all, more or less, like, I should think, and not one of them more than half done. Why have I been treated so cavalierly, Miss Maud?"

The fair artist's colour deepened a little; but her smile was quite as sweet as it was saucy, as she replied--

"Girlish caprice, I suppose. I like neither of them; and of that which a woman dislikes, she will have none. To be candid, however, I hardly think there is one of them all that does you justice."

"No?--what fault have you to find with this? This might be worked up to something very natural."

"It would be *a* natural, then--it wants expression, fearfully."

"And this, which is still better. That might be finished while I am here, and I will give you some sittings."

"Even mother dislikes *that*--there is too much of the Major of Foot in it. Mr. Woods says it is a martial picture."

"And ought not a soldier to look like a soldier? To me, now, that seems a capital beginning."

"It is not what mother, or Beulah--or father--or even any of us wants. It is too full of Bunker's Hill. Your friends desire to see you as you appear to *them*; not as you appear to your enemies."

"Upon my word, Maud, you have made great advances in the art! This is a view of the Knoll, and the dam--and here is another of the mill, and the water-fall--all beautifully done, and in water-colours, too. What is this?--Have you been attempting a sketch of yourself!--The glass must have been closely consulted, my fair coquette, to enable you to do this!"

The blood had rushed into Maud's face, covering it with a rich tell-tale mantle, when her companion first alluded to the half-finished miniature he held in his hand; then her features resembled ivory, as the revulsion of feeling, that overcame her confusion, followed. For some little time she sate, in breathless stillness, with her looks cast upon the floor, conscious that Robert Willoughby was glancing from her own face to the miniature, and from the miniature to her face again, making his observations and comparisons. Then she ventured to raise her eyes timidly towards his, half-imploringly, as if to beseech him to proceed to something else. But the young man was too much engrossed with the exceedingly pretty sketch he held in his hand, to understand her meaning, or to comply with her wishes.

"This is yourself, Maud!" he cried--"though in a strange sort of dress--why have you spoilt so beautiful a thing, by putting it in this masquerade?"

"It is not myself--it is a copy of--a miniature I possess."

"A miniature you possess!--Of whom can you possess so lovely a miniature, and I never see it?"

A faint smile illumined the countenance of Maud, and the blood began to return to her cheeks. She stretched her hand over to the sketch, and gazed on it, with intense feeling, until the tears began to stream from her eyes.

"Maud--dear, *dearest* Maud--have I said that which pains you?--I do not understand all this, but I confess there are secrets to which I can have no claim to be admitted--"

"Nay, Bob, this is making too much of what, after all, must sooner or later be spoken of openly among us. I believe that to be a copy of a miniature of my mother."

"Of mother, Maud--you are beside yourself--it has neither her features, expression, nor the colour of her eyes. It is the picture of a far handsomer woman, though mother is still pretty; and it is perfection!"

"I mean of *my* mother--of Maud Yeardley; the wife of my father, Major Meredith."

This was said with a steadiness that surprised our heroine herself, when she came to think over all that had passed, and it brought the blood to her companion's heart, in a torrent.

"This is strange!" exclaimed Willoughby, after a short pause. "And *my* mother--*our* mother has given you the original, and told you this? I did not believe she could muster the resolution necessary to such an act."

"She has not. You know, Bob, I am now of age; and my father, a month since, put some papers in my hand, with a request that I would read them. They contain a marriage settlement and other things of that sort, which show I am mistress of more money than I should know what to do with, if it were not for dear little Evert--but, with such a precious being to love, one never can have too much of anything. With the papers were many trinkets, which I suppose father never looked at. This beautiful miniature was among the last; and I feel certain, from some remarks I ventured to make, mother does not know of its existence."

As Maud spoke, she drew the original from her bosom, and placed it in Robert Willoughby's hands. When this simple act was performed, her mind seemed relieved; and she waited, with strong natural interest, to hear Robert Willoughby's comments.

"This, then, Maud, was your *own*--your *real* mother!" the young man said, after studying the miniature, with a thoughtful countenance, for near a minute. "It is *like* her--like you."

"Like *her*, Bob?--How can you know anything or that?--I suppose it to be my mother, because I think it like myself, and because it is not easy to say who else it can be. But you cannot know anything of this?"

"You are mistaken, Maud--I remember both your parents well--it could not be otherwise, as they were the bosom friends of my own. You will remember that I am now eight-and-twenty, and that I had seen seven of these years when you were born. Was my first effort in arms never spoken of in your presence?"

"Never--perhaps it was not a subject for me to hear, if it were in any manner connected with my parents."

"You are right--that must be the reason it has been kept from your ears."

"Surely, surely, I am old enough to hear it *now*--*you* will conceal nothing from me, Bob?"

"If I would, I could not, now. It is too late, Maud. You know the manner in which Major Meredith died?--"

"He fell in battle, I have suspected," answered the daughter, in a suppressed, doubtful tone--"for no one has ever directly told me even that."

"He did, and I was at his side. The French and savages made an assault on us, about an hour earlier than this, and our two fathers rushed to the pickets to repel it--I was a reckless boy, anxious even at that tender age to see a fray, and was at their side. Your father was one of the first that fell; but Joyce and *our* father beat the Indians back from his body, and saved it from mutilation. Your mother was buried in the same grave, and then you came to us, where our have been ever since."

Maud's tears flowed fast, and yet it was not so much in grief as in a gush of tenderness she could hardly explain to herself. Robert Willoughby understood her emotions, and perceived that he might proceed.

"I was old enough to remember both your parents well--I was a favourite, I believe, with, certainly was much petted by, both--I remember your birth, Maud, and was suffered to carry you in my arms, ere you were a week old."

"Then you have known me for an impostor from the beginning, Bob-- must have often thought of me as such!"

"I have known you for the daughter of Lewellen Meredith, certainly; and not for a world would I have you the real child of Hugh Willoughby--"

"Bob!" exclaimed Maud, her heart beating violently, a rush of feeling nearly overcoming her, in which alarm, consciousness, her own secret, dread of something wrong, and a confused glimpse of the truth, were all so blended, as nearly to deprive her, for the moment, of the use of her senses.

It is not easy to say precisely what would have followed this tolerably explicit insight into the state of the young man's feelings, had not an outcry on the lawn given the major notice that his presence was needed below. With a few words of encouragement to Maud, first taking the precaution to extinguish the lamp, lest its light should expose her to a shot in passing some of the open loops, he sprang towards the stairs, and was at his post again, literally within a minute. Nor was he a moment too soon. The alarm was general, and it was understood an assault was momentarily expected.

The situation of Robert Willoughby was now tantalizing in the extreme. Ignorant of what was going on in front, he saw no enemy in the rear to oppose, and was condemned to inaction, at a moment when he felt that, by training, years, affinity to the master of the place, and all the usual considerations, he ought to be in front, opposed to the enemy. It is probable he would have forgotten his many cautions to keep close, had not Maud appeared in the library, and implored him to remain concealed, at least until there was the certainty his presence was necessary elsewhere.

At that instant, every feeling but those connected with the danger, was in a degree forgotten. Still, Willoughby had enough consideration for Maud to insist on her joining her mother and Beulah, in the portion of the building where the absence of external windows rendered their security complete, so long as the foe could be kept without the palisades. In this he succeeded, but not until he had promised, again and again, to be cautious in not exposing himself at any of the windows, the day having now fairly dawned, and particularly not to let it be known in the Hut that he was present until it became indispensable.

The major felt relieved when Maud had left him. For her, he had no longer any immediate apprehensions, and he turned all his faculties to the sounds of the assault which he supposed to be going on in front. To his surprise, however, no discharges of fire-arms succeeded; and even the cries, and orders, and calling from point to point, that are a little apt to succeed an alarm in an irregular garrison, had entirely ceased; and it became doubtful whether the whole commotion did not proceed from a false alarm. The Smashes, in particular, whose vociferations for the first few minutes had been of a very decided kind, were now mute; and the exclamations of the women and children had ceased.

Major Willoughby was too good a soldier to abandon his post without orders, though bitterly did he regret the facility with which he had consented to accept so inconsiderable a command. He so far disregarded his instructions, however, as to place his whole person before a window, in order to reconnoitre; for it was now broad daylight, though the sun had not yet risen. Nothing rewarded this careless exposure; and then it flashed upon his mind that, as the commander of a separate detachment, he had a perfect right to employ any of his immediate subordinates, either as messengers or scouts. His choice of an agent was somewhat limited, it is true, lying between Mike and the Plinys; after a moment of reflection, he determined to choose the former.

Mike was duly relieved from his station at the door, the younger Pliny being substituted for him, and he was led into the library. Here he received hasty but clear orders from the major how he was to proceed, and was thrust, rather than conducted from the room, in his superior's haste to hear the tidings. Three or four minutes might have elapsed, when an irregular volley of musketry was heard in front; then succeeded an answering discharge, which sounded smothered and distant. A single musket came from the garrison a minute later, and then Mike rushed into the library, his eyes dilated with a sort of wild delight, dragging rather than carrying his piece after him.

"The news!" exclaimed the major, as soon as he got a glimpse of his messenger. "What mean these volleys, and how comes on my father in front?"

"Is it what do they mane?" answered Mike. "Well, there's but one maning to powther and ball, and that's far more sarious than shillelah wor-r-k. If the rapscallions didn't fire a whole plathoon, as serjeant Joyce calls it, right at the Knoll, my name is not Michael O'Hearn, or my nature one that dales in giving back as good as I get."

"But the volley came first from the house--why did my father order his people to make the first discharge?"

"For the same r'ason that he didn't. Och! there was a big frown on his f'atures, when he heard the rifles and muskets; and Mr. Woods never pr'ached more to the purpose than the serjeant himself, ag'in that same. But to think of them rapscallions answering a fire that was ag'in orders! Not a word did his honour say about shooting any of them, and they just pulled their triggers on the house all the same as if it had been logs growing in senseless and uninhabited trees, instead of a rational and well p'apled abode. Och! arn't they vagabonds!"

"If you do not wish to drive me mad, man, tell me clearly what has past, that I may understand you."

"Is it understand that's wanting?--Lord, yer honour, if ye can understand that Misther Strhides, that's yon, ye'll be a wise man. He calls hisself a 'son of the poor'atin's,' and poor 'ating it must have been, in the counthry of his faders, to have produced so lane and skinny a baste as that same. The orders was as partic'lar as tongue of man could utter, and what good will it all do?--Ye're not to fire, says serjeant Joyce, till ye all hear the wor-r-d; and the divil of a wor-r-d did they wait for; but blaze away did they, jist becaase a knot of savages comes on to them rocks ag'in, where they had possession all yesterday afthernoon; and sure it is common enough to breakfast where a man sups."

"You mean to say that the Indians have reappeared on the rocks, and that some of Strides's men fired at them, without orders?--Is that the history of the affair?"

"It's jist that, majjor; and little good, or little har-r-m, did it do. Joel, and his poor'atin's, blazed away at 'em, as if they had been so many Christians--and 'twould have done yer heart good to have heard the serjeant belabour them with hard wor-r-ds, for their throuble. There's none of the poor'atin' family in the serjeant, who's a mighty man wid his tongue!"

"And the savages returned the volley--which explains the distant discharge I heard."

"Anybody can see, majjor, that ye're yer father's son, and a souldier bor-r-n. Och! who would of t'ought of that, but one bred and bor-r-n in the army? Yes; the savages sent back as good as they got, which was jist not'in' at all, seem' that no one is har-r-m'd."

"And the single piece that followed--there was one discharge, by itself?"

Mike opened his mouth with a grin that might have put either of the Plinys to shame, it being rather a favourite theory with the descendants of the puritans--or "poor'atin's," as the county Leitrim-man called Joel and his set--that the Irishman was more than a match for any son of Ham at the Knoll, in the way of capacity about this portion of the human countenance. The major saw that there was a good deal of self-felicitation in the expression of Mike's visage, and he demanded an explanation in more direct terms.

"'Twas I did it, majjor, and 'twas as well fired a piece as ye've ever hear-r-d in the king's sarvice. Divil bur-r-n me, if I lets Joel get any such advantage over me, as to have a whole battle to himself. No--no--as soon as I smelt his Yankee powther, and could get my own musket cock'd, and pointed out of the forthifications, I lets 'em have it, as if it had been so much breakfast ready cooked to their hands. 'Twas well pointed, too; for I'm not the man to shoot into a fri'nd's countenance."

"And you broke the orders for a reason no better than the fact that Strides had broken them before?"

"Divil a bit, majjor--Joel had *broken* the orders, ye see and that settled the matter. The thing that is once broken is broken, and wor-r-ds can't mend it, any more than for bearin' to fire a gun will mend it."

By dint of cross-questioning, Robert Willoughby finally succeeded in getting something like an outline of the truth from Mike. The simple facts were, that the Indians had taken possession of their old bivouac, as soon as the day dawned, and had commenced their preparations for breakfast, when Joel, the miller, and a few of that set, in a paroxysm of valour, had discharged a harmless volley at them; the distance rendering the attempt futile. This fire had been partially returned, the whole concluding with the *finale* from the Irishman's gun, as has been related. As it was now too light to apprehend a surprise, and the ground in front of the palisade had no very dangerous covers, Robert Willoughby was emboldened to send one of the Plinys to request an interview with his father. In a few minutes the latter appeared, accompanied by Mr. Woods.

"The same party has reappeared, and seems disposed to occupy its old position near the mill," said the captain, in answer to his son's inquiries. "It is difficult to say what the fellows have in view; and there are moments when I think there are more or less whites among them. I suggested as much to Strides, chaplain; and I thought the fellow appeared to receive the notion as if he thought it might be true."

"Joel is a little of an enigma to me, captain Willoughby," returned the chaplain; "sometimes seizing an idea like a cat pouncing upon a rat, and then coquetting with it, as the same cat will play with a mouse, when it has no appetite for food."

"Och! he's a precious poor'atin'!" growled Mike, from his corner of the room.

"If whites are among the savages, why should they not make themselves known?" demanded Robert Willoughby. "Your character, sir, is no secret; and they must be acquainted with their own errand here."

"I will send for Strides, and get his opinion a little more freely," answered the captain, after a moment of deliberation. "You will withdraw, Bob; though, by leaving your door a little ajar, the conversation will reach you; and prevent the necessity of a repetition."

As Robert Willoughby was not unwilling to hear what the overseer might have to say in the present state of things, he did not hesitate about complying, withdrawing into his own room as requested, and leaving the door ajar, in a way to prevent suspicion of his presence, as far as possible. But, Joel Strides, like all bad men, ever suspected the worst. The innocent and pure of mind alone are without distrust; while one constituted morally, like the overseer, never permitted his thoughts to remain in the tranquillity that is a fruit of confidence. Conscious of his own evil intentions, his very nature put on armour against the same species of machinations in others, as the hedge-hog rolls himself into a ball, and thrusts out his quills, at the sight of the dog. Had not captain Willoughby been one of those who are slow to see evil, he might have detected something wrong in Joel's feelings, by the very first glance he cast about him, on entering the library.

In point of fact, Strides' thoughts had not been idle since the rencontre of the previous night. Inquisitive, and under none of the usual restraints of delicacy, he had already probed all he dared approach on the subject; and, by this time, had become perfectly assured that there was some mystery about the unknown individual whom he had met in his master's company. To own the truth, Joel did not suspect that major Willoughby had again ventured so far into the lion's den; but he fancied that some secret agent of the crown was at the Hut, and that the circumstance offered a fair opening for helping the captain down the ladder of public favour, and to push himself up a few of its rounds. He was not sorry, therefore, to be summoned to this conference, hoping it might lead to some opening for farther discoveries.

"Sit down, Strides"--said captain Willoughby, motioning towards a chair so distant from the open door of the bed-room, and so placed as to remove the danger of too close a proximity--"Sit down--I wish to consult you about the state of things towards the mills. To me it seems as If there were more pale-faces than red-skins among our visitors."

"That's not onlikely, captain--the people has got to be greatly given to paintin' and imitatin', sin' the hatchet has been dug up ag'in the British. The tea-boys were all in Indian fashion."

"True; but, why should white men assume such a disguise to come to the Knoll? I am not conscious of having an enemy on earth who could meditate harm to me or mine."

Alas! poor captain. That a man at sixty should yet have to learn that the honest, and fair-dealing, and plain-dealing, and affluent--for captain Willoughby was affluent in the eyes of those around him--that such a man should imagine he was without enemies, was to infer that the Spirit of Darkness had ceased to exercise his functions among men. Joel knew better, though he did not perceive any necessity, just then, for letting the fact reach the ears of the party principally concerned.

"A body might s'pose the captain was pop'lar, if any man is pop'lar," answered the overseer; "nor do I know that visiters in paint betoken onpopularity to a person in these times more than another. May I ask why the captain consaits these Injins a'n't Injins? To me, they have a desperate savage look, though I a'n't much accustomed to red skin usages."

"Their movements are too open, and yet too uncertain, for warriors of the tribes. I think a savage, by this time, would have made up his mind to act as friend or foe."

Joel seemed struck with the idea; and the expression of his countenance, which on entering had been wily, distrustful and prying, suddenly changed to that of deep reflection.

"Has the captain seen anything else, partic'lar, to confirm this idee?" he asked.

"Their encampment, careless manner of moving, and unguarded exposure of their persons, are all against their being Indians."

"The messenger they sent across the meadow, yesterday, *seemed* to me to be a Mohawk?"

"He was. Of *his* being a real red-skin there can be no question. But he could neither speak nor understand English. The little that passed between us was in Low Dutch. Our dialogue was short; for, apprehensive of treachery, I brought it to a close sooner than I might otherwise have done."

"Yes; treachery is a cruel thing," observed the conscientious Joel; "a man can't be too strongly on his guard ag'in it. Does the captain ra'ally calculate on defending the house, should a serious attempt be brought forward for the day?"

"Do I! That is an extraordinary question, Mr. Strides. Why have I built in this mode, if I have no such intention?--why palisaded?--why armed and garrisoned, if not in earnest?"

"I s'posed all this might have been done to prevent a surprise, but not in any hope of standin' a siege. I should be sorry to see all our women and children shut up under one roof, if the inimy came ag'in us, in airnest, with fire and sword."

"And I should be sorry to see them anywhere else. But, this is losing time. My object in sending for you, Joel, was to learn your opinion about the true character of our visiters. Have you any opinion, or information to give me, on that point?"

Joel placed his elbow on his knee, and his chin in the palm of his hand, and pondered on what had been suggested, with seeming good-will, and great earnestness.

"If any one could be found venturesome enough to go out with a flag," he at length remarked, "the whole truth might be come at, in a few minutes."

"And who shall I employ? Cheerfully would I go myself, were such a step military, or at all excusable in one in my situation."

"If the likes of myself will sarve yer honour's turn," put in Mike, promptly, and yet with sufficient diffidence as regarded his views of his own qualifications--"there'll be nobody to gainsay that same; and it isn't wilcome that I nade tell you, ye'll be to use me as ye would yer own property."

"I hardly think Mike would answer," observed Joel, not altogether without a sneer. "He scurce knows an Indian from a white man; when it comes to the paint, it would throw him into dreadful confusion."

"If ye thinks that I am to be made to believe in any more Ould Nicks, Misther Strhides, then ye're making a mistake in my nature. Let but the captain say the word, and I'll go to the mill and bring in a grist of them same, or l'ave my own body for toll."

"I do not doubt you in the least, Mike," captain Willoughby mildly observed; "but there will be no occasion, just now, of your running any such risks. I shall be able to find other truce-bearers."

"It seems the captain has his man in view," Joel said, keenly eyeing his master. "Perhaps 'tis the same I saw out with him last night. That's a reliable person, I do s'pose."

"You have hit the nail on the head. It was the man who was out last night, at the same time I was out myself, and his name is Joel Strides."

"The captain's a little musical, this morning--waal--if go I must, as there was two on us out, let us go to these savages together. I saw enough of *that* man, to know he is reliable; and if he'll go, I'll go."

"Agreed"--said Robert Willoughby, stepping into the library--"I take you at your word, Mr. Strides; you and I will run what risks there may be, in order to relieve this family from its present alarming state."

The captain was astounded, though he knew not whether to be displeased or to rejoice. As for Mike, his countenance expressed great dissatisfaction; for he ever fancied things were going wrong so long as Joel obtained his wishes. Strides, himself, threw a keen glance at the stranger, recognised him at a glance, and had sufficient self-command to conceal his discovery, though taken completely by surprise. The presence of the major, however, immediately removed all his objections to the proposed expedition; since, should the party prove friendly to the Americans, he would be safe on his own account; or, should it prove the reverse, a king's officer could not fail to be a sufficient protection.

"The gentleman's a total stranger to me," Joel hypocritically resumed; "but as the captain has belief in him, I must have the same. I am ready to do the ar'nd, therefore, as soon as it is agreeable."

"This is well, captain Willoughby," put in the major, in order to anticipate any objections from his father; "and the sooner a thing of this sort is done, the better will it be for all concerned. I am ready to proceed this instant; and I take it this worthy man--I think you called him Strides--is quite as willing."

Joel signified his assent; and the captain, perceiving no means of retreat, was fain to yield. He took the major into the bed-room, however, and held a minute's private discourse, when he returned, and bade the two go forth together.

"Your companion has his instructions, Joel," the captain observed, as they left the library together; "and you will follow his advice. Show the white flag as soon as you quit the gate; if they are true warriors, it must be respected."

Robert Willoughby was too intent on business, and too fearful of the reappearance and reproachful looks of Maud, to delay. He had passed the court, and was at the outer gate, before any of the garrison even noted his appearance among them. Here, indeed, the father's heart felt a pang; and, but for his military pride, the captain would gladly have recalled his consent. It was too late, however; and, squeezing his hand, he suffered his son to pass outward. Joel followed steadily, as to appearances, though not without misgivings as to what might be the consequences to himself and his growing family.

Chapter XVII

"I worship not the sun at noon,
The wandering stars, the changing moon,
The wind, the flood, the flame;
I will not bow the votive knee
To wisdom, virtue, liberty;
There is no god, but God for me,
Jehovah is his name."

Montgomery.

So sudden and unexpected had been the passage of Robert Willoughby through the court, and among the men on post without the inner gates, that no one recognised his person. A few saw that a stranger was in their midst; but, under his disguise, no one was quick enough of eye and thought to ascertain who that stranger was. The little white flag that they displayed, denoted the errand of the messengers; the rest was left to conjecture.

As soon as captain Willoughby ascertained that the alarm of the morning was not likely to lead to any immediate results, he had dismissed all the men, with the exception of a small guard, that was stationed near the outer gait, under the immediate orders of serjeant Joyce. The latter was one of those soldiers who view the details of the profession as forming its great essentials; and when he saw his commander about to direct a *sortie*, it formed his pride not to ask questions, and to seem to know nothing about it. To this, Jamie Allen, who composed one of the guard, quietly assented; but it was a great privation to the three or four New England-men to be commanded not to inquire into the why and wherefore.

"Wait for orders, men, wait for orders," observed the serjeant, by way of quieting an impatience that was very apparent. "If his honour, the captain, wished us to be acquainted with his movements, he would direct a general parade, and lay the matter before us, as you know he always does, on proper occasions. 'Tis a flag going out, as you can see, and should a truce follow, we'll lay aside our muskets, and seize the plough-shares; should it be a capitulation--I know our brave old commander too well to suppose it possible--but *should* it be even *that*, we'll ground arms like men, and make the best of it."

"And should Joel, and the other man, who is a stranger to me, be scalped?" demanded one of the party.

"Then we'll avenge their scalps. That was the way with us, when my Lord Howe fell--'avenge his death! cried our colonel; and on we pushed, until near two thousand of us fell before the Frenchmen's trenches. Oh! *that* was a sight worth seeing, and a day to talk of!"

"Yes, but you were threshed soundly, serjeant, as I've heard from many that were there."

"What of that, sir! we obeyed orders. 'Avenge his death!' was the cry; and on we pushed, in obedience, until there were not men enough left in our battalion to carry the wounded to the rear."

"And what did you do with them?" asked a youth, who regarded the serjeant as another Cæsar--Napoleon not having come into notice in 1776.

"We let them lie where they fell. Young man, war teaches us all the wholesome lesson that impossibilities are impossible to be done. War is the great schoolmaster of the human race; and a learned man is he who has made nineteen or twenty campaigns."

"If he live to turn his lessons to account"--remarked the first speaker, with a sneer.

"If a man is to die in battle, sir, he had better die with his mind stored with knowledge, than be shot like a dog that has outlived his usefulness. Every pitched battle carries out of the world learning upon learning that has been got in the field. Here comes his honour, who will confirm all I tell you, men. I was letting these men, sir, understand that the army and the field are the best schools on earth. Every old soldier will stick to that, your honour."

"We are apt to think so, Joyce--have the arms been inspected this morning?"

"As soon as it was light, I did that myself, sir."

"Flints, cartridge-boxes and bayonets, I hope?"

"Each and all, sir. Does your honour remember the morning we had the affair near Fort du Quesne?"

"You mean Braddock's defeat, I suppose, Joyce?"

"I call nothing a defeat, captain Willoughby. We were roughly handled that day, sir; but I am not satisfied it was a defeat. It is true, we fell back, and lost some arms and stores; but, in the main, we stuck to our colours, considering it was in the woods. No, sir; I do not call that a defeat, by any means."

"You will at least own we were hard pressed, and might have fared worse than we did, had it not been for a certain colonial corps, that manfully withstood the savages?"

"Yes, sir; that I allow. I remember the corps, and its commander, a colonel Washington, with your honour's permission."

"It was, indeed, Joyce. And do you happen to know what has became of this same colonel Washington?"

"It never crossed my mind to inquire, sir, as he was a provincial. I dare say he may have a regiment--or even a brigade by this time; and good use would he make of either."

"You have fallen far behind his fortunes, Joyce. The man is a commander-in-chief--a captain-general."

"Your honour is jesting--since many of his seniors are still living."

"This is the man who leads the American armies, in the war with England."

"Well, sir, in *that* way, he may indeed get a quick step, or two. I make no doubt, sir, so good a soldier will know how to obey orders."

"From which I infer you think him right, in the cause he has espoused?"

"Bless your honour, sir, I think nothing about it, and care nothing about it. If the gentleman has taken service with congress, as they call the new head-quarters, why he ought to obey congress; and if he serve the king, His Majesty's orders should be attended to."

"And, in this crisis, serjeant, may I ask in what particular service you conceive yourself to be, just at the present moment?"

"Captain Willoughby's, late of His Majesty's ---th Regiment of Foot, at your honour's command."

"If all act in the same spirit, Joyce, we shall do well enough at the Knoll, though twice as many savages brave us as are to be seen on yon rocks," returned the captain, smiling.

"And why should they no?" demanded Jamie Allen, earnestly. "Ye're laird here, and we've no the time, nor the grace, to study and understand the orthodoxy and heterodoxy of the quarrel atween the House of Hanover and the houses of these Americans; so, while we a'stand up for the house and household of our old maister, the Lord will smile on our efforts, and lead us to victory."

"Divil bur-r-n me, now, Jamie," said Mike, who having seen the major to the gate, now followed his father, in readiness to do him any good turn that might offer--"Divil bur-r-n me, now, Jamie, if ye could have said it better had ye just aised yer conscience to a proper praist, and were talking on a clane breast! Stick up for the captain, says I, and the Lord will be of our side!"

The serjeant nodded approbation of this sentiment, and the younger Pliny, who happened also to be within hearing, uttered the sententious word "gosh" and clenched his fist, which was taken as proof of assent also, on his part. But, the Americans of the guard, all of whom were the tools of Joel's and the miller's arts, manifested a coldness that even exceeded the usual cold manner of their class. These men meant right; but they had been deluded by the falsehoods, machinations, and frauds of a demagogue, and were no longer masters of their own opinions or acts. It struck the captain that something was wrong; but, a foreigner by birth himself, he had early observed, and long known, the peculiar exterior and phlegm of the people of the country, which so nearly resemble the stoicism of the aborigines, as to induce many writers to attribute both alike to a cause connected with climate. The present was not a moment however, nor was the impression strong enough to induce the master of the place to enter into any inquiries. Turning his eyes in the direction of the two bearers of the flag, he there beheld matter for new interest, completely diverting his thoughts from what had just passed.

"I see they have sent two men to meet our messengers serjeant," he said--"This looks as if they understood the laws of war."

"Quite true, your honour. They should now blindfold our party, and lead them within their own works, before they suffer them to see at all; though there would be no great advantage in it, as Strides is as well acquainted with every inch of that rock as I am with the manual exercise."

"Which would seem to supersede the necessity of the ceremony you have mentioned?"

"One never knows, your honour. Blindfolding is according to the rules, and I should blindfold a flag before I let him approach, though the hostile ranks stood drawn up, one on each side of a parade ground. Much is gained, while nothing is ever lost, by sticking to the rules of a trade."

The captain smiled, as did all the Americans of the guard; the last having too much sagacity not to perceive that a thing might be overdone, as well as too little attended to. As for Jamie and Mike, they both received the serjeant's opinions as law; the one from having tried the troops of the line at Culloden, and the other on account of divers experiences through which he had gone, at sundry fairs, in his own green island. By this time, however, all were too curious in watching the result of the meeting, to continue the discourse.

Robert Willoughby and Joel had moved along the lane towards the rocks, without hesitating, keeping their little flag flying. It did not appear that their approach produced any change among the savages, who were now preparing their breakfasts, until they had got within two hundred yards of the encampment, when two of the red-men, having first laid aside their arms, advanced to meet their visiters. This was the interview which attracted the attention of those at the Hut, and its progress was noted with the deepest interest.

The meeting appeared to be friendly. After a short conference, in which signs seemed to be a material agent in the communications, the four moved on in company, walking deliberately towards the rocks. Captain Willoughby had sent for his field-glass, and could easily perceive much that occuired in the camp, on the arrival of his son. The major's movements were calm and steady, and a feeling of pride passed over the father's heart, as he noted this, amid a scene that was well adapted to disturbing the equilibrium of the firmest mind. Joel certainly betrayed nervousness, though he kept close at his companion's side, and together they proceeded into the very centre of the party of strangers.

The captain observed, also, that this arrival caused no visible sensation among the red-men. Even those the major almost touched in passing did not look up to note his appearance, while no one seemed to speak, or in any manner to heed him. The cooking and other preparations for the breakfast proceeded precisely as if no one had entered the camp. The two who had gone forth to meet the flag alone attended its bearers, whom they led through the centre of the entire party; stopping only on the side opposite to the Hut, where there was an open space of flat rock, which it had not suited the savages to occupy.

Here the four halted, the major turning and looking back like a soldier who was examining his ground. Nor did any one appear disposed to interrupt him in an employment that serjeant Joyce pronounced to be both bold and against the usages of war to permit. The captain thought the stoicism of the savages amounted to exaggeration, and it renewed his distrust of the real characters of his visiters. In a minute or two, however, some three or four of the red-men were seen consulting together apart, after which they approached the bearers of the flag, and some communications passed between the two sides. The nature of these communications could not be known, of course, though the conference appeared to be amicable. After two or three minutes of conversation, Robert Willoughby, Strides, the two men who had advanced to meet them, and the four chiefs who had joined the group, left the summit of the rock in company, taking a footpath that descended in the direction of the mills. In a short time they all disappeared in a body.

The distance was not so great but these movements could easily be seen by the naked eye, though the glass was necessary to discover some of the details. Captain Willoughby had planted the instrument among the palisades, and he kept his gaze riveted on the retiring group as long as it was visible; then, indeed, he looked at his companions, as if to read their opinions in their countenances. Joyce understood the expression of his face; and, saluting in the usual military manner, he presumed to speak, in the way of reply.

"It seems all right, your honour, the bandage excepted," said the serjeant. "The flag has been met at the outposts, and led into the camp; there the officer of the day, or some savage who does the duty, has heard his errand; and, no doubt, they have all now gone to head-quarters, to report."

"I desired my son, Joyce--"

"Whom, your honour--?"

The general movement told the captain how completely his auditors were taken by surprise, at this unlooked-for announcement of the presence of the major at the Knoll. It was too late to recall the words, however, and there was so little prospect of Robert's escaping the penetration of Joel, the father saw no use in attempting further concealment.

"I say I desired my son, major Willoughby, who is the bearer of that flag," the captain steadily resumed, "to raise his hat in a particular manner, if all seemed right; or to make a certain gesture with his left arm, did he see anything that required us to be more than usually on our guard."

"And which notice has he given to the garrison, if it be your honour's pleasure to let us know?"

"Neither. I thought he manifested an intention to make the signal with the hat, when the chiefs first joined him; but he hesitated, and lowered his hand without doing as I had expected. Then, again, just as he disappeared behind the rocks, the left arm was in motion, though not in a way to complete the signal."

"Did he seem hurried, your honour, as if prevented from communicating by the enemy?"

"Not at all, Joyce. Irresolution appeared to be at the bottom of it, so far as I could judge." "Pardon me, your honour; uncertainty would be a better word, as applied to so good a soldier. Has major Willoughby quitted the king's service, that he is among us, sir, just at his moment?"

"I will tell you his errand another time, serjeant. At present, I can think only of the risk he runs. These Indians are lawless wretches; one is never sure of then faith."

"They are bad enough, sir; but no man can well be so bad as to disregard the rights of a flag," answered the serjeant, in a grave and slightly important manner. "Even the French, your honour, have always respected our *flags*."

"That is true; and, yet, I wish we could overlook that position at the mill. It's a great advantage to them, Joyce, that they can place themselves behind such a cover, when they choose!"

The serjeant looked at the encampment a moment; then his eye followed the woods, and the mountain sides, that skirted the little plain, until his back was fairly turned upon the supposed enemy, and he faced the forest in the rear of the Hut.

"If it be agreeable to your honour, a detachment can be detailed to make a demonstration"--Joyce did not exactly understand this word, but it sounded military--"in the following manner: I can lead out the party, by the rear of the house, using the brook as a covered-way. Once in the woods, it will be easy enough to make a flank movement upon the enemy's position; after which, the detachment can be guided by circumstances."

This was very martial in sound, and the captain felt well assured that Joyce was the man to attempt carrying out his own plan; but he made no answer, sighing and shaking his head, as he walked away towards the house. The chaplain followed, leaving the rest to observe the savages.

"Ye're proposition, serjeant, no seems to give his honour much satisfaction," said the mason, as soon as his superior was out of hearing. "Still, it was military, as I know by what I saw mysal' in the Forty-five. Flainking, and surprising, and obsairving, and demonstrating, and such devices, are the soul of war, and are a' on the great highway to victory. Had Chairlie's men obsairved, and particularised mair, there might have been a different family on the throne, an' the prince wad ha' got his ain ag'in. I like your idea much, serjaint, and gin' ye gang oot to practise it, I trust ye 'll no forget that ye've an auld fri'nd here, willing to be of the pairty."

"I didn't think the captain much relished the notion of being questioned about his son's feelin's, and visit up here, at a time like this," put in one of the Americans.

"There's bowels in the man's body!" cried Mike, "and it isn't the likes of him that has no falin'. Ye don't know what it is to be a father, or ye'd groan in spirit to see a child of yer own in the grip of fiery divils like them same. Isn't he a pratty man, and wouldn't I be sorrowful to hear that he had come to har-r-m? Ye've niver asked, serjeant, how the majjor got into the house, and ye a military sentry in the bargain!"

"I suppose he came by command, Michael, and it is not the duty of the non-commissioned officers to question their superiors about anything that has happened out of the common way. I take things as I find them, and obey orders. I only hope that the son, as a field-officer, will not out-rank the father, which would be unbecoming: though date of commissions, and superiority, must be respected."

"I rather think if a major in the king's service was to undertake to use authority here," said the spokesman of the Americans, a little stiffly, "he wouldn't find many disposed to follow at his heels."

"Mutiny would not fare well, did it dare to lift its head in this garrison"--answered the serjeant, with a dignity that might better have suited the mess-room of a regular regiment, than the situation in which he was actually placed. "Both captain Willoughby and myself have seen mutiny attempted, but neither has ever seen it succeed."

"Do you look on us as lawful, enlisted soldiers?" demanded one of the labourers, who had a sufficient smattering of the law, to understand the difference between a mercenary and a volunteer. "If I'm regimented, I should at least like to know in whose service it is?"

"Ye're over-quick at yer objections and sentiments," said Jamie Allen, coolly, "like most youths, who see only their ain experience in the airth, and the providence o' the Lord. Enlisted we are, a' of us, even to Michael here, and it's in the sairvice of our good master, his honour captain Willoughby; whom, with his kith and kin, may the Lord presairve from this and all other dangers."

The word master would, of itself, be very likely to create a revolt to-day, in such a corps as it was the fortune of our captain to command, though to that of "boss" there would not be raised the slightest objection. But the English language had not undergone half of its present mutations in the year 1776; and no one winced in admitting that he served a "master," though the gorges of several rose at the idea of being engaged in the service of any one, considered in a military point of view. It is likely the suggestion of the mason would have led to a hot discussion, had not a stir among the savages, just at that instant, called off the attention of all present, to matters of more importance than even an angry argument.

The movement seemed to be general, and Joyce ordered his men to stand to their arms; still he hesitated about giving the alarm. Instead of advancing towards the Hut, however, the Indians raised a general yell, and went over the cliffs, disappearing in the direction of the mill, like a flock of birds taking wing together. After waiting half an hour, in vain, to ascertain if any signs of the return of the Indians were to be seen, the serjeant went himself to report the state of things to his commander.

Captain Willoughby had withdrawn to make his toilet for the day, when he saw the last of his son and the overseer. While thus employed he had communicated to his wife all that had occurred; and Mrs. Willoughby, in her turn, had told the same to her daughters. Maud was much the most distressed, her suspicions of Joel being by far the most active and the most serious. From the instant she learned what had passed, she began to anticipate grave consequences to Robert Willoughby, though she had sufficient fortitude, and sufficient consideration for others, to keep most of her apprehensions to herself.

When Joyce demanded his audience, the family was at breakfast, though little was eaten, and less was said. The serjeant was admitted, and he told his story with military precision.

"This has a suspicious air, Joyce," observed the captain, after musing a little; "to me it seems like an attempt to induce us to follow, and to draw us into an ambuscade."

"It may be that, your honour; or, it may be a good honest retreat. *Two* prisoners is a considerable exploit for savages to achieve. I have known them count *one* a victory."

"Be not uneasy, Wilhelmina; Bob's rank will secure him good treatment, his exchange being far more important to his captors, if captors they be, than his death. It is too soon to decide on such a point, serjeant. After all, the Indians may be at the mills, in council. On a war path, all the young men are usually consulted, before any important step is taken. Then, it may be the wish of the chiefs to impress our flag-bearers with an idea of their force."

"All that is military, your honour, and quite possible. Still, to me the movement seems as if a retreat was intended, in fact, or that the *appearance* of one was in view."

"I will soon know the truth," cried the chaplain. "I, a man of peace, can surely go forth, and ascertain who these people are, and what is their object."

"You, Woods! My dear fellow, do you imagine a tribe of blood-thirsty savages will respect you, or your sacred office? You have a sufficient task with the king's forces, letting his enemies alone. You are no missionary to still a war-cry."

"I beg pardon, sir"--put in the serjeant--"his reverence is more than half right"--here the chaplain rose, and quitted the room in haste, unobserved by the two colloquists--"There is scarce a tribe in the colony, your honour, that has not some knowledge of our priesthood; and I know of no instance in which the savages have ever ill-treated a divine."

"Poh, poh, Joyce; this is much too sentimental for your Mohawks, and Oneidas, and Onondagas, and Tuscaroras. They will care no more for little Woods than they care for the great woods through which they journey on their infernal errands."

"One cannot know, Hugh"--observed the anxious mother--"Our dear Robert is in their hands; and, should Mr. Woods be really disposed to go on this mission of mercy, does it comport with our duty as parents to oppose it?"

"A mother is all mother"--murmured the captain, who rose from table, kissed his wife's cheek affectionately, and left the room, beckoning to the serjeant to follow.

Captain Willoughby had not been gone many minutes when the chaplain made his appearance, attired in his surplice, and wearing his best wig; an appliance that all elderly gentlemen in that day fancied necessary to the dignity and gravity of their appearance. Mrs. Willoughby, to own the truth, was delighted. If this excellent woman was ever unjust, it was in behalf of her children; solicitude for whom sometimes induced her to overlook the rigid construction of the laws of equality.

"We will see which best understands the influence of the sacred office, captain Willoughby, or myself;" observed the chaplain, with a little more importance of manner than it was usual for one so simple to assume. "I do not believe the ministry was instituted to be brow-beaten by tribes of savages, any more than it is to be silenced by the unbeliever, or schismatic."

It was very evident that the Rev. Mr. Woods was considerably excited; and this was a condition of mind so unusual with him, as to create a species of awe in the observers. As for the two young women, deeply as they were interested in the result, and keenly as Maud, in particular, felt everything which touched the fortunes of Robert Willoughby, neither would presume to interfere, when they saw one whom they had been taught to reverence from childhood, acting in a way that so little conformed to his ordinary manner. As for Mrs. Willoughby, her own feelings were so much awakened, that never had Mr. Woods seemed so evangelical and like a saint, as at that very moment; and it would not have been difficult to persuade her that he was acting under something very like righteous superhuman impulses.

Such, however, was far from being the case. The worthy priest had an exalted idea of his office; and, to fancy it might favorably impress even savages, was little more than carrying out his every-day notions of its authority. He conscientiously believed that he, himself, a regularly ordained presbyter, would be more likely to succeed in the undertaking before him, than a mere deacon; were a bishop present, he would cheerfully have submitted to his superior claims to sanctity and success. As for arch-bishops, arch-deacons, deans, rural deans, and all the other worldly machinery which has been superadded to the church, the truth compels us to add, that our divine felt no especial reverence since he considered them as so much clerical surplusage, of very questionable authority, and of doubtful use. He adhered strictly to the orders of divine institution, to these he attached so much weight, as to be entirely willing, in his own person, to demonstrate how little was to be apprehended, when their power was put forth, even against Indians, in humility and faith.

"I shall take this sprig of laurel in my hand, in lieu of the olive-branch," said the excited chaplain, "as the symbol of peace. It is not probable that savages can tell one plant from the other; and if they could, it will be easy to explain that olives do not grow in America. It is an eastern tree, ladies, and furnishes the pleasant oil we use on our salads. I carry with me, notwithstanding, the oil which proves a balm to many sorrows; that will be sufficient."

"You will bid them let Robert return to us, without delay?" said Mrs. Willoughby, earnestly.

"I shall bid them respect God and their consciences. I cannot now stop to rehearse to you the mode of proceeding I shall adopt; but it is all arranged in my own mind. It will be necessary to call the Deity the 'Great Spirit' or 'Manitou'--and to use many poetical images; but this can I do, on an emergency. Extempore preaching is far from agreeable to me, in general; nor do I look upon it, in this age of the world, as exactly canonical; nevertheless, it shall be seen I know how to submit even to *that*, when there is a suitable necessity."

It was so seldom Mr. Woods used such magnificent ideas, or assumed a manner in the least distinguishable from one of the utmost simplicity, that his listeners now felt really awed; and when he turned to bless them, as he did with solemnity and affection, the two daughters knelt to receive his benedictions. These delivered, he walked out of the room, crossed the court, and proceeded straightway to the outer gate.

It was, perhaps, fortunate to the design of the Rev. Mr. Woods, that neither the captain nor the serjeant was in the way, to arrest it. This the former would certainly have done, out of regard to his friend, and the last out of regard to "orders." But these military personages were in the library, in deep consultation concerning the next step necessary to take. This left the coast clear, no one belonging to the guard conceiving himself of sufficient authority to stop the chaplain, more especially when he appeared in his wig and surplice. Jamie Allen was a corporal, by courtesy; and, at the first summons, he caused the outer gate to be unlocked and unbarred, permitting the chaplain to make his egress, attended by his own respectful bows. This Jamie did, out of reverence to religion, generally; though the surplice ever excited his disgust; and, as for the Liturgy, he deemed it to be a species of solemn mockery of worship.

The captain did not reappear outside of the court, until the chaplain, who had made the best of his way towards the rocks, was actually stalking like a ghost among ruins, through the deserted shantees of the late encampment.

"What in the name of Indian artifice is the white animal that I see moving about on the rocks?" demanded the captain, whose look was first turned in the direction of the camp.

"It seems an Indian wrapped up in a shirt, your honour--as I live, sir, it has a cocked hat on its head!"

"Na--na"--interrupted Jamie, "ye'll no be guessing the truth this time, without the aid of a little profane revelation. The chiel ye see yan, yer honour, is just chaplain Woods."

"Woods--the devil!"

"Na--na--yer honour, it's the reverend gentleman, hissel', and no the de'il, at a'. He's in his white frock--though why he didn't wear his black gairment is more than I can tell ye--but there he is, walking about amang the Indian dwellings, all the same as if they were so many pews in his ain kirk."

"And, how came you to let him pass the gate, against orders?"

"Well, and it is aboot the orders of the priesthood, that he so often preaches, and seeing him in the white gairment, and knowing ye've so many fast-days, and Christmas', in the kirk o' England, I fancied it might be a bit matter o' prayer he wished to offer up, yan, in the house on the flat; and so I e'en thought church prayers better than no prayers at all, in such a strait."

As it was useless to complain, the captain was fain to submit, even beginning to hope some good might come of the adventure, when he saw

Mr. Woods walking unmolested through the deserted camp. The glass was levelled, and the result was watched in intense interest.

The chaplain first explored every shantee, fearlessly and with diligence. Then he descended the rocks, and was lost to view, like those who had preceded him. A feverish hour passed, without any symptom of human life appearing in the direction of the mills. Sometimes those who watched, fancied they beheld a smoke beginning to steal up over the brow of the rocks, the precursor of the expected conflagration; but a few moments dispersed the apprehension and the fancied smoke together. The day advanced, and yet the genius of solitude reigned over the mysterious glen. Not a sound emerged from it, not a human form was seen near it, not a sign of a hostile assault or of a friendly return could be detected. All in that direction lay buried in silence, as if the ravine had swallowed its tenants, in imitation of the grave.

Chapter XVIII

To deck my list by Nature were design'd
Such shining expletives of human kind;
Who want, while through blank life they dream along,
Sense to be right, and passion to be wrong.
Young.

The disappearance of Mr. Woods occasioned no uneasiness at first. An hour elapsed before the captain thought it necessary to relate the occurrence to his family, when a general panic prevailed among the females. Even Maud had hoped the savages would respect the sacred character of the divine, though she knew not why; and here was one of her principal grounds of hope, as connected with Robert Willoughby, slid from beneath her feet.

"What *can* we do, Willoughby?" asked the affectionate mother, almost reduced to despair. "I will go myself, in search of my son--they will respect *me*, a woman and a mother."

"You little know the enemy we have to deal with, Wilhelmina, or so rash a thought could not have crossed your mind. We will not be precipitate; a few hours may bring some change to direct us. One thing I learn from Woods' delay. The Indians cannot be far off, and he must be with them, or in their hands; else would he return alter having visited the mills and the houses beneath the cliffs."

This sounded probable, and all felt there was a relief in fancying that their friends were still near them, and were not traversing the wilderness as captives.

"I feel less apprehension than any of you," observed Beulah, in her placid manner. "If Bob is in the hands of an American party, the brother-in-law of Evert Beekman cannot come to much harm; with British Indians he will be respected for his own sake, as soon as he can make himself known."

"I have thought of all this, my child"--answered the father, musing--"and there is reason in it. It will be difficult, however, for Bob to make his real character certain, in his present circumstances. He does not appear the man he is; and should there even be a white among his captors who can read, he has not a paper with him to sustain his word."

"But, he promised me faithfully to use Evert's name, did he ever fall into American hands"--resumed Beulah, earnestly--"and Evert has said, again and again, that *my* brother could never be his enemy."

"Heaven help us all, dear child!" answered the captain, kissing his daughter--"It is, indeed, a cruel war, when such aids are to be called in for our protection. We will endeavour to be cheerful, notwithstanding; for we know of nothing yet, that ought to alarm us, out of reason; all may come right before the sun set."

The captain looked at his family, and endeavoured to smile, but he met no answering gleam of happiness on either face; nor was his own effort very successful. As for his wife, she was never known to be aught but miserable, while any she loved were in doubtful safety. She lived entirely out of herself, and altogether for her husband, children, and friends; a woman less selfish, or one more devoted to the affections, never existing. Then Beulah, with all her reliance on the magic of Evert's name, and with the deep feelings that had been awakened within her, as a wife and a mother, still loved her brother as tenderly as ever. As for Maud, the agony she endured was increased by her efforts to keep it from breaking out in some paroxysm that might betray her secret; and her features were getting an expression of stern resolution, which, blended with her beauty, gave them a grandeur her father had never before seen in her bright countenance.

"This child suffers on Bob's account more than any of us"--observed the captain, drawing his pet towards him, placing her kindly on his knee, and folding her to his bosom. "She has no husband yet, to divide her heart; all her love centres in her brother."

The look which Beulah cast upon her father was not reproachful, for that was an expression she would not have indulged with him; but it was one in which pain and mortification were so obvious, as to induce the mother to receive her into her own arms.

"Hugh, you are unjust to Beulah"--said the anxious mother--"Nothing can ever cause this dear girl, either, to forget to feel for any of us."

The captain's ready explanation, and affectionate kiss, brought a smile again to Beulah's face, though it shone amid tears. All was, however, immediately forgotten; for the parties understood each other, and Maud profited by the scene to escape from the room. This flight broke up the conference; and the captain, after exhorting his wife and daughter to set an example of fortitude to the rest of the females, left the house, to look after his duties among the men.

The absence of Joel cast a shade of doubt over the minds of the disaffected. These last were comparatively numerous, comprising most of the native Americans in the Hut, the blacks and Joyce excepted. Strides had been enabled to effect his purposes more easily with his own countrymen by working on their good qualities, as well as on their bad. Many of these men--most of them, indeed--meant well, but their attachment to the cause of their native land laid them open to assaults, against which Mike and Jamie Allen were insensible. Captain Willoughby was an Englishman, in the first place; he was an old army-officer, in the next; and he had an only son who was confessedly in open arms against the independence of America. It is easy to see how a demagogue like Joel, who had free access to the ears of his comrades, could improve circumstances like these to his own particular objects. Nevertheless, he had difficulties to contend with. If it were true that parson Woods still insisted on praying for the king, it was known that the captain laughed at him for his reverence for Cæsar; if Robert Willoughby were a major in the royal forces, Evert Beekman was a colonel in the continentals; if the owner of the manor were born in England, his wife and children were born in America; and he, himself, was often heard to express his convictions of the justice of most of that for which the provincials were contending--*all*, the worthy captain had not yet made up his mind to concede to them.

Then, most of the Americans in the Hut entertained none of the selfish and narrow views of Joel and the miller. Their wish was to do right, in the main; and though obnoxious to the charge of entertaining certain prejudices that rendered them peculiarly liable to become the dupes of a demagogue, they submitted to many of the better impulses, and were indisposed to be guilty of any act of downright injustice. The perfect integrity with which they had ever been treated, too, had its influence; nor was the habitual kindness of Mrs. Willoughby to their wives and children forgotten; nor the gentleness of Beulah, or the beauty, spirit, and generous impulses of Maud. In a word, the captain, when he went forth to review his men, who were now all assembled under arms within the palisades for that purpose, went to meet a wavering, rather than a positively disaffected or rebellious body.

"Attention!" cried Joyce, as his commanding officer came in front of a line which contained men of different colours, statures, ages, dresses, countries, habits and physiognomies, making it a sort of epitome of the population of the whole colony, as it existed in that day--"Attention! Present, arms."

The captain pulled off his hat complacently, in return to this salute, though he was obliged to smile at the array which met his eyes. Every one of the Dutchmen had got his musket to an order, following a sort of fugleman of their own; while Mike had invented a "motion" that would have puzzled any one but himself to account for. The butt of the piece was projected towards the captain, quite out of line, while the barrel rested on his own shoulder. Still, as his arms were extended to the utmost, the county Leitrim-man fancied he was performing much better than common. Jamie had correct notions of the perpendicular, from having used the plumb-bob so much, though even he made the trifling mistake of presenting arms with the lock outwards. As for the Yankees, they were all tolerably exact, in everything but time, and the line; bringing their pieces down, one after another, much as they were in the practice of following their leaders, in matters of opinion. The negroes defied description; nor was it surprising they failed, each of them thrusting his head forward to see how the "motions" looked, in a way that prevented any particular attention to his own part of the duty. The serjeant had the good sense to see that his drill had not yet produced perfection, and he brought his men to a shoulder again, as soon as possible. In this he succeeded perfectly, with the exception that just half of the arms were brought to the right, and the other half to the left shoulders.

"We shall do better, your honour, as we get a little more drill"--said Joyce, with an apologetic salute--"Corporal Strides has a tolerable idea of the manual, and he usually acts as our fugleman. When he gets back, we shall improve."

"When he gets back, serjeant--can you, or any other man, tell when that will be?"

"Yes, yer honour," sputtered Mike, with the eagerness of a boy. "I'se the man to tell yees that same."

"You?--What can you know, that is not known to all of us, my good Michael?"

"I knows what I sees; and if yon isn't Misther Strhides, then I am not acquainted with his sthraddle."

Sure enough, Joel appeared at the gate, as Mike concluded his assertions. How he got there, no one knew; for a good look-out had been kept in the direction of the mill; and, yet here was the overseer applying for admission, as if he had fallen from the clouds! Of course, the application was not denied, though made in a manner so unexpected, and Joel stood in front of his old comrades at the hoe and plough, if not in arms, in less than a minute. His return was proclaimed through the house in an incredibly short space of time, by the aid of the children, and all the females came pouring out from the court to learn the tidings, led by Mrs. Strides and her young brood.

"Have you anything to communicate to me in private, Strides?" the captain demanded, maintaining an appearance of *sang froid* that he was far from feeling--"or, can your report be made here, before the whole settlement?"

"It's just as the captain pleases," answered the wily demagogue; "though, to my notion, the people have a right to know all, in an affair that touches the common interest."

"Attention! men"--cried the serjeant--"By platoons, to the right"

"No matter, Joyce," interrupted the captain, waving his hand--"Let the men remain. You have held communications with our visiters, I know, Strides?"

"We have, captain Willoughby, and a desperate sort of visiters be they! A more ugly set of Mohawks and Onondagas I never laid eyes on."

"As for their appearance, it is matter of indifference to me--what is the object of their visit?"

"I mean ugly behaved, and they deserve all I say of 'em. Their ar'nd, according to their own tell, is to seize the captain, and his family, in behalf of the colonies."

As Joel uttered this, he cast a glance along the line of faces paraded before him, in order to read the effect it might produce. That it was not lost on some, was as evident as that it was on others. The captain, however, appeared unmoved, and there was a slight air of incredulity in the smile that curled his lip.

"This, then, you report as being the business of the party in coming to this place!" he said, quietly.

"I do, sir; and an ugly ar'nd it is, in times like these."

"Is there any person in authority in a party that pretends to move about the colony, with such high duties?"

"There's one or two white men among 'em, if that's what the captain means; they pretend to be duly authorised and appointed to act in behalf of the people."

At each allusion to the people, Joel invariably looked towards his particular partisans, in order to note the effect the use of the word might produce. On the present occasion, he even ventured to wink at the miller.

"If acting on authority, why do they keep aloof?--I have no such character for resisting the laws, that any who come clothed with its mantle need fear resistance."

"Why, I s'pose they reason in some such manner as this. There's *two* laws in operation at this time; the king's law, and the people's law. I take it, this party comes in virtue of the people's law, whereas it is likely the law the captain means is the king's law. The difference is so great, that one or t'other carries the day, just as the king's friends or the people's friends happen to be the strongest. These men don't like to trust to *their* law, when the captain may think it safest to trust a little to his'n."

"And all this was told you, Strides, in order to be repeated to me?"

"Not a word on't; it's all my own consait about the matter. Little passed between us."

"And, now," said the captain, relieving his breast by a long sigh, "I presume I may inquire about your companion. You probably have ascertained who he is?"

"Lord, captain Willoughby, I was altogether dumbfounded, when the truth came upon me of a sudden! I never should have known the major in that dress, in the world, or out of the world either; but he walks so like the captain, that as I followed a'ter him, I said to myself, who *can* it be?--and then the walk came over me, as it might be; and then I remembered last night, and the stranger that was out with the captain, and how he occupied the room next to the library, and them things; and so, when I come to look in his face, there was the major sure enough!"

Joel lied famously in this account; but he believed himself safe, as no one could very well contradict him.

"Now, you have explained the manner in which you recognised my son, Strides," added the captain, "I will thank you to let me know what has become of him?"

"He's with the savages. Having come so far to seize the father, it wasn't in natur' to let the son go free, when he walked right into the lion's den, like."

"And how could the savages know he *was* my son? Did they, too, recognise the family walk?"

Strides was taken aback at this question, and he even had the grace to colour a little. He saw that he was critically placed; for, in addition to the suggestions of conscience, he understood the captain sufficiently to know he was a man who would not trifle, in the event of his suspicions becoming active. He knew he deserved the gallows, and Joyce was a man who would execute him in an instant, did his commander order it. The idea fairly made the traitor tremble in his shoes.

"Ah! I've got a little ahead of my story," he said, hastily. "But, perhaps I had best tell everything as it happened--"

"That will be the simplest and clearest course. In order that there be no interruption, we will go into my room, where Joyce will follow us, as soon as he has dismissed his men."

This was done, and in a minute or two the captain and Joel were seated in the library, Joyce respectfully standing; the old soldier always declining to assume any familiarity with his superior. We shall give the substance of most of Joel's report in our own language; preferring it, defective as it is, to that of the overseer's, which was no bad representative of his cunning, treacherous and low mind.

It seems, then, that the bearers of the flag were amicably received by the Indians. The men towards whom they were led on the rocks, were the chiefs of the party, who treated them with proper respect. The sudden movement was explained to them, as connected with their meal; and the chiefs, accompanied by the major and Strides, proceeded to the house of the miller. Here, by means of a white man for an interpreter, the major had demanded the motive of the strangers in coming into the settlement. The answer was a frank demand for the surrender of the Hut, and all it contained, to the authorities of the continental congress. The major had endeavoured to persuade a white man, who professed to hold the legal authority for what was doing, of the perfectly neutral disposition of his father, when, according to Joel's account, to his own great astonishment, the argument was met by the announcement of Robert Willoughby's true character, and a sneering demand if it were likely a man who had a son in the royal army, and who had kept that son secreted in his own house, would be very indifferent to the success of the royal cause.

"They've got a wonderful smart man there for a magistrate, I can tell you," added Joel, with emphasis, "and he ra'ally bore as hard on the major as a lawyer before a court. How he found out that the major was at the Hut is a little strange, seein' that none of us know'd of it; but they've got extraor'nary means, now-a-days."

"And, did major Willoughby admit his true character, when charged with being in the king's service?"

"He did--and like a gentleman. He only insisted that his sole ar'nd out here was to see his folks, and that he intended to go back to York the moment he had paid his visit."

"How did the person you mention receive his explanations?"

"Waal, to own the truth, he laugh'd at it, like all natur'. I don't believe they put any great weight on a syllable the major told 'em. I never see critturs with such onbelievin' faces! After talking as long as suited themselves, they ordered the major to be shut up in a buttery, with a warrior at the door for a sentinel; a'ter which they took to examining me."

Joel then proceeded with an account--his own account, always, be it remembered--of what passed between himself and the strangers. They had questioned him closely touching the nature of the defences of the Hut, the strength of the garrison, its disposition, the number and quality of the arms, and the amount of the ammunition.

"You may depend on't, I gave a good account," continued the overseer, in a self-satisfied way. "In the first place, I told 'em, the captain had a lieutenant with him that had sarved out the whull French war; then I put the men up to fifty at once, seein' it was just as easy to say that, as thirty or thirty-three. As to the arms, I told 'em more than half the pieces were double-barrelled; and that the captain, in particular, carried a rifle that had killed nine savages in one fight."

"You were much mistaken in that, Joel. It is true, that a celebrated chief once fell by this rifle; even that is not a matter for boasting."

"Waal, them that told me on't, said that *two* had fallen before it, and I put it up to nine at once, to make a good story better. Nine men had a more desperate sound than two; and when you *do* begin to brag, a man shouldn't be backward. I thought, howsever, that they was most non-plussed, when I told 'em of the field-piece."

"The field-piece, Strides!--Why did you venture on an exaggeration that any forward movement of theirs must expose?"

"We'll see to that, captain--we'll see to that. Field-pieces are desperate dampers to Indian courage, so I thought I'd just let 'em have a six-pounder, by way of tryin' their natur's. They look'd like men goin' to execution, when I told 'em of the cannon, and what a history it had gone through."

"And what may have been this history, pray?"

"I just told 'em it was the very gun the captain had took from the French, about which we've all heer'n tell; and that, as everybody knows, was a desperate piece, havin' killed more than a hundred reg'lars, before the captain charged baggonet on it, and carried it off."

This was a very artful speech, since it alluded to the most distinguished exploit of captain Willoughby's military life; one of which it would have been more than human, had he not been a little proud. All who knew him, had heard of this adventure, and Joel cunningly turned it to account, in the manner seen. The allusion served to put to sleep, for the moment at least, certain very unpleasant suspicions that were getting to be active in his superior's mind.

"There was no necessity, Strides, for saying anything about that affair"--the captain, modestly, interposed. "It happened a long time since, and might well be forgotten. Then, you know we have no gun to support your account, when our deficiency is ascertained, it will all be set down to the true cause--a wish to conceal our real weakness."

"I beg your honour's pardon," put in Joyce--"I think Strides has acted in a military manner in this affair. It is according to the art of war for the besieged to pretend to but stronger than they are; and even besiegers sometimes put a better face than the truth will warrant, on their strength. Military accounts, as your honour well knows, never pass exactly for gospel, unless it be with the raw hands."

"Then," added Joel, "I know'd what I was about, seem that we had a cannon ready for use, as soon as it could be mounted."

"I think I understand Strides, your honour," resumed the serjeant. "I have carved a 'quaker' as an ornament for the gateway, intending to saw it in two, in the middle, and place the pieces, crosswise, over the entrance, as your honour has often seen such things in garrisons--like the brass ornaments on the artillery caps, I mean, your honour. Well, this gun is finished and painted, and I intended to split it, and have it up this very week. I suppose Joel has had it in his mind, quaker fashion."

"The Serjeant's right. That piece looks as much like a real cannon as one of our cathechisms is like another. The muzzle is more than a foot deep, and has a plaguy gunpowder look!"

"But this gun is not mounted; even if it were, it could only be set up for show," observed the captain.

"Put that cannon up once, and I'll answer for it that no Injin faces it. 'Twill be as good as a dozen sentinels," answered Joel. "As for mountin', I thought of that before I said a syllable about the crittur. There's the new truck-wheels in the court, all ready to hold it, and the carpenters can put the hinder part to the whull, in an hour or two, and that in a way no Injin could tell the difference between it and a ra'al cannon, at ten yards."

"This is plausible, your honour," said Joyce, respectfully, "and it shows that corporal Strides"--Joel insisted he was a serjeant, but the real Simon Pure never gave him a title higher than that of corporal--"and it shows that corporal Strides has an idea of war. By mounting that piece, and using it with discretion--refusing it, at the right moment, and showing it at another--a great deal might be done with it, either in a siege or an assault. If your honour will excuse the liberty, I would respectfully suggest that it might be well to set the quaker on his legs, and plant him at the gate, as an exhorter."

The captain reflected a moment, and then desired the overseer to proceed in his account. The rest of Joel's story was soon told. He had mystified the strangers, according to his own account of the matter, so thoroughly, by affecting to withhold nothing, that they considered him as a sort of ally, and did not put him in confinement at all. It is true, he was placed *en surveillance*; but the duty was so carelessly performed, that, at the right moment, he had passed down the ravine, a direction in which a movement was not expected, and buried himself in the woods, so very effectually that it would have baffled pursuit, had any been attempted. After making a very long *détour*, that consumed hours, he turned the entire valley, and actually reached the Hut, under the cover of the rivulet and its bushes, or precisely by the route in which he and Mike had gone forth, in quest of Maud, the evening of the major's arrival. This latter fact, however, Joel had reasons of his own for concealing.

"You have told us nothing of Mr. Woods, Strides," the captain observed, when Joel's account was ended.

"Mr. Woods! I can tell the captain nothing of that gentleman; I supposed he was here."

The manner in which the chaplain had left the Hut, and his disappearance in the ravine, were then explained to the overseer, who evidently had quitted the mill, on his return, before the divine performed his exploit. There was a sinister expression in Joel's eyes, as he heard the account, that might have given the alarm to men more suspicious than the two old soldiers; but he had the address to conceal all he felt or thought.

"If Mr. Woods has gone into the hands of the Injins, in his church shirt," rejoined the overseer, "his case is hopeless, so far as captivity is consarned. One of the charges ag'in the captain is, that the chaplain he keeps prays as regulairly for the king as he used to do when it was lawful, and agreeable to public feelin'."

"This you heard, while under examination before the magistrate you have named?" demanded the captain.

"As good as that, and something more to the same p'int. The 'squire complained awfully of a minister's prayin' for the king and r'yal family, when the country was fightin' 'em."

"In that, the Rev. Mr. Woods only obeys orders," said the serjeant.

"But they say not. The orders is gone out, now, *they* pretend, for no man to pray for any on 'em."

"Ay--orders from the magistrates, perhaps. But the Rev. Mr. Woods is a divine, and has his own superiors in the church, and *they* must issue the commands that he obeys. I dare to say, your honour, if the archbishop of Canterbury, or the commander-in-chief of the church, whoever he may be, should issue a general order directing all the parsons not to pray for King George, the Rev. Mr. Woods would have no scruple about obeying. But, it's a different thing when a justice of the peace undertakes to stand fugleman for the clergy. It's like a navy captain undertaking to wheel a regiment."

"Poor Woods!" exclaimed the captain--"Had he been ruled by me, he would have dropped those prayers, and it would have been better for us both. But, he is of your opinion, serjeant, and thinks that a layman can have no authority over a gownsman."

"And isn't he right, your honour! Think what a mess of it the militia officers make, when they undertake to meddle with a regular corps. Some of our greatest difficulties in the last war came from such awkward hands attempting to manage machines of which they had no just notions. As for praying, your honour, I'm no wise particular *who* I pray for, or *what* I pray for, so long as it be all set down in general orders that come from the right head-quarters; and I think the Rev. Mr. Woods ought to be judged by the same rule."

As the captain saw no use in prolonging the dialogue, he dismissed his companions. He then sought his wife, in order to make her acquainted with the actual state of things. This last was a painful duty, though Mrs. Willoughby and her daughters heard the truth with less of apprehension than the husband and father had anticipated. They had suffered so much from uncertainty, that there was a relief in learning the truth. The mother did not think the authorities of the colony would hurt her son, whom she fancied all men must, in a degree, love as she loved. Beulah thought of her own husband as Bob's safeguard; while Maud felt it to be comparative happiness to know he was unharmed, and still so near her.

This unpleasant duty discharged, the captain began to bethink him seriously of his military trust. After some reflection, and listening to a few more suggestions from Joyce, he consented to let the "quaker" be put on wheels. The carpenters were immediately set at work to achieve this job, which the serjeant volunteered to superintend, in person. As for Joel, his wife and children, with the miller, occupied most of the morning; the day turning, and even drawing towards its close, ere he became visible, as had formerly been his wont, among the men of the settlement.

All this time, everything without the palisades lay in the silence of nature. The sun cast its glories athwart the lovely scene, as in one of the

Sabbaths of the woods; but man was nowhere visible. Not a hostile Indian, or white, exhibited himself; and the captain began to suspect that, satisfied with their captures, the party had commenced its return towards the river, postponing his own arrest for some other occasion. So strong did this impression become towards the close of the day, that he was actually engaged in writing to some friends of influence in Albany and on the Mohawk to interpose their names and characters in his son's behalf, when the serjeant, about nine o'clock, the hour when he had been ordered to parade the guard for the first half of the night, presented himself at the door of his room, to make an important report.

"What now, Joyce?" demanded the captain. "Are any of our fellows sleepy, and plead illness?"

"Worse than that, your honour, I greatly fear," was the answer. Of the ten men your honour commanded me to detail for the guard, five are missing. I set them down as deserters."

"Deserters!--This is serious, indeed; let the signal be made for a general parade--the people cannot yet have gone to bed; we will look into this."

As Joyce made it matter of religion "to obey orders," this command was immediately put in execution. In five minutes, a messenger came to summon the captain to the court, where the garrison was under arms. The serjeant stood in front of the little party, with a lantern, holding his muster-roll in his hand. The first glance told the captain that a serious reduction had taken place in his forces, and he led the serjeant aside to hear his report.

"What is the result of your inquiries, Joyce?" he demanded, with more uneasiness than he would have liked to betray openly.

"We have lost just half our men, sir. The miller, most of the Yankees, and two of the Dutchmen, are not on parade; neither is one of them to be found in his quarters. They have either gone over to the enemy, captain Willoughby, or, disliking the appearance of things here, they have taken to the woods for safety."

"And abandoned their wives and children, serjeant! Men would scarcely do that."

"Their wives and children have deserted too, sir. Not a chick or child belonging to either of the runaways is to be found in the Hut."

Chapter XIX

"For all the Welshmen, hearing thou wert dead,
Are gone to Bolingbroke, dispersed and fled."

Richard III

This was startling intelligence to receive just as night had shut in, and under the other circumstances of the case. Touching the men who still remained, captain Willoughby conceived it prudent to inquire into their characters and names, in order to ascertain the ground he stood on, and to govern his future course accordingly. He put the question to the serjeant, therefore, as soon as he could lead him far enough from the little array, to be certain he was out of ear-shot.

"We have Michael O'Hearn, Jamie Allen, the two carpenters, the three niggers, Joel, and the three Dutchmen that last came into the settlement, and the two lads that Strides engaged at the beginning of the year, left," was the answer. "These, counting your honour and myself, make just fifteen men; quite enough yet, I should think, to make good the house, in case of an assault--though I fear everything like an outwork must be abandoned."

"On the whole, these are the best of our men," returned the captain; "I mean the most trustworthy. I count on Mike, Jamie, and the blacks, as being as much to be relied on as we are ourselves. Joel, too, is a man of resources, if he will but do his duty under fire."

"Corporal Strides is still an untried soldier, your honour; though recruits, even, sometimes do wonders. Of course, I shall reduce the guard to half its former strength, as the men must have some sleep, sir."

"We must depend very much on your vigilance and mine, to-night, Joyce. You shall take the guard till one, when I will stand it for the rest of the night. I will speak to the men before you dismiss them. An encouraging word, just now, may be worth a platoon to us."

The serjeant seldom dissented from any suggestion of his commanding officer, and the scheme was carried out on the spot. The lantern was so placed as to permit the captain to see the heterogeneous row of countenances that was drawn up before him, and he proceeded:

"It seems, my friends," he said, "that some of our people have been seized with a panic, and have deserted. These mistaken men have not only fled themselves, but they have induced their wives and children to follow them. A little reflection will show you to what distress all must be reduced by this ill-judged flight. Fifty miles from another settlement of any size, and more than thirty from even a single hut, beyond the cabin of a hunter, days must pass before they can reach a place of safety, even should they escape the savage foe that we know to be scouring the woods. The women and children will not have sufficient art to conceal their trail, nor sufficient strength to hold out against hunger and fatigue many hours. God forgive them for what they have done, and guide them through the difficulties and pains by which they are menaced! As for us, we must determine to do our whole duty, or, at once to retire, with the consent of each other. If there is a man among you, then, who apprehends the consequences of standing to his arms, and of defending this house, let him confess it frankly; he shall have leave to depart, with all that belongs to him, taking food and the means of subsistence and defence with him. I wish no man to remain with me and mine, but he who can do it cheerfully. The night is now dark, and, by quitting the Hut at an early hour, such a start might be gained over any pursuers, as to place him in comparative security before morning. If any such man is here, let him now speak out honestly, and fear nothing. The gate shall be opened for his march."

The captain paused, but not a soul answered. A common sentiment of loyalty seemed to bind every one of the listeners to his duty. The dark eyes of the negroes rolled along the short rank to see who would be the first to desert their master, and grins of delight showed the satisfaction with which they noted the effect of the appeal. As for Mike, he felt too strongly to keep silence, and he muttered the passing impressions aloud.

"Och!"--growled the county Leitrim-man--"Is it a good journey that I wish the runaways? That it isn't, nor many a good male either, as they trudge alang t'rough the woods, with their own consciences forenent their eyes, pricking them up to come back, like so many t'ieves of the wor-r-ld, as they are, every mother's son of 'em, women and all. I'd nivir do *that*; no, not if my head was *all* scalp, down to the soles of my fut, and an Injin was at every inch of it, to cut out his summer clothes of my own skin. Talk of religion amang sich crathures!--Why, there isn't enough moral in one of thim to carry him through the shortest prayer the Lord allows a Christian to utter. Divil burn 'em say I, and that's my kindest wish in their behalf."

The captain waited patiently for this soliloquy to terminate; then he dismissed the men, with a few more words of encouragement, and his thanks for the fidelity they, at least, had shown. By this time the night had got to be dark, and the court was much more so, on account of the shadows of the buildings, than places in the open air. As the captain turned aside to give his last instructions to Joyce, he discovered, by the light of the lantern the latter held, a figure standing at no great distance, quite dimly seen on account of its proximity to the walls of the Hut. It was clearly a man; and as all the males able to bear arms, a single sentinel outside the court excepted, were supposed to be in the group that had not yet separated, the necessity of ascertaining the character of this unlooked-for visiter flashed on the minds of both the old soldiers at the same instant. Joyce raised the lantern, as they moved quickly towards the motionless form, and its light glanced athwart a pair of wild, glowing, dark eyes, and the red visage of an Indian.

"Nick!" exclaimed the captain, "is that you?--What has brought you here again, and how have you entered the palisades?--Do you come as a friend, to aid us, or as an enemy?"

"Too much question, cap'in--too much like squaw; ask all togeder. Go to book-room; Nick follow; tell all he got to say."

The captain whispered the serjeant to ascertain whether the watch without was vigilant, when he led the way to the library, where, as he expected, he found his wife and daughters, anxiously waiting his appearance.

"Oh! Hugh, I trust it is not as bad as we feared!" cried the mother, as the captain entered the room, closely attended by the Tuscarora; "our men cannot be so heartless as to desert us at such a moment!"

The captain kissed his wife, said a word or two of encouragement, and pointed to the Indian.

"Nick!" exclaimed all three of the females, in a breath. Though the tones of their voices denoted very different sensations, at the unexpected appearance of their old acquaintance. Mrs. Willoughby's exclamation was not without pleasure, for *she* thought the man her friend. Beulah's was filled with alarm, little Evert and savage massacres suddenly crossing the sensitive mind of the young mother; while Maud's tone had much of the stern resolution that she had summoned to sustain her in a moment of such fearful trial.

"Yes, Nick--Sassy Nick," repeated the Indian, in his guttural voice--"Ole friend--you no glad see him?"

"That will depend on your errand," interposed the captain. "Are you one of the party that is now lying at the mill?--but, stop; how did you get within the palisades? First answer me *that*."

"Come in. Tree no good to stop Injin. Can't do it wid branches, how do it widout? Want plenty of musket and plenty of soldier to do *dat*. Dis no garrison, cap'in, to make Nick afeard. Always tell him too much hole to be tight."

"This is not answering my question, fellow. By what means did you pass the palisades?"

"What means?--Injin means, sartain. Came like cat, jump like deer, slide like snake. Nick great Tuscarora chief; know well how warrior march, when he dig up hatchet."

"And Nick has been a great hanger-on of garrisons, and should know the use that I can make of his back. You will remember, Tuscarora, that I have had you flogged, more than once, in my day."

This was said menacingly, and with more warmth, perhaps, than was prudent. It caused the listeners to start, as if a sudden and new danger rose before their eyes, and the anxious looks he encountered warned the captain that he was probably going too far. As for Nick, himself, the gathering thunder-cloud is not darker than his visage became at the words he heard; it seemed by the moral writhing of his spirit as if every disgracing blow he had received was at that instant torturing his flesh anew, blended with the keenest feelings of ignominy. Captain Willoughby was startled at the effect he had produced; but it was too late to change his course; and he remained in dignified quiet, awaiting the workings of the Tuscarora's mind.

It was more than a minute ere Nick made any reply. Gradually, but very slowly, the expression of his visage changed. It finally became as stoical in expression as severe training could render the human countenance, and as unmoved as marble. Then he found the language he wanted.

"Listen," said the Indian, sternly. "Cap'in ole man. Got a head like snow on rock. He bold soldier; but he no got wisdom enough for gray hair. Why he put he hand rough, on place where whip strike? Wise man nebber do *aat*. Last winter he cold; fire wanted to make him warm. Much ice, much storm, much snow. World seem bad--fit only for bear, and snake, dat hide in rock. Well; winter gone away; ice gone away; snow gone away; storm gone away. Summer come, in his place. Ebbery t'ing *good*--ebbery t'ing *pleasant*. Why t'ink of winter, when summer come, and drive him away wid pleasant sky?"

"In order to provide for its return. He who never thought of the evil day, in the hour of his prosperity, would find that he has forgotten, not only a duty, but the course of wisdom."

"He *not* wise!" said Nick, sternly. "Cap'in pale-face chief. He got garrison; got soldier; got musket. Well, he flog warrior's back; make blood come. Dat bad enough; worse to put finger on ole sore, and make 'e pain, and 'e shame, come back ag'in."

"Perhaps it would have been more generous, Nick, to have said nothing about it; but, you see how I am situated; an enemy without, my men deserting, a bad look-out, and one finding his way into my very court-yard, and I ignorant of the means."

"Nick tell cap'in all about means. If red-men outside, shoot *'em*; if garrison run away, flog garrison; if don't know, l'arn; but, don't flog back, ag'in, on ole sore!"

"Well, well, say no more about it, Nick. Here is a dollar to keep you in rum, and we will talk of other matters."

Nick heeded not the money, though it was held before his eyes, some little time, to tempt him. Perceiving that the Tuscarora was now acting as a warrior and a chief, which Nick would do, and do well, on occasion, the captain pocketed the offering, and regulated his own course accordingly.

"At all events, I have a right to insist on knowing, first, by what means you entered the palisades; and, second, what business has brought you here, at night, and so suddenly."

"Ask Nick, cap'in, all he right to ask; but, don't touch ole flog. How I cross palisade? Where your sentinel to stop Injin? One at gate; well, none all round, t'other place. Get in, up here, down dere, over yonder. Ten, twenty, t'ree spot--s'pose him tree? climb him. S'pose him palisade?--climb him, too. What help?--Soldier out at gate when Nick get over t'other end! Come in court, too, when he want. Half gate half no gate. So easy, 'shamed to brag of. Cap'in once Nick's friend--went on same war-path--dat in ole time. Both warrior; both went ag'in French garrison. Well; who crept in, close by cannon, open gate, let pale-men in. Great Tuscarora do *dat*; no flog, *den*--no talk of ole sore, dat night!"

"This is all true enough, Wyandotté"--This was Nick's loftiest appellation; and a grim, but faint smile crossed his visage, as he heard it, again, in the mouth of one who had known him when its sound carried terror to the hearts of his enemies--"This is all true, Wyandotté, and I have even given you credit for it. On that occasion you were bold as the lion, and as cunning as a fox--you were much honoured for that exploit."

"No ole sore in *dat*, um?" cried Nick, in a way so startling as to sicken Mrs. Willoughby to the heart. "No call Nick dog, dat night. He *all* warrior, den--all face; no *back*."

"I have said you were honoured for your conduct, Nick, and paid for it. Now, let me know what has brought you here to-night, and whence you come."

There was another pause. Gradually, the countenance of the Indian became less and less fierce, until it lost its expression of malignant resentment in one in which human emotions of a kinder nature predominated.

"Squaw good," he said, even gently, waving his hand towards Mrs. Willoughby--"Got son; love him like little baby. Nick come six, two time before, runner from her son."

"My son, Wyandotté!" exclaimed the mother--"Bring you any tidings, now, from my boy?"

"No bring tidin'--too heavy; Indian don't love to carry load--bring *letter*"

The cry from the three females was now common, each holding out her hand, with an involuntary impulse, to receive the note. Nick drew the missive from a fold of his garment, and placed it in the hand of Mrs. Willoughby, with a quiet grace that a courtier might have wished to equal, in vain.

The note was short, and had been written in pencil, on a leaf torn from some book of coarse paper. The handwriting however, was at once recognised as Robert Willoughby's though there was no address, nor any signature. The paper merely contained the following--

"Trust to your defences, and to nothing else. This party has many white men in it, disguised as Indians. I am suspected, if not known. You will be tampered with, but the wisest course is to be firm. If Nick is honest, he can tell you more; if false, this note will be shown, even though it be delivered. Secure the inner gates, and depend more on the house itself, than on the palisades. Fear nothing for me--my life can be in no danger."

This note was read by each, in succession, Maud turning aside to conceal the tears that fell fast on the paper, as she perused it. She read it last, and was enabled to retain it; and precious to her heart was the boon, at such a moment, when nearly every sensation of her being centred in intense feeling in behalf of the captive.

"We are told to inquire the particulars of you, Nick," observed the captain; "I hope you will tell us nothing but truth. A lie is so unworthy a warrior's mouth!"

"Nick didn't lie 'bout beaver dam! Cap'in no find him good, as Indian say?"

"In that you dealt honestly, and I give you credit for it. Has any one seen this letter but ourselves, yourself, and the person who wrote it?"

"What for ask? If Nick say no, cap'in t'ink he lie. Even fox tell trut' some time; why not Injin? Nick say no."

"Where did you leave my son, and when?--Where is the party of red-skins at this moment?"

"All pale-face in hurry! Ask ten, one, four question, altogeder. Well; answer him so. Down here, at mill; down dere, at mill; half an hour, six, two, ten o'clock."

"I understand you to say that major Willoughby was at the mill when you saw him last, and that this was only half an hour since?"

The Tuscarora nodded his head in assent, but made no other reply. Even as he did this, his keen eyes rolled over the pallid faces of the females in a way to awaken the captain's distrust, and he resumed his questions in a tone that partook more of the military severity of his ancient habits than of the gentler manner he had been accustomed to use of late years.

"You know me, Nick," he said sternly, "and ought to dread my displeasure."

"What cap'in mean, now?" demanded the Indian, quietly.

"That the same whip is in this fort that I always kept in the other, in which you knew me to dwell; nor have I forgotten how to use it."

The Tuscarora gazed at the captain with a very puzzling expression, though, in the main, his countenance appeared to be ironical rather than fierce.

"What for, talk of whip, now?" he said. "Even Yengeese gen'ral hide whip, when he see enemy. Soldier can't fight when back sore. When battle near, den all good friend; when battle over, den flog, flog, flog. Why talk so?--Cap'in nebber strike *Wyandotté*."

"Your memory must be short, to say this! I thought an Indian kept a better record of what passed."

"No man *dare* strike Wyandotté!" exclaimed the Indian, with energy. "No man--pale-face or red-skin, *can* give blow on back of Wyandotté, and see sun set!"

"Well--well--Nick; we will not dispute on this point, but let bye-gones be bye-gones. What *has* happened, *has* happened, and I hope will never occur again."

"Dat happen to Nick--Sassy Nick--poor, drunken Nick--to Wyandotté, nebber!"

"I believe I begin to understand you, now, Tuscarora, and am glad I have a chief and a warrior in my house, instead of a poor miserable outcast. Shall I have the pleasure of filling you a glass in honour of our old campaigns?"

"Nick alway dry--Wyandotté know no thirst. Nick, beggar--ask for rum--*pray* for rum--*t'ink* of rum, *talk* of rum, *laugh* for rum, *cry* for rum. Wyandotté don't know rum, when he see him. Wyandotté beg not'in'; no, not his scalp."

"All this sounds well, and I am both willing and glad, chief, to receive you in the character in which you give me to understand you have now come. A warrior of Wyandotté's high name is too proud to carry a forked tongue in his mouth, and I shall hear nothing but truth. Tell me, then, all you know about this party at the mill; what has brought it here, how you came to meet my son, and what will be the next step of his captors. Answer the questions in the order in which I put them."

"Wyandotté not newspaper to tell ebbery t'ing at once. Let cap'in talk like one chief speaking to anoder."

"Then, tell me first, what you know of this party at the mill. Are there many pale-faces in it?"

"Put 'em in the river," answered the Indian, sententiously; "water tell the trut'."

"You think that there are many among them that would wash white?"

"Wyandotté *know* so. When did red warriors ever travel on their path like hogs in drove? *One* red-man there, as Great Spirit make him; by his side *two* red-men as *paint* make 'em. This soon told on trail."

"You struck their trail, then, and joined their company, in that manner?"

Another nod indicated the assent of the Indian. Perceiving that the Tuscarora did not intend to speak, the captain continued his interrogatories.

"And how did the trail betray this secret, chief?" he asked.

"Toe turn out--step too short--trail too broad--trail too plain--march too short."

"You must have followed them some distance, Wyandotté, to learn all this?"

"Follow from Mohawk--join 'em at mill. Tuscarora don't like too much travel with Mohawk."

"But, according to your account, there cannot be a great many red-skins in the party, if the white men so much out-number them."

Nick, now, raised his right hand, showing all the fingers and the thumb, at each exhibition, four several times. Then he raised it once, showing only the fore-finger and thumb.

"This makes twenty-two, Nick--Do you include yourself in the number?"

"Wyandotté, a Tuscarora--he count *Mohawks*"

"True--Are there any other red-men among them?"

"Oneida, so"--holding up four fingers only. After which he held up a single finger, adding--"Onondaga, so."

"Twenty-two Mohawks, four Oneidas, and a single Onondaga, make twenty-seven in all. To these, how many whites am I to add?--You counted them, also?"

The Indian now showed both hands, with all the fingers extended, repeating the gestures four times; then he showed one hand entire, and two fingers on the other.

"Forty-seven. Add these to the red-skins, and we get seventy-four for the total. I had supposed them rather stronger than this, Wyandotté?"

"No stronger--no weaker--just so. Good many ole womans, too, among pale-faces."

"Old women!--You are not speaking literally, Nick? All that I have seen appear to be men."

"Got beard; but ole woman, too. Talk--talk--talk;--do not'in'. *Dat* what Injin call ole woman. Party, poor party; cap'in beat 'em, if he fight like ole time."

"Well, this is encouraging, Wilhelmina, and Nick seems to be dealing fairly with us."

"Now, inquire more about Robert, Hugh"--said the wife, in whose maternal heart her children were always uppermost.

"You hear, Nick; my wife is desirous of learning something about her son, next."

During the preceding dialogue, there had been something equivocal in the expression of the Indian's face. Every word he uttered about the party, its numbers, and his own manner of falling in with it, was true, and his countenance indicated that he was dealing fairly. Still, the captain fancied that he could detect a covert fierceness in his eye and air, and he felt uneasiness even while he yielded him credence. As soon as Mrs. Willoughby, however, interposed, the gleam of ferocity that passed so naturally and readily athwart the swarthy features of the savage, melted into a look of gentleness, and there were moments when it might be almost termed softness.

"Good to have moder"--said Nick, kindly. "Wyandotté got no squaw--wife dead, moder dead, sister dead--all gone to land of spirits--bye'm-by, chief follow. No one throw stone on his grave! Been on death-path long ago, but cap'in's squaw say 'stop, Nick; little too soon, now; take medicine, and get well.' Squaw made to do good. Chief alway like 'e squaw, when his mind not wild with war."

"And *your* mind, Wyandotté, is not wild with war, now," answered Mrs. Willoughby, earnestly. "You will help a mother, then, to get her son out of the hands of merciless enemies?"

"Why you t'ink merciless? Because pale-face dress like Injin, and try to cheat?"

"That may be one reason; but I fear there are many others. Tell me, Wyandotté, how came you to discover that Robert was a prisoner, and by what means did he contrive to give you his letter?"

The Indian assumed a look of pride, a little blended with hauteur; for he felt that he was manifesting the superiority of a red-man over the pale-face, as he related the means through which he had made his discoveries.

"Read book on ground," Nick answered gravely. "Two book alway open before chief; one in sky, t'other on ground. Book in sky, tell weather--snow, rain, wind, thunder, lightning, war--book on ground, tell what happen."

"And what had this book on the ground to do with my son, Wyandotté?"

"Tell all about him. Major's trail first seen at mill. No moccasin--much boot. Soldier boot like letter--say great deal, in few word. First t'ink it cap'in; but it too short. Den *know* it Major."

"This sounds very well, Nick," interrupted the captain, "though you will excuse me if I say it is going a little too far. It seems impossible that you should know that the print of the foot was that of my son. How *could* you be certain of this?"

"How *could*, eh? Who follow trail from house, here, to Hudson river? T'ink Nick blind, and can't see? Tuscarora read *his* book well as pale-face read bible." Here Nick looked round him a moment, raised his fore-finger, dropped his voice, and added earnestly--"see him at Bunker Hill--know him among ten, six, two t'ousand warrior. Know dat foot, if meet him in Happy Hunting Ground."

"And why my son's foot, in particular? The boot is often changed, can never be exactly like its predecessor, and one boot is so much like another, that to me the thing seems impossible. This account of the boot, Nick, makes me distrust your whole story."

"What distrust?" demanded the Indian like lightning.

"It means doubt, uncertainty--distrust."

"Don't believe, ha?"

"Yes, that is it, substantially. Don't more than *half* believe, perhaps, would be nearer to the mark."

"Why, ole soldier alway distrust; squaw nebber? Ask moder--ha!--you t'ink Nick don't know son's trail--handsome trail, like young chief's?"

"I can readily believe Nick might recognise Bob's trail, Hugh"-- expostulated Mrs. Willoughby. "He has a foot in a thousand--you may remember how every one was accustomed to speak of his beautiful foot, even when he was a boy. As a man, I think it still more remarkable."

"Ay, go on, Nick, in this way, and my wife will believe all you say. There is no distrust in a mother's partiality, certainly. You are an old courtier, and would make your way at St. James's."

"Major nebber tell about foot?" asked Nick, earnestly.

"I remember nothing; and had he spoken of any such thing, I must have heard it. But, never mind the story, now; you saw the foot-print, and knew it for my son's. Did you ask to be admitted to his prison? or was your intercourse secret?"

"Wyandotté too wise to act like squaw, or boy. See him, widout look. Talk, widout speak--hear, widout ear. Major write letter, Nick take him. All done by eye and hand; not'in' done by tongue, or at Council Fire. Mohawk blind like owl!"

"May I believe you, Tuscarora; or, incited by demons, do you come to deceive me?"

"Ole warrior look two time before he go; t'ink ten time before he say, yes. All good. Nick no affronted. Do so himself, and t'ink it right. Cap'in *may* believe all Nick say."

"Father!" cried Maud, with simple energy, "I will answer for the Indian's honesty. He has guided Robert so often, and been with him in so many trying scenes, he never *can* have the heart to betray him, or us. Trust him, then he may be of infinite service."

Even captain Willoughby, little disposed as he was to judge Nick favourably, was struck with the gleam of mamy kindness that shot across the dark face of the Indian, as he gazed at the glowing cheek and illuminated countenance of the ardent and beautiful girl.

"Nick seems disposed to make a truce with *you*, at least, Maud," he said, smiling, "and I shall now know where to look for a mediator, whenever any trouble arises between us."

"I have known Wyandotté, dear sir, from childhood, and he has ever been my friend. He promised me, in particular, to be true to Bob, and I am happy to say he has ever kept his word."

This was telling but half the story. Maud had made the Indian many presents, and most especially had she attended to his wants, when it was known he was to be the major's guide, the year previously, on his return to Boston. Nick had known her real father, and was present at his death. He was consequently acquainted with her actual position in the family of the Hutted Knoll; and, what was of far more consequence in present emergencies, he had fathomed the depths of her heart, in a way our heroine could hardly be said to have done herself. Off her guard with such a being, Maud's solicitude, however, had betrayed her, and the penetrating Tuscarora had discerned that which had escaped the observation of father, and mother, and sister. Had Nick been a pale-face, of the class of those with whom he usually associated, his discovery would have gone through the settlement, with scoffings and exaggerations; but this forest gentleman, for such was Wyandotté, in spite of his degradation and numerous failings, had too much consideration to make a woman's affections the subject of his coarseness and merriment. The secrets of Maud would not have been more sacred with her own brother, had such a relative existed to become her confidant, than it was with Saucy Nick.

"Nick gal's friend," observed the Indian, quietly; "dat enough; what Nick say, Nick mean. What Nick *mean*, he *do*. Come, cap'in; time to quit squaw, and talk about war."

At this hint, which was too plain to be misunderstood, captain Willoughby bade the Indian withdraw to the court, promising to follow him, as soon as he could hold a short conference with Joyce, who was now summoned to the council. The subject of discussion was the manner in which the Tuscarora had passed the stockade, and the probability of his being true. The serjeant was disposed to distrust all red-men, and he advised putting Nick under arrest, and to keep him in durance, until the return of light, at least.

"I might almost say, your honour, that such are orders, sir. The advice to soldiers carrying on war with savages, tells us that the best course is to pay off treachery with treachery; and treachery is a red-skin's manual exercise. There is O'Hearn will make a capital sentinel, for the fellow is as true as the best steel in the army. Mr. Woods' room is empty, and it is so far out of the way that nothing will be easier than to keep the savage snug enough. Besides, by a little management, he might fancy we were doing him honour all the while."

"We will see, serjeant," answered the captain. "It has a bad appearance, and yet it may be the wisest thing we can do. Let us first go the rounds, taking Nick with us for safety, and determine afterwards."

Chapter XX

"His hand was stay'd--he knew not why;
'Twas a presence breathed around--
A pleading from the deep-blue sky,
And up from the teeming ground.
It told of the care that lavish'd had been
In sunshine and in dew--
Of the many things that had wrought a screen
When peril round it grew."

Mrs. Seba Smith.

The desertions gave not only the captain, but his great support and auxiliary, the serjeant, the gravest apprehensions. A disposition of that nature is always contagious, men abandoning a failing cause much as rats are known to quit a sinking ship. It is not a matter of surprise, therefore, that the distrust which accompanied the unexpected appearance of the Tuscarora, became associated with this falling off in the loyalty of the garrison, in the minds of the two old soldiers.

"I do think, your honour," said Joyce, as they entered the court together, "that we may depend on O'Hearn, and Jamie, and Strides. The latter, as a matter of course, being a corporal, or serjeant as he calls himself; and the two first, as men who have no ties but such as would be likely to keep them true to this family. But here is the corporal to speak for himself."

As this was said, corporal Strides, as the serjeant persisted in terming Joel, on the ground that being but one step higher himself, the overseer could justly claim no rank of greater pretension, approached the captain, taking care to make the military salute which Joyce had never succeeded before in extracting from him, notwithstanding a hundred admonitions on the subject.

"This is a distressing affair, captain Willoughby," observed Joel, in his most jesuitical manner; "and to me it is altogether onaccountable! It does seem to me ag'in natur', for a man to desart his own household and hum' (Joel meant '*home*') in the hour of trial. If a fellow-being wunt (Anglice 'wont') stand by his wife and children, he can hardly be expected to do any of his duties."

"Quite true. Strides," answered the confiding captain, "though these deserters are not altogether as bad as you represent, since, you will remember, they have carried their wives and children with them."

"I believe they have, sir--yes, that must be allowed to be true, and that it is, which to me seems the most extr'or'nary. The very men that a person would calcilate on the most, or the heads of families, have desarted, while them that remain behind are mostly single!"

"If we single men have no wives and children of our own to fight for, Strides," observed Joyce, with a little military stiffness, "we have the wife and children of captain Willoughby; no man who wishes to sell his life dearly, need look for a better motive."

"Thank you, serjeant," the captain said, feelingly--"On *you*, I can rely as on myself. So long as I have *you*, and Joel, here, and Mike and the blacks, and the rest of the brave fellows who have stood by me thus far, I shall not despair. *We* can make good the house against ten times our own number. But, it is time to look to the Indians."

"I was going to speak to the captain about Nick," put in Joel, who had listened to the eulogium on his own fidelity with some qualms of conscience. "I can't say I like the manner he has passed between the two parties; and that fellow has always seemed to me as if he owed the captain a mortal grudge; when an Injin *does* owe a grudge, he is pretty sartain to pay it, in full."

"This has passed over my mind, too, I will confess, Joel; yet Nick and I have been on reasonably good terms, when one comes to remember his character, on the one side, and the fact that I have commanded a frontier garrison on the other. If I have had occasion to flog him a few times, I have also had occasion to give him more rum than has done him good, with now and then a dollar."

"There I think the captain miscalcilates," observed Joel with a knowledge of human nature that would have been creditable to him, had he practised on it himself. "No man is thankful for rum when the craving is off, sin' he knows he has been taking an inimy into his stomach; and as for the money, it was much the same as giving the liquor, seem' that it went for liquor as soon as he could trot down to the mill. A man will seek his revenge for rum, as soon as for anything else, when he gets to feel injuries uppermost. Besides, I s'pose the captain knows an injury will be remembered long a'ter a favour is forgotten."

"This may be true, Strides, and certainly I shall keep my eyes on the Indian. Can you mention any particular act, that excites your suspicion?"

"Don't the captain think Nick may have had suthin' to do with the desartions?--A dozen men would scarce desart all at once, as it might be, onless someone was at the bottom of it."

This was true enough, certainly, though Joel chose to keep out of view all his own machinations and arts on the subject. The captain was struck by the suggestion, and he determined to put his first intention in respect to Nick in force immediately. Still, it was necessary to proceed with caution, the state of the Hut rendering a proper watch and a suitable prison difficult to be obtained. These circumstances were mentioned to the overseer, who led the way to the part of the buildings occupied by his own family; and, throwing open the doors, ostentatiously exhibited Phoebe and her children in their customary beds, at a moment when so many others had proved recreant. His professed object was to offer a small closet in his own rooms as a prison for Nick, remarking he must be an ingenious savage indeed, if he could escape the vigilance of as many watchful eyes as would then be on him.

"I believe you, Strides," said the captain, smiling as he walked away from the place; "if he can escape Phoebe and *her* children, the fellow must be made of quicksilver. Still, I have a better prison in view. I am glad to see this proof, however, of your own fidelity, by finding all your family in their beds; for those are not wanting who would have me suspect even *you*"

"Me!--Well, if the captain can't count on his own overseer, I should like to ask such persons on whom he *can* count? Madam Willoughby and the young ladies isn't more likely to remain true than I am, myself, I should think--What in reason, or natur', or all lawful objects, could make *me*----"

Joel was about to run into that excess of vindication that is a little apt to mark guilt; but, the captain cut him short, by telling him it was unnecessary, recommending vigilance, and walking away in search of Nick.

The Indian was found standing beneath the arch of the gateway, upright, motionless, and patient. A lantern was kept burning here, the place being used as a sort of guard-house; and, by its light, it was easy to perceive the state of the still unhung leaf of the passage. This leaf, however, was propped in its place, by strong timbers; and, on the whole, many persons would think it the most secure half of the gate. Captain Willoughby observed that the Indian was studying this arrangement when he entered the place himself. The circumstance caused him uneasiness, and quickened his determination to secure the Indian.

"Well, Nick," he said, concealing his intention under an appearance of indifference, "you see our gates are well fastened, and steady hands and quick eyes will do the rest. It is getting late, and I wish to have you comfortably lodged before I lie down myself. Follow me, and I will show you to a place where you will be at your ease."

The Tuscarora understood the captain's object the instant he spoke of giving him comfortable lodgings, a bed being a thing that was virtually unknown to his habits. But, he raised no objections, quietly treading in the other's footsteps, until both were in the bed-room of the absent Mr. Woods. The apartments of the chaplain were above the library, and, being in the part of the house that was fortified by the cliff, they had dormer windows that looked toward the forest. The height of these windows the captain thought would be a sufficient security against flight; and by setting Mike and one of the Plinys on the look-out, to relieve each other at intervals of four hours, he thought the Tuscarora might be kept until the return of light. The hour when he most apprehended danger was that which just precedes the day, sleep then pressing the heaviest on the sentinel's eyelids, and rest having refreshed the assailants.

"Here, Wyandotté, I intend you shall pass the night," said the captain, assuming as much courtesy of manner as if he were doing the honours of his house to an invited and honoured guest. "I know you despise a bed, but there are blankets, and by spreading them on the floor, you can make your own arrangements."

Nick made a gesture of assent, looking cautiously around him, carefully avoiding every appearance of curiosity at the same time, more in pride of character, however, than in cunning. Nevertheless, he took in the history of the locality at a glance.

"It is well," he said; "a Tuscarora chief no t'ink of sleep. Sleep come standing, walking; *where* he will, *when* he will. Dog eats, den lie down to sleep; warrior always ready. Good bye, cap'in--to-morrow see him ag'in."

"Good night, Nick. I have ordered your old friend Mike, the Irishman, to come and sit in your room, lest you might want something in the night. You are good friends with Mike, I believe; I chose him on that account."

The Indian understood this, too; but not an angry gleam, no smile, nor any other sign, betrayed his consciousness of the captain's motives.

"Mike *good*" he answered, with emphasis. "Long tongue--short t'ink. Say much; mean little. Heart sound, like hard oak--mind, like spunk--burn quick, no too much strong."

This sententious and accurate delineation of the county Leitrim-man's characteristics induced a smile in the captain; but, O'Hearn entering at the moment, and possessing his entire confidence, he saw no use in replying. In another minute the two worthies were left in possession of the bed-room, Michael having received a most solemn injunction not to be tempted to drink.

It was now so late, the captain determined to let the regular watches of the night take their course. He held a short consultation with Joyce, who took the first ward, and then threw himself on a mattrass, in his clothes, his affectionate wife having done the same thing, by the side of her daughters and grandson in an adjoining room. In a short time, the sounds of footsteps ceased in the Hut; and, one unacquainted with the real state of the household, might have fancied that the peace and security of one of its ancient midnights were reigning about the Knoll.

It was just two in the morning, when the serjeant tapped lightly at the door of his commanding officer's room. The touch was sufficient to bring the captain to his feet, and he instantly demanded the news.

"Nothing but sentry-go, your honour," replied Joyce. "I am as fresh as a regiment that is just marching out of barracks, and can easily stand the guard till daylight. Still, as it was orders to call your honour at two, I could do no less, you know, sir."

"Very well, serjeant--I will just wash my eyes, and be with you in a minute. How has the night gone?"

"Famously quiet, sir. Not even an owl to trouble it. The sentinels have kept their eyes wide open, dread of the scalping-knife being a good wakener, and no sign of any alarm has been seen. I will wait for your honour, in the court, the moment of relieving guard being often chosen by a cunning enemy for the assault."

"Yes," sputtered the captain, his face just emerging from the water--"if he happen to know when that is."

In another minute, the two old soldiers were together in the court, waiting the return of Jamie Allen with his report, the mason having been sent round to the beds of the fresh men to call the guard. It was not long, however, before the old man was seen hastening towards the spot where Joyce had bid him come.

"The Lord ha' maircy on us, and on a' wretched sinners!" exclaimed Jamie, as soon as near enough to be heard without raising his voice on too high a key--"there are just the beds of the three Connecticut lads that were to come into the laird's guard, as empty as a robin's nest fra' which the yang ha' flown!"

"Do you mean, Jamie, that the boys have deserted?"

"It's just that; and no need of ca'ing it by anither name. The Hoose o' Hanover wad seem to have put the de'il in a' the lads, women and children included, and to have raised up a spirit o' disaffection, that is fast leaving us to carry on this terrible warfare with our ain hearts and bodies."

"With your honour's permission," said the serjeant, "I would ask corporal Allen if the deserters have gone off with their arms and accoutrements?"

"Airms? Ay, and legs, and a' belonging to 'em, with mair that is the lawfu' property of the laird. Not so much as a flint is left behind."

"Then we may count on seeing all the fellows in the enemy's ranks," the serjeant quietly remarked, helping himself to the tobacco from which he had refrained throughout the previous hours of the night, Joyce being too much of a *martinet* to smoke or chew on duty. "It's up-hill work, your honour, when every deserter counts two, in this manner. The civil wars, however, are remarkable for this sort of wheeling, and facing to the right-about; the same man often changing his colours two or three times in a campaign."

Captain Willoughby received the news of this addition to his ill luck with an air of military stoicism, though he felt, in reality, more like a father and a husband on the occasion than like a hero. Accustomed to self-command, he succeeded in concealing the extent of his uneasiness, while he immediately set about inquiring into the extent of the evil.

"Joel is to join my watch," he said, "and *he* may throw some light on this affair. Let us call him, at once, for a few minutes may prove of importance."

Even while speaking, the captain crossed the court, accompanied by the serjeant and mason; and, ceremony being little attended to on such occasions, they all entered the quarters of Strides, in a body. The place was empty! Man, woman, and children had abandoned the spot, seemingly in a body; and this, too, far from empty-handed. The manner in which the room had been stripped, indeed, was the first fact which induced the captain to believe that a man so much and so long trusted would desert him in a strait so serious. There could be no mistake; and, for a moment, the husband and father felt such a sinking of the heart as would be apt to follow the sudden conviction that his enemies must prevail.

"Let us look further, Joyce," he said, "and ascertain the extent of the evil at once."

"This is a very bad example, your honour, that corporal Strides has set the men, and we may expect to hear of more desertions. A non-commissioned officer should have had too much pride for this! I have always remarked, sir, in the army, that when a non-commissioned officer left his colours, he was pretty certain to carry off a platoon with him."

The search justified this opinion of the serjeant. A complete examination of the quarters of all the men having been made, it was ascertained that every white man in the Hut, the serjeant, Jamie Allen, and a young New England labourer of the name of Blodget excepted, had abandoned the place. Every man had carried off with him his arms and ammunition, leaving the rooms as naked of defence as they had been before they were occupied. Women and children, too, were all gone, proving that the flights had been made deliberately, and with concert. This left the Hut to be defended by its owner, the serjeant, the two Plinys and a young descendant of the same colour, Jamie Allen, Blodget and Mike, who had not yet been relieved from his ward over the Indian; eight men in all, who might possibly receive some assistance from the four black females in the kitchen.

The captain examined this small array of force, every man but Mike being up and in the line, with a saddened countenance; for he remembered what a different appearance it made only the previous day, when he had his gallant son too, with him, a host in himself. It added mortification to regret, also, when he remembered that this great loss had been made without a single blow having been struck in defence of his precious family, and his lawful rights.

"We must close the gate of the court, and bar it at once, Joyce," the captain said, as soon as fully apprised of the true state of his force. "It will be quite sufficient if we make good the house, with this handful of men; giving up all hope of doing anything with the stockade. It is the facility offered by the open gateway that has led to all this mischief."

"I don't know, your honour. When desertion once fairly gets into a man's mind, it's wonderful the means he will find to bring about his wishes. Corporal Strides, no doubt has passed his family and his kit through both gates; for, being in authority, our people were hardly disciplined enough to understand the difference between a non-commissioned officer *on* guard and one *off* guard; but, there were a hundred ways to mischief, even had there been no gate. Jamie, take one of the blacks, and bar the inner gate. What is your honour's pleasure next?"

"I wish my mind were at ease on the subject of the Tuscarora. With Nick's assistance as a runner and spy, and even as a sharp-shooter, we should be vastly stronger. See to the gate yourself, serjeant, then follow me to Mr. Woods' room."

This was done, the captain waiting for his companion on the threshold of the outer door. Ascending the narrow stairs, they were soon on the floor above, and were happy to find the door of the Tuscarora's prison fastened without, as they had left it; this precaution having been taken as a salutary assistance to O'Hearn's sagacity. Undoing these fastenings, the serjeant stepped aside to allow his superior to precede him, as became their respective stations. The captain advanced, holding the lantern before him, and found an empty room. Both Nick and Mike were gone, though it was not easy to discover by what means they had quitted the place. The door was secure, the windows were down, and the chimney was too small to allow of the passage of a human body. The defection of the Irishman caused the captain great pain, while it produced surprise even in the serjeant. Mike's fidelity had been thought of proof; and, for an instant, the master of the place was disposed to believe some evil spirit had been at work to corrupt his people.

"This is more than I could have expected, Joyce!" he said, as much in sorrow as in anger. "I should have as soon looked for the desertion of old Pliny as that of Mike!"

"It is extr'or'nary, sir; but one is never safe without in-and-in discipline. A drill a week, and that only for an hour or two of a Saturday afternoon, captain Willoughby, may make a sort of country militia, but it will do nothing for the field. 'Talk of enlisting men for a year, serjeant Joyce,' said old colonel Flanker to me, one day in the last war--'why it will take a year to teach a soldier how to eat. Your silly fellows in the provincial assemblies fancy because a man has teeth, and a stomach, and an appetite, that he knows how to *eat*; but eating is an *art*, serjeant; and military eating above all other branches of it; and I maintain a soldier can no more learn how to eat, as a soldier, the colonel meant, your honour, than he can learn to plan a campaign by going through the manual exercise.' For my part, captain Willoughby, I have always thought it took a man his first five years' enlistment to learn how to obey orders."

"I had thought that Irishman's heart in the right place, Joyce, and counted as much on him as I did on you!"

"On me, captain Willoughby!" answered the serjeant, in a tone of mortification. "I should think your honour would have made some difference between your old orderly--a man who had served thirty years in your own regiment, and most of the time in your own company, and a bit of a wild Hibernian of only ten years' acquaintance, and he a man who never saw a battalion paraded for real service!"

"I see my error now, Joyce; but Michael had so much blundering honesty about him, or seemed to have, that I have been his dupe. It is too late, however, to repine; the fellow is gone; it only remains to ascertain the manner of his flight. May not Joel have undone the fastenings of the door, and let him and the Indian escape together, in common with the rest of the deserters?"

"I secured that door, sir, with my own hands, in a military manner, and know that it was found as I left it. The Rev. Mr. Woods' bed seems to have been disturbed; perhaps that may furnish a clue."

A clue the bed did furnish, and it solved the problem. The bed-cord was removed, and both the sheets and one of the blankets were missing. This directed the inquiry to the windows, one of which was not closed entirely. A chimney stood near the side of this window, and by its aid it was not difficult to reach the ridge of the roof. On the inner side of the roof was the staging, or walk, already mentioned; and, once on that, a person could make the circuit of the entire roof, in perfect safety. Joyce mounted to the ridge, followed by the captain, and gained the staging with a little effort, whence they proceeded round the buildings to ascertain if the rope was not yet hanging over the exterior, as a means of descent. It was found as expected, and withdrawn lest it might be used to introduce enemies within the house.

These discoveries put the matter of Michael's delinquency at rest. He had clearly gone off with his prisoner, and might next be looked for in the ranks of the besiegers. The conviction of this truth gave the captain more than uneasiness; it caused him pain, for the county Leitrim-man had been a favourite with the whole family, and most especially with his daughter Maud.

"I do not think you and the blacks will leave me, Joyce," he observed, as the serjeant and himself descended, by the common passage, to the court. "On *you* I can rely, as I would rely on my noble son, were he with me at this moment."

"I beg your honour's pardon--few words tell best for a man, deeds being his duty--but, if your honour will have the condescension just to issue your orders, the manner in which they shall be obeyed will tell the whole story."

"I am satisfied of that, serjeant; we must put shoulder to shoulder, and die in the breach, should it be necessary, before we give up the place."

By this time the two old soldiers were again in the court, where they found all their remaining force, of the male sex; the men being too uneasy, indeed, to think of going to their pallets, until better assured of their safety. Captain Willoughby ordered Joyce to draw them up in line again, when he addressed them once more in person.

"My friends," the captain commenced, "there would be little use in attempting to conceal from you our real situation; nor would it be strictly honest. You see here every man on whom I can now depend for the defence of my fireside and family. Mike has gone with the rest, and the Indian has escaped in his company. You can make up your own opinions of our chances of success, but my resolution is formed. Before I open a gate to the merciless wretches without, who are worse than the savages of the wilderness, possessing all their bad and none of their redeeming qualities, it is my determination to be buried under the ruins of this dwelling. But you are not bound to imitate my example; and, if any man among you, black or white, regrets being here at this moment, he shall still have arms and ammunition, and food given him, the gates shall be opened and he may go freely to seek his safety in the forest. For God's sake let there be no more desertions; he that wishes to quit me, may now quit me unmolested; but, after this moment, martial law will *be*, enforced, and I shall give orders to shoot down any man detected in treachery, as I would shoot down a vicious dog."

This address was heard in profound silence. No man stirred, nor did any man speak.

"Blodget," continued the captain, "you have been with me a shorter time than any other person present, and cannot feel the same attachment to me and mine as the rest. You are the only native American among us, Joyce excepted--for we count the blacks as nothing in respect to country--may feel that I am an Englishman born, as I fear has been the case with the rest of your friends. Perhaps I ought not to ask you to remain. Take your arms, then, and make the best of your way to the settlements. Should you reach Albany, you might even serve me essentially by delivering a letter I will confide to you, and which will bring us effectual succour."

The young man did not answer, though his fingers worked on the barrel of his musket, and he shifted his weight, from leg to leg, like one whose inward feelings were moved.

"I believe I understand you, captain Willoughby," he said, at length, "though I think you don't understand me. I know you old country people think meanly of us new country people, but I suppose that's in the nature of things; then, I allow Joel Strides' conduct has been such as to give you reason to judge us harshly. But there is a difference among *us*, as well as among the English; and some of us--won't say I am such a man, but actions speak louder than words, and all will be known in the end--but *some* of us will be found true to our bargains, as well as other men."

"Bravely answered, my lad," cried the serjeant, heartily, and looking round at his commander with exultation, to congratulate him on having such a follower--"This is a man who will obey orders through thick and thin, I'll answer for it, your honour. Little does he care who's king or who's governor, so long as he knows his captain and his corps."

"There you are mistaken, serjeant Joyce," the youth observed, firmly. "I'm for my country, and I'd quit this house in a minute, did I believe captain Willoughby meant to help the crown. But I have lived long enough here to know he is at the most neutral; though I think he rather favours the side of the colonies than that of the crown."

"You have judged rightly, Blodget," observed the captain. "I do not quite like this declaration of independence, though I can scarce blame congress for having made it. Of the two, I think the Americans nearest right, and I now conceive myself to be more of an American than an Englishman. I wish this to be understood, Joyce."

"Do you, sir?--It's just as your honour pleases. I didn't know which side it was your pleasure to support, nor does it make any great difference with most of us. Orders are orders, let them come from king or colonies. I would take the liberty of recommending, your honour, that this young man be promoted. Strides' desertion has left a vacancy among the corporals, and we shall want another for the guard. It would hardly do to make a nigger a corporal."

"Very well, Joyce, have it as you wish," interrupted the captain, a little impatiently; for he perceived he had a spirit to deal with in Blodget that must hold such trifles at their true value. "Let it be corporal Allen and corporal Blodget in future."

"Do you hear, men?--These are general orders. The relieved guard will fall out, and try to get a little sleep, as we shall parade again half an hour before day."

Alas! the relieved guard, like the relief itself, consisted of only two men, corporal Blodget and Pliny the younger; old Pliny, in virtue of his household work, being rated as an idler. These five, with the captain and the serjeant, made the number of the garrison seven, which was the whole male force that now remained.

Captain Willoughby directed Joyce and his two companions to go to their pallets, notwithstanding, assuming the charge of the look-out himself, and profiting by the occasion to make himself better acquainted with the character of his new corporal than circumstances had hitherto permitted.

Chapter XXI

"For thee they fought, for thee they fell, And their oath was
on thee laid; To thee the clarions raised their swell, And the
dying warriors pray'd."

Percival.

The distaste for each other which existed between the people of New
England and those of the adjoining colonies, anterior to the war of the
revolution, is a matter of history. It was this feeling that threw Schuyler, one
of the ablest and best men in the service of his country, into the shade, a year
later than the period of which we are writing. This feeling was very naturally
produced, and, under the circumstances, was quite likely to be active in
a revolution. Although New England and New York were contiguous
territories, a wide difference existed between their social conditions. Out
of the larger towns, there could scarcely be said to be a gentry at all, in the
former; while the latter, a conquered province, had received the frame-work
of the English system, possessing Lords of the Manor, and divers other of the
fragments of the feudal system. So great was the social equality throughout
the interior of the New England provinces, indeed, as almost to remove
the commoner distinctions of civilised associations, bringing all classes
surprisingly near the same level, with the exceptions of the very low, or
some rare instance of an individual who was raised above his neighbours by
unusual wealth, aided perhaps by the accidents of birth, and the advantages
of education.

The results of such a state of society are easily traced. Habit had taken
the place of principles, and a people accustomed to see even questions of
domestic discipline referred, either to the church or to public sentiment,
and who knew few or none of the ordinary distinctions of social intercourse,
submitted to the usages of other conditions of society, with singular distaste
and stubborn reluctance. The native of New England deferred singularly
to great wealth, in 1776 as he is known to defer to it to-day; but it was
opposed to all his habits and prejudices to defer to social station. Unused to
intercourse with what was then called the great world of the provinces, he
knew not how to appreciate its manners or opinions; and, as is usual with
the provincial, he affected to despise that which he neither practised nor

understood. This, at once, indisposed him to acknowledge the distinctions of classes; and, when accident threw him into the adjoining province, he became marked, at once, for decrying the usages he encountered, comparing them, with singular self-felicitation, to those he had left behind him; sometimes with justice beyond a doubt, but oftener in provincial ignorance and narrow bigotry.

A similar state of things, on a larger scale, has been witnessed, more especially in western New York, since the peace of '83; the great inroads of emigrants from the New England states having almost converted that district of country into an eastern colony. Men of the world, while they admit how much has been gained in activity, available intelligence of the practical school, and enterprise, regret that the fusion has been quite so rapid and so complete; it being apparently a law of nature that nothing precious that comes of man shall be enjoyed altogether without alloy.

The condition in which captain Willoughby was now placed, might have been traced to causes connected with the feelings and habits above alluded to. It was distasteful to Joel Strides, and one or two of his associates, to see a social chasm as wide as that which actually existed between the family of the proprietor of the Knoll and his own, growing no narrower; and an active cupidity, with the hopes of confiscations, or an abandonment of the estate, came in aid of this rankling jealousy of station; the most uneasy, as it is the meanest of all our vices. Utterly incapable of appreciating the width of that void which separates the gentleman from the man of coarse feelings and illiterate vulgarity, he began to preach that doctrine of exaggerated and mistaken equality which says "one man is as good as another," a doctrine that is nowhere engrafted even on the most democratic of our institutions to-day, since it would totally supersede the elections, and leave us to draw lots for public trusts, as men are drawn for juries. On ordinary occasions, the malignant machinations of Strides would probably have led to no results; but, aided by the opinions and temper of the times, he had no great difficulty in undermining his master's popularity, by incessant and well-digested appeals to the envy and cupidity of his companions. The probity, liberality, and manly sincerity of captain Willoughby, often counteracted his schemes, it is true; but, as even the stone yields to constant attrition, so did Joel finally succeed in overcoming the influence of these high qualities, by dint of perseverance, and cunning, not a little aided by certain auxiliaries freely obtained from the Father of Lies.

As our tale proceeds, Joel's connection with the late movement will become more apparent, and we prefer leaving the remainder of the explanations to take their proper places in the course of the narrative.

Joyce was so completely a matter of drill, that he was in a sound sleep three minutes after he had lain down, the negro who belonged to his guard imitating his industry in this particular with equal coolness. As for the thoughtful Scotchman, Jamie Allen, sleep and he were strangers that night. To own the truth, the disaffection of Mike not only surprised, but it disappointed him. He remained in the court, therefore, conversing on the subject with the "laird," after his companions had fallen asleep.

"I wad na hae' thought that o' Michael," he said, "for the man had an honest way with him, and was so seeming valiant, that I could na hae' supposed him capable of proving a desairter. Mony's the time that I've heard him swear--for Michael was an awfu' hand at that vice, when his betters were no near to rebuke him--but often has he swore that Madam, and her winsome daughters, were the pride of his een; ay, and their delight too!"

"The poor fellow has yielded to my unlucky fortune, Jamie," returned the captain, "and I sometimes think it were better had you all imitated his example."

"Begging pairdon, captain Willoughby, for the familiarity, but ye're just wrang, fra' beginning to end, in the supposition. No man with a hairt in his body wad desairt ye in a time like this, and no mair 's to be said in the matter. Nor do I think that luuk has had anything to do with Michael's deficiency, unless ye ca' it luuk to be born and edicated in a misguiding religion. Michael's catholicity is at the bottom of his backsliding, ye'll find, if ye look closely into the maiter."

"I do not see how that is to be made out, Allen; all sects of the Christian religion, I believe, teaching us to abide by our engagements, and to perform our duties."

"Na doubt--na doubt, 'squire Willoughby--there's a seeming desire to teach as much in a' churches; but ye'll no deny that the creatur' o' Rome wears a mask, and that catholicity is, at the best, but a wicked feature to enter into the worship of God."

"Catholicism, Jamie, means adherence to the catholic church--"

"Just that--just that"--interrupted the Scot, eagerly--and it's that o' which I complain. All protestants--wather fully disposed, or ainly half-disposed, as may be the case with the English kirk--all protestants agree in condemning the varry word catholic, which is a sign and a symbol of the foul woman o' Babylon."

"Then, Jamie, they agree in condemning what they don't understand. I should be sorry to think I am not a member of the catholic church myself."

Yersal'!--No, captain Willoughby, ye're no catholic, though you are a bit akin to it, perhaps. I know that Mr. Woods, that's now in the hands o' the savages, prays for the catholics, and professes to believe in what he ca's the 'Holy Catholic Kirk;' but, then, I've always supposed that was in the way o' Christian charity like; for one is obleeged to use decent language, ye'll be acknowledging, sir, in the pulpit, if it's only for appearance's sake."

"Well--well--Jamie; a more fitting occasion may occur for discussing matters of this nature, and we will postpone the subject to another time. I may have need of your services an hour or two hence, and it will be well for every man to come to the work fresh and clear-headed. Go to your pallet then, and expect an early call."

The mason was not a man to oppose such an order coming from the 'laird;' and he withdrew, leaving the captain standing in the centre of the court quite alone. We say alone, for young Blodget had ascended to the gallery or staging that led around the inner sides of the roofs, while the negro on guard was stationed at the gateway, as the only point where the Hut could be possibly carried by a *coup-de-main*. As the first of these positions commanded the best exterior view from the inside of the buildings, the captain mounted the stairs he had so recently descended, and joined the young Rhode Islander at his post.

The night was star-light, but the elevation at which the two watchers were placed, was unfavourable to catching glimpses of any lurking enemy. The height confounded objects with the ground on which they were placed, though Blodget told the captain he did not think a man could cross the palisades without his being seen. By moving along the staging on the southern side of the quadrangle, he could keep a tolerable look-out, on the front and two flanks, at the same time. Still, this duty could not be performed without considerable risk, as the head and shoulders of a man moving along the ridge of the building would be almost certain to attract the eye of any Indian without. This was the first circumstance that the captain remarked on joining his companion, and gratitude induced him to point it out, in order that the other might, in a degree at least, avoid the danger.

"I suppose, Blodget, this is the first of your service," said captain Willoughby, "and it is not easy to impress on a young man the importance of unceasing vigilance against savage artifices."

"I admit the truth of all you say, sir," answered Blodget, "though I do not believe any attempt will be made on the house, until the other side has sent in what the serjeant calls another flag."

"What reason have you for supposing this?" asked the captain, in a little surprise.

"It seems unreasonable for men to risk their lives when an easier way to conquest may seem open to them. That is all I meant, captain Willoughby."

"I believe I understand you, Blodget. You think Joel and his friends have succeeded so well in drawing off my men, that they may be inclined to wait a little, in order to ascertain if further advantages may not be obtained in the same way."

Blodget confessed that he had some such thoughts in his mind, while, at the same time, he declared that he believed the disaffection would go no further.

"It is not easy for it to do so," returned the captain, smiling a little bitterly, as he remembered how many who had eaten of his bread, and had been cared for by him, in sickness and adversity, had deserted him in his need, "unless they persuade my wife and daughters to follow those who have led the way."

Respect kept Blodget silent for a minute; then uneasiness induced him to speak.

"I hope captain Willoughby don't distrust any who now remain with him," he said. "If so, I know I must be the person."

"Why you, in particular, young man? With you, surely, have every reason to be satisfied."

"It cannot be serjeant Joyce, for he will stay until he get your orders to march," the youth replied, not altogether without humour in his manner; "and, as for the Scotchman, he is old, and men of his years are not apt to wait so long, if they intend to be traitors. The negroes all love you, as if you were their father, and there is no one but me left to betray you."

"I thank you for this short enumeration of my strength, Blodget, since it gives me new assurance of my people's fidelity. You I *will* not distrust; the others I *cannot*, and there is a feeling of high confidence--What do you see?--why do you lower your piece, and stand at guard, in this manner?"

"That is a man's form, sir, on the right of the gate, trying to climb the palisades. I have had my eye on it, for some time, and I feel sure of my aim."

"Hold an instant, Blodget; let us be certain before we act."

The young man lowered the butt of his piece, waiting patiently and calmly for his superior to decide. There was a human form visible, sure enough, and it was seen slowly and cautiously rising until it reached the summit of the stockade, where it appeared to pause to reconnoitre. Whether it were a pale-face or a red-skin, it was impossible to distinguish, though the whole movement left little doubt that an assailant or a spy was attempting to pass the outer defences.

"We cannot spare that fellow," said the captain, with a little regret in his manner; "it is more than we can afford. You must bring him down, Blodget. The instant you have fired, come to the other end of the stage, where we will watch the result."

This arranged, the captain prudently passed away from the spot, turning to note the proceedings of his companion, the moment he was at the opposite angle of the gallery. Blodget was in no haste. He waited until his aim was certain; then the stillness of the valley was rudely broken by the sharp report of a rifle, and a flash illumined its obscurity. The figure fell outward, like a bird shot from its perch, lying in a ball at the foot of the stockade. Still, no cry or groan gave evidence of nature surprised by keen and unexpected anguish. At the next instant Blodget was by captain Willoughby's side. His conduct was a pledge of fidelity that could not be mistaken, and a warm squeeze of the hand assured the youth of his superior's approbation.

It was necessary to be cautious, however, and to watch the result with ceaseless vigilance. Joyce and the men below had taken the alarm, and the serjeant with his companions were ordered up on the stage immediately, leaving the negro, alone, to watch the gate. A message was also sent to the females, to give them confidence, and particularly to direct the blacks to arm, and to repair to the loops.

All this was done without confusion, and with so little noise as to prevent those without from understanding what was in progress. Terror kept the negroes silent, and discipline the others. As every one had lain down in his or her clothes, it was not a minute before every being in the Hut was up, and in motion. It is unnecessary to speak of the mental prayers and conflicting emotions with which Mrs. Willoughby and her daughters prepared themselves for the struggle; and, yet, even the beautiful and delicate Maud braced her nerves to meet the emergency of a frontier assault. As for Beulah, gentle, peaceful, and forgiving as she was by nature, the care of little Evert aroused all the mother within her, and something like a frown that betokened resolution was, for a novelty, seen on her usually placid face.

A moment sufficed to let Joyce and his companions into the state of affairs. There now being four armed men on the stage, one took each of the three exposed sides of the buildings to watch, leaving the master of the house to move from post to post, to listen to suggestions, hear reports, and communicate orders.

The dark object that lay at the foot of the palisades was pointed out to the serjeant the instant he was on the stage, and one of his offices was to observe it, in order to ascertain if it moved, or whether any attempts were made to carry off the body. The American Indians attach all the glory or shame of a battle to the acquisition or loss of scalps, and one of their practices was to remove those who had fallen, at every hazard, in order to escape the customary mutilation. Some tribes even believed it disgrace to suffer a dead body to be struck by the enemy, and many a warrior has lost his life in the effort to save the senseless corpse of a comrade from this fancied degradation.

As soon as the little stir created in the Hut by the mustering of the men was over, a stillness as profound as that which had preceded the alarm reigned around the place. No noise came from the direction of the mill; no cry, or call, or signal of battle was heard; everything lay in the quiet of midnight. Half an hour thus passed, when the streak of light that appeared in the east announced the approach of day.

The twenty minutes that succeeded were filled with intense anxiety. The slow approach of light gradually brought out object after object in the little panorama, awakening and removing alike, conjectures and apprehensions. At first the grey of the palisades became visible; then the chapel, in its sombre outlines; the skirts of the woods; the different cabins that lined them; the cattle in the fields, and the scattering trees. As for Joyce, he kept his gaze fastened on the object at the foot of the stockade, expecting every instant there would be an attempt to carry it off.

At length, the light became so strong as to allow the eye to take in the entire surface of the natural *glacis* without the defences, bringing the assurance that no enemy was near. As the ground was perfectly clear, a few fruit-trees and shrubs on the lawn excepted, and by changing positions on the stage, these last could now be examined on all sides, nothing was easier than to make certain of this fact. The fences, too, were light and open, rendering it impossible for any ambush or advancing party to shelter itself behind them. In a word, daylight brought the comfortable assurance to those within the palisades that another night was passed without bringing an assault.

"We shall escape this morning, I do believe, Joyce," said the captain, who had laid down his rifle, and no longer felt it necessary to keep the upper portions of his body concealed behind the roof--"Nothing can be seen that denotes an intention to attack, and not an enemy is near."

"I will take one more thorough look, your honour," answered the serjeant, mounting to the ridge of the building, where he obtained the immaterial advantage of seeing more at the same time, at the risk of exposing his whole person, should any hostile rifle be in reach of a bullet--"then we may be certain."

Joyce was a man who stood just six feet in his stockings, and, losing no part of this stature by his setting up, a better object for a sharp-shooter could not have been presented than he now offered. The crack of a rifle soon saluted the ears of the garrison; then followed the whizzing of the bullet as it came humming through the air towards the Hut. But the report was so distant as at once to announce that the piece was discharged from the margin of the forest; a certain evidence of two important facts; one, that the enemy had fallen back to a cover; the other, that the house was narrowly watched.

Nothing tries the nerves of a young soldier more than the whizzing of a distant fire. The slower a bullet or a shot approaches, the more noise it makes; and, the sound continuing longer than is generally imagined, the uninitiated are apt to imagine that the dangerous missile is travelling on an errand directly towards themselves. Space appears annihilated, and raw hands are often seen to duck at a round shot that is possibly flying a hundred yards from them.

On the present occasion, the younger Pliny fairly squatted below the root Jamie thought it prudent to put some of his own masonry, which was favourably placed in an adjacent chimney for such a purpose, between him and the spot whence the report proceeded; while even Blodget looked up into the air, as if he expected to *see* where the bullet was going. Captain Willoughby had no thought of the missile he was looking for the smoke in the skirts of the woods, to note the spot; while Joyce, with folded arms, stood at rest on the ridge, actually examining the valley in another direction, certain that a fire so distant could not be very dangerous.

Jamie's calculation proved a good one. The bullet struck against the chimney, indented a brick, and fell upon the shingles of the roof. Joyce descended at the next instant, and he coolly picked up, and kept tossing the flattened bit of lead in his hand, for the next minute or two, with the air of a man who seemed unconscious of having it at all.

"The enemy is besieging us, your honour," said Joyce, "but he will not attack at present. If I might presume to advise, we shall do well to leave a single sentinel on this stage, since no one can approach the palisades without being seen, if the man keeps in motion."

"I was thinking of this myself, serjeant; we will first post Blodget here. We can trust him; and, as the day advances, a-less intelligent sentinel will answer. At the same time, he must be instructed to keep an eye in the rear of the Hut, danger often coming from the quarter least expected."

All this was done, and the remainder of the men descended to the court. Captain Willoughby ordered the gate unbarred, when he passed outside, taking the direction towards the lifeless body, which still lay where it had fallen, at the foot of the stockades. He was accompanied by Joyce and Jamie Allen, the latter carrying a spade, it being the intention to inter the savage as the shortest means of getting rid of a disagreeable object. Our two old soldiers had none of the sensitiveness on the subject of exposure that is so apt to disturb the tyro in the art of war. With sentinels properly posted, they had no apprehensions of dangers that did not exist, and they moved with confidence and steadily wherever duty called. Not only was the inner gate opened and passed, but the outer also, the simple precaution of stationing a man at the first being the only safeguard taken.

When outside of the palisades, the captain and his companions proceeded at once towards the body. It was now sunrise, and a rich light was illuminating the hill-tops, though the direct rays of the luminary had not yet descended to the valley. There lay the Indian, precisely as he had fallen, no warrior having interposed to save him from the scalping-knife. His head had reached the earth first, and the legs and body were tumbled on it, in a manner to render the form a confused pile of legs and blanket, rather than a bold savage stretched in the repose of death.

"Poor fellow!" exclaimed the captain, as the three approached the spot; "it is to be hoped Blodget's bullet did its commission faithfully, else the fall must have hurt him sadly."

"By Jove, 'tis nothing but a stuffed soldier!" cried Joyce, rolling the ingeniously contrived bundle over with his foot; "and here, the lad's ball has passed directly through its head! This is Injin deviltry, sir; it has been tried, in order to see whether our sentinels were or were not asleep."

"To me, Joyce, it seems more like a white man's clumsiness. The fellow has been made to resemble an Indian, but people of our own colour have had a hand in the affair."

"Well, sir, let that be as it may, it is lucky our youngster had so quick, an eye, and so nimble a finger. See, your honour; here is the pole by which the effigy was raised to the top of the palisades, and here is the trail on the grass yet, by which his supporter has crept off. The fellow seems to have scrambled along in a hurry; his trail is as plain as that of a whole company."

The captain examined the marks left on the grass, and was of opinion that more than one man had been employed to set up the decoy figure, a circumstance that seemed probable in itself, when the weight of the image and the danger of exposure were remembered.--Let that be as it might, he was rejoiced on reflection that no one was hurt, and he still retained the hope of being able to come to such an understanding with his invaders as to supersede the necessity of actual violence.

"At all events, your honour, I will carry the quaker in," said Joyce, tossing the stuffed figure on a shoulder. "He do to man the quaker gun at least, and may be of use in frightening some one of the other side, more than he has yet frightened us."

Captain Willoughby did not object, though he reminded Joyce that the desertions had probably put the enemy in possession of a minute statement of their defences and force, including the history of the wooden gun. If Joel and his fellow-delinquents had joined the party at the mill, the name, age, character and spirit of every man remaining in the garrison were probably known to its leaders; and neither quakers nor paddies would count for much in opposing an assault.

The captain came within the gate of the palisades last, closing, barring, and locking it with his own hands, when all immediate apprehensions from the enemy ceased. He knew, certainly, that it would probably exceed his present means of resistance, to withstand a vigorous assault; but, on the other hand, he felt assured that Indians would never approach a stockade in open day, and expose themselves to the hazards of losing some fifteen or twenty of their numbers, before they could carry the place. This was opposed to all their notions of war, neither honour nor advantage tempting them to adopt it. As for the first, agreeably to savage notions, glory was to be measured by the number of scalps taken and lost; and, counting all the women left in the Hut, there would not be heads enough to supply a sufficient number to prove an offset to those which would probably be lost in the assault.

All this did the captain discuss in few words, with the serjeant, when he proceeded to join his anxious and expecting wife and daughters.

"God has looked down upon us in mercy, and protected us this night," said the grateful Mrs. Willoughby, with streaming eyes, as she received and returned her husband's warm embrace. "We cannot be too thankful, when we look at these dear girls, and our precious little Evert. If Robert were only with us now, I should be entirely happy!"

"Such is human nature, my little Maud"--answered the captain, drawing his darling towards himself and kissing her polished forehead. "The very thoughts of being in our actual strait would have made your mother as miserable as her worst enemy could wish--if, indeed, there be such a monster on earth as *her* enemy--and, now she protests she is delighted because our throats were not all cut last night. We are safe enough for the day I think, and not another night shall one of you pass in the Hut, if I can have my way. If there be such a thing as desertion, there is such a thing as evacuation also."

"Hugh!--What *can* you, *do* you mean! Remember, we are surrounded by a wilderness."

"I know our position reasonably well, wife of mine, and intend to turn that knowledge to some account, God willing, and aiding. I mean to place old Hugh Willoughby by the side of Xenophon and Washington, and let the world see what a man is capable of, on a retreat, when he has such a wife, two such daughters, and a grandson like that, on his hands. As for Bob, I would not have him here, on any account. The young dog would run away with half the glory."

The ladies were too delighted to find their father and husband in such spirits, to be critical, and all soon after sat down to an early breakfast, to eat with what appetite they could.

Chapter XXII

Yet I well remember
The favours of these men: were they not mine?
Did they not sometimes cry, all hail! to me?
So Judas did to Christ: but he, in twelve
Found truth in all but one; I in twelve thousand none.

Richard II.

That which captain Willoughby had said in seeming pleasantry he seriously meditated. The idea of passing another night in the Hut, supported by only six men, with more than ten times that number besieging him, and with all the secrets of his defences known, through the disaffection of his retainers, was, to the last degree, painful to him. Had his own life, alone, been at risk, military pride might have tempted him to remain; but his charge was far too precious to be exposed on account of considerations so vain.

No sooner, therefore, was the breakfast over, than captain summoned Joyce to a consultation on the contemplated movement. The interview took place in the library, whither the serjeant repaired, on receiving his superior's orders. As to the party without, no apprehension was felt, so long as the sentinels were even moderately vigilant, and the day lasted.

"I suppose, serjeant," commenced captain Willoughby, "a soldier of your experience is not to be taught what is the next resort of a commanding officer, when he finds himself unable to make good his ground against his enemy in front?"

"It is to retreat, your honour. The road that cannot be passed, must be turned."

"You have judged rightly. It is now my intention to evacuate the Hut, and to try our luck on a march to the rear. A retreat, skilfully executed, is a creditable thing; and any step appears preferable to exposing the dear beings in the other room to the dangers of a night assault."

Joyce appeared struck with the suggestion; though, if one might have judged from the expression of his countenance, far from favourably. He reflected a moment ere he answered.

"Did your honour send for me," he then inquired, "to issue orders for this retreat, or was it your pleasure to hear anything I might have to say about it?"

"The last--I shall give no orders, until I know your opinion of the measure."

"It is as much the duty of an inferior to speak his mind freely, when he is called for an opinion, captain Willoughby, as it is to obey in silence, when he gets nothing but orders. According to my views of the matter, we shall do better to stand our ground, and try to make good the house against these vagabonds, than to trust to the woods."

"Of course you have your reasons for this opinion, Joyce?"

"Certainly, your honour. In the first place, I suppose it to be against the rules of the art of war to evacuate a place that is well provisioned, without standing an assault. This we have not yet done. It is true, sir, that our ranks are thinned by desertions; but I never heard of a garrisoned town, or a garrisoned house, capitulating on account of a few deserters; and, I take it, evacuation is only the next step before capitulation."

"But our desertions, Joyce, have not been *few*, but *many*. Three times as many have left us, if we include our other losses, as remain. It matters not whence the loss proceeds, so long as it is a loss."

"A retreat, with women and baggage, is always a ticklish operation, your honour, especially if an enemy is pressing your rear! Then we have a wilderness before us, and the ladies could hardly hold out for so long a march as that from this place to the Mohawk; short of which river they will hardly be as safe as they are at present."

"I have had no such march in view, Joyce. You know there is a comfortable hut, only a mile from this very spot on the mountain side, where we commenced a clearing for a sheep-pasture, only three summers since. The field is in rich grass; and, could we once reach the cabin, and manage to drive a cow or two up there, we might remain a month in security. As for provisions and clothes, we could carry enough on our backs to serve us all several weeks; especially if assisted by the cows."

"I'm glad your honour has thought of this idea," said the serjeant, his face brightening as he listened; "it will be a beautiful operation to fall back on that position, when we can hold out no longer in this. The want of some such arrangement has been my only objection to this post, captain Willoughby; for, we have always seemed to me, out here in the wilderness, like a regiment drawn up with a ravine or a swamp in its rear."

"I am glad to find you relishing the movement for any cause, serjeant. It is my intention at present to make the necessary arrangements to evacuate the Hut, while it is light; and, as soon as it is dark, to retreat by the gates, the palisades, and the rivulet--How now, Jamie? You look as if there were news to communicate?"

Jamie Allen, in truth, had entered at that instant in so much haste as to have overlooked the customary ceremony of sending in his name, or even of knocking.

"News!" repeated the mason, with a sort of wondering smile "and it's just that I've come to bring. Wad ye think it, baith, gentlemen, that our people are in their am cabins ag'in, boiling their pots, and frying their pork, a' the same as if the valley was in a state of tranquillity, and we so many lairds waiting for them to come and do our pleasure!"

"I do not understand you, Jamie--whom do you mean by 'our people'?"

"Sure, just the desairters; Joel, and the miller, and Michael, and the rest."

"And the cabins--and the pots--and the pork--it is gibberish to me."

"I hae what ye English ca' an aiccent, I know; but, in my judgment, captain Willoughby, the words may be comprehended without a dictionary. It's just that Joel Strides, and Daniel the miller, and the rest o' them that fleed, the past night, have gane into their ain abodes, and have lighted their fires, and put over their pots and kettles, and set up their domestic habitudes, a' the same as if this Beaver Dam was ain o' the pairks o' Lonnon!"

"The devil they have! Should this be the case, serjeant, our sortie may be made at an earlier hour than that mentioned. I never will submit to such an insult."

Captain Willoughby was too much aroused to waste many words; and, seizing his hat, he proceeded forthwith to take a look for himself. The stage, or gallery on the roofs, offering the best view, in a minute he and his two companions were on it.

"There; ye'll be seein' a smoke in Joel's habitation, with your own een; and, yon is anither, in the dwelling of his cousin Seth," said Jamie, pointing in the direction he named.

"Smoke there is, of a certainty; but the Indians may have lighted fires in the kitchen, to do their own cooking. This looks like investing us, serjeant, rather more closely than the fellows have done before."

"I rather think not, your honour--Jamie is right, or my eyes do not know a man from a woman. That is certainly a female in the garden of Joel, and I'll engage it's Phoebe, pulling onions for his craving stomach, the scoundrel!"

Captain Willoughby never moved without his little glass, and it was soon levelled at the object mentioned.

"By Jupiter, you are right, Joyce"--he cried. "It is Phoebe, though the hussy is coolly weeding, not culling the onions! Ay--and now I see Joel himself! The rascal is examining some hoes, with as much philosophy as if he were master of them, and all near them. This is a most singular situation to be in!"

This last remark was altogether just. The situation of those in the Hut was now singular indeed. Further examination showed that every cabin had its tenant, no one of the party that remained within the palisades being a householder. By using the glass, and pointing it, in succession, at the different dwellings, the captain in due time detected the presence of nearly every one of the deserters. Not a man of them all, in fact, was missing, Mike alone excepted. There they were, with their wives and children, in quiet possession of their different habitations. Nor was this all; the business of the valley seemed as much on their minds as had been their practice for years. Cows were milked, the swine were fed, poultry was called and cared for, and each household was also making the customary preparations for the morning meal.

So absorbed was the captain with this extraordinary scene, that he remained an hour on the staging, watching the course of events. The breakfasts were soon over, having been later than common, and a little hurried; then commenced the more important occupations of the day. A field was already half ploughed, in preparation for a crop of winter grain; thither Joel himself proceeded, with the necessary cattle, accompanied by the labourers who usually aided him in that particular branch of husbandry. Three ploughs were soon at work, with as much regularity and order as if nothing had occurred to disturb the tranquillity of the valley. The axes of the wood-choppers were next heard, coming out of the forest, cutting fuel for the approaching winter; and a half-finished ditch had its workmen also, who were soon busy casting up the soil, and fashioning their trench. In a word, all the suspended toil was renewed with perfect system and order.

"This beats the devil himself, Joyce!" said the captain, after a half-hour of total silence. "Here are all these fellows at work as coolly as if I had just given them their tasks, and twice as diligently. Their unusual industry is a bad symptom of itself!"

"Your honour will remark one circumstance. Not a rascal of them all comes within the fair range of a musket, for, as to throwing away ammunition at such distances, it would be clearly unmilitary, and might be altogether useless."

"I have half a mind to scatter them with a volley"--said the captain, doubtingly. "Bullets would take effect among those ploughmen, could they only be made to hit."

"And amang the cattle, too," observed the Scotsman, who had an eye on the more economical part of the movement, as well as on that which was military. "A ball would slay a horse as well as a man in such a skairmish."

"This is true enough, Jamie; and it is not exactly the sort of warfare I could wish, to be firing at men who were so lately my friends. I do not see, Joyce, that the rascals have any arms with them?"

"Not a musket, sir. I noticed that, when Joel first detailed his detachments. Can it be possible that the savages have retired?"

"Not they; else would Mr. Strides and his friends have gone with them. No, serjeant, there is a deep plan to lead us into some sort of ambush in this affair, and we will be on the look-out for them."

Joyce stood contemplating the scene for some, time, in profound silence, when he approached the captain formally, and made the usual military salute; a ceremony he had punctiliously observed, on all proper occasions, since the garrison might be said to be placed under martial law.

"If it's your honour's pleasure," he said, "I will detail a detachment, and go out and bring in two or three of these deserters; by which means we shall get into their secrets."

"A detachment, Joyce!" answered the captain, eyeing his subordinate a little curiously--"What troops do you propose to tell-off for the service?"

"Why, your honour, there's corporal Allen and old Pliny off duty; I think the thing might be done with them, if your honour would have the condescension to order corporal Blodget, with the two other blacks, to form as a supporting party, under the cover of one of the fences."

"A disposition of my force that would leave captain Willoughby for a garrison! I thank you, serjeant, for your offer and gallantry, but prudence will not permit it. We may set down Strides and his companions as so many knaves, and----"

"That may ye!" cried Mike's well-known voice, from the scuttle that opened into the garrets, directly in front of which the two old soldiers were conversing--"That may ye, and no har-r-m done the trut', or justice, or for that matther, meself. Och! If I had me will of the blackguards, every rogue of 'em should be bound hand and fut and laid under that pratthy wather-fall, yon at the mill, until his sins was washed out of him. Would there be confessions then?--That would there; and sich letting out of sacrets as would satisfy the conscience of a hog!"

By the time Mike had got through this sentiment he was on the staging, where he stood hitching up his nether garment, with a meaning grin on his face that gave a peculiar expression of heavy cunning to the massive jaw and capacious mouth, blended with an honesty and good-nature that the well-meaning fellow was seldom without when he addressed any of the captain's family. Joyce glanced at the captain, expecting orders to seize the returned run-away; but his superior read at once good faith in the expression of his old retainer's countenance.

"You have occasioned us a good deal of surprise, O'Hearn, on more accounts than one," observed the captain, who thought it prudent to assume more sternness of manner than his feelings might have actually warranted. "You have not only gone off yourself, but you have suffered your prisoner to escape with you. Then your manner of getting into the house requires an explanation. I shall hear what you have to say before I make up my mind as to your conduct."

"Is it spake I will?--That will I, and as long as it plase yer honour to listen. Och! Isn't that Saucy Nick a quare one? Divil burn me if I thinks the likes of him is to be found in all Ameriky, full as it is of Injins and saucy fellies! Well, now, I suppose, sarjeant, ye've set me down as sin riding off with Misther Joel and his likes, if ye was to open yer heart, and spake yer thrue mind?"

"You have been marked for a deserter, O'Hearn, and one, too, that deserted from post."

"Post! Had I been *that*, I shouldn't have stirred, and ye'd be wanting in the news I bring ye from the Majjor, and Mr. Woods, and the savages, and the rest of the varmints."

"My son!--Is this possible, Michael? Have you seen *him*, or can you tell us anything of his state?"

Mike now assumed a manner of mysterious importance, laying a finger on his nose, and pointing towards the sentinel and Jamie.

"It's the sarjeant that I considers as one of the family," said the county Leitrim-man, when his pantomime was through, "but it isn't dacent to be bawling out sacrets through a whole nighbourhood; and then, as for *Ould Nick*--or Saucy Nick, or whatever ye calls him--Och! isn't he a *pratthy* Injin! Ye'll mar-r-ch t'rough Ameriky, and never see his aiquel!"

"This will never do, O'Hearn. Whatever you have to say must be said clearly, and in the simplest manner. Follow to the library, where I will hear your report. Joyce, you will accompany us."

"Let him come, if he wishes to hear wonderful achaivements!" answered Mike, making way for the captain to descend the steps; then following himself, talking as he went. "He'll niver brag of his campaigns ag'in to the likes of me, seeing that I've outdone him, ten--ay, forty times, and boot. Och! that Nick's a divil, and no har-r-m said!"

"In the first place, O'Hearn," resumed the captain, as soon as the three were alone in the library--"you must explain your own desertion."

"Me!--Desart! Sure, it isn't run away from yer honour, and the Missus, and Miss Beuly, and pratthy Miss Maud, and the child, that's yer honour's m'aning?"

This was said with so much nature and truth, that the captain had not the heart to repeat the question, though Joyce's more drilled feelings were less moved. The first even felt a tear springing to his eye, and he no longer distrusted the Irishman's fidelity, as unaccountable as his conduct did and must seem to his cooler judgment. But Mike's sensitiveness had taken the alarm, and it was only to be appeased by explanations.

"Yer honour's not sp'aking when I questions ye on that same?" he resumed, doubtingly.

"Why, Mike, to be sincere, it did look a little suspicious when you not only went, off yourself, but you let the Indian go off with you."

"Did it?"--said Mike, mus'ng--"No, I don't allow that, seein' that the intent and object was good. And, then, I never took the Injin wid *me*; but 'twas I, meself, that went wid *him*."

"I rather think, your honour," said Joyce, smiling, "we'll put O'Hearn's name in its old place on the roster, and make no mark against him at pay-day."

"I think it will turn out so, Joyce. We must have patience, too, and let Mike tell his story in his own way."

"Is it tell a story, will I? Ah!--Nick's the cr'ature for that same! See, he has given me foor bits of sticks, every one of which is to tell a story, in its own way. This is the first; and it manes let the captain into the sacret of your retrait; and how you got out of the windie, and how you comes near to breaking yer neck by a fall becaase of the fut's slipping; and how ye wint down the roof by a rope, the divil a bit fastening it to yer neck, but houlding it in yer hand with sich a grip as if 'twere the fait' of the church itself; and how Nick led ye to the hole out of which ye hot' wint, as if ye had been two cats going t'rough a door!"

Mike stopped to grin and look wise, as he recounted the manner of the escape, the outlines of which, however, were sufficiently well known to his auditors before he, began.

"Throw away that stick, now, and let us know where this hole is, and what you mean by it."

"No"--answered Mike, looking at the stick, in a doubting manner--"I'll not t'row it away, wid yer honour's l'ave, 'till I've told ye how we got into the brook, forenent the forest, and waded up to the woods, where we was all the same as if we had been two bits of clover tops hid in a haymow. That Nick is a cr'ature at consailment!"

"Go on," said the captain, patiently, knowing that there was no use in hurrying one of Mike's peculiar mode of communicating his thoughts. "What came next?"

"That will I; and the r'ason comes next, as is seen by this oder stick. And, so, Nick and meself was in the chaplain's room all alone, and n'ither of us had any mind to dhrink; Nick becaase he was a prisoner and felt crass, and full of dignity like; and meself becaase I was a sentinel; and sarjeant Joyce, there, had tould me, the Lord knows how often, that if I did my duty well, I might come to be a corporal, which was next in rank to himself; barring, too, that I was a sentinel, and a drunken sentinel is a disgrace to a man, sowl and body, and musket."

"And so neither of you drank?"--put in the captain, by way of a reminder.

"For that same r'ason, and one betther still, as we had nothin' *to* dhrink. Well, says Nick--'Mike,' says he--'you like cap'in, and Missus, and Miss Beuly, and Miss Maud, and the babby?' Divil burn ye, Nick,' says I, 'why do ye ask so foolish a question? Is it likes ye would know? Well--then just ask yerself if you likes yer own kith and kin, and ye've got yer answer.'"

"And Nick made his proposal, on getting this answer," interrupted the captain, "which was--"

"Here it is, on the stick. 'Well,' says Nick, says he--'run away wid Nick, and see Majjor; bring back news. Nick cap'in friend, but cap'in don't know it--won't believe'--Fait', I can't *tell* yer honour all Nick said, in his own manner; and so, wid yer Pave, I'll just tell it in my own way."

"Any way, Mike, so that you do but tell it."

"Nick's a cr'ature! His idee was for us two to get out of the windie, and up on the platform, and to take the bedcord, and other things, and slide down upon the ground--and we *did* it! As sure as yer honour and the sarjeant is there, we did *that same*, and no bones broke! 'Well,' says I, 'Nick, ye're here, sure enough, but how do you mane to get *out* of here? Is it climb the palisades ye will, and be shot by a sentinel?'--if there was one, which there wasn't, yer honour, seeing that all had run away--'or do ye mane to stay here,' says I, 'and be taken a prisoner of war ag'in, in which case ye'll be two prisoners, seem' that ye've been taken wonst already, will ye Nick?' says I. So Nick never spoke, but he held up his finger, and made a sign for me to follow, as follow I did; and we just crept through the palisade, and a mhighty phratty walk we had of it, alang the meadies, and t'rough the lanes, the rest of the way."

"You crept through the palisades, Mike! There is no outlet of sufficient size."

"I admits the hole is a tight squaze, but 'twill answer. And then it's just as good for an inlet as it is for an outlet, seein' that I came t'rough it this very marnin'. Och! Nick's a cr'ature! And how d'ye think that hole comes there, barring all oversights in setting up the sticks?"

"It has not been made intentionally, I should hope, O'Hearn?"

"'Twas made by Joel, and that by just sawing off a post, and forcin' out a pin or two, so that the palisade works like a door. Och! it's nately contrived, and it manes mischief."

"This must be looked to, at once," cried the captain; "lead the way, Mike, and show us the spot."

As the Irishman was nothing loth, all three were soon in the court, whence Mike led the way through the gate, round to the point where the stockade came near the cliffs, on the eastern side of the buildings. This was the spot where the path that led down to the spring swept along the defences, and was on the very route by which the captain contemplated retreating, as well as on that by which Maud had entered the Hut, the night of the invasion. At a convenient place, a palisade had been sawed off, so low in the ground that the sods, which had been cut and were moveable, concealed the injury, while the heads of the pins that ought to have bound the timber to the cross-piece, were in their holes, leaving everything apparently secure. On removing the sods, and pushing the timber aside, the captain ascertained that a man might easily pass without the stockade. As this corner was the most retired within the works, there was no longer any doubt that the hole had been used by all the deserters, including the women and children. In what manner it became known to Nick, however, still remained matter of conjecture.

Orders were about to be given to secure this passage, when it occurred to the captain it might possibly be of use in effecting his own retreat. With this object in view, then, he hastened away from the place, lest any wandering eye without might detect his presence near it, and conjecture the cause. On returning to the library, the examination of Mike was resumed.

As the reader must be greatly puzzled with the county Leitrim-man's manner of expressing himself, we shall relate the substance of what he now uttered, for the sake of brevity. It would seem that Nick had succeeded in persuading Mike, first, that he, the Tuscarora, was a fast friend of the captain and his family, confined by the former, in consequence of a misconception of the real state of the Indian's feelings, much to the detriment of all their interests; and that no better service could be rendered the Willoughbys than to let Nick depart, and for the Irishman to go with him. Mike, however, had not the slightest idea of desertion, the motive which prevailed on him to quit the Hut being a desire to see the major, and, if possible, to help him escape. As soon as this expectation was placed before his eyes, Mike became a convert to the Indian's wishes. Like all exceedingly zealous men, the Irishman had an itching propensity to be doing, and he was filled with a sort of boyish delight at the prospect of effecting a great service to those whom he so well loved, without their knowing it. Such was the history of Michael's seeming desertion; that of what occurred after he quitted the works remains to be related.

The Tuscarora led his companion out of the Hut, within half an hour after they had been left alone together, in the room of Mr. Woods. As this was subsequently to Joel's flight, Nick, in anticipation of this event, chose to lie in ambush a short time, in order to ascertain whether the defection was likely to go any further. Satisfied on this head, he quietly retired towards the mill. After making a sufficient *dêtour* to avoid being seen from the house, Nick gave himself no trouble about getting into the woods, or of practising any of the expedients of a time of real danger, as had been done by all of the deserters; but he walked leisurely across the meadows, until he struck the highway, along which he proceeded forthwith to the rocks. All this was done in a way that showed he felt himself at home, and that he had no apprehensions of falling into an ambush. It might have arisen from his familiarity with the ground; or, it might have proceeded from the consciousness that he was approaching friends, instead of enemies.

At the rocks, however, Nick did not deem it wise to lead Mike any farther, without some preliminary caution. The white man was concealed in one of the clefts, therefore, while the Indian pursued his way alone. The latter was absent an hour; at the end of that time he returned, and, after giving Mike a great many cautions about silence and prudence, he led him to the cabin of the miller, in the buttery of which Robert Willoughby was confined. To this buttery there was a window; but, as it was so small as to prevent escape, no sentinel had been placed on the outside of the building. For his own comfort, too, and in order to possess his narrow lodgings to himself, the major had given a species of parole, by which he was bound to remain in duresse, until the rising of the next sun. Owing to these two causes, Nick had been enabled to approach the window, and to hold communications with the prisoner. This achieved, he returned to the rocks, and led Mike to the same spot.

Major Willoughby had not been able to write much, in consequence of the darkness. That which he communicated, accordingly, had to pass through the fiery ordeal of the Irishman's brains. As a matter of course it did not come with particular lucidity, though Mike did succeed in making his auditors comprehend this much.

The major was substantially well treated, though intimations had been given that he would be considered as a spy. Escape seemed next to impossible; still, he should not easily abandon the hope. From all he had seen, the party was one of that irresponsible character that would render capitulation exceedingly hazardous, and he advised his father to hold out to the last. In a military point of view, he considered his captors as contemptible, being without a head; though many of the men:--the savages in particular--appeared to be ferocious and reckless. The whole party was guarded in discourse, and little was said in English, though he was convinced that many more whites were present than he had at first believed. Mr. Woods he had not seen, nor did he know anything of his arrest or detention.

This much Mike succeeded in making the captain comprehend, though a great deal was lost through the singular confusion that prevailed in the mind of the messenger. Mike however, had still another communication, which we reserve for the ears of the person to whom it was especially sent.

This news produced a pause in captain Willoughby's determination. Some of the fire of youth awoke within him, and he debated with himself on the possibility of making a sortie, and of liberating his son, as a step preliminary to victory; or, at least, to a successful retreat. Acquainted with every foot of the ground, which had singular facilities for a step so bold, the project found favour in his eyes each minute, and soon became fixed.

Chapter XXIII

--"Another love
In its lone woof begun to twine;
But, ah! the golden thread was wove
That bound my sister's heart in mine!"
Willis.

While the captain and Joyce were digesting their plans Mike proceeded on an errand of peculiar delicacy with which he had been entrusted by Robert Willoughby. The report that he had returned flew through the dwellings, and many were the hearty greetings and shakings of the hand that the honest fellow had to undergo from the Plinys and Smashes, ere he was at liberty to set about the execution of this trust. The wenches, in particular, having ascertained that Mike had not broken his fast, insisted on his having a comfortable meal, in a sort of servants' hall, before they would consent to his quitting their sight. As the county Leitrim-man was singularly ready with a knife and fork, he made no very determined opposition, and, in a few minutes, he was hard at work, discussing a cold ham, with the other collaterals of a substantial American breakfast.

The blacks, the Smashes inclusive, had been seriously alarmed at the appearance of the invading party. Between them and the whole family of red-men there existed a sort of innate dislike; an antipathy that originated in colour, and wool, and habits, and was in no degree lessened by apprehensions on the score of scalps.

"How you look, ole Plin, widout wool?" Big Smash had reproachfully remarked, not five minutes before Mike made his appearance in the kitchen, in answer to some apologetic observation of her husband, as to the intentions of the savages being less hostile than he had at first imagined; "why you say dey *no* murder, and steal and set fire, when you know dey's Injin! Natur' be natur'; and dat I hear dominie Woods say t'ree time one Sunday. What 'e dominie say *often*, he mean, and dere no use in saying dey don't come to do harm."

As Great Smash was an oracle in her own set, there was no gainsaying her dogmas, and Pliny the elder was obliged to succumb. But the presence of Mike, one who was understood to have been out, *near*, if not actually *in*, the enemy's camp, and a great favourite in the bargain, was a circumstance likely to revive the discourse. In fact, all the negroes, crowded into the hall, as soon as the Irishman was seated at table, one or two eager to talk, the rest as eager to listen.

"How near you been to sabbage, Michael?" demanded Big Smash, her two large coal-black eyes seeming to open in a degree proportioned to her interest in the answer.

"I wint as nigh as there was occasion, Smash, and that was nigher than the likes of yer husband there would be thinking of travelling. Maybe 'twas as far as from my plate here to yon door; maybe not quite so far. They 're a dhirty set, and I wish to go no nearer."

"What dey look like, in 'e dark?" inquired Little Smash--"Awful as by daylight?"

"It's not meself that stopped to admire 'em. Nick and I had our business forenent us, and when a man is hurried, it isn't r'asonable to suppose he can kape turning his head about to see sights."

"What dey do wid Misser Woods?--What sabbage want wid dominie?"

"Sure enough, little one; and the question is of yer own asking. A praist, even though he should be only a heretic, can have no great call for his sarvices, in *sich* a congregation. And, I don't think the fellows are blackguards enough to scalp a parson."

Then followed a flood of incoherent questions that were put by all the blacks in a body, accompanied by divers looks ominous of the most serious disasters, blended with bursts of laughter that broke out of their risible natures in a way to render the medley of sensations as ludicrous as it was strange. Mike soon found answering a task too difficult to be attempted, and he philosophically came to a determination to confine his efforts to masticating.

Notwithstanding the terror that actually prevailed among the blacks, it was not altogether unmixed with a resolution to die with arms in their hands, in preference to yielding to savage clemency. Hatred, in a measure, supplied the place of courage, though both sexes had insensibly imbibed some of that resolution which is the result of habit, and of which a border life is certain to instil more or less into its subjects, in a form suited to border emergencies. Nor was this feeling confined to the men; the two Smashes, in particular, being women capable of achieving acts that would be thought heroic under circumstances likely to arouse their feelings.

"Now, Smashes," said Mike, when, by his own calculation, he had about three minutes to the termination of his breakfast before him, "ye'll do what I tells ye, and no questions asked. Ye'll find the laddies, Missus, and Miss Beuly, and Miss Maud, and ye'll give my humble respects to 'em all--divil the bit, now, will ye be overlooking either of the t'ree, but ye'll do yer errand genteely and like a laddy yerself--and ye'll give my jewty and respects to 'em *all*, I tells ye, and say that Michael O'Hearn asks the honour of being allowed to wish 'em good morning."

Little Smash screamed at this message; yet she went, forthwith, and delivered it, making reasonably free with Michael's manner and gallantry in so doing.

"O'Hearn has something to tell us from Robert"--said Mrs. Willoughby, who had been made acquainted with the Irishman's exploits and return; "he must be suffered to come in as soon as he desires."

With this reply, Little Smash terminated her mission.

"And now, laddies and gentlemen," said Mike, with gravity, as he rose to quit the servants' hall, "my blessing and good wishes be wid ye. A hearty male have I had at yer hands and yer cookery, and good thanks it desarves. As for the Injins, jist set yer hearts at rest, as not one of ye will be scalp'd the day, seeing that the savages are all to be forenent the mill this morning, houlding a great council, as I knows from Nick himself. A comfortable time, then, ye may all enjoy, wid yer heads on yer shoulters, and yer wool on yer heads."

Mike's grin, as he retreated, showed that he meant to be facetious, having all the pleasantry that attends a full stomach uppermost in his animal nature at that precise moment. A shout rewarded this sally, and the parties separated with mutual good humour and good feeling. In this state of mind, the county Leitrim man was ushered into the presence of the ladies. A few words of preliminary explanations were sufficient to put Mike in the proper train, when he came at once to his subject.

"The majjor is no way down-hearted," he said, "and he ordered me to give his jewty and riverence, and obligations, to his honoured mother and his sisters. 'Tell 'em, Mike,' says he, says the majjor, 'that I feels for 'em, all the same as if I was their own fader; and tell 'em,' says he, 'to keep up their spirits, and all will come right in the ind. This is a throublesome wor-r-ld, but they that does their jewties to God and man, and the church, will not fail, in the long run, to wor-r-k their way t'rough purgatory even, into paradise.'"

"Surely my son--my dear Robert--never sent us such a message as this, Michael?"

"Every syllable of it, and a quantity moor that has slipped my memory," answered the Irishman, who was inventing, but who fancied he was committing a very pious fraud--"'Twould have done the Missuses heart good to have listened to the majjor, who spoke more in the charackter of a praist, like, than in that of a souldier."

All three of the ladies looked a little abashed, though there was a gleam of humour about the mouth of Maud, that showed she was not very far from appreciating the Irishman's report at its just value. As for Mrs. Willoughby and Beulah, less acquainted with Mike's habits, they did not so readily penetrate his manner of substituting his own desultory thoughts for the ideas of others.

"As I am better acquainted with Mike's language, dear mother"-- whispered Maud--"perhaps it will be well if I take him into the library and question him a little between ourselves about what actually passed. Depend on it, I shall get the truth."

"Do, my child, for it really pains me to hear Robert so much misrepresented--and, as Evert must now begin to have ideas, I really do not like that his uncle should be so placed before the dear little fellow's mind."

Maud did not even smile at this proof of a grandmother's weakness, though she felt and saw all its absurdity. Heart was ever so much uppermost with the excellent matron, that it was not easy for those she loved to regard anything but her virtues; and least of all did her daughter presume to indulge in even a thought that was ludicrous at her expense. Profiting by the assent, therefore, Maud quietly made a motion for Mike to follow, and proceeded at once to the room she had named.

Not a word was exchanged between the parties until both were in the library, when Maud carefully closed the door, her face pale as marble, and stood looking inquiringly at her companion. The reader will understand that, Mr. Woods and Joyce excepted, not a soul at the Hut, out of the limits of the Willoughby connection, knew anything of our heroine's actual relation to the captain and his family. It is true, some of the oldest of the blacks had once some vague notions on the subject; but *their* recollections had become obscured by time, and habit was truly second nature with all of the light-hearted race.

"*That* was mighty injanious of you, Miss Maud!" Mike commenced, giving one of his expressive grins again, and fairly winking. "It shows how fri'nds wants no spache but their own minds. Barrin' mistakes and crass-accidents, I'm sartain that Michael O'Hearn can make himself understood any day by Miss Maud Willoughby, an' niver a word said."

"Your success then, Mike, will be greater at dumb-show than it always is with your tongue," answered the young lady, the blood slowly returning to her cheek, the accidental use of the name of Willoughby removing the apprehension of anything immediately embarrassing; "what have you to tell me that you suppose I have anticipated?"

"Sure, the like o' yees needn't be tould, Miss Maud, that the majjor bad me spake to ye by yerself, and say a word that was not to be overheerd by any one else."

"This is singular--extraordinary even--but let me know more, though the messenger be altogether so much out of the common way!"

"I t'ought ye 'd say *that*, when ye come to know me. Is it meself that 's a messenger? and where is there another that can carry news widout spilling any by the way? Nick's a cr'ature, I allows; but the majjor know'd a million times bhetter than to trust an Injin wid sich a jewty. As for Joel, and *that* set of vagabonds, we'll grind 'em all in the mill, before we've done wid 'em. Let 'em look for no favours, if they wishes no disapp'intment."

Maud sickened at the thought of having any of those sacred feelings connected with Robert Willoughby that she had so long cherished in her inmost heart, rudely probed by so unskilful a hand; though her last conversation with the young soldier had told so much, even while it left so much unsaid, that she could almost kneel and implore Mike to be explicit. The reserve of a woman, notwithstanding, taught her how to preserve her sex's decorum, and to maintain appearances.

"If major Willoughby desired you to communicate anything to me, in particular," she said, with seeming composure, "I am ready to hear it."

"Divil the word did he desire, Miss Maud, for everything was in whispers between us, but jist what I'm about to repait. And here's my stick, that Nick tould me to kape as a reminderer; it 's far bhetter for me than a book, as I can't read a syllable. 'And now, Mike,' says the majjor, says he, 'conthrive to see phratty Miss Maud by herself'----"

"*Pretty* Miss Maud!" interrupted the young lady, involuntarily.

"Och! it's meself that says *that*, and sure there 's plenty of r'ason for it; so we'll agree it's all right and proper--'phratty Miss Maud by herself, letting no mortal else know what you are about. *That* was the majjor's."

"It is very extraordinary!--Perhaps it will be better Michael, if you tell me nothing but what is strictly the major's. A message should be delivered as nearly like the words that were actually sent as possible."

"Wor-r-ds!--And it isn't wor-r-ds at all, that I have to give ye."

"If not a message in words, in what else can it be?--Not in sticks, surely."

"In *that*"--cried Mike, exultingly--"and, I'll warrant, when the trut' comes out, that very little bit of silver will be found as good as forty Injin scalps."

Although Mike put a small silver snuff-box that Maud at once recognised as Robert Willoughby's property into the young lady's hand, nothing was more apparent than the circumstance that he was profoundly ignorant of the true meaning of what he was doing. The box was very beautiful, and his mother and Beulah had often laughed at the major for using an article that was then deemed *de rigueur* for a man of extreme *ton*, when all his friends knew he never touched snuff. So far from using the stimulant, indeed, he never would show how the box was opened, a secret spring existing; and he even manifested or betrayed shyness on the subject of suffering either of his sisters to search for the means of doing so.

The moment Maud saw the box, her heart beat tumultuously. She had a presentiment that her fate was about to be decided. Still, she had sufficient self-command to make an effort to learn all her companion had to communicate.

"Major Willoughby gave you this box," she said, her voice trembling in spite of herself. "Did he send any message with it? Recollect yourself; the words may be very important."

"Is it the wor-r-ds? Well, it's little of *them* that passed between us, barrin' that the Injins was so near by, that it was whisper we did, and not a bit else."

"Still there *must* have been *some* message."

"Ye are as wise as a sarpent, Miss Maud, as Father O'Loony used to tell us all of a Sunday! Was it wor-r-ds!--Give *that* to Miss Maud,' says the majjor, says he, 'and tell her she is now *misthress of my sacret.*"

"Did he say this, Michael?--For heaven's sake, be certain of what you tell me."

"Irish Mike--Masser want you in monstrous hurry," cried the youngest of the three black men, thrusting his glistening lace into the door, announcing the object of the intrusion, and disappearing almost in the same instant.

"Do not leave me, O'Hearn," said Maud, nearly gasping for breath, "do not leave me without an assurance there is no mistake."

"Divil bur-r-n me if I 'd brought the box, or the message, or anything like it, phretty Miss Maud, had I t'ought it would have done this har-r-m."

"Michael O'Hearn," called the serjeant from the court, in his most authoritative military manner, and that on a key that would not brook denial.

Mike did not dare delay; in half a minute Maud found herself standing alone, in the centre of the library, holding the well-known snuff-box of Robert Willoughby in her little hand. The renowned caskets of Portia had scarcely excited more curiosity in their way than this little silver box of the major's had created in the mind of Maud. In addition to his playful evasions about letting her and Beulah pry into its mysteries, he had once said to herself, in a grave and feeling manner, "When you get at the contents of this box, dear girl, you will learn the great secret of my life." These words had made a deep impression at the time--it was in his visit of the past year--but they had been temporarily forgotten in the variety of events and stronger sensations that had succeeded. Mike's message, accompanied by the box itself, however, recalled them, and Maud fancied that the major, considering himself to be in some dangerous emergency, had sent her the bauble in order that she might learn what that secret was. Possibly he meant her to communicate it to others. Persons in our heroine's situation feel, more than they reason; and it is possible Maud might have come to some other conclusion had she been at leisure, or in a state of mind to examine all the circumstances in a more logical manner.

Now she was in possession of this long-coveted box--coveted at least so far as a look into its contents were concerned--Maud not only found herself ignorant of the secret by which it was opened, but she had scruples about using the means, even had she been in possession of them. At first she thought of carrying the thing to Beulah, and of asking if she knew any way of getting at the spring; then she shrunk from the exposure that might possibly attend such a step. The more she reflected, the more she felt convinced that Robert Willoughby would not have sent *her* that particular box, unless it were connected with herself, in some way more than common; and ever since the conversation in the painting-room she had seen glimmerings of the truth, in relation to his feelings. These glimmerings too, had aided her in better understanding her own heart, and all her sentiments revolted at the thought of having a witness to any explanation that might relate to the subject. In every event she determined, after a few minutes of thought, not to speak of the message, or the present, to a living soul.

In this condition of mind, filled with anxiety, pleasing doubts, apprehensions, shame, and hope, all relieved, however, by the secret consciousness of perfect innocence, and motives that angels might avow, Maud stood, in the very spot where Mike had left her, turning the box in her hands, when accidentally she touched the spring, and the lid flew open. To glance at the contents was an act so natural and involuntary as to anticipate reflection.

Nothing was visible but a piece of white paper, neatly folded, and compressed into the box in a way to fill its interior. "Bob has written," thought Maud--"Yet how could he do this? He was in the dark, and had not pen or paper!" Another look rendered this conjecture still more improbable, as it showed the gilt edge of paper of the quality used for notes, an article equally unlikely to be found in the mill and in his own pocket. "Yet it must be a note," passed through her mind, "and of course it was written before he left the Hut--quite likely before he arrived--possibly the year before, when he spoke of the box as containing the evidence of the great secret of his life."

Maud now wished for Mike, incoherent, unintelligible, and blundering as he was, that she might question him still further as to the precise words of the message. "Possibly Bob did not intend me to open the-box at all," she thought, "and meant merely that I should keep it until he could return to claim it. It contains a great secret; and, because he wishes to keep this secret from the Indians, it does not follow that he intends to reveal it to me. I will shut the box again, and guard his secret as I would one of my own."

This was no sooner *thought* than it was *done*. A pressure of the lid closed it, and Maud heard the snap of the spring with a start. Scarcely was the act performed ere she repented it. "Bob would not have sent the box without some particular object," she went on to imagine; "and had he intended it not to be opened, he would have told as much to O'Hearn. How easy would it have been for him to say, and for Mike to repeat, 'tell her to keep the box till I ask for it--it contains a secret, and I wish my captors not to learn it.' No, he has sent the box with the design that I should examine its contents. His very life may depend on my doing so; yes, and on my doing so this minute!"

This last notion no sooner glanced athwart our heroine's mind, than she began diligently to search for the hidden spring. Perhaps curiosity had its influence on the eagerness to arrive at the secret, which she now manifested; possibly a tenderer and still more natural feeling lay concealed behind it all. At any rate, her pretty little fingers never were employed more nimbly, and not a part of the exterior of the box escaped its pressure. Still, the secret spring eluded her search. The box had two or three bands of richly chased work on each side of the place of opening, and amid these ornaments Maud felt certain that the little projection she sought must lie concealed. To examine these, then, she commenced in a regular and connected manner, resolved that not a single raised point should be neglected. Accident, however, as before, stood her friend; and, at a moment when she least expected it, the lid flew back, once more exposing the paper to view.

Maud had been too seriously alarmed about re-opening the box, to hesitate a moment now, as to examining its contents. The paper was removed, and she began to unfold it slowly, a slight tremor passing through her frame as she did so. For a single instant she paused to scent the delightful and delicate perfume that seemed to render the interior sacred; then her fingers resumed their office. At each instant, her eyes expected to meet Robert Willoughby's well known handwriting. But the folds of the paper opened on a blank. To Maud's surprise, and, for a single exquisitely painful moment, she saw that a lock of hair was all the box contained, besides the paper in which it was enveloped. Her look became anxious, and her face pale; then the eyes brightened, and a blush that might well be likened to the tints with which the approach of dawn illumines the sky, suffused her cheeks, as, holding the hair to the light, the long ringlets dropped at length, and she recognised one of those beautiful tresses, of which so many were falling at that very moment, in rich profusion around her awn lovely face. To unloosen her hair from the comb, and to lay the secret of Bob Willoughby by its side, in a way to compare the glossy shades, was the act of only a moment; it sufficed, however, to bring a perfect conviction of the truth. It was a memorial of herself, then, that Robert Willoughby so prized, had so long guarded with care, and which he called the secret of his life!

It was impossible for Maud not to understand all this. Robert Willoughby loved her; he had taken this mode of telling his passion. He had been on the point of doing this in words the very day before; and now he availed himself of the only means that offered of completing the tale. A flood of tenderness gushed to the heart of Maud, as she passed over all this in her mind; and, from that moment, she ceased to feel shame at the recollection of her own attachment. She might still have shrunk a little from avowing it to her father, and mother, and Beulah; but, as to herself the world, and the object of her affections, she now stood perfectly vindicated in her own eyes.

That was a precious half-hour which succeeded. For the moment, all present dangers were lost sight of, in the glow of future hopes. Maud's imagination portrayed scenes of happiness, in which domestic duties, Bob beloved, almost worshipped, and her father and mother happy in the felicity of their children, were the prominent features; while Beulah and little Evert filled the back-ground of the picture in colours of pleasing softness. But these were illusions that could not last, for ever, the fearful realities of her situation returning with the greater consciousness of existence. Still, Bob might now be loved, without wounding any of the sensitiveness of her sex's opinions; and dearly, engrossingly, passionately was he rewarded, for the manner in which he had thought of letting her know the true state of his heart, at a moment when he had so much reason to think only of himself.

It was time for Maud to return to her mother and sister. The box was carefully concealed, leaving the hair in its old envelope, and she hurried to the nursery. On entering the room, she found that her father had just preceded her. The captain was grave, more thoughtful than usual, and his wife, accustomed to study his countenance for so much of her happiness, saw at once that something lay heavy on his mind.

"Has anything out of the way happened, Hugh?" she asked, "to give you uneasiness?"

Captain Willoughby drew a chair to the side of that of his wife, seated himself, and took her hand before he answered. Little Evert, who sat on her knee, was played with, for a moment, as if to defer a disagreeable duty; not till then did he even speak.

"You know, dearest Wilhelmina," the captain finally commenced, "that there have never been any concealments between us, on the score of danger, even when I was a professed soldier, and might be said to carry my life in my hand."

"You have ever found me reasonable, I trust, while feeling like a woman, mindful of my duty as a wife?"

"I have, love; this is the reason I have always dealt with you so frankly."

"We understand each other, Hugh. Now tell me the worst at once."

"I am not certain you will think there is any worst about it, Wilhelmina, as Bob's liberty is the object. I intend to go out myself, at the head of all the white men that remain, in order to deliver him from the hands of his enemies. This will leave you, for a time--six or seven hours perhaps--in the Hut, with only the three blacks as a guard, and with the females. You need have no apprehension of an assault, however, everything indicating a different intention on the part of our enemies; on that score you may set your hearts at rest."

"All my apprehensions and prayers will be for you, my husband--for ourselves, we care not."

"This I expected; it is to lessen these very apprehensions that I have come to tell you my whole plan."

Captain Willoughby now related, with some minuteness, the substance of Mike's report, and his own plan, of the last of which we have already given an outline. Everything had been well matured in his mind, and all promised success. The men were apprised of the service on which they were to be employed, and every one of them had manifested the best spirit. They were then busy in equipping themselves; in half an hour they would be ready to march.

To all this Mrs. Willoughby listened like a soldier's wife, accustomed to the risks of a frontier warfare, though she felt like a woman. Beulah pressed little Evert to her heart, while her pallid countenance was turned to her father with a look that seemed to devour every syllable. As for Maud, a strange mixture of dread and wild delight were blended in her bosom. To have Bob liberated, and restored to them, was approaching perfect happiness, though it surpassed her powers not to dread misfortunes. Nevertheless, the captain was so clear in his explanations, so calm in his manner, and of a judgment so approved, that his auditors felt far less concern than might naturally have been expected.

Chapter XXIV

"March--march--march!
Making sounds as they tread,
Ho-ho! how they step,
Going down to the dead."

Coxe.

The time Maud consumed in her meditations over the box and its contents, had been employed by the captain in preparations for his enterprise. Joyce, young Blodget, Jamie and Mike, led by their commander in person, were to compose the whole force on the occasion; and every man had been busy in getting his arms, ammunition and provisions ready, for the last half-hour. When captain Willoughby, therefore, had taken leave of his family, he found the party in a condition to move.

The first great desideratum was to quit the Hut unseen. Joel and his followers were still at work, in distant fields; but they all carefully avoided that side of the Knoll which would have brought them within reach of the musket, and this left all behind the cliff unobserved, unless Indians were in the woods in that direction. As Mike had so recently passed in by that route, however, the probability was the whole party still remained in the neighbourhood of the mills, where all accounts agreed in saying they mainly kept. It was the intention of the captain, therefore, to sally by the rivulet and the rear of the house, and to gain the woods under cover of the bushes on the banks of the former, as had already been done by so many since the inroad.

The great difficulty was to quit the house, and reach the bed of the stream, unseen. This step, however, was a good deal facilitated by means of Joel's sally-port, the overseer having taken, himself, all the precautions against detection of which the case well admitted. Nevertheless, there was the distance between the palisades and the base of the rocks, some forty or fifty yards, which was entirely uncovered, and had to be passed under the notice of any wandering eyes that might happen to be turned in that quarter. After much reflection, the captain and serjeant came to the conclusion to adopt the following mode of proceeding.

Blodget passed the hole, by himself, unarmed, rolling down the declivity until he reached the stream. Here a thicket concealed him sufficiently, the bushes extending along the base of the rocks, following the curvature of the rivulet. Once within these bushes, there was little danger of detection. As soon as it was ascertained that the young man was beneath the most eastern of the outer windows of the northern wing, the only one of the entire range that had bushes directly under it, all the rifles were lowered down to him, two at a time, care being had that no one should appear at the window during the operation. This was easily effected, jerks of the rope sufficing for the necessary signals to haul in the line. The ammunition succeeded; and in this manner, all the materials of offence and defence were soon collected on the margin of the stream.

The next step was to send the men out, one by one, imitating the precautions taken by Blodget. Each individual had his own provisions, and most of the men carried some sort of arms, such as a pistol, or a knife, about his person. In half an hour the four men were armed, and waited for the leader, concealed by the bushes on the border of the brook. It only remained for captain Willoughby to give some instructions to those he left in the Hut, and to follow.

Pliny the elder, in virtue of his years, and some experience in Indian warfare, succeeded to the command of the garrison, in the absence of its chief. Had there remained a male white at the Knoll, this trust never could have devolved on him, it being thought contrary to the laws of nature for a negro to command one of the other colour; but such was not the fact, and Pliny the elder succeeded pretty much as a matter of course. Notwithstanding, he was to obey not only his particular *old* mistress, but both his *young* mistresses, who exercised an authority over him that was not to be disputed, without doing violence to all the received notions of the day. To him, then, the captain issued his final orders, bidding him be vigilant, and above all to keep the gates closed.

As soon as this was done, the husband and father went to his wife and children to take a last embrace. Anxious not to excite too strong apprehensions by his manner, this was done affectionately--solemnly, perhaps--but with a manner so guarded as to effect his object.

"I shall look for no other signal, or sign of success, Hugh," said the weeping wife, "than your own return, accompanied by our dearest boy. When I can hold you both in my arms, I shall be happy, though all the Indians of the continent were in the valley."

"Do not miscalculate as to time, Wilhelmina. That affectionate heart of yours sometimes travels over time and space in a way to give its owner unnecessary pain. Remember we shall have to proceed with great caution, both in going and returning; and it will require hours to make the *détour* I have in view. I hope to see you again before sunset, but a delay may carry us into the night. It may even become necessary to defer the final push until after dark."

This was melancholy intelligence for the females; but they listened to it with calmness, and endeavoured to be, as well as to seem, resigned. Beulah received her father's kiss and blessing with streaming eyes, straining little Evert to her heart as he left her. Maud was the last embraced, He even led her, by gentle violence, to the court, keeping her in discourse by the way, exhorting her to support her mother's spirits by her own sense and steadiness.

"I shall have Bob in the Hut, soon," he added, "and this will repay us all for more than twice the risks--all but you, little vixen; for your mother tells me you are getting, through some caprice of that variable humour of your sex, to be a little estranged from the poor fellow."

"Father!"

"O! I know it is not very serious still, even Beulah tells me you once called him a Major of Foot."

"Did I?" said Maud, trembling in her whole frame lest her secret had been prematurely betrayed by the very attempt to conceal it. "My tongue is not always my heart."

"I know it, darling, unless where I am concerned. Treat the son as you will, Maud, I am certain that you will always love the father." A pressure to the heart, and kisses on the forehead, eyes, and cheeks followed. "You have all your own papers, Maud, and can easily understand your own affairs. When examined into, it will be seen that every shilling of your fortune has gone to increase it; and, little hussy, you are now become something like a great heiress."

"What does this mean, dearest, dearest father? Your words frighten me!"

"They should not, love. Danger is never increased by being prepared to meet it. I have been a steward, and wish it to be known that the duty has not been unfaithfully discharged. That is all. A hundred-fold am I repaid by possessing so dutiful and sweet a child."

Maud fell on her father's bosom and sobbed. Never before had he made so plain allusions to the true relations which existed between them; the papers she possessed having spoken for themselves, and having been given in silence. Nevertheless, as he appeared disposed to proceed no further, at present, the poor girl struggled to command herself, succeeded in part, rose, received her father's benediction, most solemnly and tenderly delivered, and saw him depart, with an air of calmness that subsequently astonished even herself.

We must now quit the interesting group that was left behind in the Hut, and accompany the adventurers in their march.

Captain Willoughby was obliged to imitate his men, in the mode of quitting the palisades. He had dressed himself in the American hunting-shirt and trowsers for the occasion, and, this being an attire he now rarely used, it greatly diminished the chances of his being recognised, if seen. Joyce was in a similar garb, though neither Jamie nor Mike could ever be persuaded to assume a style that both insisted so much resembled that of the Indians. As for Blodget, he was in the usual dress of a labourer.

As soon as he had reached the bottom of the cliff, the captain let the fact be known to Old Pliny, by using his voice with caution, though sufficiently loud to be heard on the staging of the roof, directly above his head. The black had been instructed to watch Joel and his companions, in order to ascertain if they betrayed, in their movements, any consciousness of what was in progress at the Hut. The report was favourable, Pliny assuring his master that "all 'e men work, sir, just as afore. Joel hammer away at plough-handle, tinkerin' just like heself. Not an eye turn dis away, massa."

Encouraged by this assurance, the whole party stole through the bushes, that lined this part of the base of the cliffs, until they entered the bed of the stream. It was September, and the water was so low, as to enable the party to move along the margin of the rivulet dry-shod, occasionally stepping from stone to stone. The latter expedient, indeed, was adopted wherever circumstances allowed, with a view to leave as few traces of a trail as was practicable. Otherwise the cover was complete; the winding of the rivulet preventing any distant view through its little reaches, and the thick fringe of the bushes on each bank, effectually concealing the men against any passing, lateral, glimpse of their movements.

Captain Willoughby had, from the first, apprehended an assault from this quarter. The house, in its elevation, however, possessed an advantage that would not be enjoyed by an enemy on the ground; and, then, the cliff offered very serious obstacles to anything like a surprise on that portion of the defences. Notwithstanding, he now led his men, keeping a look riveted on the narrow lane in his front, far from certain that each turn might not bring him in presence of an advancing party of the enemy. No such unpleasant encounter occurred; and the margin of the forest was gained, without any appearance of the foe, and seemingly without discovery.

Just within the cover of the woods, a short reach of the rivulet lay fairly in sight, from the rear wing of the dwellings. It formed a beautiful object in the view; the ardent and tasteful Maud having sketched the silvery ribbon of water, as it was seen retiring within the recesses of the forest, and often calling upon others to admire its loveliness and picturesque effect. Here the captain halted, and made a signal to Old Pliny, to let him know he waited for an answer. The reply was favourable, the negro showing the sign that all was still well. This was no sooner done, than the faithful old black hurried down to his mistress, to communicate the intelligence that the party was safely in the forest; while the adventurers turned, ascended the bank of the stream, and pursued their way on more solid ground.

Captain Willoughby and his men were now fairly engaged in the expedition, and every soul of them felt the importance and gravity of the duty he was on. Even Mike was fain to obey the order to be silent, as the sound of a voice, indiscreetly used, might betray the passage of the party to some outlying scouts of the enemy. Caution was even used in treading on dried sticks, lest their cracking should produce the same effect.

The sound of the axe was heard in the rear of the cabins coming from a piece of woodland the captain had ordered cleared, with the double view of obtaining fuel, and of increasing his orchards. This little clearing was near a quarter of a mile from the flats, the plan being, still to retain a belt of forest round the latter; and it might have covered half-a-dozen acres of land, having now been used four or five years for the same purpose. To pass between this clearing and the cabins would have been too hazardous, and it became necessary to direct the march in a way to turn the former.

The cow-paths answered as guides for quite a mile, Mike being thoroughly acquainted with all their sinuosities. The captain and serjeant, however, each carried a pocket compass, an instrument without which few ventured far into the forests. Then the blows of the axes served as sounds to let the adventurers know their relative position, and, as they circled the place whence they issued, they gave the constant assurance of their own progress, and probable security.

The reader will probably comprehend the nature of the ground over which our party was now marching. The 'flats' proper, or the site of the old Beaver Dam, have already been described. The valley, towards the south, terminated at the rocks of the mill, changing its character below that point, to a glen, or vast ravine. On the east were mountains of considerable height, and of unlimited range; to the north, the level land extended miles, though on a platform many feet higher than the level of the cleared meadows; while, to the west, along the route the adventurers were marching, broad slopes of rolling forest spread their richly-wooded surfaces, filled with fair promise for the future. The highest swell of this undulating forest was that nearest to the Hut, and it was its elevation only that gave the home-scene the character of a valley.

Captain Willoughby's object was to gain the summit of this first ridge of land, which would serve as a guide to his object, since it terminated at the line of rocks that made the water-fall, quite a mile, however, in the rear of the mills. It would carry him also quite beyond the clearing of the wood-choppers, and be effectually turning the whole of the enemy's position. Once at the precipitous termination caused by the face of rock that had been thrown to the surface by some geological phenomenon, he could not miss his way, since these rugged marks must of themselves lead him directly to the station known to be occupied by the body of his foes.

Half an hour served to reach the desired ridge, when the party changed its march, pursuing a direction nearly south, along its summit.

"Those axes sound nearer and nearer, serjeant," Captain Willoughby observed, after the march had lasted a long time in profound silence. "We must be coming up near the point where the men are at work."

"Does your honour reflect at all on the reason why these fellows are so particularly industrious in a time like this?--To me it has a very ambuscadish sort of look!"

"It cannot be connected with an ambuscade, Joyce, inasmuch as we are not supposed to be on a march. There can be no ambuscade, you will remember, practised on a garrison."

"I ask your honour's pardon--may not a sortie be ambushed, as well as a march?"

"In that sense, perhaps, you may be right. And, now you mention it, I think it odd there should be so much industry at wood-chopping, in a moment like this. We will halt as soon as the sounds are fairly abreast of us, when you and I can reconnoitre the men, and ascertain the appearance of things for ourselves."

"I remember, sir, when your honour led out two companies of ours, with one of the Royal Irish, a major's command, of good rights, to observe the left flank of the French, the evening before we stormed the enemy's works at Ty--"

"Your memory is beginning to fail you, Joyce," interrupted the captain, smiling. "We were far from storming those works, having lost two thousand men before them, and failed of seeing their inside at all."

"I always look upon a soldierly attempt, your honour, the same as a thing that is done. A more gallant stand than we made I never witnessed; and, though we were driven back, I will allow, yet I call that assault as good as storming!"

"Well, have it your own way, Joyce.--The morning before your storming, I remember to have led out three companies; though it was more in advance, than on either flank. The object was to unmask a suspected ambush."

"That's just what I wanted to be at, your honour. The general sent you, as an old captain, with three companies, to spring the trap, before he should put his own foot into it."

"He certainly did--and the movement had the desired effect."

"Better and better, sir.--I remember we were fired on, and lost some ten or fifteen men, but I would not presume to say whether the march succeeded or not; for nothing was said of the affair, next day, in general orders, sir--"

"Next day we had other matters to occupy our minds. It was a bloody and a mournful occasion for England and her colonies."

"Well, your honour, that does not affect our movement, which, you say, yourself, was useful."

"Very true, Joyce, though the great calamity of the succeeding day prevented the little success of the preceding morning from being mentioned in general orders. But to what does all this tend; as I know it must lead to something?"

"It was merely meant as a respectful hint, your honour, that the inferior should be sent out, now, according to our own ancient rules, to reconn'itre the clearing, while the commander-in-chief remain with the main body, to cover the retreat."

"I thank you, serjeant, and shall not fail to employ you, on all proper occasions. At present, it is my intention that we go together, leaving the men to take breath, in a suitable cover."

This satisfied Joyce, who was content to wait for orders. As soon as the sounds of the axes showed that the party were far enough in advance, and the formation of the land assured the captain that he was precisely where he wished to be, the men were halted, and left secreted in a cover made by the top of a fallen tree. This precaution was taken, lest any wandering savage might get a glimpse of their persons, if they stood lounging about in the more open forest, during the captain's absence.

This disposition made, the captain and serjeant, first examining the priming of their pieces, moved with the necessary caution towards the edge of the wood-chopper's clearing. The axe was a sufficient guide, and ere they had proceeded far the light began to shine through the trees, proof in itself that they were approaching an opening in the forest.

"Let us incline to the left, your honour," said Joyce, respectfully; "there is a naked rock hereabouts, that completely overlooks the clearing, and where we can get even a peep at the Hut. I have often sat on it, when out with the gun, and wearied; for the next thing to being at home, is to see home."

"I remember the place, serjeant, and like your suggestion," answered the captain, with an eagerness that it was very unusual for him to betray. "I could march with a lighter heart, after getting another look at the Knoll, and being certain of its security."

The parties being both of a mind, it is not surprising that each looked eagerly for the spot in question. It was an isolated rock that rose some fifteen or twenty feet above the surface of the ground, having a width and depth about double its height--one of those common excrescences of the forest that usually possess interest for no one but the geologist. Such an object was not difficult to find in an open wood, and the search was soon rewarded by a discovery. Bending their steps that way, our two soldiers were quickly at its base. As is usual, the summit of this fragment of rock was covered with bushes; others shooting out, also, from the rich, warm earth at its base, or, to speak more properly, at its junction with the earth.

Joyce ascended first, leaving his rifle in the captain's charge. The latter followed, after having passed up his own and his companion's arms; neither being disposed to stir without having these important auxiliaries at command. Once on the rock, both moved cautiously to its eastern brow, care being had not to go beyond the cover. Here they stood, side by side, gazing on the scene that was outspread before them, through openings in the bushes.

To the captain's astonishment, he found himself within half musket shot of the bulk of the hostile party. A regular bivouac had been formed round a spring in the centre of the clearing, and bodies of trees had been thrown together, so as to form a species of work which was rudely, but effectually abbatied by the branches. In a word, one of those strong, rough forest encampments had been made, which are so difficult to carry without artillery, more especially if well defended. By being placed in the centre of the clearing, an assault could not be made without expensing the assailants, and the spring always assured to the garrison the great requisite, water.

There was a method and order in this arrangement that surprised both our old soldiers. That Indians had resorted to this expedient, neither believed;

nor would the careless, untaught and inexperienced whites of the Mohawk be apt to adopt it, without a suggestion from some person acquainted with the usages of frontier warfare. Such persons were not difficult to find, it is true; and it was a proof that those claiming to be in authority, rightfully or not, were present.

There was something unlooked for, also, in the manner in which the party of strangers were lounging about, at a moment like that, seemingly doing nothing, or preparing for no service. Joyce, who was a man of method, and was accustomed to telling off troops, counted no less than forty-nine of these idlers, most of whom were lounging near the log entrenchment, though a few were sauntering about the clearing, conversing with the wood-choppers, or making their observations listlessly, and seemingly without any precise object in view.

"This is the most extr'or'nary sight, for a military expedition, I have ever seen, your honour," whispered Joyce, after the two had stood examining the position for quite a minute in silence. "A tolerable good log breast-work, I will allow, sir, and men enough to make it good against a sharp assault; but nothing like a guard, and not so much as a single sentinel. This is an affront to the art. Captain Willoughby; and it is such an affront to us, that I feel certain we might carry the post by surprise, if all felt the insult as I do myself."

"This is no time for rash acts or excited feelings, Joyce. Though, were my gallant boy with us, I do think we might make a push at these fellows, with very reasonable chances of success."

"Yes, your honour, and without him, too. A close fire, three cheers, and a vigorous charge would drive every one of the rascals into the woods!"

"Where they would rally, become the assailants in their turn, surround us, and either compel us to surrender, or starve us out. At all events, nothing of the sort must be undertaken until we have carried out the plan for the rescue of Major Willoughby. My hopes of success are greatly increased since I find the enemy has his principal post up here, where he must be a long half-mile from the mill, even in a straight line. You have counted the enemy?"

"There are just forty-nine of them in sight, and I should think some eight or ten more sleeping about under the logs, as I occasionally discover a new one raising his head.--Look, sir, does your honour see that manoeuvre?"

"Do I see what, serjeant?--There is no visible change that I discover."

"Only an Indian chopping wood, Captain Willoughby which is some such miracle as a white man painting."

The reader will have understood that all the hostile party that was lounging about this clearing were in Indian guise, with faces and hands of the well-known reddish colour that marks the American aborigines. The two soldiers could discover many evidences that there was deception in these appearances, though they thought it quite probable that real red men were mingled with the pale-faces. But, so little did the invaders respect the necessity of appearances in their present position, that one of these seeming savages had actually mounted a log, taken the axe from the hands of its owner, and begun to chop, with a vigour and skill that soon threw off chips in a way that no man can successfully imitate but the expert axe-man of the American interior.

"Pretty well that, sir, for a red-skin," said Joyce, smiling "If there isn't white blood, ay, and Yankee blood in that chap's arm, I'll give him some of my own to help colour it. Step this way, your honour--only a foot or two--there, sir; by looking through the opening just above the spot where that very make-believe Injin is scattering his chips as if they were so many kernels of corn that he was tossing to the chickens, you will get a sight of the Hut."

The fact was so. By altering his own position a little on the rock, Captain Willoughby got a full view of the entire buildings of the Knoll. It is true, he could not see the lawn without the works, nor quite all of the stockade, but the whole of the western wing, or an entire side-view of the dwellings, was obtained. Everything seemed as tranquil and secure, in and around them, as if they vegetated in a sabbath in the wilderness. There was something imposing even, in the solemn silence of their air, and the captain now saw that if he had been struck, and rendered uneasy by the mystery that accompanied the inaction and quiet of his invaders, they, in their turns, might experience some such sensations as they gazed on the repose of the Hut, and the apparent security of its garrison. But for Joel's desertion, indeed, and the information he had carried with him, there could be little doubt that the stranger must have felt the influence of such doubts to a very material extent. Alas! as things were, it was not probable they could be long imposed on, by any seeming calm.

Captain Willoughby felt a reluctance to tear himself away from the spectacle of that dwelling which contained so many that were dear to him. Even Joyce gazed at the house with pleasure, for it had been his quarters, now, so many years, and he had looked forward to the time when he should breathe his last in it. Connected with his old commander by a tie that was inseparable, so far as human wishes could control human events, it was impossible that the serjeant could go from the place where they had left so many precious beings almost in the keeping of Providence, at a moment like that, altogether without emotion. While each was thus occupied in mind, there was a perfect stillness. The men of the party had been so far drilled, as to speak in low voices, and nothing they said was audible on the rock. The axes alone broke the silence of the woods, and to ears so accustomed to their blows, they offered no intrusion. In the midst of this eloquent calm, the bushes of the rock rustled, as it might be with the passage of a squirrel, or a serpent. Of the last the country had but few, and they of the most innocent kind, while the former abounded. Captain Willoughby turned, expecting to see one of these little restless beings, when his gaze encountered a swarthy face, and two glowing eyes, almost within reach of his arm. That this was a real Indian was beyond dispute, and the crisis admitting of no delay, the old officer drew a dirk, and had already raised his arm to strike, when Joyce arrested the blow.

"This is Nick, your honour;" said the serjeant, inquiringly--"is he friend, or foe?"

"What says he himself?" answered the captain, lowering his hand in doubt. "Let him speak to his own character."

Nick now advanced and stood calmly and fearlessly at the side of the two white men. Still there was ferocity in his look, and an indecision in his movements. He certainly might betray the adventurers at any instant, and they felt all the insecurity of their situation. But accident had brought Nick directly in front of the opening through which was obtained the view of the Hut. In turning from one to the other of the two soldiers, his quick eye took in this glimpse of the buildings, and it became riveted there as by the charm of fascination. Gradually the ferocity left his countenance, which grew human and soft.

"Squaw in wigwam"--said the Tuscarora, throwing forward a hand with its fore-finger pointing towards the house. "Ole squaw--young squaw. Good. Wyandotté sick, she cure him. Blood in Injin body; thick blood-- nebber forget good--nebber forget bad."

Chapter XXV

"Every stride--every stamp, Every footfall is bolder; 'Tis a
skeleton's tramp, With a skull on its shoulder! But ho, how
he steps With a high-tossing head, That clay-covered bone,
Going down to the dead!"

Coxe.

Nick's countenance was a fair index to his mind; nor were his words
intended to deceive. Never did Wyandotté forget the good, or evil, that was
done him. After looking intently, a short time, at the Hut, he turned and
abruptly demanded of his companions,--

"Why come here? Like to see enemy between you and wigwam?"

As all Nick said was uttered in a guarded tone, as if he fully entered
into the necessity of remaining concealed from those who were in such a
dangerous vicinity, it served to inspire confidence, inducing the two soldiers
to believe him disposed to serve them.

"Am I to trust in you as a friend?" demanded the captain, looking the
Indian steadily in the eye.

"Why won't trust? Nick no hero--gone away--Nick nebber come ag'in-
-Wyandotté hero--who no trust Wyandotté? Yengeese always trust great
chief."

"I shall take you at your word, Wyandotté, and tell you everything,
hoping to make an ally of you. But, first explain to me, why you left the Hut,
last night--friends do not desert friends."

"Why leave wigwam?--Because wanted to. Wyandotté come when he
want; go when he want. Nick go too.--Went to see son--come back; tell story;
eh?"

"Yes, it has happened much as you say, and I am willing to think it all
occurred with the best motives. Can you tell me anything of Joel, and the
others who have left me?"

"Why tell?--Cap'in look; he see. Some chop--some plough--some weed-
-some dig ditch. All like ole time Bury hatchet--tired of war-path--why
cap'in ask?"

"I see all you tell me. You know, then, that those fellows have made friends with the hostile party?"

"No need know--see. Look--Injin chop, pale-face look on! Call that war?"

"I do see that which satisfies me the men in paint yonder are not all red men."

"No--cap'in right--tell him so at wigwam. But dat Mohawk--dog--rascal--Nick's enemy!"

This was said with a gleam of fierceness shooting across the swarthy face, and a menacing gesture of the hand, in the direction of a real savage who was standing indolently leaning against a tree, at a distance so small as to allow those on the rock to distinguish his features. The vacant expression of this man's countenance plainly denoted that he was totally unconscious of the vicinity of danger. It expressed the listless vacancy of an Indian in a state of perfect rest--his stomach full, his body at ease, his mind peaceful.

"I thought Nick was not here," the captain quietly observed, smiling on the Tuscarora a little ironically.

"Cap'in right--Nick no here. Well for dog 'tis so. Too mean for Wyandotté to touch. What cap'in come for? Eh! Better tell chief--get council widout lightin' fire."

"As I see no use in concealing my plan from you, Wyandotté,"--Nick seemed pleased whenever this name was pronounced by others--"I shall tell it you, freely. Still, you have more to relate to me. Why are *you* here?--And how came you to discover us?"

"Follow trail--know cap'in foot--know serjeant foot--know Mike foot--see so many foot, follow him. Leave so many" holding up three fingers "in bushes--so many" holding up two fingers "come here. Foot tell *which* come here--Wyandotté chief--he follow chief."

"When did you first strike, or see our trail, Tuscarora?"

"Up here--down yonder--over dere." Captain Willoughby understood this to mean, that the Indian had crossed the trail, or seen it in several places. "Plenty trail; plenty foot to tell all about it. Wyandotté see foot of friend--why he don't follow, eh?"

"I hope this is all so, old warrior, and that you will prove yourself a friend indeed. We are out in the hope of liberating my son, and we came here to see what our enemies are about."

The Tuscarora's eyes were like two inquisitors, as he listened; but he seemed satisfied that the truth was told him. Assuming an air of interest, he inquired if the captain knew where the major was confined. A few words explained everything, and the parties soon understood each other.

"Cap'in right," observed Nick. "Son in cupboard still; but plenty warrior hear, to keep eye on him."

"You know his position, Wyandotté, and can aid us materially, if you will. What say you, chief; will you take service, once more, under your old commander?"

"Who *he* sarve--King George--Congress--eh?"

"Neither. I am neutral, Tuscarora, in the present quarrel. I only defend myself, and the rights which the laws assure to me, let whichever party govern, that may."

"Dat bad. Nebber neutral in hot war. Get rob from bot' side. Alway be one or t'oder, cap'in."

"You may be right, Nicholas, but a conscientious man may think neither wholly right, nor wholly wrong. I wish never to lift the hatchet, unless my quarrel be just."

"Injin no understand *dat*. Throw hatchet at *enemy*--what matter what he say--good t'ing, bad t'ing. He *enemy*--dat enough. Take scalp from *enemy*-- don't touch *friend*"

"That may do for *your* mode of warfare, Tuscarora, but It will hardly do for *mine*. I must feel that I have right of my side, before I am willing to take life."

"Cap'in always talk so, eh? When he soldier, and general say shoot ten, forty, t'ousand Frenchmen, den he say; stop, general--no hurry--let cap'in t'ink.' Bye'm-by he'll go and take scalp; eh!"

It exceeded our old soldier's self-command not to permit the blood to rush into his face, at this home-thrust; for he felt the cunning of the Indian had involved him in a seeming contradiction.

"That was when I was in the army, Wyandotté," he answered, notwithstanding his confusion, "when my first, and highest duty, was to obey the orders of my superiors. Then I acted as a soldier; now, I hope to act as a man."

"Well, Indian chief alway in army. Always high duty, and obey superior--obey Manitou, and take scalp from enemy. War-path alway open, when enemy at t'other end."

"This is no place to discuss such questions, chief; nor have we the time. Do you go with us?"

Nick nodded an assent, and signed for the other to quit the rocks. The captain hesitated a moment, during which he stood intently studying the scene in the clearing.

"What say you, Tuscarora; the serjeant has proposed assaulting that breast-work?"

"No good, cap'in. You fire, halloo, rush on--well, kill four, six, two--rest run away. Injin down at mill hear rifle; follow smoke--where major, den? Get major, first--t'ink about enemy afterwards."

As Nick said this, he repeated the gesture to descend; and he was obeyed in silence. The captain now led the way back to his party; and soon rejoined it. All were glad to see Nick, for he was known to have a sure rifle; to be fearless as the turkey-cock; and to possess a sagacity in the woods, that frequently amounted to a species of intuition.

"Who lead, cap'in or Injin?" asked the Tuscarora, in his sententious manner.

"Och, Nick, ye're a cr'ature!" muttered Mike. "Divil bur-r-rn me, Jamie, but I t'inks the fallie would crass the very three-tops, rather than miss the majjor's habitation."

"Not a syllable must be uttered," said the captain, raising a hand in remonstrance. "I will lead, and Wyandotté will march by my side, and give me his council, in whispers. Joyce will bring up the rear. Blodget, you will keep a sharp look-out to the left, while Jamie will do the same to the right. As we approach the mills, stragglers may be met in the woods, and our march must be conducted with the greatest caution. Now follow, and be silent."

The captain and Nick led, and the whole party followed, observing the silence which had been enjoined on them. The usual manner of marching on a war-path, in the woods, was for the men to follow each other singly; an order that has obtained the name of 'Indian file,' the object being to diminish the trail, and conceal the force of the expedition, by each man treading in his leader's footsteps. On the present occasion, however, the captain induced Nick to walk at his side, feeling an uneasiness on the subject of the Tuscarora's fidelity that he could not entirely conquer. The pretext given was very different, as the reader will suppose. By seeing the print of a moccasin in company with that of a boot, any straggler that crossed the trail might be led to suppose it had been left by the passage of a party from the clearing or the mill. Nick quietly assented to this reasoning, and fell in by the side of the captain without remonstrance.

Vigilant eyes were kept on all sides of the line of march, though it, was hoped and believed that the adventurers had struck upon a route too far west to be exposed to interruption. A quarter of a mile nearer to the flats might have brought them within the range of stragglers; but, following the summit of the ridge, there was a certain security in the indolence which would be apt to prevent mere idlers from sauntering up an ascent. At all events, no interruption occurred, the party reaching in safety the rocks that were a continuation of the range which formed the precipice at the falls--the sign that they had gone far enough to the south. At this period, the precipice was nearly lost in the rising of the lower land, but its margin was sufficiently distinct to form a good mask.

Descending to the plateau beneath, the captain and Nick now inclined to the east, the intention being to come in upon the mills from the rear. As the buildings lay in the ravine, this could only be done by making a rapid descent immediately in their vicinity; a formation of the ground that rendered the march, until within pistol-shot of its termination, reasonably secure. Nick also assured his companions that he had several times traversed this very plateau, and that he had met no signs of footsteps on it; from which he inferred that the invaders had not taken the trouble to ascend the rugged cliffs that bounded the western side of the glen.

The approach to the summit of the cliff was made with caution, though the left flank of the adventurers was well protected by the abrupt descent they had already made from the terrace above. This left little more than the right flank and the front to be watched, the falling away of the land forming, also, a species of cover for the rear. It is not surprising, then, that the verge of the ravine or glen was attained, and no discovery was made. The spot being favourable, the captain immediately led down a winding path, that was densely fringed with bushes, towards the level of the buildings.

The glen of the mills was very narrow; so much so, as barely to leave sites for the buildings themselves, and three or four cabins for the workmen. The mills were placed in advance, as near as possible to the course of the water; while the habitations of the workmen were perched on shelves of the rocks, or such level bits of bottom-land as offered. Owing to this last circumstance, the house of Daniel the miller, or that in which it was supposed the major was still confined, stood by itself, and fortunately, at the very foot of the path by which the adventurers were descending. All this was favourable, and had been taken into the account as a material advantage, by Captain Willoughby when he originally conceived the plan of the present sortie.

When the chimney of the cabin was visible over the bushes, Captain Willoughby halted his party, and repeated his instruction to Joyce, in a voice very little raised above a whisper; The serjeant was ordered to remain in his present position, until he received a signal to advance. As for the captain, himself, he intended to descend as near as might be to the buttery of the cabin, and reconnoitre, before he gave the final order. This buttery was in a lean-to, as a small addition to the original building was called in the parlance of the country; and, the object being shade and coolness, on account of the milk with which it was usually well stored at this season of the year, it projected back to the very cliff, where it was half hid in bushes and young trees. It had but a single small window, that was barred with wood to keep out cats, and such wild vermin as affected milk, nor was it either lathed or plastered; these two last being luxuries not often known in the log tenements of the frontier. Still it was of solid logs, chinked in with mortar, and made a very effectual prison, with the door properly guarded; the captive being deprived of edged tools. All this was also known to the father, when he set forth to effect the liberation of his son, and, like the positions of the buildings themselves, had been well weighed in his estimate of the probabilities and chances.

As soon as his orders were given, Captain Willoughby proceeded down the path, accompanied only by Nick. He had announced his intention to send the Tuscarora ahead to reconnoitre, then to force himself among the bushes between the lean-to and the rocks, and there to open a communication with the major through the chinks of the logs After receiving Nick's intelligence, his plan was to be governed by circumstances, and to act accordingly.

"God bless you, Joyce," said the captain, squeezing the Serjeant's hand as he was on the point of descending. "We are on ticklish service, and require all our wits about us. If anything happen to me, remember that my wife and daughter will mainly depend on you for protection."

"I shall consider that as your honour's orders, sir, and no more need be said to me, Captain Willoughby."

The captain smiled on his old follower, and Joyce thought that never had he seen the fine manly face of his superior beam with a calmer, or sweeter expression, than it did as he returned his own pressure of the hand. The two adventurers were both careful, and their descent was noiseless. The men above listened, in breathless silence, but the stealthy approach of the cat upon the bird could not have been more still, than that, of these two experienced warriors.

The place where Joyce was left with the men, might have been fifty feet above the roof of the cabin, and almost perpendicularly over the narrow vacancy that was known to exist between the rocks and the lean-to. Still the bushes and trees were so thick as to prevent the smallest glimpse at objects below, had the shape of the cliff allowed it, while they even intercepted sounds. Joyce fancied, nevertheless, that he heard the rustling bushes, as the captain forced his way into the narrow space he was to occupy, and he augured well of the fact, since it proved that no opposition had been encountered. Half an hour of forest silence followed, that was only interrupted by the tumbling of the waters over the natural dam. At the end of that weary period, a shout was heard in front of the mills, and the party raised their pieces, in a vague apprehension that some discovery had been made that was about to bring on a crisis. Nothing further occurred, however, to confirm this impression, and an occasional burst of laughter, that evidently came from white men, rather served to allay the apprehension.

Another half-hour passed, during which no interruption was heard. By this time Joyce became uneasy, a state of things having arrived for which no provision had been made in his instructions. He was about to leave his command under the charge of Jamie, and descend himself to reconnoitre, when a footstep was heard coming up the path. Nothing but the deep attention, and breathless stillness of the men could have rendered the sound of a tread so nearly noiseless, audible; but heard it was, at a moment when every sense was wrought up to its greatest powers. Rifles were lowered, in readiness to receive assailants, but each was raised again, as Nick came slowly into view. The Tuscarora was calm in manner, as if no incident had occurred to disconcert the arrangement, though his eyes glanced around him, like those of a man who searched for an absent person.

"Where cap'in?--Where major?" Nick asked, as soon as his glance had taken in the faces of all present.

"We must ask that of you, Nick," returned Joyce. "We have not seen the captain, nor had any orders from him, since he left us."

This answer seemed to cause the Indian more surprise than it was usual for him to betray, and he pondered a moment in obvious uneasiness.

"Can't stay here, alway," he muttered. "Best go see. Bye'm-by trouble come; then, too late."

The serjeant was greatly averse to moving without orders. He had his instructions how to act in every probable contingency, but none that covered the case of absolute inaction on the part of those below. Nevertheless, twice the time necessary to bring things to issue had gone by, and neither signal, shot, nor alarm had reached his ears.

"Do you know anything of the major, Nick?" the serjeant demanded, determined to examine the case thoroughly ere he came to a decision.

"Major dere--see him at door--plenty sentinel. All good--where cap'in?"

"Where did you leave him?--You can give the last account of him."

"Go in behind cupboard--under rock--plenty bushes--all right--son dere."

"This must be looked to--perhaps his honour has fallen into a fit--such things sometimes happen--and a man who is fighting for his own child, doesn't feel, Jamie, all the same as one who fights on a general principle, as it might be."

"Na--ye 're right, sairjeant J'yce, and ye'll be doing the kind and prudent act, to gang doon yersal', and investigate the trainsaction with yer ain een."

This Joyce determined to do, directing Nick to accompany him, as a guide. The Indian seemed glad to comply, and there was no delay in proceeding. It required but a minute to reach the narrow passage between the cliff and the lean-to. The bushes were carefully shoved aside, and Joyce entered. He soon caught a glimpse of the hunting-shirt, and then he was about to withdraw, believing that he was in error, in anticipating orders. But a short look at his commander removed all scruples; for he observed that he was seated on a projection of the rocks, with his body bowed forward, apparently leaning on the logs of the building. This seemed to corroborate the thought about a fit, and the serjeant pressed eagerly forward to ascertain the truth.

Joyce touched his commander's arm, but no sign of consciousness came from the latter. He then raised his body upright, placing the back in a reclining attitude against the rocks, and started back himself when he caught a glimpse of the death-like hue of the face. At first, the notion of the fit was strong with the serjeant; but, in changing his own position, he caught a glimpse of a little pool of blood, which at once announced that violence had been used.

Although the serjeant was a man of great steadiness of nerves, and unchangeable method, he fairly trembled as he ascertained the serious condition of his old and well-beloved commander. Notwithstanding, he was too much of a soldier to neglect anything that circumstances required. On examination, he discovered a deep and fatal wound between two of the ribs, which had evidently been inflicted with a common knife. The blow had passed into the heart, and Captain Willoughby was, out of all question, dead! He had breathed his last, within six feet of his own gallant son, who, ignorant of all that passed, was little dreaming of the proximity of one so dear to him, as well as of his dire condition.

Joyce was a man of powerful frame, and, at that moment, he felt he was master of a giant's strength. First assuring himself of the fact that the wounded man had certainly ceased to breathe, he brought the arms over his own shoulders, raised the body on his back, and walked from the place, with less attention to caution than on entering, but with sufficient care to prevent exposure. Nick stood watching his movements with a wondering look, and as soon as there was room, he aided in supporting the corpse.

In this manner the two went up the path, bearing their senseless burden. A gesture directed the party with Jamie to precede the two who had been below, and the serjeant did not pause even to breathe, until he had fairly reached the summit of the cliff; then he halted in a place removed from the danger of immediate discovery. The body was laid reverently on the ground, and Joyce renewed his examination with greater ease and accuracy, until perfectly satisfied that the captain must have ceased to breathe, nearly an hour.

This was a sad and fearful blow to the whole party. No one, at such a moment, thought of inquiring into the manner in which their excellent master had received his death-blow; but every thought was bent either on the extent of the calamity, or on the means of getting back to the Hut. Joyce was the soul of the party. His rugged face assumed a stern, commanding expression; but every sign of weakness had disappeared. He gave his orders promptly, and the men even started when he spoke, so bent on obtaining obedience did he appear to be.

The rifles were converted into a bier, the body was placed upon it, and the four men then raised the burthen, and began to retrace their footsteps, in melancholy silence. Nick led the way, pointing out the difficulties of the path, with a sedulousness of attention, and a gentleness of manner, that none present had ever before witnessed in the Tuscarora He even appeared to have become woman, to use one of his own peculiar expressions.

No one speaking, and all the men working with good will, the retreat, notwithstanding the burthen with which it was encumbered, was made with a rapidity greatly exceeding the advance. Nick led the way with an unerring eye, even selecting better ground than that which the white men had been able to find on their march. He had often traversed all the hills, in the character of a hunter, and to him the avenues of the forest were as familiar as the streets of his native town become to the burgher. He made no offer to become one of the bearers; this would have been opposed to his habits; but, in all else, the Indian manifested gentleness and solicitude. His apprehension seemed to be, and so he expressed it, that the Mohawks might get the scalp of the dead man; a disgrace that he seemed as solicitous to avoid as Joyce himself; the serjeant, however, keeping in view the feelings of the survivors, rather than any notions of military pride.

Notwithstanding the stern resolution that prevailed among the men, that return march was long and weary. The distance, of itself, exceeded two miles, and there were the inequalities and obstacles of a forest to oppose them. Per severance and strength, however, overcame all difficulties; and, at the end of two hours, the party approached the point where it became necessary to enter the bed of the rivulet, or expose their sad procession by marching in open view of any who might be straggling in the rear of the Hut. A species of desperate determination had influenced the men in their return march, rendering them reckless of discovery, or its consequences; a circumstance that had greatly favoured their object; the adventurous and bold frequently encountering fewer difficulties, in the affairs of war, than the cautious and timid. But an embarrassment now presented itself that was far more difficult to encounter than any which proceeded from personal risks. The loving family of the deceased was to be met; a wife and daughters apprised of the fearful loss that, in the providence of God, had suddenly alighted on their house.

"Lower the body, men, and come to a halt," said Joyce, using the manner of authority, though his voice trembled "we must consult together, as to our next step."

There was a brief and decent pause, while the party placed the lifeless body on the grass, face uppermost, with the limbs laid in order, and everything about it, disposed of in a seemliness that betokened profound respect for the senseless clay, even after the noble spirit had departed. Mike alone could not resist his strong native propensity to talk. The honest fellow raised a hand of his late master, and, kissing it with strong affection, soliloquized as follows, in a tone that was more rebuked by feeling, than any apprehension of consequences.

"Little need had ye of a praist, and extreme unction," he said. "The likes of yerself always kapes a clane breast; and the knife that went into yer heart found nothing that ye need have been ashamed of! Sorrow come over me, but yer lass is as great a one to meself, as if I had tidings of the sinking of ould Ireland into the salt say, itself; a thing that niver *can* happen, and niver will happen; no, not even at the last day; as all agree the wor-r-ld is to be burned and not drowned. And who'll there be to tell this same to the Missus, and Miss Beuly, and phratty Miss Maud, and the babby, in the bargain? Divil bur-r-n me, if 't will be Michael O'Hearn, who has too much sorrow of his own, to be running about, and d'aling it out to other people. Sarjeant, that will be ver own jewty, and I pities the man that has to perform it."

"No man will see me shrink from a duty, O'Hearn," said Joyce, stiffly, while with the utmost difficulty he kept the tears from breaking out of a fountain that had not opened, in this way, for twenty years. "It may bear hard on my feelings--I do not say it will *not*--but duty is duty, and it must be done. Corporal Allen, you see the state of things; the commanding officer is among the casualties, and nothing would be simpler than our course, were it not for Madam Willoughby--God bless her, and have her in His holy keeping--and the young ladies. It is proper to deliberate a little about *them*. To you then, as an elderly and experienced man, I first apply for an opinion."

"Sorrow's an unwelcome guest, whether it comes expected, or without any previous knowledge. The hairts o the widow and fairtherless must be stricken, and it's little that a' our consolations and expairiments will prevail ag'in the feelin's o' natur'. Pheeloosophy and religion tall us that the body's no mair than a clod o' the valley when the speerit has fled; but the hairt is unapt to listen to wisdom while the grief is fraish, and of the severity of an unlooked-for sairtainty. *I* see little good, therefore, in doing mair than just sending in a messenger, to clear the way a little for the arrival of truth, in the form o' death, itsal'."

"I have been thinking of this--will you take the office, Jamie, as a man of years and discretion?"

"Na--na--ye'll be doing far better by sending a younger man. Age has weakened my memory, and I'll be overlooking some o' the saircumstances in a manner that will be unseemly for the occasion. Here is Blodget, a youth of ready wit, and limber tongue."

"I wouldn't do it, mason, to be the owner of ten such properties as this!" exclaimed the young Rhode Islander, actually recoiling a step, as if he retreated before a dreaded foe.

"Well, sairjeant, ye've Michael here, who belangs to a kirk that has so little seempathy with protestantism as to lessen the pain o' the office. Death is a near ally to religion, and Michael, by taking a religious view o' the maither, might bring his hairt into such a condition of insensibility as wad give him little to do but to tell what has happened, leaving God, in his ain maircy, to temper the wind to the shorn lamb."

"You hear, O'Hearn?" said the serjeant, stiffly--"Everybody seems to expect that you will do this duty."

"Jewty!--D 'ye call it a jewty for a man in my situation to break the hearts of Missus, and Miss Beuly, and phratty Miss Maud, and the babby? for babbies has hearts as well as the stoutest man as is going. Divil bur-r-n me, then, if ye gets out of my mout' so much as a hint that the captain's dead and gone from us, for ever and ever, amen! Ye may send me in, for ye 're corporals, and serjeants, and the likes of yees, and I'll obey as a souldier, seem' that he would have wished as much himself, had the breat' staid in his body, which it has not, on account of its l'aving his sowl on 'arth, and departing with his corporeal part for the mansions of happiness, the Blessed Mary have mercy on him, whether here or *there*--but the captain was not the man to wish a fait'ful follower to afflict his own wife; and so I'll have not'in' to do with such a message, at all at all."

"Nick go"--said the Indian, calmly--"Used to carry message--carry him for cap'in, once more."

"Well, Nick, you may do it certainly, if so disposed," answered Joyce, who would have accepted the services of a Chinese rather than undertake the office in person. "You will remember and speak to the ladies gently, and not break the news too suddenly."

"Yes--squaw soft heart--Nick know--had moder--had wife, once--had darter."

"Very well; this will be an advantage, men, as Nick is the only married man among us; and married men should best understand dealing with females."

Joyce then held a private communication with the Tuscarora, that lasted some five or six minutes, when the last leaped nimbly into the bed of the stream, and was soon concealed by the bushes of one of its reaches.

Chapter XXVI

"Heart leaps to heart--the sacred flood
That warms us is the same;
That good old man--his honest blood
Alike we fondly claim."

Sprague.

Although Nick commenced his progress with so much seeming zeal and activity, his speed abated, the moment he found himself beyond the sight of those he had left in the woods. Before he reached the foot of the cliff, his trot had degenerated to a walk; and when he actually found he was at its base, he seated himself on a stone, apparently to reflect on the course he ought to pursue.

The countenance of the Tuscarora expressed a variety of emotions while he thus remained stationary. At first, it was fierce, savage, exulting; then it became gentler, soft, perhaps repentant. He drew his knife from its buckskin sheath, and eyed the blade with a gaze expressive of uneasiness. Perceiving that a clot of blood had collected at the junction with the handle, it was carefully removed by the use of water. His look next passed over his whole person, in order to ascertain if any more of these betrayers of his fearful secret remained; after which he seemed more at ease.

"Wyandotté's back don't ache now," he growled to himself. "Ole sore heal up. Why Cap'in touch him? T'ink Injin no got feelin'? Good man, sometime; bad man, sometime. Sometime, live; sometime, die. Why tell Wyandotté he flog ag'in, just as go to enemy's camp? No; back feel well, now--nebber smart, any more."

When this soliloquy was ended, Nick arose, cast a look up at the sun, to ascertain how much of the day still remained, glanced towards the Hut, as if examining the nature of its defences, stretched himself like one who was weary, and peeped out from behind the bushes, in order to see how those who were afield, still occupied themselves. All this done, with singular deliberation and steadiness, he arranged his light dress, and prepared to present himself before the wife and daughters of the man, whom, three hours before, he had remorselessly murdered. Nick had often meditated this treacherous deed, during the thirty years which had elapsed between his first flogging and the present period; but circumstances had never placed its execution safely in his power. The subsequent punishments had increased the desire, for a few years; but time had so far worn off the craving for revenge, that it would never have been actively revived, perhaps, but for the unfortunate allusions of the victim himself, to the subject. Captain Willoughby had been an English soldier, of the school of the last century. He was naturally a humane and a just man, but he believed in the military axiom that "the most flogging regiments were the best fighting regiments;" and perhaps he was not in error, as regards the lower English character. It was a fatal error, however, to make in relation to an American savage; one who had formerly exercised the functions, and who had not lost all the feelings, of a chief. Unhappily, at a moment when everything depended on the fidelity of the Tuscarora, the captain had bethought him of his old expedient for insuring prompt obedience and, by way of a reminder, he made an allusion to his former mode of punishment. As Nick would have expressed it, "the old sores smarted;" the wavering purpose of thirty years was suddenly and fiercely revived, and the knife passed into the heart of the victim, with a rapidity that left no time for appeals to the tribunal of God's mercy. In half a minute, Captain Willoughby had ceased to breathe.

Such had been the act of the man who now passed through the opening of the palisade, and entered the former habitation of his victim. A profound stillness reigned in and around the Hut, and no one appeared to question the unexpected intruder. Nick passed, with his noiseless step, round to the gate, which he found secured. It was necessary to knock, and this he did in a way effectually to bring a porter.

"Who dere?" demanded the elder Pliny, from within.

"Good friend--open gate. Come wid message from cap'in."

The natural distaste to the Indians which existed among the blacks of the Knoll, included the Tuscarora. This disgust was mingled with a degree of dread; and it was difficult for beings so untutored and ignorant, at all times to draw the proper distinctions between Indian and Indian. In *their* wonder-loving imaginations, Oneidas, Tuscaroras, Mohawks, Onondagas, and Iroquois were all jumbled together in inextricable confusion, a red man being a red man, and a savage a savage. It is not surprising, therefore, that Pliny the elder should hesitate about opening the gate, and admitting one of the detested race, though a man so well known to them all, in the peculiar situation of the family. Luckily, Great Smash happened to be near, and her husband called her to the gate by one of the signals that, was much practised between them.

"Who you t'ink out-dere?" asked Pliny the elder of his consort, with a very significant look.

"How you t'ink guess, ole Plin?--You 'spose nigger wench like Albonny wise woman, dat she see t'rough a gate, and know ebbery t'ing, and little more!"

"Well, *dat* Sassy Nick. What you say *now?*"

"You sartain, ole Plin?" asked Mistress Smash, with a face ominous of evil.

"Sartain as ear. Talk wid him--he want to come in. What you t'ink?"

"Nebber open gate, ole Plin, till mistress tell you. You stay here--dere; lean ag'in gate wid all you might; dere; now I go call Miss Maud. She all alone in librarim, and will know what best. Mind you lean ag'in gate well, ole Plin."

Pliny the elder nodded assent, placed his shoulders resolutely against the massive timbers, and stood propping a defence that would have made a respectable resistance to a battering-ram, like another Atlas, upholding a world. His duty was short, however, his 'lady' soon returning with Maud, who was hastening breathlessly to learn the news.

"Is it you, Nick?" called out the sweet voice of our heroine through the crevices of the timber.

The Tuscarora started, as he so unexpectedly heard those familiar sounds; for an instant, his look was dark; then the expression changed to pity and concern, and his reply was given with less than usual of the abrupt, guttural brevity that belonged to his habits.

"'Tis Nick--Sassy Nick--Wyandotté, Flower of the Woods," for so the Indian often termed Maud.--"Got news--cap'in send him. Meet party and go along. Nobody here; only Wyandotté. Nick see major, too--say somet'ing to young squaw."

This decided the matter. The gate was unbarred, and Nick in the court in half-a-minute. Great Smash stole a glance without, and beckoned Pliny the elder to join her, in order to see the extraordinary spectacle of Joel and his associates toiling in the fields. When they drew in their heads, Maud and her companion were already in the library. The message from Robert Willoughby had induced our heroine to seek this room; for, placing little confidence in the delicacy of the messenger, she recoiled from listening to his words in the presence of others.

But Nick was in no haste to speak. He took the chair to which Maud motioned, and he sate looking at her, in a way that soon excited her alarm.

"Tell me, if your heart has any mercy in it, Wyandotté; has aught happened to Major Willoughby?"

"He well--laugh, talk, feel good. Mind not'ing. He prisoner; don't touch he scalp."

"Why, then, do you wear so ominous a look--your face is the very harbinger of evil."

"Bad news, if trut' must come. What you' name, young squaw?"

"Surely, surely, you must know that well, Nick! I am Maud--your old friend, Maud."

"Pale-face hab two name--Tuscarora got t'ree. Some time, Nick--sometime, Sassy Nick--sometime, Wyandotté."

"You know my name is Maud Willoughby," returned our heroine, colouring to the temples with a certain secret consciousness of her error, but preferring to keep up old appearances.

"Dat call you' fader's name, Meredit'; no Willoughby."

"Merciful Providence! and has this great secret been known to *you*, too, Nick!"

"He no secret--know all about him. Wyandotté dere. See Major Meredit' shot. *He* good chief--nebber flog--nebber strike Injin. Nick know fader, know moder--know squaw, when pappoose."

"And why have you chosen this particular moment to tell me all this? Has it any relation to your message--to Bob--to Major Willoughby, I mean?" demanded Mauo, nearly gasping for breath.

"No relation, tell you," said Nick, a little angrily. "Why make relation, when no relation at all. Meredit'; no Willoughby. Ask moder; ask major; ask chaplain--all tell trut'! No need to be so feelin'; no you fader, at all."

"What *can* you--what *do* you mean, Nick? Why do you look so wild--so fierce--so kind--so sorrowful--so angry? You must have bad news to tell me."

"Why bad to *you*--he no fader--only fader friend. You can't help it--fader die when you pappoose--why you care, now, for dis?"

Maud now actually gasped for breath. A frightful glimpse of the truth gleamed before her imagination, though it was necessarily veiled in the mist of uncertainty. She became pale as death, and pressed her hand upon her heart, as if to still its beating. Then, by a desperate effort, she became more calm, and obtained the power to speak.

"Oh! is it so, Nick!--*can* it be so!" she said; "my father has fallen in this dreadful business?"

"Fader kill twenty year ago; tell you *dat,* how often?" answered the Tuscarora, angrily; for, in his anxiety to lessen the shock to Maud, for whom this wayward savage had a strange sentiment of affection, that had grown out of her gentle kindnesses to himself, on a hundred occasions, he fancied if she knew that Captain Willoughby was not actually her father, her grief at his loss would be less. "Why you call *dis* fader, when *dat* fader. Nick know fader and moder.--Major no broder."

Notwithstanding the sensations that nearly pressed her to the earth, the tell-tale blood rushed to Maud's cheeks, again, at this allusion, and she bowed her face to her knees. The action gave her time to rally her faculties; and catching a glimpse of the vast importance to all for her maintaining self-command, she was enabled to raise her face with something like the fortitude the Indian hoped to see.

"Trifle with me no longer, Wyandotté, but let me know the worst at once. Is my father dead?--By father, I mean captain Willoughby?"

"Mean wrong, den--no fader, tell you. Why young quaw so much like Mohawk?"

"Man--is captain Willoughby killed?"

Nick gazed intently into Maud's face for half a minute, and then he nodded an assent. Notwithstanding all her resolutions to be steady, our heroine nearly sank under the blow. For ten minutes she spoke not, but sat, her head bowed to her knees, in a confusion of thought that threatened a temporary loss of reason. Happily, a flood of tears relieved her, and she became more calm. Then the necessity of knowing more, in order that she might act intelligently, occurred to her mind, and she questioned Nick in a way to elicit all it suited the savage to reveal.

Maud's first impulse was to go out to meet the body of the captain, and to ascertain for herself that there was actually no longer any hope. Nick's account had been so laconic as to leave much obscurity, and the blow had been so sudden she could hardly credit the truth in its full extent. Still, there remained the dreadful tidings to be communicated to those dear beings, who, while they feared so much, had never anticipated a calamity like this. Even Mrs. Willoughby, sensitive as she was, and wrapped up in those she loved so entirely, as she was habitually, had been so long accustomed to see and know of her husband's exposing himself with impunity, as to begin to feel, if not to think, that he bore a charmed life. All this customary confidence was to be overcome, and the truth was to be said. Tell the fact to her mother, Maud felt that she could not then; scarcely under any circumstances would she have consented to perform this melancholy office; but, so long as a shadow of doubt remained on the subject of her father's actual decease, it seemed cruel even to think of it. Her decision was to send for Beulah, and it was done by means of one of the negresses.

So long as we feel that there are others to be sustained by our fortitude, even the feeblest possess a firmness to which they might otherwise be strangers. Maud, contrary to what her delicate but active frame and sweetness of disposition might seem to indicate, was a young woman capable of the boldest exertions, short of taking human life. Her frontier training had raised her above most of the ordinary weaknesses of her sex; and, so far as determination went, few men were capable of higher resolution, when circumstances called for its display. Her plan was now made up to go forth and meet the body, and nothing short of a command from her mother could have stopped her. In this frame of mind was our heroine, when Beulah made her appearance.

"Maud!" exclaimed the youthful matron, "what has happened!--why are you so pale!--why send for me? Does Nick bring us any tidings from the mill?"

"The worst possible, Beulah. My father--my dear, dear father is hurt. They have borne him as far as the edge of the woods, where they have halted, in order not to take us by surprise. I am going to meet the--to meet the men, and to bring father in. You must prepare mother for the sad, sad tidings--yes, Beulah, for the worst, as everything depends on the wisdom and goodness of God!"

"Oh! Maud, this is dreadful!" exclaimed the sister, sinking into a chair--"What will become of mother--of little Evert--of us all!"

"The providence of the Ruler of heaven and earth will care for us. Kiss me, dear sister--how cold you are--rouse yourself, Beulah, for mother's sake. Think how much more *she* must feel than we possibly can, and then be resolute."

"Yes, Maud--very true--no woman can feel like a wife--unless it be a mother--"

Here Beulah's words were stopped by her fainting.

"You see, Smash," said Maud, pointing to her sister with a strange resolution, "she must have air, and a little water--and she has salts about her, I know. Come, Nick; we have no more time to waste--you must be my guide."

The Tuscarora had been a silent observer of this scene, and if it did not awaken remorse in his bosom, it roused feelings that had never before been its inmates. The sight of two such beings suffering under a blow that his own hand had struck, was novel to him, and he knew not which to encourage most, a sentiment allied to regret, or a fierce resentment, that any should dare thus to reproach, though it were only by yielding to the grief natural to their situation. But Maud had obtained a command over him, that he knew not how to resist, and he followed her from the room, keeping his eyes riveted the while on the pallid face of Beulah. The last was recalled from her insensibility, however, in the course of a few minutes, through the practised attentions of the negresses.

Maud waited for nothing. Motioning impatiently for the Tuscarora to lead the way, she glided after him with a rapidity that equalled his own loping movement. She made no difficulties in passing the stockade, though Nick kept his eyes on the labourers, and felt assured their *exeunt* was not noticed. Once by the path that led along the rivulet, Maud refused all precautions, but passed swiftly over it, partially concealed by its bushes. Her dress was dark, and left little liability to exposure. As for Nick, his forest attire, like the hunting shirt of the whites, was expressly regulated by the wish to go to and fro unseen.

In less than three minutes after the Indian and Maud had passed the gate, they were drawing near to the melancholy group that had halted in the forest. Our heroine was recognised as she approached, and when she came rushing up to the spot, all made way, allowing her to fall upon her knees by the side of the lifeless body, bathing the placid face of the dead with her tears, and covering it with kisses.

"Is there no hope--oh! Joyce," she cried, "*can* it be possible that my father is actually dead?"

"I fear, Miss Maud, that his honour has made his last march. He has received orders to go hence, and, like a gallant soldier as he was, he has obeyed, without a murmur;" answered the serjeant, endeavouring to appear firm and soldier-like, himself. "We have lost a noble and humane commander, and you a most excellent and tender father."

"No fader,"--growled Nick, at the serjeant's elbow, twitching his sleeve, at the same time, to attract attention. 'Serjeant know *her* fader. He by; I by, when Iroquois shoot him."

"I do not understand you, Tuscarora, nor do I think you altogether understand *us*; the less you say, therefore, the better for all parties. It is our duty, Miss Maud, to say 'God's will be done,' and the soldier who dies in the discharge of his duty is never to be pitied. I sincerely wish that the Rev. Mr. Woods was here; he would tell you all this in a manner that would admit of no dispute; as for myself, I am a plain man, Miss Maud, and my tongue cannot utter one-half that my heart feels at this instant."

"Ah! Joyce, what a friend--what a parent has it pleased God to call to himself!"

"Yes, Miss Maud, that may be said with great justice--if his honour has left us in obedience to general orders, it is to meet promotion in a service that will never weary, and never end."

"So kind; so true; so gentle; so just; so affectionate!" said Maud, wringing her hands.

"And so brave, young lady. His honour, captain Willoughby, wasn't one of them that is always talking, and writing, and boasting about fighting; but when anything was to be *done*, the Colonel always knew whom to send on the duty. The army couldn't have lost a braver gentleman, had he remained in it."

"Oh! my father--my father,"--cried Maud, in bitterness of sorrow, throwing herself on the body and embracing it, as had been her wont in childhood--"would that I could have died for you!"

"Why you let go on so," grumbled Nick, again. "*No* her fader--you know *dat*, serjeant."

Joyce was not in a state to answer. His own feelings had been kept in subjection only by military pride, but they now had become so nearly uncontrollable, that he found himself obliged to step a little aside in order to conceal his weakness. As it was, large tears trickled down his rugged face, like water flowing from the fissures of the riven oak Jamie Allen's constitutional prudence, however, now became active, admonishing the party of the necessity of their getting within the protection of the Hut.

"Death is at a' times awfu'," said the mason, "but it must befall young and auld alike. And the affleection it brings cometh fra' the heart, and is a submission to the la' o' nature. Nevertheless we a' hae our duties, so lang as we remain in the flesh, and it is time to be thinking o' carryin' the body into some place o' safety, while we hae a prudent regard to our ain conditions also."

Maud had risen, and, hearing this appeal, she drew back meekly, assumed a manner of forced composure, and signed to the men to proceed. On this intimation, the body was raised, and the melancholy procession resumed its march.

For the purpose of concealment, Joyce led the way into the bed of the stream, leaving Maud waiting their movements, a little deeper within the forest. As soon as he and his fellow-bearers were in the water, Joyce turned and desired Nick to escort the young lady in, again, on dry land, or by the path along which she had come out. This said, the serjeant and his companions proceeded. Maud stood gazing on the sad spectacle like one entranced, until she felt a sleeve pulled, and perceived the Tuscarora at her side.

"No go to Hut," said Nick, earnestly; "go wid Wyandotté."

"Not follow my dear father's remains--not go to my beloved mother in her anguish. You know not what you ask, Indian--move, and let me proceed."

"No go home--no use--no good. Cap'in dead--what do widout commander. Come wid Wyandotté--find major--den do some good."

Maud fairly started in her surprise. There seemed something so truly useful, so consoling, so dear in this proposal, that it instantly caught her ear.

"Find the Major!" she answered. "Is that possible, Nick? My poor father perished in making that attempt--what hope can there be then for *my* success?" "Plenty hope--much as want--all, want. Come wid Wyandotté--he great chief--show young squaw where to find broder."

Here was a touch of Nick's consummate art. He knew the female bosom so well that he avoided any allusion to his knowledge of the real relation between Robert Willoughby and Maud, though he had so recently urged her want of natural affinity to the family, as a reason why she should not grieve. By keeping the Major before her eyes as a brother, the chances of his own success were greatly increased. As for Maud, a tumult of feeling came over her heart at this extraordinary proposal. To liberate Bob, to lead him into the Hut, to offer his manly protection to her mother, and Beulah, and little Evert, at such an instant, caught her imagination, and appealed to all her affections.

"Can you do this, Tuscarora"--she asked, earnestly, pressing her hand on her heart as if to quiet its throbbings. "Can you really lead me to Major Willoughby, so that I may have some hope of liberating him?"

"Sartain--you go, he come. I go, he no come. Don't love Nick--t'ink all Injin, one Injin--t'ink one Injin, all Injin. You go, he come--he stay, find more knife, and die like Cap'in. Young squaw follow Wyandotté, and see."

Maud needed no more. To save the life of Bob, her well-beloved, he who had so long been beloved in secret, she would have gone with one far less known and trusted than the Tuscarora. She made an eager gesture for him to proceed, and they were soon on their way to the mill, threading the mazes of the forest.

Nick was far from observing the precautions that had been taken by the captain, in his unfortunate march out. Acquainted with every inch of ground in the vicinity of the Dam, and an eye-witness of the dispositions of the invaders, he had no occasion for making the long *détour* already described, but went to work in a much more direct manner. Instead of circling the valley, and the clearing, to the westward, he turned short in the contrary direction, crossed the rivulet on the fallen tree, and led the way along the eastern margin of the flats. On this side of the valley he knew there were no enemies, and the position of the huts and barns enabled him to follow a path, that was just deep enough in the forest to conceal his movements. By taking this course, besides having the advantage of a clear and beaten path, most of the way, the Tuscarora brought the whole distance within a mile.

As for Maud, she asked no questions, solicited no pauses, manifested no physical weakness. Actively as the Indian moved among the trees, she kept close in his footsteps; and she had scarcely begun to reflect on the real nature of the undertaking in which she was engaged, when the roar of the rivulet, and the formation of the land, told her they had reached the edge of the glen below the mills. Here Nick told her to remain stationary a moment, while he advanced to a covered point of the rocks, to reconnoitre. This was the place where the Indian had made his first observations of the invaders of the valley, ascertaining their real character before he trusted his person among them. On the present occasion, his object was to see if all remained, in and about the mills, as when he had last left the spot.

"Come"--said Nick, signing for Maud to follow him--"we go--fools sleep, and eat, and talk. Major prisoner now; half an hour, Major free."

This was enough for the ardent, devoted, generous-hearted Maud. She descended the path before her as swiftly as her guide could lead, and, in five more minutes, they reached the bank of the stream, in the glen, at a point where a curvature hid the rivulet from those at the mill. Here an enormous pine had been laid across the torrent; and, flattened on its upper surface, it made a secure bridge for those who were sure of foot, and steady of eye. Nick glanced back at his companion, as he stepped upon this bridge, to ascertain if she were equal to crossing it, a single glance sufficing to tell him apprehensions were unnecessary. Half a minute placed both, in safety, on the western bank.

"Good!" muttered the Indian; "young squaw make wife for warrior."

But Maud heard neither the compliment nor the expression of countenance which accompanied it. She merely made an impatient gesture to proceed. Nick gazed intently at the excited girl; and there was an instant when he seemed to waver in his own purpose; but the gesture repeated, caused him to turn, and lead the way up the glen.

The progress of Nick now, necessarily, became more guarded and slower. He was soon obliged to quit the common path, and to incline to the left, more against the side of the cliff, for the purposes of concealment. From the time he had struck the simple bridge, until he took this precaution, his course had lain along what might have been termed the common highway, on which there was always the danger of meeting some messenger, travelling to or from the valley.

But Nick was at no loss for paths. There were plenty of them; and the one he took soon brought him out into that by which Captain Willoughby had descended to the lean-to. When the spot was reached where Joyce had halted, Nick paused; and, first listening intently, to catch the sound of noises, if any might happen to be in dangerous proximity, he addressed his companion:

"Young squaw bold," he said, encouragingly; "now want heart of warrior."

"I can follow, Nick--having come so far, why distrust me, now?"

"'Cause he here--down dere--woman love man; man love woman--dat right; but, no show it, when scalp in danger."

"Perhaps I do not understand you, Tuscarora--but, my trust is in God; he is a support that can uphold any weakness."

"Good!--stay here--Nick come back, in minute."

Nick now descended to the passage between the rocks and the lean-to, in order to make certain that the major still remained in his prison, before he incurred any unnecessary risk with Maud. Of this fact he was soon assured; after which he took the precaution to conceal the pool of blood, by covering it with earth and stones. Making his other observations with care, and placing the saw and chisel, with the other tools, that had fallen from the captain's hand, when he received his death-wound, in a position to be handy, he ascended the path, and rejoined Maud. No word passed between our heroine and her guide. The latter motioned for her to follow; then he led the way down to the cabin. Soon, both had entered the narrow passage; and Maud, in obedience to a sign from her companion, seated herself on the precise spot where her father had been found, and where the knife had passed into his heart. To all this, however, Nick manifested the utmost indifference. Everything like ferocity had left his face; to use his own figurative language, his sores smarted no longer; and the expression of his eye was friendly and gentle. Still it showed no signs of compunction.

Chapter XXVII

"Her pallid face displayed
Something, methought, surpassing mortal beauty.
She presently turn'd round, and fixed her large, wild eyes.
Brimming with tears, upon me, fetch'd a sigh,
As from a riven heart, and cried: He's dead!"

Hillhouse.

Maud had been so earnest, and so much excited, that the scarcely reflected on the singularity and novelty of her situation, until she was seated, as described at the close of the last chapter. Then, indeed, she began to think that she had embarked in an undertaking of questionable prudence, and to wonder in what manner she was to be useful. Still her heart did not fail her, or her hopes altogether sink. She saw that Nick was grave and occupied, like a man who intended to effect his purpose at every hazard; and that purpose she firmly believed was the liberation of Robert Willoughby.

As for Nick, the instant his companion was seated, and he had got a position to his mind, he set about his business with great assiduity. It has been said that the lean-to like the cabin, was built of logs; a fact that constituted the security of the prisoner. The logs of the lean-to, however, were much smaller than those of the body of the house, and both were of the common white pine of the country; a wood of durable qualities, used as it was here, but which yielded easily to edged tools. Nick had a small saw, a large chisel, and his knife. With the chisel, he cautiously commenced opening a hole of communication with the interior, by removing a little of the mortar that filled the interstices between the logs. This occupied but a moment. When effected, Nick applied an eye to the hole and took a look within. He muttered the word "good," then withdrew his own eye, and, by a sign, invited Maud to apply one of hers. This our heroine did, and saw Robert Willoughby, reading within a few feet of her, with a calmness of air, that at once announced his utter ignorance of the dire event that had so lately occurred, almost within reach of his arm.

"Squaw speak," whispered Nick; "voice sweet as wren--go to Major's ear like song of bird.--Squaw speak music to young warrior."

Maud drew back, her heart beat violently, her breathing became difficult, and the blood rushed to her temples. But an earnest motion from Nick reminded her this was no time for hesitation, and she applied her mouth to the hole.

"Robert--*dear* Robert," she said, in a loud whisper, "we are here--have come to release you."

Maud's impatience could wait no longer; but her eye immediately succeeded her mouth. That she was heard was evident from the circumstance that the book fell from the Major's hand, in a way to show how completely he was taken by surprise. "He knows even my whispers," thought Maud, her heart beating still more violently, as she observed the young soldier gazing around him, with a bewildered air, like one who fancied he had heard the whisperings of some ministering angel. By this time, Nick had removed a long piece of the mortar; and he too, was looking into the buttery. By way of bringing matters to an understanding, the Indian thrust the chisel through the opening, and, moving it, he soon attracted Willoughby's attention. The latter instantly advanced, and applied his own eye to the wide crack, catching a view of the swarthy face of Nick.

Willoughby knew that the presence of this Indian, at such a place, and under such circumstances, indicated the necessity of caution. He did not speak, therefore; but, first making a significant gesture towards the door of his narrow prison, thus intimating the close proximity of sentinels, he demanded the object of this visit, in a whisper.

"Come to set major free," answered Nick.

"Can I trust you, Tuscarora? Sometimes you seem a friend, sometimes an enemy. I know that you appear to be on good terms with my captors."

"Dat good--Injin know how to look two way--warrior *must*, if great warrior."

"I wish I had some proof, Nick, that you are dealing with me in good faith."

"Call *dat* proof, den!" growled the savage, seizing Maud's little Land, and passing it through the opening, before the startled girl was fully aware of what he meant to do.

Willoughby knew the hand at a glance. He would have recognised it, in that forest solitude, by its symmetry and whiteness, its delicacy and its fullness; but one of the taper fingers wore a ring that, of late, Maud had much used; being a diamond hoop that she had learned was a favourite ornament of her real mother's. It is not surprising, therefore, that he seized the pledge that was thus strangely held forth, and had covered it with kisses, before Maud had presence of mind sufficient, or strength to reclaim it. This she would not do, however, at such a moment, without returning all the proofs of ardent affection that were lavished on her own hand, by giving a gentle pressure to the one in which it was clasped.

"This is so strange, Maud!--so every way extraordinary, that I know not what to think," the young man whispered soon as he could get a glimpse of the face of the sweet girl. "Why are you here, beloved, and in such company?"

"You will trust *me*, Bob--Nick comes as your friend. Aid him all you can, now, and be silent. When free, then will be the time to learn all."

A sign of assent succeeded, and the major withdrew a step, in order to ascertain the course Nick meant to pursue. By this time, the Indian was at work with his knife, and he soon passed the chisel in to the prisoner, who seized it, and commenced cutting into the logs, at a point opposite to that where the Tuscarora was whittling away the wood. The object was to introduce the saw, and it required some labour to effect such a purpose. By dint of application, however, and by cutting the log above as well as that below, sufficient space was obtained in the course of a few minutes. Nick then passed the saw in, through the opening, it exceeding his skill to use such a tool with readiness.

By this time, Willoughby was engaged with the earnestness and zeal of the captive who catches a glimpse of liberty. Notwithstanding, he proceeded intelligently and with caution. The blanket given him by his captors, as a pallet, was hanging from a nail, and he took the precaution to draw this mil, and to place it above the spot selected for the cut, that he might suspend the blanket so as to conceal what he was at, in the event of a visit from without. When all was ready, and the blanket was properly placed, he began to make long heavy strokes with the tool, in a way to deaden the sound. This was a delicate operation; but the work's being done behind the blanket, had some effect in lessening the noise. As the work proceeded, Willoughby's hopes increased; and he was soon delighted to hear from Nick, that it was time to insert the saw in another place. Success is apt to induce carelessness; and, as the task proceeded, Willoughby's arm worked with greater rapidity, until a noise at the door gave the startling information that he was about to be visited. There was just time to finish the last cut, and to let the blanket fall, before the door opened. The saw-dust and chips had all been carefully removed, as the work proceeded, and of these none were left to betray the secret.

There might have been a quarter of a minute between the moment when Willoughby seated himself, with his book in his hand, and that in which the door opened. Short as was this interval, it sufficed for Nick to remove the piece of log last cut, and to take away the handle of the saw; the latter change permitting the blanket to hang so close against the logs as completely to conceal the hole. The sentinel who appeared was an Indian in externals, but a dull, white countryman in fact and character.

"I thought I heard the sound of a saw, major," he said listlessly; "yet everything looks quiet, and in its place here!"

"Where should I get such a tool?" Willoughby coolly replied; "and what is there here to saw?"

"'Twas as nat'ral, too, as the carpenter himself could make it, in sound!"

"Possibly the mill has been set in motion by some of your idlers, and you have heard the large saw, which, at a distance, may sound like a smaller one near by."

The man looked incredulously at his prisoner for a moment; then he drew to the door, with the air of one who was determined to assure himself of the truth, calling aloud as he did so, to one of his companions to join him. Willoughby knew that no time was to be lost. In half-a-minute, he had passed the hole, dropped the blanket before it, had circled the slender waist of Maud with one arm, and was shoving aside the bushes with the other, as he followed Nick from the straitened passage between the lean-to and the rock. The major seemed more bent on bearing Maud from the spot, than on saving himself. Her feet scarce touched the ground, as he ascended to the place where Joyce had halted. Here Nick stood an instant, with a finger raised in intense listening. His practised ears caught the sound of voices in the lean-to, then scarce fifty feet distant. Men called to each other by name, and then a voice directly beneath them, proclaimed that a head was already thrust through the hole.

"Here is your saw, and here is its workmanship!" exclaimed this voice.

"And here is blood, too," said another. "See! the ground has been a pool beneath those stones."

Maud shuddered, as if the soul were leaving its earthly tenement, and Willoughby signed impatiently for Nick to proceed. But the savage, for a brief instant, seemed bewildered The danger below, however, increased, and evidently drew so near, that he turned and glided up the ascent. Presently, the fugitives reached the descending path, that diverged from the larger one they were on, and by which Nick and Maud had so recently come diagonally up this cliff. Nick leaped into it, and then the intervening bushes concealed their persons from any who might continue on the upward course. There was an open space, however, a little lower down; and the quick-witted savage came to a stand under a close cover, believing flight to be useless should their pursuers actually follow on their heels.

The halt had not been made half-a-dozen seconds, when the voices of the party ascending in chase, were heard above the fugitives. Willoughby felt an impulse to dash down the path, bearing Maud in his arms, but Nick interposed his own body to so rash a movement. There was not time for a discussion, and the sounds of voices, speaking English too distinctly to pass for any but those of men of English birth, or English origin, were heard disputing about the course to be taken, at the point of junction between the two paths.

"Go by the lower," called out one, from the rear; "he will run down the stream, and make for the settlements on the Hudson. Once before, he has done this, as I know from Strides himself."

"D---n Strides!" answered another, more in front. "He is a sniveling scoundrel, who loves liberty, as a hog loves corn for the sake of good living. I say go the *upper*, which will carry him on the heights, and bring him out near his father's garrison."

"Here are marks of feet on the upper," observed a third, "though they seem to be coming *down*, instead of going *up* the hill."

"It is the trail of the fellows who have helped him to escape. Push *up* the hill, and we shall have them all in ten minutes. Push *up*--push *up*."

This decided the matter. It appeared to Willoughby that at least a dozen men ran up the path, above his head, eager in the pursuit, and anticipating success. Nick waited no longer, but glided down the cliff, and was soon in the broad path which led along the margin of the stream, and was the ordinary thoroughfare in going to or from the Knoll. Here the fugitives, as on the advance, were exposed to the danger of accidental meetings; but, fortunately, no one was met, or seen, and the bridge was passed in safety. Turning short to the north, Nick plunged into the woods again, following the cow-path by which he had so recently descended to the glen. No pause was made even here. Willoughby had an arm round the waist of Maud, and bore her forward, with a rapidity to which her own strength was altogether unequal. In less than ten minutes from the time the prisoner had escaped, the fugitives reached the level of the rock of the water-fall, or that of the plain of the Dam. As it was reasonably certain that none of the invaders had passed to that side of the valley, haste was no longer necessary, and Maud was permitted to pause for breath.

The halt was short, however, our heroine, herself, now feeling as if the major could not be secure until he was fairly within the palisades. In vain did Willoughby try to pacify her fears and to assure her of his comparative safety; Maud's nerves were excited, and then she had the dreadful tidings, which still remained to be told pressing upon her spirits, and quickening all her natural impulses and sentiments.

Nick soon made the signal to proceed, and then the three began to circle the flats, as mentioned in the advance of Maud and her companion. When they reached a favourable spot, the Indian once more directed a halt, intimating his own intention to move to the margin of the woods, in order to reconnoitre. Both his companions heard this announcement with satisfaction, for Willoughby was eager to say to Maud directly that which he had so plainly indicated by means of the box, and to extort from her a confession that she was not offended; while Maud herself felt the necessity of letting the major know the melancholy circumstance that yet remained to be told. With these widely distinct feelings uppermost, our two lovers saw Nick quit them, each impatient, restless and uneasy.

Willoughby had found a seat for Maud, on a log, and he now placed himself at her side, and took her hand, pressing it silently to his heart.

"Nick has then been a true man, dearest Maud," he said, "notwithstanding all my doubts and misgivings of him."

"Yes; he gave me to understand you would hardly trust him, and that was the reason I was induced to accompany him. We both thought, Bob, you would confide in *me*!"

"Bless you--bless you--beloved Maud--but have you seen Mike--has *he* had any interview with you--in a word, did he deliver you my box?"

Maud's feelings had been so much excited, that the declaration of Willoughby's love, precious as it was to her heart failed to produce the outward signs that are usually exhibited by the delicate and sensitive of her sex, when they listen to the insinuating language for the first time. Her thoughts were engrossed with her dreadful secret, and with the best and least shocking means of breaking it to the major. The tint on her cheek, therefore, scarce deepened, as this question was put to her, while her eye, full of earnest tenderness, still remained riveted on the face of her companion.

"I have seen Mike, dear Bob," she answered, with a steadiness that had its rise in her singleness of purpose--"and he *has* shown me--*given* me, the box."

"But have you understood me, Maud?--You will remember that box contained the great secret of my life!"

"This I well remember--yes, the box contains the great secret of your life."

"But--you cannot have understood me, Maud--else would you not look so unconcerned--so vacantly--I am not understood, and am miserable!"

"No--no--no"--interrupted Maud, hurriedly--"I understand *all* you have wished to say, and you have no cause to be--" Maud's voice became choked, for she recollected the force of the blow that she had in reserve.

"This is so strange!--altogether so unlike your usual manner, Maud, that there must be some mistake. The box contained nothing but your own hair, dearest."

"Yes; nothing else. It was *my* hair; I knew it the instant I saw it."

"And did it tell you no secret?--Why was Beulah's hair not with it? Why did I cherish *your* hair, Maud, and your's alone? You have not understood me!"

"I have, dear, dear Bob!--You love me--you wished to say we are not brother and sister, in truth; that we have an affection that is far stronger--one that will bind us together for life. Do not look so wretched, Bob; I understand everything you wish to say."

"This is so very extraordinary!--So unlike yourself, Maud, I know not what to make of it! I sent you that box, beloved one, to say that you had my whole heart; that I thought of you day and night; that you were the great object of my existence, and that, while misery would be certain without you, felicity would be just as certain with you; in a word, that I love you, Maud, and can never love another."

"Yes, so I understood you, Bob."--Maud, spite of her concentration of feeling on the dreadful secret, could not refrain from blushing--"It was too plain to be mistaken."

"And how was my declaration received? Tell me at once, dear girl, with your usual truth of character, and frankness--*can* you, *will* you love me in return?"

This was a home question, and, on another occasion, it might have produced a scene of embarrassment and hesitation. But Maud was delighted with the idea that it was in her power to break the violence of the blow she was about to inflict, by setting Robert Willoughby's mind at ease on this great point.

"I *do* love you, Bob," she said, with fervent affection beaming in every lineament of her angel face--"*have* loved you, for years--how could it be otherwise? I have scarce seen any other to love; and how see you, and refrain?"

"Blessed, blessed, Maud--but this is so strange--I fear you do not understand me--I am not speaking of such affection as Beulah bears me, as brother and sister feel; I speak of the love that my mother bore my father--of the love of man and wife"----

A groan from Maud stopped the vehement young man, who received his companion in his arms, as she bowed her head on his bosom, half fainting.

"Is this resentment, dearest, or is it consent?" he asked, bewildered by all that passed.

"Oh! Bob--Father--father--father!"

"My father!--what of him, Maud? Why has the allusion to him brought you to this state?"

"They have killed him, dearest, dearest Bob; and you must now be father, husband, brother, son, all in one. We have no one left but you!"

A long pause succeeded. The shock was terrible to Robert Willoughby, but he bore up against it, like a man. Maud's incoherent and unnatural manner was now explained, and while unutterable tenderness of manner--a tenderness that was increased by what had just passed--was exhibited by each to the other, no more was said of love. A common grief appeared to bind their hearts closer together, but it was unnecessary to dwell on their mutual affection in words. Robert Willoughby's sorrow mingled with that of Maud, and, as he folded her to his heart, their faces were literally bathed in each other's tears.

It was some time before Willoughby could ask, or Maud give, an explanation. Then the latter briefly recounted all she knew, her companion listening with the closest attention. The son thought the occurrence as extraordinary as it was afflicting, but there was not leisure for inquiry.

It was, perhaps, fortunate for our lovers that Nick's employment kept him away. For nearly ten minutes longer did he continue absent; then he returned, slowly, thoughtful, and possibly a little disturbed. At the sound of his footstep, Willoughby released Maud from his arms, and both assumed an air of as much tranquillity as the state of their feelings would allow.

"Better march"--said Nick, in his sententious manner--"Mohawk very mad."

"Do you see the signs of this?" asked the major, scarce knowing what he said.

"Alway make Injin mad; lose scalp. Prisoner run away, carry scalp with him."

"I rather think, Nick, you do my captors injustice; so far from desiring anything so cruel, they treated me well enough, considering the circumstances, and that we are in the woods."

"Yes; spare scalp, 'cause t'ink rope ready. Nebber trust Mohawk--all bad Injin."

To own the truth, one of the great failings of the savages of the American forests, was to think of the neighbouring tribes, as the Englishman is known to think of the Frenchman, and vice versa; as the German thinks of both, and all think of the Yankee. In a word, his own tribe contains everything that is excellent, with the Pawnee, the Osage and Pottawattomie, as Paris contains all that is perfect in the eyes of the *bourgeois*, London in those of the cockney, and this virtuous republic in those of its own enlightened citizens; while the hostile communities are remorselessly given up to the tender solicitude of those beings which lead nations, as well as individuals, into the sinks of perdition. Thus Nick, liberalized as his mind had comparatively become by intercourse with the whites, still retained enough of the impressions of childhood, to put the worst construction on the acts of all his competitors, and the best on his own. In this spirit, then, he warned his companions against placing any reliance on the mercy of the Mohawks.

Major Wilioughby, however, had now sufficient inducements to move, without reference to the hostile intentions of his late captors. That his escape would excite a malignant desire for vengeance, he could easily believe; but his mother, his revered heart-broken mother, and the patient, afflicted Beulah, were constantly before him, and gladly did he press on, Maud leaning on his arm, the instant Nick led the way. To say that the lovely, confiding being who clung to his side, as the vine inclines to the tree, was forgotten, or that he did not retain a vivid recollection of all that she had so ingenuously avowed in his favour, would not be rigidly accurate, though the hopes thus created shone in the distance, under the present causes of grief, as the sun's rays illumine the depths of the heavens, while his immediate face is entirely hidden by an eclipse.

"Did you see any signs of a movement against the house, Nick?" demanded the major, when the three had been busily making their way, for several minutes, round the margin of the forest.

The Tuscarora turned, nodded his head, and glanced at Maud.

"Speak frankly, Wyandotté--"

"Good!" interrupted the Indian with emphasis, assuming a dignity of manner the major had never before witnessed. "Wyandotté come--Nick gone away altogeder. Nebber see Sassy Nick, ag'in, at Dam."

"I am glad to hear this, Tuscarora, and as Maud says, you may speak plainly."

"T'ink, den, best be ready. Mohawk feel worse dan if he lose ten, t'ree, six scalp. Injin know Injin feelin'. Pale-face can't stop red-skin, when blood get up."

"Press on, then, Wyandotté, for the sake of God--let me, at least, die in defence of my beloved mother!"

"Moder; good!--Doctor Tuscarora, when death grin in face! She *my* moder, too!"

This was said energetically, and in a manner to assure his listeners that they had a firm ally in this warlike savage. Little did either dream, at that instant, that this same wayward being--the creature of passion, and the fierce avenger of all his own fancied griefs, was the cause of the dreadful blow that had so recently fallen on them.

The sun still wanted an hour of setting, when Nick brought his companions to the fallen tree, by which they were again to cross the rivulet. Here he paused, pointing to the roofs of the Hut, which were then just visible through the trees; as much as to say that his duty, as a guide, was done.

"Thank you, Wyandotté," said Willoughby; "if it be the will of God to carry us safely through the crisis, you shall be well rewarded for this service."

"Wyandotté chief--want no dollar. Been Injin runner--now be Injin warrior. Major follow--squaw follow--Mohawk in hurry."

This was enough. Nick passed out of the forest on a swift walk--but for the female, it would have been his customary, loping trot--followed by Willoughby; his arm, again, circling the waist of Maud, whom he bore along scarce permitting her light form to touch the earth. At this instant, four or five conches sounded, in the direction of the mills, and along the western margin of the meadows. Blast seemed to echo blast; then the infernal yell, known as the war-whoop, was heard all along the opposite face of the buildings. Judging from the sounds, the meadows were alive with assailants, pressing on for the palisades.

At this appalling moment, Joyce appeared on the ridge of the roof, shouting, in a voice that might have been heard to the farthest point in the valley--

"Stand to your arms, my men," he cried; "here the scoundrels come; hold your fire until they attempt to cross the stockade."

To own the truth, there was a little bravado in this, mingled with the stern courage that habit and nature had both contributed to lend the serjeant. The veteran knew the feebleness of his garrison, and fancied that warlike cries, from himself, might counterbalance the yells that were now rising from all the fields in front of the house.

As for Nick and the major, they pressed forward, too earnest and excited, to speak. The former measured the distance by his ear; and thought there was still time to gain a cover, if no moment was lost. To reach the foot of the cliff, took just a minute; to ascend to the hole in the palisade, half as much time; and to pass it, a quarter. Maud was dragged ahead, as much as she ran; and the period when the three were passing swiftly round to the gate, was pregnant with imminent risk. They were seen, and fifty rifles were discharged, as it might be, at a command. The bullets pattered against the logs of the Hut, and against the palisades, but no one was hurt. The voice of Willoughby opened the gate, and the next instant the three were within the shelter of the court.

Chapter XXVIII

"They have not perish'd--no!
Kind words, remembered voices, once so sweet,
Smiles, radiant long ago,
And features, the great soul's apparent seat;

"All shall come back, each tie
Of pure affection shall be knit again;
Alone shall evil die,
And sorrow dwell a prisoner in thy reign.

"And then shall I behold
Him, by whose kind paternal side I sprung,
And her, who still and cold,
Fills the next grave--the beautiful and young."

Bryant's Past.

The scene that followed passed like a hurricane sweeping over the valley. Joyce had remained on the ridge of the roof, animating his little garrison, and endeavouring to intimidate his enemies, to the last moment. The volley of bullets had reached the palisades and the buildings, and he was still unharmed. But the sound of the major's voice below, and the cry that Miss Maud and Nick were at the gate, produced a sudden change in all his dispositions for the defence. The serjeant ran below himself, to report and receive his orders from the new commander, while all the negroes, females as well as males, rushed down into the court, to meet their young master and mistress.

It is not easy to describe the minute that succeeded, after Willoughby and Maud were surrounded by the blacks. The delight of these untutored beings was in proportion to their recent sorrow. The death of their master, and the captivity of Master Bob and Miss Maud, had appeared to them like a general downfall of the family of Willoughby; but here was a revival of its hopes, that came as unexpectedly as its previous calamities. Amid the clamour, cries, tears, lamentations, and bursts of uncontrollable delight, Joyce could scarce find a moment in which to discharge his duty.

"I see how it is, serjeant," exclaimed Willoughby; "the assault is now making, and you desire orders."

"There is not an instant to lose, Major Willoughby; the enemy are at the palisades already, and there is no one at his station but Jamie and young Blodget."

"To your posts, men--to your posts, everybody. The house shall be made good at all hazards. For God's sake, Joyce, give me arms. I feel that my father's wrongs are to be revenged."

"Robert--dear, dear Robert," said Maud, throwing her arms on his shoulders, "this is no moment for such bitter feelings. Defend us, as I know you will, but defend us like a Christian."

One kiss was all that the time allowed, and Maud rushed into the house to seek her mother and Beulah, feeling as if the tidings of Bob's return might prove some little alleviation to the dreadful blow under which they must be suffering.

As for Willoughby, he had no time for pious efforts at consolation. The Hut was to be made good against a host of enemies; and the cracking of rifles from the staging and the fields, announced that the conflict had begun in earnest. Joyce handed him a rifle, and together they ascended rapidly to the roofs. Here they found Jamie Allen and Blodget, loading and firing as fast as they could, and were soon joined by all the negroes. Seven men were now collected on the staging; and placing three in front, and two on each wing, the major's dispositions were made; moving, himself, incessantly, to whatever point circumstances called. Mike, who knew little of the use of fire-arms, was stationed at the gate, as porter and warder. It was so unusual a thing for savages to attack by daylight, unless they could resort to surprise, that the assailants were themselves a little confused. The assault was made, under a sudden feeling of resentment at the escape of the prisoner, and contrary to the wishes of the principal white men in the party, though the latter were dragged in the train of events, and had to seem to countenance that of which they really disapproved. These sudden outbreakings were sufficiently common in Indian warfare, and often produced memorable disasters. On the present occasion, however, the most that could occur was a repulse, and to this the leaders, demagogues who owed their authority to the excesses and necessities of the times, were fain to submit, should it happen.

The onset had been fierce and too unguarded. The moment the volley was fired at the major, the assailants broke cover, and the fields were alive with men. This was the instant when the defence was left to Allen and Blodget, else might the exposure have cost the enemy dear. As it was, the last brought down one of the boldest of the Indians while the mason fired with good will, though with less visible effect. The yell that followed this demonstration of the apparent force of the garrison, was a wild mixture of anger and exultation, and the rush at the palisades was general and swift. As Willoughby posted his reinforcement, the stockade was alive with men, some ascending, some firing from its summit, some aiding others to climb, and one falling within the enclosure, a second victim to Blodget's unerring aim.

The volley that now came from the roofs staggered the savages, most of whom fell outward, and sought cover in their usual quick and dexterous manner. Three or four, however, thought it safer to fall within the palisades, seeking safety immediately under the sides of the buildings. The view of these men, who were perfectly safe from the fire of the garrison so long as the latter made no sortie, gave an idea to those without, and produced, what had hitherto been wanting, something like order and concert in the attack. The firing now became desultory and watchful on both sides, the attacking party keeping themselves covered by the trees and fences as well as they could, while the garrison only peered above the ridge of the roof, as occasions required.

The instant the outbreak occurred, all the *ci-devant* dependants of captain Willoughby, who had deserted, abandoned their various occupations in the woods and fields, collecting in and around the cabins, in the midst of their wives and children. Joel, alone, was not to be seen. He had sought his friends among the leaders of the party, behind a stack of hay, at a respectful distance from the house, and to which there was a safe approach by means of the rivulet and its fringe of bushes. The little council that was held at this spot took place just as the half-dozen assailants who had fallen within the palisades were seen clustering along under the walls of the buildings.

"Natur' gives you a hint how to conduct," observed Joel, pointing out this circumstance to his principal companions, as they all lay peering over the upper portions of the stack, at the Hut. "You see them men under the eaves--they're a plaguy sight safer up there, than we be down here; and; if 'twere'n't for the look of the thing, I wish I was with 'em. That house will never be taken without a desperate sight of fightin'; for the captain is an old warrior, and seems to like to snuff gunpowder"--the reader will understand none knew of the veteran's death but those in the house--"and won't be for givin' up while he has a charge left. If I had twenty men--no, thirty would be better, where these fellows be, I think the place could be carried in a few minutes, and then liberty would get its rights, and your monarchy-men would be put down as they all desarve."

"What do then?" demanded the leading Mohawk, in his abrupt guttural English. "No shoot--can't kill log."

"No, chief, that's reasonable, an' ongainsayable, too; but only one-half the inner gate is hung, and I've contrived matters so, on purpose, that the props of the half that isn't on the hinges can be undone, all the same as onlatching the door. If I only had the right man here, now, the business should be done, and that speedily."

"Go 'self," answered the Mohawk, not without an expression of distrust and contempt.

"Every man to his callin', chief. My trade is peace, and politics, and liberty, while your's is war. Howsever, I can put you, and them that likes fightin', on the trail, and then we'll see how matters can be done. Mortality! How them desperate devils on the roof do keep blazin' away! It wouldn't surprise me if they shot somebody, or get hurt themselves!"

Such were the deliberations of Joel Strides on a battle. The Indian leaders, however, gave some of their ordinary signals, to bring their 'young men' more under command and, sending messengers with orders in different directions, they left the haystack, compelling Joel to accompany them.

The results of these movements were soon apparent. The most daring of the Mohawks made their way into the rivulet, north of the buildings, and were soon at the foot of the cliff. A little reconnoitring told them that the hole which Joel had pointed out, had not been closed since the entrance of Willoughby and his companions. Led by their chief, the warriors stole up the ascent, and began to crawl through the same inlet which had served as an outlet to so many deserters, the previous night, accompanied by their wives and children.

The Indians in front had been ordered to occupy the attention of the garrison, while this movement was in the course of execution. At a signal, they raised a yell, unmasked them, fired one volley, and seemed to make another rush at the works. This was the instant chosen for the passage of the hole, and the seven leading savages effected their entrance within the stockade, with safety. The eighth man was shot by Blodget, in the hole itself. The body was instantly withdrawn by the legs, and all in the rear fell back under the cover of the cliff.

Willoughby now understood the character of the assault. Stationing Joyce, with a party to command the hole, he went himself into the library, accompanied by Jamie and Blodget, using a necessary degree of caution. Fortunately the windows were raised, and a sudden volley routed all the Indians who had taken shelter beneath the rocks. These men, however, fled no further than the rivulet, where they rallied under cover of the bushes, keeping up a dropping fire at the windows. For several minutes, the combat was confined to this spot; Willoughby, by often shifting from window to window along the rear of the house, getting several volleys that told, at the men under the cover.

As yet, all the loss had been on the side of the assailants, though several of the garrison, including both Willoughby and Joyce, had divers exceedingly narrow escapes. Quite a dozen of the assailants had suffered, though only four were killed outright. By this time, the assault had lasted an hour, and the shades of evening were closing around the place. Daniel, the miller, had been sent by Joel to spring the mine they had prepared together, but, making the mistake usual with the uninitiated, he had hung back, to let others pass the hole first, and was consequently carried down in the crowd, within the cover of the bushes of the rivulet.

Willoughby had a short consultation with Joyce, and then he set seriously about the preparations necessary for a light defence. By a little management, and some persona, risk, the bullet-proof shutters of the north wing of the Hut were all closed, rendering the rear of the buildings virtually impregnable. When this was done, and the gates of the area were surely shut, the place was like a ship in a gale, under short canvass and hove-to. The enemy within the palisades were powerless, to all appearance, the walls of stone preventing anything like an application of fire. Of the last, however, there was a little danger on the roof, the Indians frequently using arrows for this purpose, and water was placed on the staging in readiness to be used on occasion.

All these preparations occupied some time, and it was quite dark ere they were completed. Then Willoughby had a moment for reflection; the firing having entirely ceased, and nothing further remaining to do.

"We are safe for the present, Joyce," the major observed, as he and the serjeant stood together on the staging, after having consulted on the present aspect of things; "and I have a solemn duty, yet, to perform--my dear mother--and the body of my father--"

"Yes, sir; I would not speak of either, so long as it was your honour's pleasure to remain silent on the subject. Madam Willoughby is sorely cut down, as you may imagine, sir; and, as for my gallant old commander, he died in his harness, as a soldier should."

"Where have you taken the body?--has my mother seen it?"

"Lord bless you, sir, Madam Willoughby had his honour carried into her own room, and there she and Miss Beulah"--so all of the Hut still called the wife of Evert Beekman--"she and Miss Beulah, kneel, and pray, and weep, as you know, sir, ladies will, whenever anything severe comes over their feelings--God bless them both, we all say, and think, ay, and pray, too, in our turns, sir."

"Very well, Joyce. Even a soldier may drop a tear over the dead body of his own father. God only knows what this night will bring forth, and I may never have a moment as favourable as this, for discharging so solemn a duty."

"Yes, your honour"--Joyce fancied that the major had succeeded to this appellation by the decease of the captain--"yes, your honour, the commandments, that the Rev. Mr. Woods used to read to us of a Sunday, tell us all about that; and it is quite as much the duty of a Christian to mind the commandments, I do suppose, as it is for a soldier to obey orders. God bless you, sir, and carry you safe through the affair. I had a touch of it with Miss Maud, myself, and know what it is. It's bad enough to lose an old commander in so sudden a way like, without having to *feel* what has happened in company with so sweet ladies, as these we have in the house. As for these blackguards down inside the works, let them give you no uneasiness; it will be light work for us to keep them busy, compared to what your honour has to do."

It would seem by the saddened manner in which Willoughby moved away, that he was of the same way of thinking as the serjeant, on this melancholy subject. The moment, however, was favourable for the object, and delay could not be afforded. Then Willoughby's disposition was to console his mother, even while he wept with her over the dead body of him they had lost.

Notwithstanding the wild uproar that had so prevailed, not only without, but within the place, the portion of the house that was occupied by the widowed matron and her daughters, was silent as the grave. All the domestics were either on the staging, or at the loops, leaving the kitchens and offices deserted. The major first entered a little ante-chamber, that opened between a store-room, and the apartment usually occupied by his mother; this being the ordinary means of approach to her room. Here he paused, and listened quite a minute, in the hope of catching some sound from within that might prepare him for the scene he was to meet. Not a whisper, a moan, or a sob could be heard; and he ventured to tap lightly at the door. This was unheeded; waiting another minute, as much in dread as in respect, he raised the latch with some such awe, as one would enter into a tomb of some beloved one. A single lamp let him into the secrets of this solemn place.

In the centre of the room, lay stretched on a large table, the manly form of the author of his being. The face was uppermost, and the limbs had been laid, in decent order, as is usual with the dead that have been cared for. No change had been made in the dress, however, the captain lying in the hunting-shirt in which he had sallied forth; the crimson tint which disfigured one breast, having been sedulously concealed by the attention of Great Smash. The passage from life to eternity had been so sudden, as to leave the usual benignant expression on the countenance of the corpse; the paleness which had succeeded the fresh ruddy tint of nature, alone denoting that the sleep was not a sweet repose, but that of death.

The body of his father was the first object that met the gaze of the major. He advanced, leaned forward, kissed the marble-like forehead, with reverence, and groaned in the effort to suppress an unmanly outbreaking of sorrow. Then he turned to seek the other well-beloved faces. There sat Beulah, in a corner of the room, as if to seek shelter for her infant, folding that infant to her heart, keeping her look riveted, in anguish, on the inanimate form that she had ever loved beyond a daughter's love. Even the presence of her brother scarce drew a glance away from the sad spectacle; though, when it at length did, the youthful matron bowed her face down to that of her child, and wept convulsively. She was nearest to the major, who moved to her side, and kissed the back of her neck, with kind affection. The meaning was understood; and Beulah, while unable to look up, extended a hand to meet the fraternal pressure it received.

Maud was near, kneeling at the side of the bed. Her whole attitude denoted the abstraction of a mind absorbed in worship and solicitation. Though Willoughby's heart yearned to raise her in his arms; to console her, and bid her lean on himself, in future, for her earthly support, he too much respected her present occupation, to break in upon it with any irreverent zeal of his own. His eye turned from this loved object, therefore, and hurriedly looked for his mother.

The form of Mrs. Willoughby had escaped the first glances of her son, in consequence of the position in which she had placed herself. The stricken wife was in a corner of the room, her person partly concealed by the drapery of a window-curtain; though this was evidently more the effect of accident, than of design. Willoughby started, as he caught the first glance of his beloved parent's face; and he felt a chill pass over his whole frame. There she sat upright, motionless, tearless, without any of the alleviating weaknesses of a less withering grief, her mild countenance exposed to the light of the lamp, and her eyes riveted on the face of the dead. In this posture had she remained for hours; no tender cares on the part of her daughters; no attentions from her domestics; no outbreaking of her own sorrows, producing any change. Even the clamour of the assault had passed by her like the idle wind.

"My mother--my poor--dear--heart-broken mother!" burst from Willoughby, at this sight, and he stepped quickly forward, and knelt at her feet.

But Bob--the darling Bob--his mother's pride and joy, was unheeded. The heart, which had so long beaten for others only; which never seemed to feel a wish, or a pulsation, but in the service of the objects of its affection, was not sufficiently firm to withstand the blow that had lighted on it so suddenly. Enough of life remained, however, to support the frame for a while; and the will still exercised its power over the mere animal functions. Her son shut out the view of the body, and she motioned him aside with an impatience of manner he had never before witnessed from the same quarter. Inexpressibly shocked, the major took her hands, by gentle compulsion, covering them with kisses, and literally bathing them in tears.

"Oh! mother--dearest, dearest mother!" he cried, "*will* you not--*do* you not know *me*--Robert--Bob--your much-indulged, grateful, affectionate son. If father is gone into the immediate presence of the God he revered and served, I am still left to be a support to your declining years. Lean on me, mother, next to your Father in Heaven."

"Will he ever get up, Robert?" whispered the widowed mother. "You speak too loud, and may rouse him before his time. He promised me to bring you back; and he ever kept his promises. He had a long march, and is weary, See, how sweetly he sleeps!"

Robert Willoughby bowed his head to his mother's knees, and groaned aloud. When he raised his face again, he saw the arms of Maud elevated towards heaven, as if she would pluck down that consolation for her mother, that her spirit was so fervently asking of the Almighty. Then he gazed into the face of his mother again; hoping to catch a gleam of some expression and recognition, that denoted more of reason. It was in vain; the usual placidity, the usual mild affection were there; but both were blended with the unnatural halo of a mind excited to disease, if not to madness. A slight exclamation, which sounded like alarm, came from Beulah; and turning towards his sister, Willoughby saw that she was clasping Evert still closer to her bosom, with her eyes now bent on the door. Looking in the direction of the latter, he perceived that Nick had stealthily entered, the room.

The unexpected appearance of Wyandotté might well alarm the youthful mother. He had applied his war-paint since entering the Hut; and this, though it indicated an intention to fight in defence of the house, left a picture of startling aspect. There was nothing hostile intended by this visit, however. Nick had come not only in amity, but in a kind concern to see after the females of the family, who had ever stood high in his friendship, notwithstanding the tremendous blow he had struck against their happiness. But he had been accustomed to see those close distinctions drawn between individuals and colours; and, the other proprieties admitted, would not have hesitated about consoling the widow with the offer of his own hand. Major Willoughby, understanding, from the manner of the Indian, the object of his visit, suffered him to pursue his own course, in the hope it might rouse his mother to a better consciousness of objects around her.

Nick walked calmly up to the table, and gazed at the face of his victim with a coldness that proved he felt no compunction. Still he hesitated about touching the body, actually raising his hand, as if with that intent, and then withdrawing it, like one stung by conscience. Willoughby noted the act; and, for the first time, a shadowy suspicion glanced on his mind. Maud had told him all she knew of the manner of his father's death, and old distrusts began to revive, though so faintly as to produce no immediate results.

As for the Indian, the hesitating gesture excepted, the strictest scrutiny, or the keenest suspicion could have detected no signs of feeling. The senseless form before him was not less moved than he appeared to be, so far as the human eye could penetrate. Wyandotté *was* unmoved. He believed that, in curing the sores on his own back in this particular manner, he had done what became a Tuscarora warrior and a chief. Let not the self-styled Christians of civilized society affect horror at this instance of savage justice, so long as they go the whole length of the law of their several communities, in avenging their own fancied wrongs, using the dagger of calumny instead of the scalping-knife, and rending and tearing *their* victims, by the agency of gold and power, like so many beasts of the field, in all the forms and modes that legal vindictiveness will either justify or tolerate; often exceeding those broad limits, indeed, and seeking impunity behind perjuries and frauds.

Nick's examination of the body was neither hurried nor agitated. When it was over, he turned calmly to consider the daughters of the deceased.

"Why you cry--why you 'fear'd," he said, approaching Beulah, and placing his swarthy hand on the head of her sleeping infant.--"Good squaw--good pappoose. Wyandotté take care 'em in woods. Bye'm-by go to paleface town, and sleep quiet."

This was rudely said, but it was well meant. Beulah so received it; and she endeavoured to smile her gratitude in the face of the very being from whom, more than from all of earth, she would have turned in horror, could her mental vision have reached the fearful secret that lay buried in his own bosom. The Indian understood her look; and making a gesture of encouragement, he moved to the side of the woman whom his own hand had made a widow.

The appearance of Wyandotté produced no change in the look or manner of the matron. The Indian took her hand, and spoke.

"Squaw *berry* good," he said, with emphasis. "Why look so sorry--cap'in gone to happy huntin'-ground of his people. All good dere--chief time come, *must* go."

The widow knew the voice, and by some secret association it recalled the scenes of the past, producing a momentary revival of her faculties.

"Nick, *you* are my friend," she said, earnestly. "Go speak to him, and see if *you* can wake him up."

The Indian fairly started, as he heard this strange proposal. The weakness lasted only for a moment, however, and he became as stoical, in appearance at least, as before.

"No," he said; "squaw quit cap'in, now. Warrior go on last path, all alone--no want companion.--She look at grave, now and den, and be happy."

"Happy!" echoed the widow, "what is *that*, Nick?--what is *happy*, my son? It seems a dream--I *must* have known what it was; but I forget it all now. Oh! it was cruel, cruel, cruel, to stab a husband, and a father--wasn't it, Robert?--What say you, Nick--shall I give you more medicine?--You'll die, Indian, unless you take it--mind what a Christian woman tells you, and be obedient.--Here, let me hold the cup--there; now you'll live!"

Nick recoiled an entire step, and gazed at the still beautiful victim of his ruthless revenge, in a manner no one had ever before noted in his mien. His mixed habits left him in ignorance of no shade of the fearful picture before his eyes, and he began better to comprehend the effects of the plow he had so hastily struck--a blow meditated for years, though given at length under a sudden and vehement impulse. The widowed mother, however, was past noting these changes.

"No--no--no--Nick," she added, hurriedly, scarce speaking above a whisper, "do not awake him! God will do that, when he summons his blessed ones to the foot of his throne. Let us all lie down, and sleep with him. Robert, do you lie there, at his side, my noble, noble boy; Beulah, place little Evert and yourself at the other side; Maud, your place is by the head; I will sleep at his feet; while Nick shall watch, and let us know when it will be time to rise and pray"

The general and intense--almost spell-bound--attention with which all in the room listened to these gentle but touching wanderings of a mind so single and pure, was interrupted by yells so infernal, and shrieks so wild and fearful, that it seemed, in sooth, as if the last trump had sounded, and men were passing forth from their graves to judgment. Willoughby almost leaped out of the room, and Maud followed, to shut and bolt the door, when her waist was encircled by the arm of Nick, and she found herself borne forward towards the din.

Chapter XXIX

"O, Time and Death! with certain pace,
Though still unequal, hurrying on,
O'erturning, in your awful race,
The cot, the palace, and the throne!"

Sands.

Maud had little leisure for reflection. The yells and shrieks were followed by the cries of combatants, and the crack of the rifle. Nick hurried her along at a rate so rapid that she had not breath to question or remonstrate, until she found herself at the door of a small store-room, in which her mother was accustomed to keep articles of domestic economy that required but little space. Into this room Nick thrust her, and then she heard the key turn on her egress. For a single moment, Wyandotté stood hesitating whether he should endeavour to get Mrs. Willoughby and her other daughter into the same place of security; then, judging of the futility of the attempt, by the approach of the sounds within, among which he heard the full, manly voice of Robert Willoughby, calling on the garrison to be firm, he raised an answering yell to those of the Mohawks, the war-whoop of his tribe, and plunged into the fray with the desperation of one who ran a muck, and with the delight of a demon.

In order to understand the cause of this sudden change, it will be necessary to return a little, in the order of time. While Willoughby was with his mother and sisters, Mike had charge of the gate. The rest of the garrison was either at the loops, or was stationed on the roofs. As the darkness increased, Joel mustered sufficient courage to crawl through the hole, and actually reached the gate. Without him, it was found impossible to spring his mine, and he had been prevailed on to risk this much, on condition it should not be asked of him to do such violence to his feelings as to enter the court of a house in which he had seen so many happy days.

The arrangement, by which this traitor intended to throw a family upon the tender mercies of savages, was exceedingly simple. It will be remembered that only one leaf of the inner gate was hung, the other being put in its place, where it was sustained by a prop. This prop consisted of a single piece of timber, of which one end rested on the ground, and the other on the centre of the gate; the last being effectually prevented from slipping by pins of wood, driven into the massive wood-work of the gate, above its end. The lower end of the prop rested against a fragment of rock that nature had placed at this particular spot. As the work had been set up in a hurry, it was found necessary to place wedges between the lower end of the prop and the rock, in order to force the leaf properly into its groove, without which it might have been canted to one side, and of course easily overturned by the exercise of sufficient force from without.

To all this arrangement, Joel had been a party, and he knew, as a matter of course, its strong and its weak points. Seizing a favourable moment, he had loosened the wedges, leaving them in their places, however, but using the precaution to fasten a bit of small but strong cord to the most material one of the three, which cord he buried in the dirt, and led half round a stick driven into the earth, quite near the wall, and thence through a hole made by one of the hinges, to the outer side of the leaf. The whole had been done with so much care as to escape the vigilance of casual observers, and expressly that the overseer might assist his friends in entering the place, after he himself had provided for his own safety by flight. The circumstance that no one trod on the side of the gateway where the unhung leaf stood, prevented the half-buried cord from being disturbed by any casual footstep.

As soon as Joel reached the wall of the Hut, his first care was to ascertain if he were safe from missiles from the loops. Assured of this fact, he stole round to the gate, and had a consultation with the Mohawk chief, on the subject of springing the mine. The cord was found in its place; and, hauling on it gently, Joel was soon certain that he had removed the wedge, and that force might speedily throw down the unhung leaf. Still, he proceeded with caution. Applying the point of a lever to the bottom of the leaf, he hove it back sufficiently to be sure it would pass inside of its fellow; and then he announced to the grave warrior, who had watched the whole proceeding, that the time was come to lend his aid.

There were a dozen reckless whites, in the cluster of savages collected at the gate; and enough of these were placed at handspikes to effect the intended dislodgement. The plan was this: while poles were set against the upper portion of the leaf, to force it within the line of the suspended part, handspikes and crowbars, of which a sufficiency had been provided by Joel's forethought, were to be applied between the hinge edge and the wall, to cast the whole over to the other side.

Unluckily, Mike had been left at the gate as the sentinel. A more upfortunate selection could not have been made; the true-hearted fellow having so much self-confidence, and so little forethought, as to believe the gates impregnable. He had lighted a pipe, and was smoking as tranquilly as he had ever done before, in his daily indulgences of this character, when the unhung leaf came tumbling in upon the side where he sat; nothing saving his head but the upper edge's lodging against the wall. At the same moment, a dozen Indians leaped through the opening, and sprang into the court, raising the yells already described. Mike followed, armed with his shillelah, for his musket was abandoned in the surprise, and he began to lay about him with an earnestness that in nowise lessened the clamour. This was the moment when Joyce, nobly sustained by Blodget and Jamie Allen, poured a volley into the court, from the roofs; when the fray became general. To this point had the combat reached, when Willoughby rushed into the open air followed, a few instants later, by Nick.

The scene that succeeded is not easily described. It was a *mélée* in the dark, illuminated, at instants, by the flashes of guns, and rendered horrible by shrieks, curses, groans and whoops. Mike actually cleared the centre of the court, where he was soon joined by Willoughby, when, together, they made a rush at a door, and actually succeeded in gaining their own party on the roof. It was not in nature for the young soldier to remain here, however, while his mother, Beulah, and, so far as he knew, Maud, lay exposed to the savages below. Arnid a shower of bullets he collected his whole force, and was on the point of charging into the court, when the roll of a drum without, brought everything to a stand. Young Blodget, who had displayed the ardour of a hero, and the coolness of a veteran throughout the short fray, sprang down the stairs unarmed, at this sound, passed through the astonished crowd in the court, unnoticed, and rushed to the outer gate. He had barely time to unbar it, when a body of troops marched through, led by a tall, manly-looking chief, who was accompanied by one that the young man instantly recognised, in spite of the darkness, for Mr. Woods, in his surplice. At the next moment, the strangers had entered, with military steadiness, into the court, to the number of, at least, fifty, ranging themselves in order across its area.

"In the name of Heaven, who are you?" called out Willoughby, from a window. "Speak at once, or we fire."

"I am Colonel Beekman, at the head of a regular force," was the answer, "and if, as I suspect, you are Major Willoughby, you know you are safe. In the name of Congress, I command all good citizens to keep the peace, or they will meet with punishment for their contumacy."

This announcement ended the war, Beekman and Willoughby grasping each other's hands fervently, at the next instant.

"Oh! Beekman!" exclaimed the last, "at what a moment has God sent you hither! Heaven be praised! notwithstanding all that has happened, you will find your wife and child safe. Place sentinels at both gates; for treachery has been at work here, and I shall ask for rigid justice."

"Softly--softly--my good fellow," answered Beekman, pressing his hand. "Your own position is a little delicate, and we must proceed with moderation. I learned, just in time, that a party was coming hither, bent on mischief; and obtaining the necessary authority, I hastened to the nearest garrison, obtained a company, and commenced my march as soon as possible. Had we not met with Mr. Woods, travelling for the settlements in quest of succour, we might have been too late. As it was, God be praised!--I think we have arrived in season."

Such were the facts. The Indians had repelled the zealous chaplain, as a madman; compelling him to take the route toward the settlements, however; their respect for this unfortunate class of beings, rendering them averse to his rejoining their enemies. He could, and did impart enough to Beekman to quicken his march, and to bring him and his followers up to the gate at a time when a minute might have cost the entire garrison their lives.

Anxious as he was to seek Beulah and his child, Beekman had a soldier's duties to perform, and those he would not neglect. The sentinels were posted, and orders issued to light lanterns, and to make a fire in the centre of the court, so that the actual condition of the field of battle might be ascertained. A surgeon had accompanied Beekman's party, and he was already at work, so far as the darkness would allow. Many hands being employed, and combustibles easy to be found, ere long the desired light was gleaming on the terrible spectacle.

A dozen bodies wexre stretched in the court, of which, three or four were fated never to rise again, in life. Of the rest, no less than four had fallen with broken heads, inflicted by O'Hearn's shillelah. Though these blows were not fatal, they effectually put the warriors *hors de combat*. Of the garrison, not one was among the slain, in this part of the field. On a later investigation, however, it was ascertained that the poor old Scotch mason had received a mortal hurt, through a window, and this by the very last shot that had been fired. On turning over the dead of the assailants, too, it was discovered that Daniel the Miller was of the number. A few of the Mohawks were seen, with glowing eyes, in corners of the court, applying their own rude dressings to their various hurts; succeeding, on the whole, in effecting the great purpose of the healing art, about as well as those who were committed to the lights of science.

Surprisingly few uninjured members of the assaulting party, however, were to be found, when the lanterns appeared. Some had slipped through the gate before the sentinels were posted; others had found their way to the roof, and thence, by various means to the ground; while a few lay concealed in the buildings, until a favourable moment offered to escape. Among all those who remained, not an individual was found who claimed to be in any authority. In a word, after five minutes of examination, both Beekman and Willoughby were satisfied that there no longer existed a force to dispute with them the mastery of the Hut.

"We have delayed too long relieving the apprehensions of those who are very dear to us, Major Willoughby," Beekman at length observed. "If you will lead the way to the parts of the buildings where your--*my* mother, and wife, are to be found, I will now follow you."

"Hold, Beekman--there yet remains a melancholy tale to be told--nay, start not--I left our Beulah, and your boy, in perfect health, less than a quarter of an hour since. But my honoured, honourable, revered, beloved father has been killed in a most extraordinary manner, and you will find his widow and daughters weeping over his body."

This appalling intelligence produced a halt, during which Willoughby explained all he knew of the manner of his father's death, which was merely the little he had been enabled to glean from Maud. As soon as this duty was performed, the gentlemen proceeded together to the apartment of the mourners, each carrying a light.

Willoughby made an involuntary exclamation, when he perceived that the door of his mother's room was open. He had hoped Maud would have had the presence of mind to close and lock it; but here he found it, yawning as if to invite the entrance of enemies. The light within, too, was extinguished, though, by the aid of the lanterns, he saw large traces of blood in the ante-room, and the passages he was obliged to thread. All this hastened his steps. Presently he stood in the chamber of death.

Short as had been the struggle, the thirst for scalps had led some of the savages to this sanctuary. The instant the Indians had gained the court, some of the most ferocious of their number had rushed into the building, penetrating its recesses in a way to defile them with slaughter. The first object that Willoughby saw was one of these ruthless warriors, stretched on the floor, with a living Indian, bleeding at half a dozen wounds, standing over him; the eye-balls of the latter were glaring like the tiger's that is suddenly confronted to a foe. An involuntary motion was made towards the rifle he carried, by the major; but the next look told him that the living

Indian was Nick. Then it was, that he gazed more steadily about him, and took in all the horrible truths of that fatal chamber.

Mrs. Willoughby was sealed in the chair where she had last been seen, perfectly dead. No mark of violence was ever found on her body, however, and there is no doubt that her constant spirit had followed that of her husband to the other world, in submission to the blow which had separated them. Beulah had been shot; not, as was afterwards ascertained, by any intentional aim, but by one of those random bullets, of which so many had been flying through the buildings. The missile had passed through her heart, and she lay pressing the little Evert to her bosom, with that air of steady and unerring affection which had marked every act of her innocent and feeling life. The boy himself, thanks to the tiger-like gallantry of Nick, had escaped unhurt. The Tuscarora had seen a party of six take the direction of this chamber, and he followed with an instinct of their intentions. When the leader entered the room, and found three dead bodies, he raised a yell that betokened his delight at the prospect of gaining so many scalps; at the next instant, while his fingers were actually entwined in the hair of Captain Willoughby, he fell by a blow from Wyandotté. Nick next extinguished the lamp, and then succeeded a scene, which none of the actors, themselves, could have described. Another Mohawk fell, and the remainder, ailer suffering horribly from the keen knife of Nick, as well as from blows received from each other, dragged themselves away, leaving the field to the Tuscarora. The latter met the almost bewildered gaze of the major with a smile of grim triumph, as he pointed to the three bodies of the beloved ones, and said--

"See--all got scalp! Deat', nothin'--scalp, ebbery t'ing."

We shall not attempt to describe the outbreaking of anguish from the husband and brother. It was a moment of wild grief, that bore down all the usual restraints of manhood, though it was such a moment as an American frontier residence has often witnessed. The quiet but deep-feeling nature of Beekman received a shock that almost produced a dissolution of his earthly being. He succeeded, however, in raising the still warm body of Beulah from the floor, and folding it to his heart. Happily for his reason, a flood of tears, such as women shed, burst from his soul, rather than from his eyes, bedewing her still sweet and placid countenance.

To say that Robert Willoughby did not feel the desolation, which so suddenly alighted on a family that had often been quoted for its mutual affection and happiness, would be to do him great injustice. He even staggered under the blow; yet his heart craved further information. The Indian was gazing intently on the sight of Beekman's grief, partly in wonder, but more in sympathy, when he felt an iron pressure of his arm.

"Maud--Tuscarora"--the major rather groaned than whispered in his ear, "know you anything of Maud?"

Nick made a gesture of assent; then motioned for the other to follow. He led the way to the store-room, produced the key, and throwing open the door, Maud was weeping on Robert Willoughby's bosom in another instant. He would not take her to the chamber of death, but urged her, by gentle violence, to follow him to the library.

"God be praised for this mercy!" exclaimed the ardent girl, raising her hands and streaming eyes to heaven. "I know not, care not, who is conqueror, since *you* are safe!"

"Oh! Maud--beloved one--we must now be all in all to each other. Death has stricken the others."

This was a sudden and involuntary announcement, though it was best it should be so under the circumstances. It was long before Maud could hear an outline, even, of the details, but she bore them better than Willoughby could have hoped. The excitement had been so high, as to brace the mind to meet any human evil. The sorrow that came afterwards, though sweetened by so many tender recollections, and chastened hopes, was deep and enduring.

Our picture would not have been complete, without relating the catastrophe that befell the Hutted Knoll; but, having discharged this painful duty, we prefer to draw a veil over the remainder of that dreadful night. The cries of the negresses, when they learned the death of their old and young mistress, disturbed the silence of the place for a few minutes and then a profound stillness settled on the buildings, marking them distinctly as the house of mourning. On further inquiry, too, it was ascertained that Great Smash, after shooting an Oneida, had been slain and scalped. Pliny the younger, also, fell fighting like a wild beast to defend the entrance to his mistresses' apartments.

The following day, when light had returned, a more accurate idea was obtained of the real state of the valley. All of the invading party, the dead and wounded excepted, had made a rapid retreat, accompanied by most of the deserters and their families. The name, known influence, and actual authority of Colonel Beekman had wrought this change; the irregular powers that had set the expedition in motion, preferring to conceal their agency in the transaction, rather than make any hazardous attempt to claim the reward of patriotic service, as is so often done in revolutions, for merciless deeds and selfish acts. There had been no real design on the part of the whites to injure any of the family in their persons; but, instigated by Joel, they had fancied the occasion favourable for illustrating their own public virtue, while they placed themselves in the way of receiving fortune's favours. The assault that actually occurred, was one of those uncontrollable outbreakings of Indian ferocity, that have so often set at defiance the restraints of discipline.

Nick was not to be found either. He had been last seen dressing his wounds, with Indian patience, and Indian skill, preparing to apply herbs and roots, in quest of which he went into the forest about midnight. As he did not return Willoughby feared that he might be suffering alone, and determined to have a search made, as soon as he had performed the last sad offices for the dead.

Two days occurred, however, before this melancholy duty was discharged. The bodies of all the savages who had fallen were interred the morning after the assault; but that of Jamie Allen, with those of the principal persons of the family, were kept for the pious purposes of affection, until the time mentioned.

The funeral was a touching sight. The captain, his wife, and daughter, were laid, side by side, near the chapel; the first and last of their race that ever reposed in the wilds of America. Mr. Woods read the funeral service, summoning all his spiritual powers to sustain him, as he discharged this solemn office of the church. Willoughby's arm was around the waist of Maud, who endeavoured to reward his tender assiduities by a smile, but could not. Colonel Beekman held little Evert in his arms, and stood over the grave with the countenance of a resolute man stricken with grief--one of the most touching spectacles of our nature.

"*I am the resurrection and the life, saith the Lord,*" sounded in the stillness of that valley like a voice from heaven, pouring out consolation on the bruised spirits of the mourners. Maud raised her face from Willoughby's shoulder, and lifted her blue eyes to the cloudless vault above her; soliciting mercy, and offering resignation in the look. The line of troops in the back-ground moved, as by a common impulse, and then a breathless silence showed the desire of these rude beings not to lose a syllable.

A round red spot formed on each of the cheeks of Mr. Woods as he proceeded, and his voice gathered strength, until its lowest intonations came clear and distinct on every ear. Just as the bodies were about to be lowered into their two receptacles, the captain, his wife and daughter being laid in the same grave, Nick came with his noiseless step near the little group of mourners. He had issued from the forest only a few minutes before, and understanding the intention of the ceremony, he approached the spot as fast as weakness and wounds would allow. Even he listened with profound attention to the chaplain, never changing his eye from his face, unless to glance at the coffins as they lay in their final resting-place.

"*I heard a voice from Heaven, saying unto me, write, From henceforth blessed are the dead who die in the Lord; even so saith the Spirit, for they rest from their labours,*" continued the chaplain, his voice beginning to betray a tremor; then the gaze of the Tuscarora became keen as the panther's glance at his discovered victim. Tears followed, and, for a moment, the voice was choked.

"Why you woman?" demanded Nick, fiercely. "Save all 'e scalp!"

This strange interruption failed to produce any effect. First Beekman yielded; Maud and Willoughby followed; until Mr. Woods, himself, unable to resist the double assaults of the power of sympathy and his own affection, closed the book and wept like a child.

It required minutes for the mourners to recover their self-command. When the latter returned, however, all knelt on the grass, the line of soldiers included, and the closing prayers were raised to the throne of God.

This act of devotion enabled the mourners to maintain an appearance of greater tranquillity until the graves were filled. The troops advanced, and fired three volleys over the captain's grave, when all retired towards the Hut. Maud had caught little Evert from the arms of his father, and, pressing him to her bosom, the motherless babe seemed disposed to slumber there. In this manner she walked away, attended closely by the father, who now cherished his boy as an only treasure.

Willoughby lingered the last at the grave, Nick alone remaining near him. The Indian had been struck by the exhibition of deep sorrow that he had witnessed, and he felt an uneasiness that was a little unaccountable to himself. It was one of the caprices of this strange nature of ours, that he should feel a desire to console those whom he had so deeply injured himself. He drew near to Robert Willoughby, therefore, and, laying a hand on the latter's arm, drew his look in the direction of his own red and speaking face.

"Why so sorry, major?" he said. "Warrior nebber die but once--*must* die sometime."

"There lie my father, my mother, and my only sister, Indian--is not that enough to make the stoutest heart bend? You knew them, too, Nick--did you ever know better?"

"Squaw good--both squaw good--Nick see no pale-face squaw he like so much."

"I thank you, Nick! This rude tribute to the virtues of my mother and sister, is far more grateful to me than the calculating and regulated condolence of the world."

"No squaw *so* good as ole one--she, all heart--love every body, but self."

This was so characteristic of his mother, that Willoughby was startled by the sagacity of the savage, though reflection told him so long an acquaintance with the family must have made a dog familiar with this beautiful trait in his mother.

"And my father, Nick!" exclaimed the major, with feeling--"my noble, just, liberal, gallant father!--He, too, you knew well, and must have loved."

"No so good as squaw," answered the Tuscarora, sententiously, and not altogether without disgust in his manner.

"We are seldom as good as our wives, and mothers, and sisters, Nick, else should we be angels on earth. But, allowing for the infirmities of us men, my father was just and gocd."

"Too much flog"--answered the savage, sternly--"make Injin's back sore."

This extraordinary speech struck the major less, at the time, than it did, years afterwards, when he came to reflect on all the events and dialogues of this teeming week. Such was also the case as to what followed.

"You are no flatterer, Tuscarora, as I have always found in our intercourse. If my father ever punished you with severity, you will allow, me, at least, to imagine it was merited."

"Too much flog, I say," interrupted the savage, fiercely. "No difference, chief or not. Touch ole sore too rough. Good, some; bad, some. Like weather--now shine; now storm."

"This is no time to discuss these points, Nick. You have fought nobly for us, and I thank you. Without your aid, these beloved ones would have been mutilated, as well as slain; and Maud--my own blessed Maud--might now have been sleeping at their sides."

Nick's face was now all softness again, and he returned the pressure of Willoughby's hand with honest fervor. Here they separated. The major hastened to the side of Maud, to fold her to his heart, and console her with his love. Nick passed into the forest, returning no more to the Hut. His path led him near the grave. On the side where lay the body of Mrs. Willoughby, he threw a flower he had plucked in the meadow; while he shook his finger menacingly at the other, which hid the person of his enemy. In this, he was true to his nature, which taught him never to forget a favour, or forgive an injury.

Chapter XXX

"I shall go on through all eternity,
Thank God, I only am an embryo still:
The small beginning of a glorious soul,
An atom that shall fill immensity."

Coxe.

A fortnight elapsed ere Willoughby and his party could tear themselves from a scene that had witnessed so much domestic happiness; but on which had fallen the blight of death. During that time, the future arrangements of the survivors were completed. Beekman was made acquainted with the state of feeling that existed between his brother-in-law and Maud, and he advised an immediate union.

"Be happy while you can," he said, with bitter emphasis. "We live in troubled times, and heaven knows when we shall see better. Maud has not a blood-relation in all America, unless there may happen to be some in the British army. Though we should all be happy to protect and cherish the dear girl, she herself would probably, prefer to be near those whom nature has appointed her friends. To me, she will always seem a sister, as you must ever be a brother. By uniting yourselves at once, all appearances of impropriety will be avoided; and in time, God averting evil, you can introduce your wife to her English connections."

"You forget, Beekman, that you are giving this advice to one who is a prisoner on parole, and one who may possibly be treated as a spy."

"No--that is impossible. Schuyler, our noble commander, is both just and a gentleman. He will tolerate nothing of the sort. Your exchange can easily be effected, and, beyond your present difficulties, I can pledge myself to be able to protect you."

Willoughby was not averse to following this advice; and he urged it upon Maud, as the safest and most prudent course they could pursue. Our heroine, however, was so reluctant even to assuming the appearance of happiness, so recently after the losses she had experienced, that the lover's task of persuasion was by no means easy. Maud was totally free from affectation, while she possessed the keenest sense of womanly propriety.

Her intercourse with Robert Willoughby had been of the tenderest and most confidential nature, above every pretence of concealment, and was rendered sacred by the scenes through which they had passed. Her love, her passionate, engrossing attachment, she did not scruple to avow; but she could not become a bride while the stains of blood seemed so recent on the very hearth around which they were sitting. She still saw the forms of the dead, in their customary places, heard their laughs, the tones of their affectionate voices, the maternal whisper, the playful, paternal reproof, or Beulah's gentle call.

"Yet, Robert," said Maud, for she could now call him by that name, and drop the desperate familiarity of 'Bob,'--"yet, Robert, there would be a melancholy satisfaction in making our vows at the altar of the little chapel, where we have so often worshipped together--the loved ones who are gone and we who alone remain."

"True, dearest Maud; and there is another reason why we should quit this place only as man and wife. Beekman has owned that a question will probably be raised among the authorities at Albany concerning the nature of my visit here. It might relieve him from an appeal to more influence than would be altogether pleasant, did I appear as a bridegroom rather than as a spy."

The word "spy" settled the matter. All ordinary considerations were lost sight of, under the apprehensions it created, and Maud frankly consented to become a wife that very day. The ceremony was performed by Mr. Woods accordingly, and the little chapel witnessed tears of bitter recollections mingling with the smiles with which the bride received the warm embrace of her husband, after the benediction was pronounced. Still, all felt that, under the circumstances, delay would have been unwise. Maud saw a species of holy solemnity in a ceremony so closely connected with scenes so sad.

A day or two after the marriage, all that remained of those who had so lately crowded the Hut, left the valley together. The valuables were packed and transported to boats lying in the stream below the mills. All the cattle, hogs, &c., were collected and driven towards the settlements; and horses were prepared for Maud and the females, who were to thread the path that led to Fort Stanwix. In a word, the Knoll was to be abandoned, as a spot unfit to be occupied in such a war. None but labourers, indeed, could, or would remain, and Beekman thought it wisest to leave the spot entirely to nature, for the few succeeding years.

There had been some rumours of confiscations by the new state, and Willoughby had come to the conclusion that it would be safer to transfer this property to one who would be certain to escape such an infliction, than to retain it in his own hands. Little Evert was entitled to receive a portion of the captain's estate by justice, if not by law. No will had been found, and the son succeeded as heir-at-law. A deed was accordingly drawn up by Mr. Woods, who understood such matters, and being duly executed, the Beaver Dam property was vested in fee in the child. His own thirty thousand pounds, the personals he inherited from his mother, and Maud's fortune, to say nothing of the major's commission, formed an ample support for the new-married pair. When all was settled, and made productive, indeed, Willoughby found himself the master of between three and four thousand sterling a year, exclusively of his allowances from the British government, an ample fortune for that day. In looking over the accounts of Maud's fortune, he had reason to admire the rigid justice, and free-handed liberality with which his father had managed her affairs. Every farthing of her income had been transferred to capital, a long minority nearly doubling the original investment. Unknown to himself, he had married one of the largest heiresses then to be found in the American colonies. This was unknown to Maud, also; though it gave her great delight on her husband's account, when she came to learn the truth.

Albany was reached in due time, though not without encountering the usual difficulties. Here the party separated. The remaining Plinys and Smashes were all liberated, handsome provisions made for their little wants, and good places found for them, in the connection of the family to which they had originally belonged. Mike announced his determination to enter a corps that was intended expressly to fight the Indians. He had a long score to settle, and having no wife or children, he thought he might amuse himself in this way, during a revolution, as well as in any other.

"If yer honour was going anywhere near the county Leitrim," he said, in answer to Willoughby's offer to keep him near himself, "I might travel in company; seein' that a man likes to look on ould faces, now and then. Many thanks for this bag of gold, which will sarve to buy scalps wid'; for divil bur-r-n me, if I don't carry on *that* trade, for some time to come. T'ree cuts wid a knife, half a dozen pokes in the side, and a bullet scraping; the head, makes a man mindful of what has happened; to say nothing of the captain, and Madam Willoughby, and Miss Beuly--God for ever bless and presarve 'em all t'ree--and, if there was such a thing as a bit of a church in this counthry, wouldn't I use this gould for masses?--*dat* I would, and let the scalps go to the divil!"

This was an epitome of the views of Michael O'Hearn. No arguments of Willoughby's could change his resolution; but he set forth, determined to illustrate his career by procuring as many Indian scalps, as an atonement for the wrongs done "Madam Willoughby and Miss Beuly," as came within his reach.

"And you, Joyce," said the major, in an interview he had with the serjeant, shortly after reaching Albany; "I trust *we* are not to part. Thanks to Colonel Beekman's influence and zeal, I am already exchanged, and shall repair to New York next week. You are a soldier; and these are times in which a *good* soldier is of some account. I think I can safely promise you a commission in one of the new provincial regiments, about to be raised."

"I thank your honour, but do not feel at liberty to accept the offer. I took service with Captain Willoughby for life; had he lived, I would have followed wherever he led. But that enlistment has expired; and I am now like a recruit before he takes the bounty. In such cases, a man has always a right to pick his corps. Politics I do not much understand; but when the question comes up of pulling a trigger *for* or *against* his country, an *unengaged* man has a right to choose. Between the two, meaning no reproach to yourself, Major Willoughby, who had regularly taken service with the other side, before the war began--but, between the two, I would rather fight an Englishman, than an American."

"You may possibly be right, Joyce; though, as you say, my service is taken. I hope you follow the dictates of conscience, as I am certain I do myself. We shall never meet in arms, however, if I can prevent it. There is a negotiation for a lieutenant-colonelcy going on, which, if it succeed, will carry me to England. I shall never serve an hour longer against these colonies, if it be in my power to avoid it."

"*States*, with your permission, Major Willoughby," answered the serjeant, a little stiffly. "I am glad to hear it, sir; for, though I wish my enemies good soldiers, I would rather not have the son of my old captain among them. Colonel Beekman has offered to make me serjeant-major of his own regiment; and we both of us join next week."

Joyce was as good as his word. He became serjeant-major, and, in the end, lieutenant and adjutant of the regiment he had mentioned. He fought in most of the principal battles of the war, and retired at the peace, with an excellent character. Ten years later, he fell, in one of the murderous Indian affairs, that occurred during the first oresidential term, a grey-headed captain of foot. The manner of his death was not to be regretted, perhaps, as it was what he had always wished might happen; but, it was a singular fact, that Mike stood over his body, and protected it from mutilation; the County Leitrim-man having turned soldier by trade, re-enlisting regularly, as soon as at liberty, and laying up scalps on all suitable occasions.

Blodget, too, had followed Joyce to the wars. The readiness and intelligence of this young man, united to a courage of proof, soon brought him forward, and he actually came out of the revolution a captain. His mind, manners and information advancing with himself, he ended his career, not many years since, a prominent politician in one of the new states; a general in the militia--no great preferment, by the way, for one who had been a corporal at the Hut--and a legislator. Worse men have often acted in all these capacities among us; and it was said, with truth, at the funeral of General Blodget, an accident that does not always occur on such occasions, that "another revolutionary hero is gone." Beekman was never seen to smile, from the moment he first beheld the dead body of Beulah, lying with little Evert in her arms. He served faithfully until near the close of the war, falling in battle only a few months previously to the peace. His boy preceded him to the grave, leaving, as confiscations had gone out of fashion by that time, his uncle heir-at-law, again, to the same property that he had conferred on himself.

As for Willoughby and Maud, they were safely conveyed to New York, where the former rejoined his regiment. Our heroine here met her great-uncle, General Meredith, the first of her own blood relations whom she had seen since infancy. Her reception was grateful to her feelings; and, there being a resemblance in years, appearance and manners, she transferred much of that affection which she had thought interred for ever in the grave of her reputed father, to this revered relative. He became much attached to his lovely niece, himself; and, ten years later, Willoughby found his income quite doubled, by his decease.

At the expiration of six months, the gazette that arrived from England, announced the promotion of "Sir Robert Willoughby, Bart., late major in the ---th, to be lieutenant colonel, by purchase, in His Majesty's ---th regiment of foot." This enabled Willoughby to quit America; to which quarter of the world he had no occasion to be sent during the remainder of the war.

Of that war, itself, there is little occasion to speak. Its progress and termination have long been matters of history. The independence of America was acknowledged by England in 1783; and, immediately after, the republicans commenced the conquest of their wide-spread domains, by means of the arts of peace. In 1785, the first great assaults were made on the wilderness, in that mountainous region which has been the principal scene of our tale. The Indians had been driven off, in a great measure, by the events of the revolution; and the owners of estates, granted under the crown, began to search for their lands in the untenanted woods. Such isolated families, too, as had taken refuge in the settlements, now began to return to their deserted possessions; and soon the smokes of clearings were obscuring the sun. Whitestown, Utica, on the site of old Fort Stanwix, Cooperstown, for years the seat of justice for several thousand square miles of territory, all sprang into existence between the years 1785 and 1790. Such places as Oxford, Binghamton, Norwich, Sherburne, Hamilton, and twenty more, that now dot the region of which we have been writing, did not then exist, even in name; for, in that day, the appellation and maps came after the place; whereas, now, the former precede the last.

The ten years that elapsed between 1785 and 1795, did wonders for all this mountain district. More favourable lands lay spread in the great west, but the want of roads, and remoteness from the markets, prevented their occupation. For several years, therefore, the current of emigration which started out of the eastern states, the instant peace was proclaimed, poured its tide into the counties mentioned in our opening chapter--*counties* as they are to-day; *county* ay, and fragment of a county, too, as they were then.

The New York Gazette, a journal that frequently related facts that actually occurred, announced in its number of June 11th, 1795, "His Majesty's Packet that has just arrived"--it required half a century to teach the journalists of this country the propriety of saying "His *Britannic* Majesty's Packet," instead of "His Majesty's," a bit of good taste, and of good sense, that many of them have yet to learn--"has brought *out*," *home* would have been better "among her passengers, Lieutenant-General Sir Robert Willoughby, and his lady, both of whom are natives of this state. We welcome them back to their land of nativity where we can assure them they will be cordially received notwithstanding old quarrels. *Major* Willoughby's kindness to American prisoners is gratefully remembered; nor is it forgotten that he desired to exchange to another regiment in order to avoid further service in this country."

It will be conceded, this was a very respectable puff for the year 1795, when something like moderation, truth, and propriety were observed upon such occasions. The effect was to bring the English general's name into the mouths of the whole state; a baronet causing a greater sensation then, in America, than a duke would produce to-day. It had the effect, however, of bringing around General Willoughby many of his father's, and his own old friends, and he was as well received in New York, twelve years after the termination of the conflict, as if he had fought on the other side. The occurrence of the French revolution, and the spread of doctrines that were termed Jacobinical, early removed all the dissensions between a large portion of the whigs of America and the tories of England, on this side of the water at least; and Providence only can tell what might have been the consequences, had this feeling been thoroughly understood on the other.

Passing over all political questions, however, our narrative calls us to the relation of its closing scene. The visit of Sir Robert and Lady Willoughby to the land of their birth was, in part, owing to feeling; in part, to a proper regard for the future provision of their children. The baronet had bought the ancient paternal estate of his family in England, and having two daughters, besides an only son, it occurred to him that the American property, called the Hutted Knoll, might prove a timely addition to the ready money he had been able to lay up from his income. Then, both he and his wife had a deep desire to revisit those scenes where they had first learned to love each other, and which still held the remains of so many who were dear to them.

The cabin of a suitable sloop was therefore engaged, and the party, consisting of Sir Robert, his wife, a man and woman servant, and a sort of American courier, engaged for the trip, embarked on the morning of the 25th of July. On the afternoon of the 30th, the sloop arrived in safety at Albany, where a carriage was hired to proceed the remainder of the way by land. The route by old Fort Stanwix, as Utica was still generally called, was taken. Our travellers reached it on the evening of the third day; the 'Sands, which are now traversed in less than an hour, then occupying more than half of the first day. When at Fort Stanwix, a passable country road was found, by which the travellers journeyed until they reached a tavern that united many of the comforts of a coarse civilisation, with frontier simplicity. Here they were given to understand they had only a dozen miles to go, in order to reach the Knoll.

It was necessary to make the remainder of the journey on horseback. A large, untenanted estate lay between the highway and the valley, across which no public road had yet been made. Foot-paths, however, abounded, and the rivulet was found without any difficulty. It was, perhaps, fortunate for the privacy of the Knoll, that it lay in the line of no frequented route, and, squatters being rare in that day, Willoughby saw, the instant he struck the path that followed the sinuosities of the stream, that it had been seldom trodden in the interval of the nineteen-years which had occurred since he had last seen it himself. The evidences of this fact increased, as the stream was ascended, until the travellers reached the mill, when it was found that the spirit of destruction, which so widely prevails in the loose state of society that exists in all new countries, had been at work. Every one of the buildings at the falls had been burnt; probably as much because it was in the power of some reckless wanderer to work mischief, as for any other reason. That the act was the result of some momentary impulse, was evident in the circumstance that the mischief went no further. Some of the machinery had been carried away, however, to be set up in other places, on a principle that is very widely extended through all border settlements, which considers the temporary disuse of property as its virtual abandonment.

It was a moment of pain and pleasure, strangely mingled, when Willoughby and Maud reached the rocks, and got a first view of the ancient Beaver Dam. All the buildings remained, surprisingly little altered to the eye by the lapse of years. The gates had been secured when they left the place, in 1776; and the Hut, having no accessible external windows, that dwelling remained positively intact. It is true, quite half the palisadoes were rotted down; but the Hut, itself, had resisted the ravages of time. A fire had been kindled against its side, but the stone walls had opposed an obstacle to its ravages; and an attempt, by throwing a brand upon the roof, had failed of its object, the shingles not igniting. On examination, the lock of the inner gate was still secure. The key had been found, and, on its application, an entrance was obtained into the court.

What a moment was that, when Maud, fresh from the luxuries of an English home, entered this long and well remembered scene of her youth! Rank grasses were growing in the court, but they soon disappeared before the scythes that had been brought, in expectation of the circumstance. Then, all was clear for an examination of the house. The Hut was exactly in the condition in which it had been left, with the exception of a little, and a very little, dust collected by time.

Maud was still in the bloom of womanhood, feminine, beautiful, full of feeling, and as sincere as when she left these woods, though her feelings were tempered a little by intercourse with the world. She went from room to room, hanging on Willoughby's arm, forbidding any to follow. All the common furniture had been left in the house, in expectation it would be inhabited again, ere many years; and this helped to preserve the identity. The library was almost entire; the bed-rooms, the parlours, and even the painting-room, were found very much as they would have appeared, after an absence of a few months. Tears flowed in streams down the cheeks of Lady Willoughby, as she went through room after room, and recalled to the mind of her husband the different events of which they had been the silent witnesses. Thus passed an hour or two of unutterable tenderness, blended with a species of holy sorrow. At the end of that time, the attendants, of whom many had been engaged, had taken possession of the offices, &c., and were bringing the Hut once more into a habitable condition. Soon, too, a report was brought that the mowers, who had been brought in anticipation of their services being wanted, had cut a broad swathe to the ruins of the chapel, and the graves of the family.

It was now near the setting of the sun, and the hour was favourable for the melancholy duty that remained. For bidding any to follow, Willoughby proceeded with Maud to the graves. These had been dug within a little thicket of shrubs, planted by poor Jamie Allen, under Maud's own directions. She had then thought that the spot might one day be wanted. These bushes, lilacs, and ceringos, had grown to a vast size, in that rich soil. They completely concealed the space within, an area of some fifty square feet, from the observation of those without. The grass had been cut over all, however, and an opening made by the mowers gave access to the graves. On reaching this opening, Willoughby started at hearing voices within the inclosure; he was about to reprove the intruders, when Maud pressed his arm, and whispered--

"Listen, Willoughby--those voices sound strangely to my ears! We have heard them before."

"I tell ye, Nick--ould Nicky, or Saucy Nick, or whatever's yer name," said one within in a strong Irish accent "that Jamie, the mason that was, is forenent ye, at this minute, under that bit of a sod--and, it's his honour, and Missus, and Miss Beuly, that is buried here. Och! ye're a cr'ature, Nick; good at takin' scalps, but ye knows nothin' of graves; barrin' the quhantity ye've helped to fill."

"Good"--answered the Indian. "Cap'in here; squaw here; darter here. Where son?--where t'other gal?"

"Here," answered Willoughby, leading Maud within the hedge. "I am Robert Willoughby, and this is Maud Meredith, my wife."

Mike fairly started; he even showed a disposition to seize a musket which lay on the grass. As for the Indian, a tree in the forest could not have stood less unmoved than he was at this unexpected interruption. Then all four stood in silent admiration, noting the changes which time had, more or less, wrought in all.

Willoughby was in the pride of manhood. He had served with distinction, and his countenance and frame both showed it, though neither had suffered more than was necessary to give him a high military air, and a look of robust vigour. As for Maud, with her graceful form fully developed by her riding-habit, her soft lineaments and polished expression, no one would have thought her more than thirty, which was ten years less than her real age. With Mike and Nick it was very different. Both had grown old, not only in fact, but in appearance. The Irishman was turned of sixty, and his hard, coarse-featured face, burnt as red as the sun in a fog, by exposure and Santa Cruz, was getting to be wrinkled and a little emaciated. Still, his frame was robust and powerful. His attire was none of the best, and it was to be seen at a glance that it was more than half military. In point of fact, the poor fellow had been refused a reinlistment in the army, on account of his infirmities and years, and America was not then a country to provide retreats for her veterans. Still, Mike had an ample pension for wounds, and could not be said to be in want. He had suffered in the same battle with Joyce, in whose company he had actually been corporal O'Hearn, though his gallant commander had not risen to fight again, as had been the case with the subordinate.

Wyandotté exhibited still greater changes. He had seen his threescore and ten years; and was fast falling into the "sere and yellow leaf." His hair was getting grey, and his frame, though still active and sinewy, would have yielded under the extraordinary marches he had once made. In dress, there was nothing to remark; his ordinary Indian attire being in as good condition as was usual for the man. Willoughby thought, however, that his eye was less wild than when he knew him before; and every symptom of intemperance had vanished, not only from his countenance, but his person.

From the moment Willoughby appeared, a marked change came over the countenance of Nick. His dark eye, which still retained much of its brightness, turned in the direction of the neighbouring chapel, and he seemed relieved when a rustling in the bushes announced a footstep. There had not been another word spoken when the lilacs were shoved aside, and Mr. Woods, a vigorous little man, in a green old age, entered the area. Willoughby had not seen the chaplain since they parted at Albany, and the greetings were as warm as they were unexpected.

"I have lived a sort of hermit's life, my dear Bob, since the death of your blessed parents," said the divine, clearing his eyes of tears; "now and then cheered by a precious letter from yourself and Maud--I call you both by the names I gave you both in baptism--and it was, 'I, *Maud*, take thee, *Robert*,' when you stood before the altar in that little edifice--you will pardon me if I am too familiar with a general officer and his lady"

"Familiar!" exclaimed both in a breath;--and Maud's soft, white hand was extended towards the chaplain, with reproachful earnestness;--"We, who were made Christians by you, and who have so much reason to remember and love you always!"

"Well, well; I see you are Robert and Maud, still"--dashing streaming tears from his eyes now. "Yes, I did bring you both into God's visible church on earth, and you were baptised by one who received his ordination from the Archbishop of Canterbury himself,"--Maud smiled a little archly--"and who has never forgotten his ordination vows, as he humbly trusts. But you are not the only Christians I have made--I now rank Nicholas among the number"--

"Nick!" interrupted Sir Robert--"Wyandotté!" added his wife, with a more delicate tact.

"I call him Nicholas, now, since he was christened by that name--there is no longer a Wyandotté, or a Saucy Nick. Major Willoughby, I have a secret to communicate--I beg pardon, Sir Robert--but you will excuse old habits --if you will walk this way."

Willoughby was apart with the chaplain a full half-hour, during which time Maud wept over the graves, the rest standing by in respectful silence. As for Nick, a stone could scarcely have been more fixed than his attitude. Nevertheless, his mien was rebuked, his eye downcast; even his bosom was singularly convulsed. He knew that the chaplain was communicating to Willoughby the manner in which he had slain his father. At length, the gentlemen returned slowly towards the graves; the general agitated, frowning, and flushed. As for Mr. Woods, he was placid and full of hope. Willoughby had yielded to his expostulations and arguments a forgiveness, which came reluctantly, and perhaps as much for the want of a suitable object for retaliation, as from a sense of Christian duty.

"Nicholas," said the chaplain, "I have told the general all."

"He know him!" cried the Indian, with startling energy.

"I do, Wyandotté; and sorry have I been to learn it. You have made my heart bitter."

Nick was terribly agitated. His youthful and former opinions maintained a fearful struggle with those which had come late in life; the result being a wild admixture of his sense of Indian justice, and submission to the tenets of his new, and imperfectly-comprehended faith. For a moment, the first prevailed. Advancing, with a firm step, to the general, he put his own bright and keen tomahawk into the other's hands, folded his arms on his bosom, bowed his head a little, and said, firmly--

"Strike--Nick kill cap'in--Major kill Nick."

"No, Tuscarora, no," answered Sir Robert Willoughby, his whole soul yielding before this act of humble submission--"May God in heaven forgive the deed, as I now forgive you."

There was a wild smile gleaming on the face of the Indian; he grasped both hands of Willoughby in his own. He then muttered the words, "God forgive," his eye rolled upward at the clouds, and he fell dead on the grave of his victim. It was thought, afterwards, that agitation had accelerated the crisis of an incurable affection of the heart.

A few minutes of confusion followed. Then Mike, bare-headed, his old face flushed and angry, dragged from his pockets a string of strange-looking, hideous objects, and laid them by the Indian's side. They were human scalps, collected by himself, in the course of many campaigns, and brought, as a species of hecatomb, to the graves of the fallen.

"Out upon ye, Nick!" he cried. "Had I known the like of that, little would I have campaigned in yer company! Och! 'twas an undacent deed, and a hundred confessions would barely wipe it from yer sowl. It's a pity, too, that ye've died widout absolution from a praist, sich as I've tould ye off. Barrin' the brache of good fellieship, I could have placed yer own scalp wid the rest, as a p'ace-offering, to his Honour, the Missus and Miss Beuly----"

"Enough," interrupted Sir Robert Willoughby, with an authority of manner that Mike's military habits could not resist; "the man has repented, and is forgiven. Maud, love, it is time to quit this melancholy scene; occasions will offer to revisit it."

In the end, Mr. Woods took possession of the Hut, as a sort of hermitage, in which to spend the remainder of his days. He had toiled hard for the conversion of Nick, in gratitude for the manner in which he had fought in defence of the females. He now felt as keen a desire to rescue the Irishman from the superstitions of what he deemed an error quite as fatal as heathenism. Mike consented to pass the remainder of his days at the Knoll, which was to be, and in time, *was*, renovated, under their joint care.

Sir Robert and Lady Willoughby passed a month in the valley. Nick had been buried within the bushes; and even Maud had come to look upon this strange conjunction of graves, with the eye of a Christian, blended with the tender regrets of a woman. The day that the general and his wife left the valley for ever, they paid a final visit to the graves. Here Maud wept for an hour. Then her husband, passing an arm around her waist, drew her gently away; saying, as they were quitting the inclosure--

"They are in Heaven, dearest--looking down in love, quite likely, on us, the objects of so much of their earthly affection. As for Wyandotté, he lived according to his habits and intelligence, and happily died under the convictions of a conscience directed by the lights of divine grace. Little will the deeds of this life be remembered, among those who have been the true subjects of its blessed influence. If this man were unmerciful in his revenge, he also remembered my mother's kindnesses, and bled for her and her daughters. Without his care, my life would have remained unblessed with your love, my ever-precious Maud! He never forgot a favour, or forgave an injury."